The
Three
Graces

The Three Graces

Elizabeth Wix

SOHO

Copyright © 1989 by Elizabeth Wix.
All rights reserved under International, Berne and Pan American
Copyright Conventions. Published in the United States by
Soho Press, Inc.
1 Union Square
New York, NY 10003

Library of Congress Cataloging-in-Publication Data

Wix, Elizabeth, 1950–
The three graces / Elizabeth Wix.
p.   cm.
ISBN 0-939149-29-X
I.   Title.
PR6073.I87T48 1989
813'.54—dc20   89-34556
CIP

Book design and composition by The Sarabande Press

Manufactured in the United States of America

FIRST EDITION

Acknowledgements

I would like to thank David Unwin and Jack Ludwig for their encouragement, Jill McKay and Celeste Wenzel for their friendship, and Robert, Bobby and Claudia Schmid for their patience during the writing of this book. My thanks also go to my editor, Laura Hruska.

Part One

One

Elinor Fane collected prizes as easily as her sister's clothes collected
dabs of paint. Last year she had won a scholarship to Lady Margaret
Hall and this year Simon Varley's heart. On this glimmering Oxford
afternoon, as she gazed out of the window of his room, she wondered
what more life could offer.

"Should we do anything special for Clare do you think?" Simon
asked, as he bent to pick up a tortoiseshell comb which had fallen to the
floor beside his bed.

"Good Lord, no! I should think she would find all this impressive
enough." Elinor continued brushing her luxuriant hair, her head bent
sideways to accommodate its length.

"And is all this impressive?" Simon looked at his austere room with
its battered furniture and walls which were badly in need of paint.

"Of course it is. Don't you think so?" Elinor laughed, twisting her
hair up into a loose knot with casual competence as she surveyed the
room. "The very top of a tower in Balliol; rooms once lived in by Aldous
Huxley; you and me."

3

"The rest of it might be, but are we so very remarkable?" In Simon's world, Oxford followed Eton as predictably as life imitated art.

"We are to Clare," said Elinor. "She's not at all sophisticated, although of course she pretends to be."

"I thought, being your sister, she would have been born sophisticated and intimidating."

"Hmm," murmured Elinor, tucking up a stray strand of hair. "Do you know what Clare's favourite adjective for describing me is at the moment?"

"No, tell me." Simon handed her a lit cigarette.

"Worldly," said Elinor, blowing a perfect smoke ring.

"How lovely," he said. "I rather look forward to seeing her."

There was a knock at the door of the outer room and Elinor jumped up. "Do I look awfully rumpled?"

"Not a bit. Perhaps a little worldly though." He bent forward to kiss her broad lovely brow.

"Thank you. I expect that's her now. I do hope you like her."

But it was not Clare. Instead, Elinor let in Max Cousins and Conrad Elton who, though utterly dissimilar to one another in looks and demeanor, Elinor tended to think of as a sort of composite Max-and-Conrad since they were almost always together. Max was very fair and dressed entirely in black, his slight limp imperceptible as he strode into the room exuding vitality. Simon said that Max was the most phenomenally intelligent person he had ever met. And Conrad was the son of a lord. *Just* who Clare would want to meet, thought Elinor.

"How very fortuitous!" she said. "You're just in time for Clare. You must stay."

"But who is Clare?" asked Max, kissing Elinor's cheek and settling himself comfortably on the threadbare sofa.

"My talented and romantic sister. Do promise not to laugh at her. She's really very charming. I think so anyway."

Moments later Clare, who had leaped up the steps, taking them two at a time, arrived outside Simon's door rather pink and slightly out of breath. "Heavens, El! Couldn't Simon have found a nice dank basement somewhere? I'm exhausted from all those stairs!" she announced as she entered the room. After kissing her sister she plumped herself down on the other end of the sofa and smiled beatifically around her. Sunlight from the tall windows glanced off her upturned face.

"Well?" said Elinor. "How did it go?"

"Can't you guess from my radiant mien?"

"I could, but you must tell me all about it.

"Oh," said Clare, "they wanted me. Just like that. They told me straight away, as if there wasn't really any question about it. They just looked at my paintings and said I could have a place in the autumn. I feel very honoured." Though she was trying to sound casual, Clare couldn't stop grinning.

"I'm so glad for you, Clare. Simon, do open some wine. And you must all be properly introduced."

Clare sat sipping her drink thinking her day was going extraordinarily well. First, escaping from school in the morning, then having her work admired after lunch and now drinking wine in Simon's room in the middle of the afternoon with Elinor's friends who did not seem as intimidating to her as she had thought they might. Perhaps she could become a part of their world, albeit a very minor one of course; art school was not university, not quite as real as that, but it was something after all.

Max watched Clare as she sat drenched in the sunlight and tried to trace her likeness to Elinor. The Fane sisters seemed to radiate confidence, a knowledge of being wanted, of somehow having a secure niche in a known world. In Clare, though, it was more tremulous and undefined, a more temporary state, perhaps brought on by her recent success. She looked out at him with great round eyes which were made up to look even larger and glowed with pleasure; the rest of her face was quite insignificant in contrast.

Max turned to her. "You smell of turpentine," he said.

"Oh, Lord! Do I really? That was the awful bit you see. I knocked great quantities of it all over the place. Quite by mistake."

"I hardly suppose you would do so on purpose." He smiled at Clare as if this first conversation was the continuation of many. "Tell me about it," he continued.

"Well, you know the Ashmolean Museum of course. Where you first go in? And it is quite chock-full of limbless statues, very colourless and calm? But then, when I walked into the schoolroom, there was a model quite naked and pink with all her limbs intact, being stared at by a roomful of people. It seemed very shocking somehow and I didn't look where I was going and my folder hit this great jam jar full of turps which shattered all over the floor. You don't often see people quite bare in the middle of the day, do you?" Clare blushed. Perhaps Max did.

But he said quite kindly, "No, I don't very often as it happens." And Clare felt better.

Simon poured more wine. Clare wondered if it was the unaccustomed alcohol which was making her so happy. Either that or getting into the William Morris School of Drawing and Fine Art, or being here with these people, or talking to Max, or any random combination of the above.

Max said, "And so you want to become a painter?"

"Yes, I want to very much."

"And what will you paint?"

"Oh, quite ordinary things. Fruit and flowers. Kitchen tables and windows with the view showing through them. Dull stuff like that because I haven't any imagination at all. But I will make all these ordinary things extraordinary, like Morandi painting the same old bottles over and over again."

"And how will you live?"

"In a garret somewhere surrounded by flowers and empty wine bottles, suffering terribly and creating beautiful things, being very decadent and leading a fascinating life. I'd like that I think."

"So would I," said Max, and Clare wondered if, though he sounded quite serious, he was laughing at her. "And where will your garret be?"

"Paris perhaps, or Rome. Not England anyway. I'm fed up with England. Though actually I haven't been out of it very much," she added, truth vying with romance at the last moment.

"And will you have children?" Max asked.

"Yes, dozens of them," said Clare, whose glass was now empty. "All of them very free and unfettered and un-English who will run about barefoot in all weathers and never be asked to tidy up at all. And they will have wonderful names like Augusta and Amaranthie and never go to school." Clare smiled and wondered what Max would ask her next.

They seemed to be playing some absurd game where only they knew the rules and everyone else was excluded. A sort of mental Ping Pong which nobody won or even attempted to. The truth didn't seem particularly important just then. All that mattered was the pleasure his attention gave her. It was quite unlike anything she had felt before.

"May I see your drawings?" Conrad asked. Clare had almost forgotten there was anyone else in the room.

"Of course you may, if you want to. But I think you'll be dreadfully disappointed. Terrible schoolgirl stuff," she said, producing landscapes and still lifes and flower paintings vibrant with colour and painted with a conviction and solidity which made the fruit almost tangible.

"I think they are wonderful," said Conrad. "How talented you are!"

"Thank you," Clare said and looked at Max. He was studying the paintings with close attention.

"Well, Clare," he said eventually. "I'm so glad you can paint. I would have been very let down if you couldn't. My room is always full of flowers. You must come and visit me when you are next in Oxford."

Max and Conrad left soon after and Elinor relaxed on the sofa where Max had sat and turned to Clare. "You seem to have made a great hit with Max."

"Did I? I do feel remarkably cheerful. Are all your friends as dazzling as that?"

"Some of them are dreadfully dull. You struck lucky. Max is one of the un-dull ones."

"I am lucky, aren't I," said Clare.

"We both are, very." Elinor kissed Simon and picked up his car keys. "But come along, we must hurry. Mummy will worry if we are late for supper."

To Clare Fane the world was a safe and benign place, dull at times and constricting but essentially manageable and sane. But at the age of seventeen this was the last thing she wanted it to be; she longed to be swept away by some all-consuming passion which would illuminate and elucidate the very nature of existence. The reality of life as it was—an interminable round of lessons and meals and healthy walks in the country — gave Clare ample opportunity to ponder her fate. She thought her problems could be roughly divided into three categories. The first was Love (or the absence thereof), which left an aching void, a vacuum that both Clare and nature abhorred. She wrote, of course, to boys, callow youths from the better-known public schools in whose sweaty grasp she had writhed in the dark at teenage dances but whose faces she could no longer clearly reconstruct. Even she was sophisticated enough to realise the limits of such postal passion as their letters afforded. They wrote things like "We played Merton House on Saturday. We won. I scored a try," and would end them, "Longing to see you next hols. Love Michael." Or sometimes merely, "Yours, Tim," or "Christopher," or whatever. Clare carried these talismans in her tunic pocket, but they were not Byronic at all however much she wished they were.

The second problem was fat and the awfulness of it in this summer of emaciated beauties whose corrugated chests stared out at her from the pages of *Vogue* and *Honey*. Those willowy ectomorphs were not subjected to the constant onslaught of rice pudding and toad-in-the-hole (which Clare ate because, secretly, she liked them). Clare studied the sturdy legs of her contemporaries and drew consolation from the fact that hers were not half so hefty as Carolyn Wilkes' — might be considered almost elegant in comparison. She wished she had the wistful fragility of a Botticelli beauty and the streaming hair of Marianne Faithful but had to be content with her mother saying, "But you have the most wonderful eyes, darling." All plain girls were told they had lovely eyes. Whatever other bits might be publicly regretted, no one ever, ever, said anyone's eyes were piggy. Not to their faces at least.

In fact, Clare was not plain. She did indeed have beautiful eyes, quite remarkably large and clear and expressive and she was tall with a graceful long neck and well-modelled shoulders which gave promise of what might be revealed when the effects of school food had worn off. Her hair was light brown, lacking the vivid tints which distinguished her sister and made people stop in the street to watch Elinor as she passed. Elinor was an acknowledged beauty and Clare was not. Elinor was also staggeringly intelligent and responsible, which led Clare to ponder the third of her problems. She felt dimmed and diminished by her sister's loveliness and sophistication and by the fact that Elinor did everything first and almost everything better.

Elinor drove well and made it seem easy, neither nervous like their mother nor reckless like some of their friends; Clare felt safe with her sister.

"Do you think Mummy will be pleased with me?"

Elinor hesitated for a moment. "I should think so, Clare, if it's really what you want to do. That's all they ever say they want, you know. For us to be happy."

"But what does she really think?"

"Oh, in her heart of hearts I think she would have preferred one of us to do something 'sensible,' like going to domestic science college and learning how to cook. Though she would never dare say it of course."

"But I'd hate that. You know I would."

"Of course you'd hate it. So would I."

"I wish I was clever like you, El."

"You could be if you wanted. I sometimes think you don't try very hard. You get discouraged too easily."

"But I can paint."

Elinor accelerated to overtake a lorry which was belching fumes into their faces as they swept along the wide road in the open car. "You just have to decide what you want and ignore all the rest of it."

"I know what I don't want," said Clare, observing the rows of stuccoed or pebble-dashed semidetached houses lining the road, Ford Cortinas parked neatly in their driveways. Vivid climbing roses clashed with the colours of their window frames. "I would die if I had to live like that!"

"I don't think anyone would force you to, Clare, if you didn't want to."

"No, but Mummy's life is like that, isn't it? Not quite so awful of course, but all bound up with meals and domesticity and sending things to the laundry and making sure that the silver is polished. She has never actually done anything in her whole life."

9

"I think she's happy though, don't you? That's why she wants it for us. Because it's safe."

"But unbearably dull."

"To you perhaps," said Elinor, overtaking another lorry and enjoying the sensation of speed; Simon very rarely allowed her to drive when he was with her. His last bastion of male egotism.

The Fane house stood solid and suburban in its acre of neatly tended garden, its red brick walls softened by climbing roses and the now flowerless winter jasmine. Architecturally it was impossible to determine its exact antecedents. It was the result, perhaps, of an odd marriage between the style of Lutyens and the milder mode of stockbroker Tudor; better not to enquire too closely into its provenance.

Mrs. Fane sat in the drawing room with the curtains partially drawn against the late afternoon sun, the *Daily Telegraph* in a crumpled heap in her lap. She wondered if she had done everything she had meant to do. That morning she had collected the joint from the butcher's, put vinegar and sugar to soak for the mint sauce and made a gooseberry fool. But had she any of those little sponge fingers to dip into it? She put the paper aside and went to look in the tin in the larder. There were none. If she rang the village shop now they would just have time to deliver them before they closed.

She rang the shop from the telephone in the hall, the number as familiar to her as those of her closest friends (she rang it more frequently after all). She looked about her with satisfaction as she waited for the shop to answer. A few rose petals had fallen onto the polished tabletop and she smelled the mingled scent of flowers and polish. A most welcoming and lovely smell, she thought. She had put fresh flowers in all the rooms, even the bedrooms. Long years of practice doing the church flowers in their awkward huge vases had made doing ones for the house quite easy, a pleasure in fact. She occasionally wondered if her family noticed what she did for them, little things like flowers and putting clean towels in the downstairs loo. They would only notice, she thought, if she didn't do them. When she was seventeen she certainly had not cared about fish knives and soup tureens. She hoped Elinor was driving carefully.

"Mrs. Johnstone? Mrs. Fane here. I'm frightfully sorry to bother you again today but I just wondered if you had any of those little sponge fingers for puddings? And if you could put them in with my order? The girls are coming home this evening and they do love them."

Everything perfect at last.

Elinor parked Simon's MG by the front door like a visitor. "It's rather comforting that it's always the same, isn't it?" she said.

"I suppose so, but I sometimes wish it wouldn't be. Let's lay bets on supper. I guess lamb and summer pudding."

"Too early. No raspberries. Gooseberry fool I should think."

"Darlings!" Their mother rushed out to greet them. "Did you have a ghastly journey? Are you terribly tired?"

"Not at all tired, Mummy. A bit hot though."

"Do let me help you with your bags!"

"No, it's all right, really it is." Clare bent down to pat the Labradors who were milling about grinning idiotically, wagging their tails.

Mr. Fane, a happy and methodical man, threw his briefcase into the hall chair at precisely six forty-two. He glanced up at the grandfather clock when he came in as he had done for the past twenty years, and it was almost always six forty-two unless British Railways let him down, which it occasionally did. Though precise, he was stoical; he would not let things like railways upset him. On top of his briefcase he balanced the day's copy of the *Times*, neatly folded, with the crossword completed in ink uppermost. He achieved this between Guildford and Waterloo every morning. He handed the *Evening Standard* to his wife. "Well, I see Simmonds has been. I wasn't looking forward to doing the lawns at the weekend."

"No, wasn't it lucky? He managed to come for the whole day."

Mr. Fane kissed his wife. "And how are they? Your little chickabiddies?"

"In the garden. Longing to see you."

"And what about Clare? Did she get into her art school?" He did not want to say the wrong thing if she had not.

"Yes. And she's awfully thrilled about it though I can't say I am really. I hope she'll be all right." Visions of unbridled sex and mind-altering drugs careened through Mrs. Fane's mind.

"Of course she'll be all right. You worry too much! Shall we have wine with dinner? What are we having?"

"Lamb."

"Oh, yes, I remember you told me this morning. How stupid of me to forget!"

Mrs. Fane never knew whether he genuinely forgot or said he did so on purpose to provoke her. Luckily Frank would eat anything. Baked beans or caviar were all the same to him.

Clare appeared in the hall wearing a dress even shorter than the one she had arrived home in, but her father did not comment this time or launch into his famous dissertation on the fact that the knee was an ugly joint. (Clare argued occasionally that her knees were made by God like the rest of her and were not ugly in a swimsuit or a tennis dress. Why should they be in an ordinary one? Actually, short everyday dresses came under the category of "flaunting oneself," which was different.)

"And how is the artist?" His kiss prickled her cheek. He still had a moustache, grayish, and neatly trimmed like the lawns, which gave him an almost military air. It was odd to think that her father, the most gentle of men, might once have killed people. Clare hoped he had not. She had never asked.

"I'm terrifically well, Daddy, and very cheerful. Did Mummy tell you?"

He squeezed her arm. "Yes, and we're very happy for you."

"I thought Mummy might not be."

"She'll get used to the idea in the end."

Elinor sat reading the paper. "This war just seems to go on and on, doesn't it?"

"Which war, darling?" said her mother vaguely.

"The war in Vietnam of course, Mummy." Elinor wondered if her mother could find Vietnam on the map.

"I used to wonder what they would put in the paper when there wasn't a war," said Mrs. Fane. "How they would manage to fill up all the space. But there are so many awful things: rapes, murders, strikes. There seems no end to them."

"But there isn't anything we can do about them just now." Francis Fane sipped his gin and tonic, pushing away thoughts of death and destruction.

"But I wish someone could, Daddy. They ought to," said Clare, who, at intervals, wished fervently to change the world.

"There's a great difference, my darling, between what people ought to do and what they actually do. That's the pity of it."

Wanting familial peace at all costs, Mrs. Fane said, "Oh, Clare! Do pick some mint. I quite forgot."

How quickly her mother's mind travelled from the general to the particular! How easy for her to think mint more important than death.

Clare took the green leaves into the kitchen and chopped them. The mint crunched stickily amidst the grains of sugar. How nice it would be not to think at all; just to feel and be seduced by sensation! The dark green fragments smelled wonderful. She licked her fingers and wondered if little bits of them had got stuck between her teeth. Home!

Clare sat looking out of Elinor's bedroom window on to the shadowy lawn which was not quite dark even at eleven o'clock. "Elinor?" she asked tentatively, not quite sure whether her sister was asleep or not.

"Yes?"

"What do you want to do with your life?"

"What a question, Clare. It's too enormous to think about just now. Why? What do *you* want to do?"

Clare clasped her knees to her chest and looked out into the night at the bright stars infinitely far above her. "I think I want to live poetry, if that's at all possible. Do you think it might be?" She was thinking of what Rupert Brooke had once written, that there were only three things in the world worth doing: one was to read poetry, another was to write poetry and the best of all was to live poetry. She did not want to mention Rupert Brooke. Elinor, she knew, considered him juvenile and sentimental.

"I suppose it might be, Clare. But think of all the bits in between. The washing up and the posting of letters. I think there is much more of that sort of thing, really."

"But if one really tried hard enough and wanted it enough?"

"Anything is possible. But I don't think one should actually *try* to live poetry. I think it would just come as a by-product of something else and would creep up on one unexpectedly when one was least prepared."

"Then you don't think it would be totally impossible?"

Elinor was getting sleepy. "It depends upon how you define both poetry and possibility, I think."

"Oh, Lord, El. I don't want to define it! I just want to live it!"

"Well, good luck, Claretta. You must let me know how you get on." Elinor rolled over and fell asleep.

Clare remained at the window watching her mother crossing the lawn and calling softly to the dogs. She heard the back door slam and then her mother putting the early morning tea things on a tray and the rattle of the cups as her mother mounted the stairs. She hesitated outside the room and Clare willed her not to come in. Her mother had once said that when she and Elinor were small one of her chief delights was to creep in when they were both asleep and watch them dreaming with their hands clenched above their heads. Clare wondered if she would ever want to watch someone when they were asleep. It seemed rather a dull occupation, like many of her mother's pleasures.

Clare heard her mother's bathwater gurgling down the plug hole. She climbed into her soft bed and lay trying to recapture some of the things she and Max had talked about and how he had looked when he had said them. But soon she felt that warm soft falling through space which heralded oblivion.

Two

When Clare returned to Ashwell House for the few remaining weeks of term, school seemed to her quite transformed. She was reluctant to admit that she was enjoying it now that it did not matter. She was allowed to draw in the gardens whenever she wanted and had been given a key to the studio. She felt she could see the staff clearly for the first time, as they really were, spinsters, mostly, with horribly circumscribed lives. She even felt capable of feeling sorry for them, something she had never before considered possible.

Clare enjoyed acting (showing off, her mother would have said). Darcy, in *Pride and Prejudice*, was not the role she would have chosen, but since she was tall and, some people felt, rather formidable, she had been given the part. But if a man, at least she was a glamourous one. The choice for Elizabeth at first surprised Clare (who would have rather enjoyed the part herself). Antonia Acton was only fifteen after all, a rather insubstantial child who had previously been quite inconspicuous. But, Clare noted, she was quite altered when pretending to be someone else. By adopting Elizabeth's qualities of liveliness and intelligence she seemed to make them her own. And she was very lovely, Clare thought, with her light eyes and mass of dark hair, the very picture of a romantic heroine from the cover of a Gothic romance. Clare would have liked to draw her but knew she could not, separated as they were by two years and institutional disapproval. They were thrown together quite often during rehearsals and Clare realised she knew very little about Antonia although they had slept under the same roof for four years.

"Will your parents come to the play?" Clare asked one evening as they walked back to their house quite late (one of the perks of being a star).

"Yes—or rather my father will. He never usually does, but this time he promised he would. He's so often abroad, you know."

Clare did not know. "And your mother?"

"No." Antonia asked, "Will yours come?"

"Yes. They always do. I can't imagine anyone actually enjoying watching a school play, but they say they wouldn't miss it for anything. You must point out your father to me." They parted on the steps, Antonia climbing to a higher floor.

Clare would not need to point out her parents to Antonia. Not that they were in any way remarkable, rather the reverse. To Antonia, however, they were the embodiment of proper parents—Mrs. Fane, round and cheerful, with her hair set like the Queen's, and Mr. Fane, determined to enjoy himself, his eyes lighting up when he greeted his daughters. Antonia had first studied them when Elinor had been headgirl and she had had a sort of crush on her. At first she had been disappointed by their ordinariness, but they were always *there*.

When Antonia was getting ready for bed that night she looked at the photograph of her father which was propped up on her dressing table. It had been taken in front of the house in Cornwall in which Antonia had spent her childhood. He smiled out at her (or rather at her mother, who had taken the picture) as he stood outside Field End with a proprietorial air. He was the handsomest man she had ever seen. Even with his eyes squinting against the sun you could see the grandeur of his features, the perfection of them. Both the house and her mother were gone, but the image remained from the time when they had all been together.

It was for her father she had wanted to be in the play. To impress him and make him notice her. Perhaps if she did something conspicuous he would realise she was worthy of his attention.

The play went off as well as might reasonably be expected. Briony Atkinson forgot her lines and giggled. The girl playing Mrs. Bennett tripped over a chair. Clare didn't look particularly manly in her wig (nor would she have wanted to). On the stage with the spotlight upon her Antonia wondered how she looked to her father. She dared not scan the audience during the performance. She knew he must be there somewhere, sitting on a hard chair, surrounded by other parents all eager for glimpses of their talented offspring or their friends' daughters. During the interval he would smoke a Turkish cigarette standing outside near the rosebeds. Perhaps he would meet the Fanes and they would compare notes on the performance and he would tell them whose father he was.

When the lights came up and the play was over and Antonia had curtsied to the applause (polite but not tumultuous, she decided), she dared look out into the sea of faces at last.

She could not see him anywhere. She retreated behind the curtains.

"Do tell me which he is," whispered Briony. "I've longed to see him. Your glamourous and elusive father."

"But I can't see him anywhere, Bry. Really I can't."

"Of course he must be here. Wasn't that him sitting next to the Searles?"

"No, that was Caroline's father."

The curtain rose again and Antonia knew for certain that he was not there. Not at the back nor in the front nor in the middle.

"He isn't here, Briony." Antonia rushed from the stage and fled to the lavatory and wept. Then she was sick. She washed her face in cold water and went to rejoin the rest of the cast.

"My father is a very busy man," she said. "He doesn't have much time for school plays. I think he must be in Bolivia still, or Paris or somewhere."

But no one was listening; they were too intent upon greeting their own families. He might have come just this once, thought Antonia. But of course he had not.

The morning after the play, Clare's parents dropped her in Oxford where, she had said, she was going to look for a place to live next term. By eleven she stood outside Max's door. The bright sunlight bathed her as she gathered the courage to knock.

"Come in," he said.

Clare opened the door to the darkened room and saw Max sitting in a chair with a book in his lap. She knew he had not been reading it but waiting. He stood up.

"Clare! How lovely to see you." Clare knew he had not been waiting for her. He kissed her cheek. As her eyes became accustomed to the gloom, she saw that there were no flowers.

"But Max, I thought you said your room was always filled with flowers."

"I've found someone to give them to."

"I'm glad," Clare said, though she was not.

"What brings you to Oxford so soon?"

"Oh, visiting Elinor and looking for a room for next term. But I can't find any suitable garrets this morning."

"You look very well though, in this heat."

Clare was glad that he had noticed. She had dressed with great care to see him, though she was not quite sure that looking well was exactly what she had had in mind.

Just then the door opened again and Conrad walked in arm in arm with a slight dark girl whose olive skin and almond eyes gave an exotic cast to her unusual features.

"Conrad gave me the most enormous breakfast," she said to Max, ignoring Clare. She smiled at Max, "What would we do without the estimable Conrad?" She glanced at the tousled bed and put her hand on Max's arm.

"I must go upstairs to meet Elinor now," said Clare.

"Then let me come with you," said Conrad. "You know I always long to see Elinor."

Clare wanted to cry, but couldn't of course. "Who was that, Conrad?"

"Sasha Bakhlavi. She's at St. Hugh's." Conrad took Clare's arm as he had done Sasha's and they climbed the many steps to Simon's room.

Elinor smiled at them both. "Did you see Max, Clare?"

"Yes," Clare replied as the day deadened about her.

A month passed before Clare ventured up to Oxford again.

Elinor had a summer job dusting and tending and cataloguing old volumes in an antiquarian bookshop. The bindings were often of more interest than the contents; myriads of books, few of whose words would mean anything to anyone ever again: the flora and fauna of Asia Minor, missionaries' travels to remote regions of China, Hittite remains and collected sermons (there were a lot of these).

Clare, visiting for the day, asked, "Do you ever think you ought to read them? All the books I mean? That one *ought* to know everything, everything that has ever been thought?"

"Of course not. You'd end up with a mind like the contents of *Reader's Digest*, a complete mishmash of useless information, most of it dull. All that stuff they fill you up with at school is bad enough. What are the principal industries of Hull?"

"Fish paste and Elastoplast."

"You see. How far will that get you?" Elinor took out a pale blue index card and wrote down the author, the date of publication, the title, the size and condition of the last book in her pile and then placed the card in a box with a mock leather cover. "The last time this book will be touched by human hands for the next thousand years. The marbled endpapers were nice though." She added the squat volume to a pile to her right. "You ought to look at some of the art books, Clare. You might find something you like."

Clare wandered through the stacks. "Who on earth was Sir Hubert von Herkomer, El?"

"Don't ask me. Oh, actually I think he was some foreigner who got in with Queen Victoria and got knighted like Winterhalter. I think she knighted Germans a lot to please Albert. Or perhaps Albert was dead already and not using his soap."

"What soap?"

"The soap laid out in his dressingroom in case he came back very smelly from the grave and needed a wash."

"Did she really?"

"Well, not her personally of course. The valet probably."

"Another thing I didn't know . . . to add to my collection of useless facts."

"As you see, quite a lot of it isn't worth knowing." Elinor looked at her hands, which were filmed with grayish dust. "God, I'm filthy. I think I'll slink off and wash. Could you hold the fort for a moment?"

Clare sat down in Elinor's chair and tried out her pen. She wrote, "This pen is nice" for want of anything better to say. The way she had written it, it looked like "this penis"; she scribbled over it but the words still seemed to show through. She looked up to see Conrad watching her and blushed.

"I thought you were Elinor for a moment," he said.

"How flattering," Clare pushed her hair back behind her ears. "She'll be back in a minute." She caught sight of Max, who had taken out a huge book on Indian sculpture.

"Do you know anything about sculpture, Clare?" Max asked.

"Not much really. Mostly, I think, because it isn't coloured." She looked briefly at the book. There were figures entwined in heaps, in columns like Gothic flowers.

"But a lot of it was coloured at first, you know. The ancients were much more gaudy than you would imagine."

"Oh." Clare wished Elinor would get back. If they wanted to buy anything she wouldn't know what to do.

"I didn't expect to find you here, Clare. Elinor is one of the very few worthwhile people left in Oxford. It feels like a city in the grip of the plague. And I am von Aschenbach."

Clare wondered if von Aschenbach was related to Sir Hubert von Herkomer, a sort of cousin perhaps, or a member of some club you could only join if you had a complicated, Germanic and unspellable name.

Elinor's hands were now clean, long-fingered and lightly brown. "What have you done with Sasha, Max?"

"Oh, she's gone to Baghdad and I haven't heard from her."

"She might write."

"But then again, she might not." Max looked tired. "I thought of following her there but decided against it and came to look for you instead. Clare is a sort of bonus, a consolation prize for the deserted. Do they ever let you out of your cage to eat?"

Elinor glanced at her watch. "In about half an hour I should think. You could lurk about here or on the other hand you could take Clare somewhere for a bit and I would join you. She talks all the time and I can't concentrate."

"I rather enjoy listening to Clare," said Max.

"Oh, so do I, but not all the time." Elinor went back to her index cards, pinning down facts in her bold italic script like butterflies caught and mounted uselessly.

Clare walked between Max and Conrad matching her step to theirs.

"Shall we eat?" asked Conrad.

"I think I'd rather walk," said Clare. "My lungs feel full of dust."

"Where do you want to walk to?"

"Anywhere. It's so lovely to be outside. I suppose in hot places one would want to be indoors in the height of summer. Here, to stay inside would be a crime."

"You are like Elinor," said Max. "Very bracing. Aren't you ever miserable?"

"Constantly. But I try not to be in public." They turned into Broad Street and Clare felt the sun seeping through the skin on her arms, trying to invade her bones; she did not feel at all miserable.

"You vanished very suddenly when I last saw you," said Max.

"I had things to do. I had to see Elinor."

"You had nothing to do and you can see Elinor whenever you like."

"But *she* didn't want me there, did she?"

"Oh, Sasha. No, I suppose she didn't. She has a very bad effect on women."

"And there weren't any flowers."

"There had been, roses and lilies. Ones that you would have liked. I'm sorry you missed them."

Clare wondered if she had sounded petulant, but Max added, "Actually, Sasha has a very bad effect upon me, too, sometimes."

Clare wondered why she hated Sasha so much, having only seen her for less than five minutes and never having exchanged so much as a word with her. To change the subject she said, "I'm going to Provence next week," wishing that it was somewhere more exotic. Baghdad was rather a hard act to follow. "Perhaps I'll come back very thin and brown and spouting Baudelaire." Clare looked down at her long lily white legs. "Perhaps I should use some of that instant tan before I go."

"I wouldn't bother if I were you," said Max. "Conrad thinks your legs are very nice as they are. Don't you, Conrad?"

"I can't remember saying so though I may have done," Conrad said.

Perhaps Max knew what people were thinking before they said anything. He was altogether strange and comfortable at the same time.

"But I always think I ought to be able to cope with things like that. Hair spray and girdles and nail polish. Feminine disguises. Some people manage them very well."

"Of course they do. But you don't need to, surely?"

That was the good thing about Max, Clare thought. He made her think she was all right as she was and she could talk to him as if she had known him for a long time. That nothing she said, however trivial, was totally absurd and that he found her amusing. She wanted to amuse Max because he looked so sad, but couldn't think how to. He had said she was bracing like Elinor, but she wasn't sure how to set about being bracing either.

When they had been silent for some time Max remarked, "Elinor says you talk all the time."

"I usually do. But I seem to have run out of things to say."

It was time to collect Elinor, and they walked down to Addison's Walk among the tall trees. The sunlight, falling from a sky enormously far above them, freckled their path in variegated patches.

Elinor walked with Conrad, her gait a sort of stately glide which Clare had once tried to copy.

Max said, "It can't be easy having a sister like Elinor."

"Most people seem to think it would be a wonderful advantage to have someone who does everything first, but it makes me into a feeble sort of echo. Actually, I used to mind very much. I think I would loathe her if she wasn't so nice. She does everything so much better than I do."

"Except paint," said Max. "I liked your paintings very much."

"But painting is creating things secondhand. It's not really making things. Making a picture of an orange isn't making the orange itself."

"Well, if you could actually make oranges you would have to be God, which I imagine would be an even harder feat than emulating Elinor."

Clare laughed and sat down on a fallen treetrunk next to her intimidating sister. Elinor was throwing twigs into the greasy green water which looked to Clare like the liquid that seeped out of school mince when they had put herbs into it to disguise the flavour of decomposition.

As if echoing her thought Max said, "What is the most revolting thing they dished up at your school?"

Clare reflected for a moment and then said, "Spam fritters, all pink inside and oozing grease. Or, alternately, date crunch so dry it stuck to the roof of your mouth."

"You forgot the burnt porridge with the mucouslike lumps," said Elinor.

"Or the gristle in stew of indeterminate origin which was impossible to swallow because one's throat refused to open up to let it pass and it bounced back," suggested Conrad.

"The oddest thing," said Max, "was that our parents actually paid for it and all the other peculiar things they did to us whilst trying to turn us into little Empire builders when there wasn't any Empire left."

"Well," said Elinor, "I think they believed that suffering ennobles the soul. Just look at us. How well we all turned out!"

"It just taught me how to survive under the most trying circumstances and to be devious and underhanded and not admit to suffering," said Max.

"Perhaps they were trying to teach us not to feel when they dished up that garbage instead of food," said Clare.

"But of course we do still feel, though I suppose some people have forgotten how to," said Max.

Clare thought that, in fact, school food was all the same, Empire-building establishments or not. The only difference was that at day schools you could go home and moan about it to a sympathetic audience. If eating gristle was all the suffering she had done it wasn't much. She suddenly ran in front of Max who was still gazing into the water and turned a cartwheel: a perfect circle in the air, hand-hand, foot-foot—a skill she had not thought would necessarily stand her in good stead in the real world. She ended up very close to the water.

Max touched her arm. "Could you swim in that water, Clare?"

She looked down at her face staring back at her, hair tumbled about her cheeks, little bits of grass passing over her lips. Max's reflected face was close beside hers, shimmering in the current as if he were underwater looking out at her.

"I wouldn't want to," she said. "But I could if I had to."

"I sometimes think I would like to be part of something which never ends, that goes on forever like the river and never changes. That always remains the same," said Max.

"We will all be in the end," she said. "Whether we want to or not." To shake off the feeling of cold which had come upon her unexpectedly she turned another cartwheel, not wanting the afternoon to end.

"I didn't know you were good at gymnastics," said Conrad.

"Oh, I'm not," said Clare, "only the showing-off bits."

They walked back to the town discussing politics, which Clare found rather dull. If people were not so greedy and selfish the world's problems would merely fade away. The world was rife with possibilities.

Clare hoped Max would take her arm but he did not.

Three

The plane trees behind the mews were just beginning to turn colour, their green leaves becoming blotched with a venomous yellow. Eileen Acton put the breakfast plates into the washing-up machine so Mrs. Harding wouldn't have to do them. She wished, in fact, that Mrs. Harding didn't have to "do" anything at all. Mrs. Harding had informed Eileen that Mr. Harding had ulcers the size of soup plates and was in hospital. Couldn't she spend the day there with him instead? Surely it would be more amusing for her. "Triple fracture from off of a bike. And one 'ad 'alf 'is stomach out, miles of it unravelled like knitting wool. One next to 'Enry 'as got piles." A roomful of people with bits cut off them or leaking. "Better than 'The Archers,'" she had said. Better than the Actons, too, thought Eileen.

Rex had left early that morning for Brussels after placing an envelope on the table for Antonia.

"Gone, 'as 'e?" said Mrs. Harding.

"Yes."

"Always off somewhere, isn't 'e? Surprised 'e doesn't take you with

25

'im more often. Cheer you up a bit, abroad." Mrs. Harding stubbed out her cigarette into a saucer and staggered off under the weight of the Hoover to do the lounge (which Antonia called the sitting room).

Antonia squeezed past Mrs. Harding in the hall. Though not massive exactly, Mrs. Harding's overalled bulk seemed to spread and shift uncontrollably.

"Reading, are you?"

"Yes." Antonia smiled briefly at Mrs. Harding.

"Good, is it? What's it about, then?"

"A T.B. sanatorium," Antonia shouted above the roar of the vacuum cleaner.

"Ooh, I wouldn't want to read about that. Too morbid. They've got injections for that now."

Antonia took a cup from the cupboard and poured herself some black coffee. She sat down, not appearing to notice Eileen at all. Eileen glanced at the title of the book while Antonia's back was turned. It was *The Magic Mountain* by Thomas Mann. Last summer Antonia had read Daphne du Maurier and Georgette Heyer and it had been a bit better, a very slight thaw but not much.

"Your father left you this." Eileen handed Antonia the envelope.

"Thank you." Two new ten-pound notes slipped out and a note which said "Good luck with the new term. Love, Daddy." Antonia continued reading and a tear dropped onto the page. Her hair fell forward so it formed a curtain in front of her face. She got up and put on the radio.

"Shall we go shopping, Toni?" Eileen asked. "We could get you something lovely and autumnish. There's a lot of plum about, very rich-looking. It would suit you, I think. Or some sweaters would be nice."

"I can't wear them at school, you know."

"But you could save them for the holidays. It would be something to look forward to."

"But I don't want to *buy* anything. There isn't any point."

"It's your last day, Toni. Don't you want to do anything special? I would come with you if you like."

"No, thanks. Really. You needn't bother."

"It wouldn't be any bother. I'd like to do something with you."

Eileen wanted to go out. She couldn't stay in the house all day. She had nothing to do in it. She couldn't even clean it. Justin was back at school, had slipped back willingly into that alien world of little boys. Rex would not return until Wednesday week, if then. He had stopped giving her exact dates and she had stopped asking. And she was left with Antonia, who patently didn't want her company. Eileen retreated upstairs and sat at her dressing table and looked at herself in the mirror. Her hair, newly set, was frozen round her face. She was twenty-nine, almost thirty, and she thought she looked old already. Little hard lines had formed near her mouth. The skin round her eyes looked brittle to her as she painted on her face and attached her eyelashes. When she had finished she looked quite different, not mousey at all, perhaps almost glamourous, and not at all how she felt underneath.

It was very important to her, this morning ritual: rising from sleep where she had disturbing dreams and making herself into what she should be. "Our Eileen wants to be posh," Sandra had said years ago whilst she sat on the settee in the front room in Forest Hill, eating chips out of a bag. "Fancy yourself, don't you?"

It was true. Eileen had been fastidious even then, reading all the tips in *Woman's Own* on how to make herself look nice. Trying all the new colours. Keeping herself neat. And then Rex. She had not imagined that he would notice her, though she was good at her job: the efficient Miss Tubman who didn't mind working late. He had a wife of course, and a daughter, though he didn't mention them. They lived too far away for her to see them, but Eileen heard him on the phone to them sounding placating to his wife and cheerful to his daughter.

She took messages occasionally from Mrs. Acton, whose voice alarmed her—it was so soft, so smooth, so educated. She would like to talk like Mrs. Acton. Perhaps she could if she tried. She had learned to dress as if she was better off than she was, perhaps she could change her voice, too.

They had envied her, those other girls in the office, working for Mr. Acton, who was the most glamourous thing they had ever set eyes on. He went abroad all the time to South America and Japan when the most they managed was a fortnight in Spain. But they didn't like her and she wasn't asked to the party when Carole left to get married. Not that she would have wanted to go, but it would have been nice to be asked. She had cut herself off from all that. She had, instead, odd nights at undistinguished hotels where he would meet no one he knew. And once, only once, a whole weekend in Milan where Mrs. Acton had rung up to say Antonia had chicken pox and wanted to talk to him.

He would never have married her if she hadn't been pregnant and if Mrs. Acton hadn't died. She knew that. It wasn't right to be glad that someone was dead, even someone you had never met. And now he regretted it though she still adored him. If it wasn't for Justin he would be gone, but you don't abandon your children twice without comment.

Eileen put on a red dress, then thought it made her skin look sallow and took it off again. Perhaps she was too old for red. She had worn it a lot when she had first met Rex because he had said it suited her. "A real scarlet woman and everyone will envy me!" He had liked her to look nice and had stared at her with admiration.

She had worn red the first time she had met Antonia; a well-cut coat which had almost concealed the bump that was to be Justin. They had had tea at Harrods and Eileen had poured the milk in first, which Antonia had noticed and Rex had pretended not to. Antonia had been silent, answering only when she had been directly addressed and then only in monosyllables. Eileen had wanted to like her and had imagined she would but when confronted with her in the flesh she had been stumped.

"Your father says it's a lovely school, right in the country."

"It's all right," Antonia said. She had been trying to spread a scone which had crumbled and bits of it had become stuck to the knife.

"I expect you have lots of little friends there longing to see you."

"Some." Antonia's mouth was full of scone; she could not have said more even if she had wanted to.

"Your father has told me all about you." Eileen smiled at the small serious figure and hoped to win a smile in return. But Antonia continued to eat in silence.

Eileen had felt sick, unable to eat. It should have worn off by lunchtime but it never did. She had had to put on a lot of makeup to stop herself looking pasty. The meal seemed to be taking a very long time and Rex was no help at all just sitting there smoking, blowing fumes over the food. Eileen thought she might really be sick.

"Well, I must get back to the office. I'll leave you two girls together." He handed Eileen some money. "Perhaps you could help Antonia choose a dress to take back to school to wear on Sundays." He seemed rather pleased that he had remembered something about Antonia's life, that they let the children wear home dresses after tea on Sundays. He kissed them both briefly and escaped.

"That's very nice of him I must say. Shall we go and look for something?"

"If you want to," said Antonia politely, as if she didn't care.

"I would have been very excited at your age to be able to choose what I wanted. I think I would have chosen something with a sticking-out skirt that made me look like a princess."

Antonia looked at her as if she were mad. "I think I would prefer to look quite ordinary," she said.

The saleslady produced two dresses in Antonia's size, one a soft blue which echoed her eyes and the other a rich red with smocking. She tried them both on impassively.

"You look lovely in the red," said Eileen when Antonia emerged from the changing room with the saleslady in tow. "It brightens you up."

"I think I prefer the other one."

"Well, that looks very nice on you, too, dear," the saleslady remarked. "Your mother was just saying what a nice shade it was."

"She's not my mother," said Antonia. "But I'll have the blue anyway."

They had walked and looked at the puppies rolling together in the pet department and at last Antonia had smiled. "But it's a pity they have to grow up into poodles."

"But aren't they cute now? Just little bundles of fluff. I've never had a dog," Eileen admitted.

"I had one," said Antonia. "They had to put it to sleep. They said Granny was too old to look after it, but she wasn't really."

After Antonia went off to school Eileen had gone back and bought one of the puppies. She had never been able to train it. Even now she had to clean up after it and scrub the shag carpet where it had messed. But Antonia liked it in spite of the fact that it was a poodle. She called upstairs, "I'm just going out to walk Mimi. I'll be back later."

Eileen thought, "She likes the dog better than she does me," and put on another layer of mascara.

Mimi was a silly affected dog who minced on tiny feet and sniffed disdainfully at scraps of paper, but she had a certain charm of expression at times, Antonia thought, and *she* did not want to talk all the time. She did not want to buy things and did not endlessly go into shops and choose things, bring them home and then send them back to be altered. She was only a dog after all, a minute manicured bitch trapped in a town.

Antonia unleashed her in the enclosed garden behind the mews and hoped she wouldn't poop right in the middle where the small children played. A little enclosed garden for a little town dog. Antonia's old dog, Punch, would have found it horribly limiting and hemmed in with no rabbits and no foxes (except draping incredibly frail old ladies in the winter). Mimi was not a real dog, just as this was not a real garden, nothing was real anymore but only a small bogus imitation of home, of Field End. A doll's house, little and neat, presided over by painted Eileen. No echoing passages and smoking fireplaces but central heating which stifled and killed the air making the winter less real: It was always the same temperature. She supposed she ought to be grateful that she was never cold there, but she was not.

Then she saw the madwoman surrounded by paper bags sitting on a bench, her eyes darting left and right at the ground as if armies of giant ants were sneaking up on her when she wasn't looking. The woman never looked up, did not notice Antonia. She hissed briefly at Mimi and snatched a paper bag away from the dog, each finger be-ringed, flashing glass stones, red, green, amethyst. Her nails were black with grime.

"I'm so sorry," said Antonia. "Mimi, come here, good dog."

The woman spat on the grass beside the bench, green phlegm mottled with white.

If I were a saint, thought Antonia, I could pick up that phlegm and eat it. Some saint somewhere had done it. Melissa had said so. Saints had done almost everything, had had almost everything done to them—a favourite topic of conversation at night when the lights were out, the gruesome fate of virgins and the plots of horror films: heads dished up on plates, people impaled on spikes. If you could remember a whole film you were popular. Perhaps if I could be nice to Eileen I would be a saint. If I could recall a whole film I'd have friends. Antonia wondered which was less likely to occur. If I will it enough perhaps I could be saintly, Antonia thought. Elinor Fane had once said at lunch that whatever you believe is true, if you really believe it. Or at least it is for you at the time. Elinor had said that by effort of will you could make things happen. She would be a member of a happy family, her father would love her, if she could believe it even for a moment. She thought that she would try very hard to be good.

"Do you really want to go out, Eileen?" she asked when she returned to the mews.

"Yes, of course."

"Shall we go to the Tate?"

"What a lovely idea. Let me get ready. I won't be a sec."

Antonia could see no point in changing. Eileen put on shoes with high heels, patent leather, shiny. They did not look comfortable.

"I like to look at pictures," said Eileen. "They make me think of things I haven't thought of before. They make things look different somehow."

"They sometimes make me feel strange," said Antonia. She identified with people in pictures: Ophelia drowned, bodies rising from the grave at Cookham, Lytton Strachey stretched out uncomfortably with those odd little figures dwarfed outside the window, isolated behind the glass. The Tate was awash with strangeness, even the restaurant with the murals of people in carriages in an ideal landscape surrounded by the very prosaic real people, drinking tea out of thick white cups.

"Rex will be very pleased when I tell him where we were. That we came out together." Eileen's lipstick had come away on the edge of her cup.

"It was nice, wasn't it?" said Antonia, though she thought she couldn't bear it every day, there was too much to take in all at once.

She bought a postcard of Richard Dadd's painting, done in Bedlam, to take back to school. Little men with manic eyes chopping at daisies, minutely detailed.

"Are you sorry to be going back?" asked Eileen in the taxi going home.

"Oh, I don't mind really," said Antonia, though she did. "But thank you for having me for the holidays anyway."

"You don't have to thank me, Toni. It's your home after all."

Eileen opened the door and stepped over the puddle made by Mimi in their absence. "Thank God Rex didn't see that. Silly Mimi, Mummy will make it all better."

The smell of Dettol, as Eileen mopped up, reminded Antonia of school corridors. She felt sick with dread.

Four

Clare's room in the Woodstock Road had been found eventually by her mother, who, with a residue of wartime fortitude, had walked along roads and knocked on the doors of likely looking houses.

Clare had said, "Oh, Mummy, I wish you wouldn't."

"But why ever not, darling? No one minds. They can only say no, after all."

"But you look so conspicuous."

Mrs. Fane was oddly brave at times. Perhaps at her age one didn't mind what people thought. Clare herself minded dreadfully.

Though glad to have found somewhere at last, Clare realised that the flat had its drawbacks, the most obvious of which was Mrs. Corbett, the landlady. She had never got used to the fact that though she owned the whole house, parts of it were now private. She would stump upstairs and comment on the unmade beds and the joss-stick burns on the mantelpiece.

Clare said to Julia, with whom she shared the flat, "She has no right to come in here and snoop about. No right at all!"

"Of course she doesn't. But the thing is that she thinks she does. And what on earth can we do about it?"

Nothing at all, thought Clare. Needless to say Mrs. Corbett had liked Mrs. Fane; people like that always did. Her mother was rather gracious to them and confiding and so they always said such things as, "But Clare your mother is such a charming woman, surely she wouldn't want you to . . ." Here Clare thought she could insert an almost endless list of things of which her mother purportedly disapproved, like leaving her clothes scattered all over the floor and staying out all night and burning incense and having a red light bulb in the sitting room. Things of such utter triviality that Clare was aghast. She also felt slightly guilty.

The museum, however, was a source of solace. Clare knew backwards and sideways and upside down every painting in the place, the colour of every Egyptian amulet and the exact state of the alimentary canal and reproductive tract of every one of the ladies who sat knitting, one to each room. The knitting ladies, guardians of the treasures, knew the states of every one of the students' affairs almost better than the students did themselves; they were a sort of Greek chorus to them all. Clare talked to them quite often and enjoyed their company but sometimes wished she could stop herself from doing so, and felt spied upon and embarrassed.

The art school itself was very small and by most standards reactionary. The students spent most of their time drawing from Greek casts and the rest painting still lifes in the "well," a dusty basement lit by skylights enormously far above them. There were sixty students all together, whom Clare was beginning to know.

Clare's drawing had improved; of that, at least, she was certain. The smell and texture of oil paint had come to be second nature to her; it hung about her like some exotic scent but much nicer. Even so, she felt her work was not very good, at least not in comparison with other people's. They all seemed so much more serious and worked much harder. She was envious of Elinor being a real undergraduate and living with Simon. She felt herself to be lonely, though she was friendly with some of the girls and one or two of the less-prepossessing boys whose adoration she fed on guiltily. She did not want to go out with un-prepossessing boys who had just left school and thought her wonderful.

"Oh, Elinor," she wailed, "where are they all? The devastating men with brilliant minds and fascinating lives? I'm fed up with boys with spots and bicycles."

"Rarer than hen's teeth, Claretta. But you'll see, things will get better."

"They don't seem to. Pass me another tea cake."

"But your work is going well, surely?"

"I suppose so. If there was any point in it."

"There's always point in working. It stops you thinking if you're miserable."

"But if I'm miserable I can't work." Clare fiddled with a little piece of sofa which was coming adrift.

Elinor lay back in her chair and blew smoke rings up into the air. "You look very picturesque anyway."

Clare's skirt was black crushed velvet with little splotches of paint on it. "I haven't seen Max for a long time," she said, trying to sound as if she didn't care.

"Oh, the great Max. No, I suppose you haven't. Didn't you know?"

"Know what? What should I know?"

Elinor hesitated. "Perhaps I shouldn't tell you, but it doesn't matter now. I think he'll come back soon."

"But where has he been?"

"Locked up in the Warneford. He went mad I think. Or at least Conrad said he did. He was very ill, anyway."

"Did you go to see him?"

"No. I would have done, but he only wanted to see Conrad. And Conrad said it was awful. Max locked up, weeping, in a room full of strange people tapping their fingers and wailing."

"How terrifying," said Clare. She could not imagine it: Max, not powerful at all. "But why, El?"

"I think she left him."

"Oh, yes . . . *her*," said Clare. How wonderful to go mad because of love!

35

Elinor poured more tea when Simon came in and they drew the curtains against the encroaching dusk.

"Are you enjoying life, Clare?" he asked.

Clare set out to be amusing and told them the latest installment in the saga of the knitting ladies.

The next Friday, as Clare sat idly doodling in Simon's room, Elinor looked up from the paper she was writing and glanced quizzically at her sister. "Max is back," she said.

"Is he?" Clare replied, feigning indifference.

"He asked after you when I saw him this morning. Oh, and another thing, do you want to come with us to Peter Lucas' party tomorrow night? It's a sort of open invitation. You could bring someone, if you wanted."

"I might," Clare said, "unless anything much more thrilling comes up."

Clare dressed for the party with infinite care, trying to make the result look careless and uncontrived. She put on lace and old silk, things that had once been lovely and which she had rescued from the oblivion of the jumble sales her mother organised. Her mother would have thrown them away because of their decrepitude. Clare twined flowers in her hair and made up her face very slowly, savouring each brushstroke, each dab of colour, with as much care as she gave to her paintings. There really is no difference, she thought, between painting oneself and painting fruit. I am just making something which was not there before, an artifact to be admired. But she felt quite blank looking at herself in the glass, her features so familiar that she could not see them. She felt sick with excitement and could not eat.

She sat in Lucilla's room down the hall watching the pale lumpish creature dress. Lucilla came from Ireland and painted miniatures and was altogether odd and never went out at all.

"It's so kind of you to take me, Clare. It will be all right, my going, won't it?"

"Of course it will. Though it will probably be most dreadfully dull. These things usually are." World-weary Clare, whose heart was beating unnaturally fast and who did not have the courage to go alone. She hoped very much that Max would be there.

"Does my dress look okay?" Lucilla pulled it tight with a belt which accented her rotundity.

"It will probably be quite dark. You look lovely to me."

"Do you really think so?"

Oh, God, thought Clare, she cares what I think. She probably imagines I am sophisticated. I don't care in the least what she looks like. She lit a cigarette and looked at the travelling clock on Lucilla's dressing table. In an hour she might see Max. She smiled encouragingly at Lucilla. "I really do think you look nice," she said and indeed Lucilla looked no odder than usual.

The room was very crowded, dimly lit and overhung with a pall of smoke. It was full of people Clare knew but did not particularly want to see, though she greeted them with an appearance of pleasure and enthusiasm. She accepted a drink and then another, and danced with a faceless young man in a flowered shirt. Lucilla stood glued to the wall. Perhaps I should introduce her to people, Clare thought, dull men in scratchy tweed jackets with slapped-on Old Spice. Perhaps she's miserable and I should never have brought her.

Clare had her photograph taken with the president of the Oxford Union, who was a friend of Elinor and Simon. She smiled into the camera, his arm around her. A picture of an ugly man who was someone and a girl who was nothing at all.

As the flash faded Clare saw Max, standing behind a group of chattering couples, looking at her. She had known for some time that he was in the room.

He walked towards her through the crush and took her arm. "What a horrible party," he said.

"It is rather," said Clare.

"Then why did you come?"

"I came to see you of course."

"Then why didn't you come to my room?"

"I couldn't do that. I had to be sure you wanted to see me. I couldn't risk it."

"But you know I never come to parties."

"I thought you might, just this once." Clare smiled.

"Shall we leave?"

Clare saw Lucilla still watching the dancers, an empty wineglass clutched in her hand. "I brought someone from the art school. She doesn't know anyone at all."

"Is that your problem?"

"Partly it is. I feel responsible for her in a way."

"Don't be. She could always leave, too." Max put his arm around Clare's shoulders and guided her towards the door.

"But she can't come with us," Clare said.

"No," said Max. "She will survive without you, whereas I might not. Let's go to my room. It's quieter there."

Max's room was tall and square, set in the corner of the building, facing the street. Orange fluorescence from the streetlights washed in through the uncurtained windows. Inside the room the flickering flame from one white candle joined the pink glow of the gas fire to relieve the gloom.

Conrad stood up when Clare came in and smiled at her. "So Max found you after all." He kissed her cheek. "How lovely you look."

Clare sat back on her heels before the fire between Max and Conrad and the room closed in upon her, black and warm. Conrad gave her a little handleless cup of China tea, very pale and smelling of flowers. Clare studied Max's face in the firelight and she suddenly knew what it was that he reminded her of. It was the face she constantly drew in the museum, the Greek cast of an ideal head with square brow, straight, well-modelled nose and wide mouth, everything balanced, even, each feature complementing the others, a harmony which was character-less, useless and dead, without animation because the eyes were blank.

"You seem amused, Clare. Tell me what you are thinking."

"Oh, it's just that I have recognised you, Max. Your face is exactly like one of the statues I draw and I can't think why I hadn't realised it before. I must bring my drawings to show you. You would be amused, too, I think."

Max smiled, a slow archaic smile. "And do you know what you look like?"

"No, tell me."

"The very apotheosis of an English schoolgirl. Not in the least pretty, but I think you will be beautiful one day. Such wonderful puddly eyes. You can't fade or change, only get better. Don't you think so, Conrad?"

"I think Clare looks very lovely now, as she is."

"Thank you," said Clare.

"And are you happy?" Max asked.

"Very happy tonight."

"But not all the time?"

"Even I think that is too much to hope for." Clare looked up at Max, who, in spite of his beauty, still looked intolerably tired. She longed to ask him what it was like to be mad, and if he still was, and what he was thinking.

"So tell me all you have been doing since we last met." He propped his hand on his cheek and looked down at her, smiling still.

Clare wondered what to tell Max, what would amuse him about her mundane existence. "There is very little to tell. I live in a flat with Julia, who is very rarely there. I go to school and sit astride a donkey, which is one of those stools to prop your drawing board up on with nothing for your back. And I draw from antique casts until my back hurts too much and then I go to pubs with spotty boys who drink too much beer and throw up. And I read a lot, and sleep and eat and all that sort of thing. And I visit Simon and Elinor, but not too often, because then they would think I was bored."

"Are you bored?"

"I know I shouldn't be but I quite often am."

"No, you certainly shouldn't be bored, Clare."

"Then tell me what I should do."

"Anything you want: seduce people, write poetry, paint marvellous pictures. It's very ordinary to be bored."

"But what I really hate most is being on my own. Some people say they like it, but I'm not very good at it at all."

"I'm not very good at it either," said Max. "But I'm surprised you admit it. Most people want you to believe they are terribly busy all the time and that they find themselves quite fascinating."

"How convenient for them. But I can't imagine it for myself."

"Neither can I," said Max.

Conrad went out to try and find some food, since none of them had eaten that night, and came back from the common room with some tepid chicken pies, colourless and glutinous. "It's all I could find, I'm sorry."

Max and Conrad ate them anyway, washed down with wine. But Clare could not eat even when they tried to persuade her to.

"You should eat something, Clare, however vile. You look much thinner than in the summer."

"But then I was horribly fat."

Max was thinner, too, Clare thought, and his eyes more deeply etched.

They discussed poetry and politics, and painting and religion, and music and philosophy and Clare realised how very ignorant she was and how little she knew about the state of the world, though they listened to her opinions as if they mattered. And they discussed their families and grisly Christmas parties where eccentric aunts gave them presents ten years out of date, and they made up spoof thank-you letters which would have been far too cruel to send. Max was very funny and Clare found it odd and comforting that Conrad's family, though much grander, was quite as dreary and comical as her own.

When they finally stopped laughing and mascara streaked Clare's face where the tears had rolled down it, she realised that the sounds of the party had melted away. It was very quiet outside the room and she could hear car tires swishing on the damp leaves in the road, their headlights flashing in the cracked glass of the windowpane. The buildings opposite were dark and Clare could no longer see the illuminated windows of the Arthur Murray School of Dance, where the shadows of overweight housewives and clumsy clerks had lumbered away their Saturday night.

Clare stood up reluctantly, one of her legs tingling with pins and needles where she had sat on it too long. "I should go now. I think it must be very late."

"But why Clare? There is a lot of night to be got through."

Clare thought of the bleak winter night, of her cold bed lying unmade in her room and of Julia, who would not care if she were there or not. Somewhere outside the room a clock struck three.

"You can't go running around at all hours in the dark by yourself," Max said.

"But I often do."

"I wish you wouldn't go. Surely you don't have to?"

"I don't *have* to do anything." Clare looked into Max's eyes. "I'll stay if you want me to." She sat down on the floor again by Max's chair while Conrad made more tea.

Max said, "There is something I must read before I go to sleep. Will it disturb you if I turn on the light?"

So Clare sat with Conrad, willing him to leave, as Max read at his desk.

Conrad was charming of course, as he always was. "You are all right, Clare, aren't you? You must always tell me if you are not. Promise me that. You will, won't you?"

"Of course I'm all right. Why shouldn't I be?"

"No reason at all." He squeezed her hand lightly and kissed her cheek. "I must go now. I will see you soon, no doubt."

Conrad went out of the room, shutting the door behind him.

"So the estimable Conrad thinks you are tired," said Max putting aside his book.

"Actually," said Clare, "I'm not so much tired as dying to wee." This was a problem since the lavatory was up three flights of stairs past twenty closed doors.

"You could always pee down the wash basin," said Max.

"How silly of me not to think of that before." The basin's porcelain rim was cold beneath her thighs. She had never peed down a sink before. She jumped down into the room.

"But you *are* tired, aren't you?" Max drew the wilted flowers from her hair and she shivered. "Come let me put you to bed." He took off her clothes, all of them, until she was quite naked before him, with goose bumps on her arms.

"Oh, Clare, I'm so glad you are staying." He buried his head in her hair and held her. Clare suddenly burst into tears, great racking sobs shaking her body.

"I'm so sorry, Max. I didn't mean to cry."

He laid her on the bed and tucked the red blanket up to her chin. "It's all right. It doesn't matter. I'm quite used to people crying, what with one thing and another."

Clare said between sobs, "Do you love me, Max?"

"Yes, of course I do. As much as I'm capable of loving any of my friends. And you are a friend, Clare, aren't you?" He pushed the hair gently back off her face. "And I know you will never betray me."

"How could I betray you?"

"That's just it. You couldn't because you are very like me, aren't you?"

"How like you?"

"Oh, a part of me when I was very young like you. I knew it when I first saw you. But please stop crying or you will make me miserable, too."

Clare sat up and put her arms around him and they sat rocking together comfortingly, frightened to let go of each other.

"Have you slept with many men, Clare?"

"No. I haven't as it happens. And you? Have you slept with most of your friends?"

"Some of them."

Max kissed her then as she had been longing for him to from the first moment she had met him in Simon's room and every moment they had spent together since.

He kissed every part of her soft body and she his, and he was both alien and familiar at the same time. She searched to make known what she had longed for, she wanted to be joined with him entirely both with her body and her mind.

"Do you mind that I've got my period?"

"No, why should I? I think it's very nice in a way. If I were a woman I would be very pleased to have it."

Clare said, later, lying enclosed in his arms, encompassed by his flesh, "Now I'll never know if I bled."

"Does it matter?"

"Not in the least. But it's funny, isn't it? Everything's changed."

"Nothing ever changes, Clare. But a little bit of you will always be

42

with me and a bit of me with you, always. Now go to sleep and I will watch you dreaming."

Clare awoke later to see Max standing over the bed gazing down at her. "Please come and lie with me. Don't leave me alone."

He slid in beside her on the sex-dampened sheets, gathering her to him. "Dear Clare, believe me, it's all right. I wouldn't let you sleep alone."

In the morning they sat up in bed, Clare wrapped in Max's red Chinese robe, and drank more tea from the little handleless cups.

"Poor Conrad is hopelessly in love with you," Max said.

"I know. I wish he wasn't. I like him so much." She laid her head against Max's shoulder and put her hand on his heart and felt it beating very fast beneath her fingers.

Max's room became Clare's whole world; she very rarely left it. It was December now and the days were short and dark, merging and mingling into one another, unbounded by meals or lessons.

She sat on the broad windowsill cataloguing the contents of the room: the ashtray shaped like a globe; the vases which had once held flowers and now did not; the plates, records and accumulated debris. She drew constantly, mostly the things in the room, but occasionally Max, trying to capture his fleeting expressions and failing miserably. Or else she lay beside him on the sheepskin rug before the fire, hugging him to her and breathing in the smell of his body. And she watched him as he wrote at his desk when he was unaware of her watching.

Conrad was their familiar, their audience. He supplied them with food. Conrad dealt with the outside world—moved in and out of the room at will—there and not there, but very welcome when he was.

When Max went out Clare was bereft and played endless games of Draughts with Conrad. They were very evenly matched. Clare could win when she concentrated. One day when Max was gone for a long time (it seemed a long time to Clare, who did not have a watch) she asked, "Does he go to see Sasha?"

"Yes. He sees her sometimes when she wants him to."

"Does he make love to her?"

"How should I know, Clare? Probably."

A tear slid down Clare's cheek and fell onto the board, and Conrad touched it with his finger. Clare saw the black and white squares wobble and reform themselves into a different pattern.

"He loves her very much, doesn't he?"

"Yes."

"What is she like?"

"How could I tell you that? How does one ever know what someone is like to someone else."

"Is she very beautiful and clever?"

"She is certainly both of those things."

"But is she the least nice?"

"Of course not." Conrad smiled. "Do concentrate, Clare. You are about to be entirely obliterated by my king. You are an absolute sitting duck."

Clare was obliterated anyway and swallowed two pills from her bag. "I feel rather peculiar, Conrad. If Max didn't want me here would he tell me to go away?"

"But he does want you here. He thinks you are wonderfully kind." Conrad set out the pieces for another game.

"Max, do you think I will ever be a real painter?" Clare lay beside him, his arm heavy across her chest, making it hard for her to breathe.

"I think you are a better person than an artist. Some people are better at living than others. I think you are one of those."

"Then should I go to university and try to learn things?"

"If you want to."

"But will they accept me?"

"Obviously they will. Think of all the ridiculous things you know, far more than most people, almost as many as I do." He rolled over and looked down at her. "I keep telling you, you can do anything."

"You make me think I can. You make me feel very powerful."

"Oh, you are, Clare, very powerful indeed." He traced the line of her belly and her breast with his fingertip. "Much more powerful than you realise. I think some people never know how to live except inside themselves, unable to connect. You know how not to hurt people, how to heal. I don't think many people have that gift."

"But I am nothing on my own."

"Look, Clare, let me tell you something. When I saw Sasha today she said that she didn't love me, couldn't love me. And she laughed at me. She is the most beautiful person God ever created and she despises me. She watches me disintegrate and she still laughs." He caught Clare's hand and held it to his face. "See, you are flesh, too, with a mind underneath it. You are a sort of perfection, but quite other. I sometimes think none of it matters at all, except that it does."

Clare lay in Max's bed whilst he read at his desk. Raindrops, like wiggling spermatozoa, were tearing diagonally down the windowpane, which rattled in the gale.

Conrad came in carrying two paper bags, wet from the storm. Clare sat up, her breasts bare. It did not matter that Conrad saw them, he was family, a part of them both, a party to their secrets. But it was cold. She slipped on Max's sweater, which lay on the floor beside the bed where he had thrown it hours before.

"What day is it, Conrad?" she asked.

"Wednesday." He threw off his wet jacket and knelt by the fire, steam rising from his hair.

"What a satisfactory day Wednesday is, even, like the number four. Do you ever match numbers to things which don't have them particularly? Like red is four, too. And Thursday is seven and Saturday is possibly eleven." She got out of bed and opened the paper bags. "Gin! How nice. But what on earth are these?"

"They are meant to be Cornish pasties, at least that's what they said they were."

"Really? What vivid imaginations they have." Clare set out three plates and put the food on them, picked up the gin bottle and placed it beside them. She walked to the sink and took one of Max's pills and poured bitter lemon into his tooth mug, swallowed the pill, then added gin to what was left in the mug.

"God what a terrible taste!" Gin, lemon, toothpaste. She sat cross-legged on the floor like a child at a picnic. "But I am very grateful really, Conrad. You do try to get things I like."

"Well eat it, Clare, don't discuss it endlessly." Max smiled.

Clare looked at the pasty but couldn't eat it.

"Do you think that whatever this is made of has been dead for a long time?"

"Years probably. It won't mind your eating it in the least," said Conrad, already eating.

"Clare tells me she is going to university to prove she is intelligent," said Max.

"Is it necessary to prove it? Don't we know that already?"

Clare felt very clever then, and admired, and very silly from all the gin she had consumed. The storm still beat against the windows, howling to be let in.

"Here, have an apple, Clare. At least that isn't dead yet." Max handed her the perfect round fruit but as she looked at it she realised that it was neither perfect nor dead. There was a worm inside, gnawing its way to the very centre of the apple.

"I think I'm going to be sick, Max."

"All right. Be sick." Clare got up, her long legs wobbling and everything went black and stopped.

"What happened?" Clare was in bed, the covers tucked tightly around her.

"Not much. You got drunk and passed out, and Conrad was furious and said it was all my fault, and I shouldn't let you take my pills. And I said what you did was entirely your affair and none of my business at all, though I would never let anything really awful happen to you if I could help it. And this is not so very awful, is it? You being here, inviolate, saved, wrapped up in warm blankets and half asleep?"

"Oh, Conrad is always worried about me. He likes to be."

"Fuck Conrad."

"I haven't, actually, though he would like me to, I think."

"Would you sleep with Conrad?"

"Not unless you wanted me to."

"I don't as it happens. *She* did you know."

"I didn't know. Oh, God, really?"

"Of course."

"Is all this getting very ridiculous, Max? Very crazy?"

"Yes, all of it. Move over, Clare. Make room for me." The mattress tilted under his weight. "Clare, I need you so much just now."

Flesh upon flesh. It was tomorrow in China already. Max wept as he came, his fingers biting into her back, leaving welts which were sore in the morning and she felt bruised and exhausted.

"I love you, Max. I love you so very much."

He looked at her in the cold morning light.

"Don't, Clare. Don't say anything." He clamped her mouth shut with his hand.

Five

Antonia Acton woke very early one morning at school. She began to read under the covers, but her head hurt and was hot, and she started to cough. She lay back and let her mind drift, feeling very strange indeed. When the rising bell sounded Antonia remained in bed, thinking it was rather pleasant to feel so peculiar.

"Antonia, you really should get up." Philippa, the head of bedroom, stalwart and officious, pulled back her blankets and glared at her.

"Well, I'm ill, and I'm not going to."

"But you know you have to even if you've got a temperature."

"But I'm not going to." Antonia stayed in bed, covered her face with the blankets and continued to cough.

Miss Bill stood at the bottom of the stairs and shouted, "Antonia Acton, come down here this minute."

Antonia did not reply.

Miss Bill called again, adding, "I'm going to tell Miss Jackson about this!"

Antonia waited to see what would happen. Nothing did for some

48

time. The other girls went off to breakfast rather sorry to miss the outcome of this unexpected defiance of the established order.

Antonia was awakened by the sound of two pairs of feet clumping up the uncarpeted stairs.

Miss Jackson said, "I can't imagine what you think you are doing. If you don't feel well you should have come down to surgery before the second bell. You know that perfectly well."

Her flat voice hurt Antonia's head. She opened her eyes and looked at the ceiling; she did not want to look at Miss Jackson's moles with the hairs sprouting out of them.

"I'll give you three minutes exactly to get dressed and then I'll take your temperature. Then you will have to give your apologies to Miss Genton for being late for breakfast. You've given us a great deal of trouble already. I can't imagine what your father would have to say about all this!"

Nothing, probably, Antonia thought. He wouldn't care any more than these women did. She had spent so long trying to please them all. She wondered why she had bothered.

She got out of bed feeling wobbly and put on her blouse and tunic. She did not put on her tie. She went downstairs.

"Go upstairs at once and put your tie on. You look a disgrace," said Miss Jackson, who would have been halfway through her cornflakes by now. She was famous for her greed; occasionally, pieces of toast got stuck in her teeth and remained fixed there all morning.

"I'm not going to put on my tie. I don't like it." Antonia felt very brave and wondered why she had obeyed them so meekly and unquestioningly for so long.

"Sit down and I'll take your temperature and we'll soon see about you!"

Antonia was glad to sit down. She put the thermometer under her tongue and waited. Miss Jackson folded her arms and looked out of the window at the leafless trees, dripping. The time passed very slowly and Antonia longed to cough.

"Well," said Miss Jackson. "You have got a temperature, which is lucky for you in a way. Go back to bed immediately and we'll bring you some breakfast later."

Miss Jackson did not tell Antonia what her temperature was; they never did.

Antonia lay in her uncomfortable, tangled bed and tried to sleep. Just when she had fallen into a sort of half doze, Miss Bill clattered up the stairs with a tray of congealing food. She tried to be nice and offered to get Antonia something to read. Antonia didn't reply. She hoped she was really ill, that would serve them right. It was remarkable how quickly they changed their tune when there was something really wrong with you. Antonia was sorry she could not take more interest in the discomfort she was causing them.

She was taken to the school sanatorium in a taxi. Miss Jackson and Miss Bill smiled and waved as she swept past them down the drive. Antonia looked the other way as if she had not noticed them.

Being ill had its compensations; it was quite different from her everyday existence. By lunchtime she had missed Latin, geography and double maths. The doctor arrived in the early afternoon and felt her glands, listened to her chest and looked down her throat. Antonia did not ask him what it was she had; she would not have been told.

In the bathroom next to Antonia's room was a pair of scales and she weighed herself. She thought that if she stopped eating she would be ill for longer. She had no particular desire to be thin, but it would be an interesting experiment to see how much weight she could lose before she had to return to her real life. Anyway, her throat hurt when she swallowed and she didn't want to eat.

Antonia's meals were brought to her room by Cora, a tall, gaunt woman with cropped black hair that looked as if it had been cut with kitchen scissors. The Sister was too lazy to come up except when she accompanied the doctor. Cora was simple; it was evident in her every gesture. Antonia was sorry Cora had to climb all those stairs with her food when all she did with it was wait until no one was about and then flush it down the lavatory. (She threw her pills out of the window; it was less effort than walking to the bathroom.)

Cora spent what little time she had free from her duties as skivvy embroidering cheap tablecloths with blue stamped-on designs which ran in her sweaty hands. They were very ugly and ill-worked. She told

Antonia she was making them for the girls at "the big school." "Do you think they will like them?" she asked.

"Of course, Cora. They're lovely," Antonia lied.

Cora showed Antonia her work every day, each cloth more wretched than the last. The girls would have laughed at them, Antonia knew, and prayed they would never have the opportunity. Antonia had time then, lying in her fetid bed, to think of her own life and of Cora's. Perhaps Cora was happy in her own way. But how could she be? Subject to the whims of a petty tyrant, never going out, never seeing the real world, bounded by rules and her own handicap. Perhaps she had been damaged even before she was born and was fixed here forever, incapable of either change or escape. Her life seemed dismal, dismal beyond Antonia's conceiving. Antonia tried to be kind to her and wondered if others were; if others would be. Perhaps they could run away together.

"Have you ever thought of getting another job?" Antonia asked one morning as Cora put down the breakfast tray, slopping milk all over the scrambled eggs.

"Sister says it's a kindness to have me here. To be with you girls. To help her."

"Does she really?"

"I do my best," said Cora, as if she were being accused of something.

"I know you do," Antonia said. "I don't know what she would do without you." She saw Cora's red hands, rough and raw from the potato water. There had been little flecks of blood on the tray cloths.

"They will wash out, Miss, won't they?" Cora had asked.

"I'm sure they will," Antonia lied again. She wanted to save Cora and knew that she would not.

So Antonia lay in bed for a week not eating anything. After three days she did not even feel hungry, but very light and distanced from everything around her. She half wondered if anyone would notice what she was doing but nobody did. She thought she ought to write to her father, but since they were only allowed to write postcards from the San—because germs would get trapped in envelopes they said—she decided not to. Instead, she decided that when she was better *she* would run away.

. . .

It was still quite dark inside the school bedroom, but outside the curtainless windows Antonia could see the cold gray light making the trees visible in the dawn. She looked around her at the hunched bodies, lying sleeping under their tartan rugs; at the plastic bowls on the chests of drawers beside the decanters; at the black floorboards with the minute rag rugs; at the metal tubes holding up the cubicle curtains— all dimly there but without definition. I will not miss all this, she thought.

She put on her clothes, the most inconspicuous she could think of to escape in, a pair of jeans which she had been allowed to wear to play goalie at hockey (the only compensation for that ignominious position), and her gym shoes, which had lain lumpily under her pillow all night. These last had been chosen for their noiselessness. The stairs always creaked alarmingly. Her mackintosh hung on a hook by the front door, but she decided to forgo its warmth for fear of the squeaking boards in the hall.

It was getting much lighter as she let herself out into the garden by the boiler-room window. The February air was cold against her face. She realised she would have to get away quickly before anyone else was awake.

With infinite relief she saw a bus coming up the road almost as soon as she was out of the gate. She sat on it counting her meagre funds. She hoped she had enough for a ticket to Oxford. It was just as well she did not want to go to London; she knew she did not have enough money for that.

Antonia sat on a hard bench in Great Malvern Station, attempting to look invisible. It was strange to be there alone and not surrounded by gaggles of chattering school-girls in itchy tweed coats. She tried not to look furtive as she gazed around her, and ended up staring at the pillars with their entwined metal flowers. She avoided catching the eyes of either of the two stout women in smart suits who were sitting on the next bench trying not to get their skirts dirty. They were obviously county matrons going up to shop for the day at Harrods and Peter Jones. One of their hats was a sort of muddy ochre and the other an undistinguished blue-gray, both quite unassertive and unutterably dull.

What liberation, Antonia thought, never to have to wear a hat again! Never to have to wear anything in particular, no more uniforms to humiliate and constrict her. I won't be made to look ugly ever again. I will wash my hair whenever I want and never even cast my eyes in the direction of a pair of galoshes. She catalogued the minutiae of what she had escaped, or was willing herself to escape, and managed to make herself almost cheerful by the time the train drew in. She realised no one was taking the least notice of her.

She climbed into a second-class carriage and breathed the stuffy British Railways smell with delight, that smell which usually made her feel sick, and permeated her clothes and her hair and which she could not rest without washing off. She sank into a corner seat, raising a puff of dust, and studied the pictures of seaside resorts, twenty years out of date, places which she had never visited and had always wished to see.

The train sped through a tunnel. Emerging again into the light, she could see the threatening hills diminishing behind her, and before her the spire of Worcester Cathedral beckoning from the valley, and freedom. She had always thought there was something terrifying and decaying about Malvern; a desolate lifelessness and a sense of captivity. She imagined Malvern filled with old people waiting to die, people who remembered the Winter Gardens in the days of Elgar, when George Bernard Shaw's plays were first performed at the Malvern Festival. She imagined the faded gentility of their stained and stuffy rooms, with medicine bottles collecting dust on bedside tables and the curtains never fully opened.

There had been houses she had walked past on the side of the hills, stucco-covered houses around which trees had grown up, dripping on them continuously, darkening the walls, making them rot. There was something terrible about living in a house that was overshadowed by hills and trees, a house that got no light and was always in shade, gloomy and dank.

The ticket inspector startled Antonia when he came into the compartment. "Next stop Oxford," he said, handing her back her ticket.

When she was very young she had always imagined that Simon Varley could do anything. Even his sister Christina said so. The Varleys lived near Field End, and as a child she had worshipped Simon.

Christina's infrequent letters had kept her up-to-date. She thought he might save her now. She could not think of anyone else who would.

When Antonia got off the train at Oxford Station she realised she had almost no money left and not the least idea where Balliol was. She eventually accosted a stout woman with a shopping basket and asked for directions.

"Is that one of the colleges, dear?"

"Yes."

"Well, there are a lot of them," said the woman trying to look helpful. "I just come in to do my shopping you see. I don't know much about students." She pointed vaguely in the general direction of the town. "I should ask a student if I were you. Or you could take a bus."

"Thank you very much," said Antonia, who was no better off than before she had asked. She decided to walk and try to find a student on the way. But how could one differentiate between a student and an ordinary person?

The streets were very dingy and awash with housewives in head scarves, looking purposeful. Antonia felt lightheaded and rather detached. She realised she had had nothing to eat since the previous night when she had managed an orange for supper, having spurned the tinned ravioli. Oxford was not at all as she had imagined it would be. She could see no dreaming spires at all, only Marks & Spencer and Woolworth's like in any other unremarkable town. When she turned into Broad Street the transformation was astonishing. It looked at last like the pictures she had seen in books, and she realised she had come to the right place after all.

She turned into the hallowed portals of Balliol at last (she had read "hallowed portals" in a book) and asked for Simon Varley at the forbidding porter's lodge.

She climbed the many stairs to his room wondering what on earth she would say to him and whether he would be pleased or horrified to see her. Perhaps he might not recognise her? Four years had passed. She knocked quickly on the door before her courage could fail her—and before she had any time to rehearse what she would say to him. But there was no reply.

She had not considered the possibility of his not being in. He had to be there; it was necessary for him to be there. She sat on the stairs and decided to wait.

The time passed very slowly indeed and it began to get dark as she tried to sleep with her head resting against the cold and clammy stone. Eventually she heard footsteps and two people's voices. She was not prepared for this. She had imagined meeting him alone.

"Hello, Simon," she said, her voice sounding surprisingly bright and normal.

It was almost dark and he squinted his eyes in the dim light. "But Antonia! How lovely to see you! How unexpected. I never knew you knew where I lived." He unlocked the door. "Come in anyway. This is Jeremy Winters, Antonia. Jeremy, Antonia Acton."

Antonia sat on the edge of the sofa and Simon smiled at her. "I ran away," she said. "I couldn't take it any more."

"How exciting, Toe. But when did you get here?"

"Oh, some time this morning I think. I sat on the stairs."

"How dull. But where are you staying?"

"I hoped I could stay with you. For a few days anyway, while I decide what to do."

"But of course you can. I long for a little diversion from my mundane existence."

Antonia had never seen him put out even when capsized or thrown from a horse, but still she was relieved that he took this imposition so well.

"Jeremy, this is a very great friend of mine who used to live near us in Cornwall, in a very old and wonderful house. But you look exhausted, Toe. Can I get you anything? Tea perhaps. Or toast and anchovy paste?"

"I really only want to wash my face and get rid of the smell of the train," Antonia said.

Simon showed her the basin in his bedroom and she looked at herself in the mirror. How nice it was to have her hair flowing down her back, free and unfettered. She washed her face with his face flannel and walked back into the other room.

Jeremy looked up. "How Pre-Raphaelite you are, Antonia. You should always wear dark colours. I wish someone like you would turn up on my doorstep." He handed her a piece of toast.

Antonia knelt before the fire. Simon sat opposite her, with his hand under his chin, watching her. His dark hair fell forward over one eye and he flicked it back, a gesture she remembered well.

"Was it so very bad, Toe?"

"Yes, quite bad. I couldn't see any point in it at all. Those women, the other girls curling their hair, and chapel and exams and nothing ever happening and all of us trapped."

"Does your father know where you are?"

"No, of course not. Nobody does."

"Are you going to tell him?"

"Why should I? I don't think he really cares much, do you?"

"Yes, I think he does. He always seemed to dote on you."

"When he was there perhaps, but he so rarely was. It doesn't matter anyway."

"I imagine they are scouring the countryside for you. You must tell someone."

"He's probably in Peru, or somewhere," said Antonia.

"Then you should ring Eileen. Or I could do it for you if you wanted me to. It would stop them all getting hysterical at least."

"I'd be terribly grateful, Simon. I never know what to say to her at the best of times, which this obviously isn't."

"But what do you want me to say?"

"That I'm not dead in a ditch, that I'll ring her in the morning, which I promise I will. I can't face it now." Antonia thought of her stepmother's voice, genteel and slightly nasal, always trying to be nice, making her cringe. Tomorrow was a long way off and she could not cope with anything else just now.

When Simon went out to telephone (taking Jeremy with him), Antonia went to sleep on the sofa and dreamed of Cornwall.

Antonia awoke to find her arm had gone to sleep beneath her and Simon was reading in his chair beside the fire.

"I didn't want to wake you. You looked so peaceful."

"What did you have for supper?" she asked.

"Athletic chicken. Why do you ask?"

Antonia propped herself up on her elbow and smiled. "I couldn't think of anything else to say."

"Jeremy said he thought you were exquisite."

"How nice of him. I don't think I'm exquisite at all. Is he always like that?"

"Like what?"

"Oh, always comparing people to other things and pictures and so on."

"Yes, usually. You see he thinks he's an aesthete, a sort of latter-day Oscar Wilde or Walter Pater. One gets quite used to him in the end. He thought you were very brave running away from school."

"So do I. I'm rather proud of myself. So many people say they will and never actually do it."

Simon put on a record of Greek music in a minor key, very lyrical and haunting and strange, as if the singer were grieving for something. Since Antonia knew no Greek, it was impossible to tell what; still, it was horribly tragic.

"I like that," said Antonia. "It rather sums up how I feel."

Simon looked at her quizzically. "How old are you now anyway, Toe?"

"Fifteen. Nearly sixteen."

"Isn't that rather young to be on your own?"

"I was always alone at that place I ran away from."

"School is hell, isn't it," Simon said, lighting a cigarette and dismissing the subject.

"But what did she say?"

"Eileen? Oh, she was just terribly glad that you were somewhere safe with someone she'd at least heard of. She hasn't phoned your father yet. I told her to tell them that you were with her. Rather clever of me, don't you think?"

"So they can't appear and capture me?"

"Not tonight anyway. You do make me laugh, Toe. What shall we do to celebrate your great bid for freedom?" He handed her a glass of wine which she drank slowly, not liking the taste.

"I think I'd like to go back to sleep if you don't mind. I think I've had enough of today. What time is it anyway?"

"Half past twelve. It's tomorrow already."

"And you really, truly, don't mind me staying with you?"

"I could hardly turn you out at this hour, could I?"

"No, I suppose not," she said, finishing her wine, feeling slightly sick but euphoric at the same time. "Do you want me to sleep with you?"

Simon looked as startled as she had ever seen him look, which, on him, came out looking more amused than anything else. "Why on earth did you say that?"

"Oh, I thought I should offer, having thrown myself on your mercy like this."

"You didn't have to offer, Toe. I'm not used to giving people pieces of toast and expecting them to sleep with me in return." He smiled.

"I only wondered," she said, rather worried that she had offended him. "I have never slept with anyone, ever, in my whole life, you know."

"I didn't really see you as an abandoned woman of the world, as it happens."

"Have you slept with lots of people?" she asked rashly.

"You do ask the most ridiculous questions. What would you like me to say?"

"Whatever you want to. I was just interested, that's all."

"You really mustn't go round asking people things like that."

"I'm sorry."

"It's all right. It just sounds terribly naive."

"I suppose I am naive if it comes to it."

"You do look exhausted still. Don't you think you ought to go to sleep? You can have my bed. I'll sleep on the sofa."

"No, please, have your own bed. I'm quite all right here, if you have a coat or a blanket or something. I won't be any trouble."

"You have been a great deal of trouble already."

Antonia did not know whether he was joking or not. "I'm sorry," she said again.

"Oh, do stop saying you're sorry. I said it was all right."

Antonia climbed into Simon's bed and he came and lay next to her and stroked her hair.

"I won't make love to you, Toe, because it would be the stupidest thing to do. Tell me, are you terribly unhappy?"

"Yes."

He kissed her cheek and held her. "You have grown quite lovely since I last saw you. I was quite stunned when I realised who you were."

"Am I pretty, really?"

"If you were hideous I would never have taken you in."

"Wouldn't you? Does it matter very much what people look like?"

"No, not really. You are exceptionally beautiful, but I have no real desire to be had up for statutory rape."

"What's that?"

"Sleeping with people under the age of consent."

"Oh, I hadn't realised. So you won't make love to me?"

"No. I'd go to sleep and not worry about it if I were you."

Antonia went to sleep thinking she had had a very successful day, all things considered. She was looking forward to her new life and her father's consternation.

Six

In the morning Antonia was awakened by Elinor Fane. Elinor had let herself into the room very quietly. She sat on the edge of the bed, smoking a cigarette, her coffee balanced precariously on the eiderdown. Simon still slept; his inert form loomed between them.

"Antonia," she said. "How extraordinary to see you here. I didn't know you knew Simon." She said this in the most ordinary conversational tone.

Antonia was quite dumbstruck and confused. But perhaps she should not have been. What was more natural than that the two people whom she most admired should know one another? She said, when she had recovered herself a little, "I've always known Simon. We were neighbours when I was a child."

"How lovely for you," said Elinor pushing back her flaming hair, which Antonia had never seen loose before. At school it had always been tucked up into the most correct of French twists.

It seemed odd to be talking to Elinor on terms of almost-equality. At Ashwell House she had been a remote and benign presence of infinite glamour and unapproachability. Antonia wondered if Elinor thought Simon had just made love to her.

"I thought it was term time. What on earth are you doing here?" Elinor said.

"I ran away."

"How very enterprising of you! Clare will be green with envy when she hears about it. She always threatened to do something that exciting but of course she never did. She's here in Oxford, too. Did you know?"

Antonia had not known. Though less remote than Elinor, the difference in their ages had rendered Clare almost as inaccessible.

Elinor poked Simon in the ribs. "Do wake up, Simon, and explain yourself."

He roused himself slightly and taking Elinor's lighted cigarette from her hand took a deep drag on it. "Now I feel better," he said stretching and then kissing Elinor lazily on the mouth while Antonia pretended not to notice. "Have you two met?" he asked sleepily.

"Yes, we met years ago as it happens, in that awful mausoleum in the hills. We were just reacquainting ourselves."

Antonia felt grateful for Elinor's casual acceptance of her presence.

"Oh, how very convenient. And how very good of you to come this morning, Elinor. You must help me find Antonia something to wear and somewhere to stay. I can't have her in my room indefinitely."

"Of course not," said Elinor.

Antonia felt very small then, as if she were something to be easily disposed of. "It's all right," she said. "I was thinking of going this morning, anyway."

"Don't be silly, Toe. Elinor will take you in hand. You can't disappear before we know what will become of you."

The prospect of being taken in hand by Elinor was not altogether displeasing once Antonia had got over the initial shock of discovering how things stood between her and Simon.

"Look, Antonia, I'll just go and try to round up Clare. I think she's more your size than I am. She's bound to have something you can wear and you could probably spend the night with her while you decide what to do."

Elinor swept out majestically and Antonia wished she could look exactly like her. She had been dressed in an Edwardian lace blouse and a brilliant scarlet skirt which should have clashed with her hair and looked awful but in fact had merely looked striking—she wore it with such careless abandon.

Antonia was left alone with Simon and suddenly felt shy as she had not felt the night before when she had not imagined his life at all.

At breakfast she steeled herself to ask Simon what she had been wanting to know ever since she had first seen him. "Have you been to Field End?"

"Yes, and I'm sure you would hate it. No doubt the Greys think they have improved it enormously, and perhaps they have in a way. But it's very much altered."

Antonia thought of her last view of her childhood home as her father had driven off quickly, not leaving her time to see the tears roll down Nanny's cheeks, tears which Antonia had seen forming as she had kissed her good-bye and clung to her. She had never seen Nanny cry, ever. She could still remember that day very clearly, and could still recapture the tires' impatient crunch on the gravel. The house had been bathed in the impersonal July sunlight. Already the decay was becoming apparent. The lawns had not been mown for some time and the wisteria flopped and drooped where it had not been trimmed. The brown foliage of the spring bulbs had not been removed from the urns which flanked the front door. The copper beech had been dark and brooding with all its spring lightness turned gloomy as if it were waiting for autumn already.

"I never want to see it again, Simon. I couldn't bear it. Are the Greys really as awful as I thought they were?"

"Pretty awful. My sister doesn't like them much either."

"I'm so glad," Antonia replied.

Although she had been at great pains to conceal it, Elinor had been horrified to discover Antonia in Simon's bed. Though it was unspoken, she had assumed that she and Simon had some sort of agreement. She, certainly, would not consider sleeping with another man. She had realised almost at once that Antonia was a diversion not a threat, but it

made her realise how much she valued the exclusivity of their relationship. On the other hand, Antonia's unexpected arrival might be a very
good thing for Clare; perhaps, for one day at least, it would give her
something to do and someone else to think about. Antonia might
consider Clare interesting, which was rather what Clare wanted people
to think, not pathetic as she appeared to Elinor now.

Elinor had not at first realised how much Max meant to Clare; she
had not known for some time where Clare had disappeared to in those
short dark days before Christmas. She was not her sister's keeper, she
was not there to protect her and tell her what to do. But Max was
undeniably mad, had been in hospital again in January and now did not
want to see Clare, particularly since the poisonous and glamourous
Sasha had reappeared. The fact that Max was ill did not deter Clare
from considering him the most powerful person she had ever met; it did
not terrify Clare as it did Elinor. Clare would only see the good side of
it: the energy, the intensity and the all-encompassing benevolence of
Max at his best. Conrad, however, was less sanguine. He had told
things to Elinor which she had not related to Clare, who kept hoping
that Max would come and find her when Elinor knew he would not.

Elinor let herself into the house on Woodstock Road and was
pounced on by Mrs. Corbett. "Oh, Elinor," she said, "I do wish you
would have a word with Clare. I can't think how she can behave like
this. Her flat is in the most awful state and I really don't know what I
can do about it."

"I'm so sorry, Mrs. Corbett, but it isn't any of my business to tell her
what to do."

"But your mother, Elinor. What would she think?"

"My mother is in Surrey, Mrs. Corbett. Still horribly cold, isn't it? I
wonder when the spring will ever come."

"But do have a word with her, dear, if you would."

Elinor drew herself up to her full height and looked at Mrs. Corbett's
bent back as she retreated into her room. Perhaps I am the only person
she has talked to today, poor woman, Elinor thought. But really I can't
worry about her, too. I cannot soothe everyone in this endless chain of
people who expect me to sort out their problems and help them.

Elinor picked up Clare's dressing gown, which was lying on the sitting-room floor, and went into the bedroom whose thin curtains were still drawn against the light.

Clare sat up, a strange figure bundled in sweaters and a scarf. "Oh, it's you. I was dreaming Max came to find me. Give me a cigarette, would you?"

Elinor searched amongst the rubble surrounding the bed and lit one. "Guess who I just found in Simon's bed?"

"Oh, God, El, who?" Clare managed to wake herself up enough to sound worried for her sister.

"Do you remember that child at school, the skinny elfin one, Antonia Acton?"

"What? Really? Of course I remember her." Clare was fully awake now and fascinated.

"It turns out she was Simon's neighbour in Cornwall and decided he would save her if no one else would. So she ran away from school and just turned up out of the blue. Of course Simon was rather flattered and amused and sorted it all out within reason. But it's funny, isn't it? I must say she was suitably alarmed when I arrived. As if she couldn't really believe it was me."

"If I were her I would have been alarmed, too. But tell me all about it."

"There isn't much to tell, except she seems to have left without any clothes and I wondered if you would have anything to fit her?"

"Is there anything between them, do you think?"

"No, I really think not. Though Simon feels responsible for her. She has the most feckless family who she says don't care in the least what she does. But I think she'll go to London tomorrow to see her father. And perhaps she could sleep here tonight because in spite of everything I don't want her in Simon's bed any longer than strictly necessary."

Clare smiled and said, "I used to imagine running away, but then I would think how upset Mummy and Daddy would be and I couldn't. I wish I had though!"

"It would only have caused the most awful pain and chaos, Clare. It wouldn't have achieved anything."

"No, but it might have been fun." Clare got out of bed and started looking for clothes for Antonia, things which she wouldn't miss very much but would seem romantic and unusual to someone used to a school uniform.

She took a bus into Oxford and met Antonia in Simon's room.

"How brave you are!" Clare said as they walked down Woodstock Road. Of course a bus passed them almost immediately, but Clare insisted it would not have come had they waited for it.

Antonia was not feeling very brave just then. The enormity of what she had done was beginning to trouble her. She imagined herself like a parcel handed from one set of people to another, none of whom really wanted her, and having to explain herself at every turn. But nothing, she decided, would have been worse than staying at school; that, at least she knew was true. The thought of two more years with nothing to look forward to and no real reason for acquiring knowledge except to pass exams, with no one to please or to share her pleasure, was too terrible. Of course she could pass exams. She had proved that by staying up late into the night reading under the covers or waking up early and reading in the bathroom before anyone else was awake. She had imagined that by doing well she would please her father, but he did not seem to notice.

"I seem to be causing everyone a great deal of trouble," she said to Clare at last.

"Oh, don't think about that. You're no trouble at all really. I wasn't going to do anything in particular today anyway."

"But Elinor said you were at art school. Don't you have to go in?"

"Oh, yes, that. Well, I'm supposed to. But there really doesn't seem to be much point in it just now."

"But at school everyone thought you were a tremendously good painter."

Clare kicked a Coke can off the pavement into the road where it was promptly crushed by a lorry. "But that was at school. And you know what we both thought of that!"

How comforting, thought Antonia, to be using the past tense about it. So it wasn't real any more and didn't matter.

"But you, Antonia. Tell me how you did it."

"Well, I just got up and walked out. Of course I had planned it very carefully, as I suppose most people do."

"But you actually did it, which is quite a different thing altogether."

Clare sounded admiring, which Antonia knew her father would not be. How odd to be treated as an equal by the Fanes.

Luckily, Mrs. Corbett's door was shut.

Clare's sitting room had almost certainly once been a bedroom and had equally certainly not been painted since. The walls which may have started out as a cheerful yellow were now a cheerless and murky beige. Linoleum, curling and cracking at the edges, crept out beyond the carpet which was a sort of blotched mulberry colour and threadbare. There was an old horsehair sofa, oozing prickly black stuffing, over which Clare had flung a vast Indian silk shawl in a vague attempt to make it look inviting, and two chairs with greasy arms and brownish loose covers which Clare had not attempted to do anything about at all.

"Ghastly, isn't it?" said Clare grabbing a bunch of very dead daffodils and throwing them into the wicker wastepaper basket. "If I'd known you were coming I would have tidied up a bit."

"But I think it's wonderful to have a place of your own," said Antonia, meaning it.

"Actually, it is rather," said Clare continuing to clear up in a rather haphazard fashion. "Only I wish it wasn't in this house. Another example of my mother's misplaced benevolence." She threw some clothes into a heap by the door. "Do remind me to go to the laundrette." Clare stuffed papers into drawers which were filled to overflowing already and spilled out again.

"Do let me help you, Clare."

"Oh, you needn't bother, really. It's my filth. I should deal with it." She sat back on her heels and looked about her. "There, that's much better, isn't it?"

It was not much better, in fact. The ashtrays were still full of butts and lay beside coffee mugs with the dregs congealing in them. But Antonia thought the room had a certain charm, so different was it from the austere, bleak rooms at school designed to be easily cleaned. This was all a great muddle but a comfortable one.

"Let me make you some tea." Clare disappeared into the kitchen and put on the kettle. "Do you mind if I wash my hair while I'm in here? I think there might be just enough hot water if that swine Julia didn't take it all. A legacy of school, this mortal dread of dirty hair; probably the thing I hated most about it. Didn't you?"

Antonia did not answer. Having dirty hair had been one of the things which she hated but scarcely the worst. Clare seemed to Antonia to be almost as intimidating as Elinor. Antonia wondered, as she sat listening to the water sloshing in the sink, what it would be like to be Elinor's sister.

Clare reappeared with her hair swathed in a bath towel, carrying two mugs of tea. "I hope you like Lapsang Souchong? You can only get it at one place in the market. Max always drinks it."

Antonia wondered who Max was but didn't like to ask. Instead she sipped her tea. Clare was busy drying her hair in front of the gas fire. When her hair was dry and formed a fair halo around her now-pink face, Clare lit a Black Russian cigarette (another legacy of Max), turned to Antonia, and said, "Now tell me what you're going to do."

"That's the worst of it. I don't know."

"But surely you must."

"I knew I wanted to get out of there, but I didn't really think beyond the getting out."

"You could always stay here. There are all sorts of absurd schools catering to odd people. Oxford is quite wonderful. Even I think that, though I'm hating it just now."

Clare made it seem a fascinating city. And it was not like London, Antonia thought, mile upon mile of houses, mean and bleak, with sooty gardens with railings around them that you had to use a key to get into.

Clare, her mother's daughter, suddenly remembered her duties as hostess. "Do you want some lunch? I think I've got some brussels sprouts somewhere. We could eat them with butter on."

After the meal, which consisted in its entirety of the sprouts washed down with more tea, Clare said, "Have you ever fallen in love, immediately, totally and irrevocably?"

"No, I never have," Antonia replied. "I've never been in love at all."

"I have," said Clare, swallowing two pills which she had dredged up from the depths of her capacious handbag.

"Was it wonderful?"

"Well, it was at the time. But it isn't now. Do I seem horribly depressed to you?"

"Not really. You seem rather the same as I remember you."

"Well, thank God for that. I'd hate to bore you." Then Clare spent the entire afternoon telling Antonia all about Max—she very rarely had a virgin audience after all—and to talk about him was to make him more real, more substantial. It was rather like painting, she sometimes thought, taking something which was real and turning it into something entirely different, but with its kernel still there, though transformed. And she also hoped to impress Antonia, which she succeeded in doing while, of course, hating herself for it. One should not do things to show off she knew, one should do them for a reason. But she wanted to talk about Max very much. Perhaps that was reason enough?

Raindrops slid noiselessly down the windows and the light began to fade.

"I think Elinor wanted me to show you the sights, and I'm sorry that I haven't. But we can't go out now can we? I shouldn't have been so selfish trapping you here and boring you to death with my miserable existence."

"It doesn't seem boring to me at all, Clare. I feel very honoured."

Antonia spent the night in the absent Julia's bed and prayed that she would not appear unexpectedly and throw her out.

The next morning Antonia went to London. She was dressed in a long black skirt of Clare's which swept the ground when she walked, and a green velvet jacket the colour of emeralds. She wondered if she did indeed look Pre-Raphaelite as Jeremy had suggested. Her gym shoes were somewhat incongruous beneath her new glamourous garments, and she wondered, sitting on the tube between Paddington and Oxford Circus, whether she ought to buy some shoes before she met her father. But she had no money, and her gym shoes would not be very noticeable beneath her skirt, she hoped.

Antonia walked down Regent Street and lingered before the windows of the china shops. She would like to have some plates of her own, she thought; real ones, big ones, the sort you have in your own home when you set the table for the family and they all sit round together. Perhaps she would ask her father for some, but would he think it very odd since she rarely wanted to eat?

Antonia walked unannounced into her father's office, where he sat behind a huge desk, an antique one with embossed leather on top. She looked at his fair head as he bent over some papers unaware of her standing there watching him.

When he eventually looked up, he came to her side of the desk and hugged her and kissed the top of her head. "My God, Toe. What if something had happened to you? Please don't do anything like that ever again. You don't know how frightened I would have been had I known what you were doing. Eileen was panic-stricken. They rang her up at lunchtime and told her you were gone. It wasn't worthy of you to make her suffer so."

Antonia looked at her father's well-cut suit and his polished shoes and the immaculate knot in his tie. "Eileen was the last person I was thinking about at the time," she said.

"Even so, you might have considered her. But anyway you're safe now, which is a relief. You don't know how glad I am to see you." He smiled his devastating smile. "Let's find you something slightly less ridiculous to wear and then we will have lunch and you can tell me all about it."

They went to Biba's, where Antonia chose a lot of clothes almost at random, which she knew her father would be glad to pay for. She tried them on in the communal changing room, comparing her body in the mirror with those of the other women. Their bodies were quite unlike the ones Antonia saw in magazines. Real women, it seemed, were often heavy-breasted and dimple-thighed. She was glad she had no breasts to speak of. She left her gym shoes behind to be thrown away.

"Daddy?" said Antonia in the taxi on the way to Rule's.

"Yes, darling?"

"It never was just us alone was it? Can't we pretend just for today that it is?"

As soon as they were seated and his drink was served Rex Acton said, "I gather you didn't think much of your school. I wish you had told me."

"You were never there to tell. I was sure you would think me ridiculous not liking what is supposed to be a very good school. And it was very convenient of course to be able to send me away like that."

"What else was I to do under the circumstances?"

"I don't know, Daddy. Surely you could have thought of something?"

The waiter brought melon and Parma ham. Antonia ate the melon alone and pushed the ham to the side of her plate.

"And so you still don't eat meat?"

"No, I don't like dead things. Though I eat fish occasionally for the protein."

"I wish you liked Eileen more, darling. You should make an effort not to be so cold to her."

"I do make an effort. Haven't you noticed? But it's rather hard to like someone who killed your mother, isn't it?"

"Is that what you really think?"

"It took me some time to work it out. I was very slow really, wasn't I?"

"Your mother died in a car accident."

"Of course she did. But it was very convenient."

Rex Acton looked at his plate to avoid meeting Antonia's eyes. "I don't want you to talk about Eileen like that ever again. Do you understand?"

"But you had left us both, hadn't you? Long before she died. Even then you were never there."

"It was your mother's idea to live in the country. She said London was smelly and filthy and no place to bring up a child."

"But that was not all of it, was it?"

"What are you trying to do, Antonia? Make me grovel? Make me say I was always wrong?"

"I don't know what I want you to say." Antonia pushed the remains of her omelette away from her, and a tear fell, plop, on the back of her hand "I'm sorry, Daddy, I didn't want to wreck our meal. I meant to be so grown-up and sophisticated for you."

"It doesn't matter, there will be other meals." He leaned forward and squeezed her hand. "And we still have to decide what to do with you next."

"You wouldn't send me back there, would you?"

"I've spoken to them and they won't have you, so that is quite out of the question. They think you should talk to someone about why you are so unhappy. Do you think you should?"

"What sort of someone?"

"A doctor."

"I'd rather not. I don't want people poking about and knowing things about me I would rather they didn't know."

"Quite."

"Perhaps I could go to school in Oxford? I thought it was beautiful and there are said to be all sorts of schools for misfits like me."

"If that is what you really want I'll look into it. I only want you to be happy, you know that." Rex sighed and called for the bill. He glanced at his watch. "I've got a meeting at four. Here, take this." He handed Antonia a note from his wallet. "Perhaps you could get yourself some more clothes."

"I have too many clothes as it is."

"Well, something anyway. And I'll see you tonight. I won't be late. I promise." He kissed her cheek and hugged her again and she breathed in his unfamiliar smell.

Antonia bought the plates she had coveted, lovely ones with birds and baskets of fruit on them, and hid them in the cupboard of her bedroom in the mews. She lay on the bed in her pink and white teenager's dream of a room which Eileen had had decorated for her thirteenth birthday. It looked almost more charming than it had in the magazine in which Eileen had first seen it. But Antonia hated its prissy white flounces and candy-striped walls. She considered Clare's room far nicer in its decrepitude.

Eileen sat in her bedroom, doing her nails and wishing Antonia would come out and talk to her, but she dared not knock on her stepdaughter's door.

Seven

Clare detested Saturdays. They were days when one ought to have something interesting and special to do, but she generally did not. When she had been with Max she had rarely known what day it was. But now, returned to her ordinary existence, things which she had thought did not matter began to matter again. She knew she had neglected her work and was sorry for it. She had been rude to Julia. And worst of all, she was bored.

It was the end of March, damp and cold with a gray overcast sky, and Clare was walking back to her flat with nothing better to do than wash her hair—that is, if she had a shilling to feed into the water heater, which she well might not have. As she passed the Martyrs' Memorial she noticed two of her fellow students sitting sketching, their hair being blown about by the wind. How noble of them, she thought, how purposeful, how ineffably dreary. But how nice it would be to want to work all the time!

Julia was not in, just when Clare had resolved to be nice to her. And she did not have a shilling. The freesias she had bought the previous week were dead in their jug and their water was beginning to turn to a malodorous green slime; Clare looked in the cupboard but there was nothing to eat.

She walked back to the memorial and sat down wrapping her cloak around her against the damp. Malcolm, who was in her half of the year, seemed pleased to see her, which she had thought likely. He was one of the boys who was taken in by her assumed air of mystery and world-weariness.

"Clare, I don't think you know David Lennox?" Malcolm said.

She smiled at David and looked at him properly for the first time. "No, I don't really, though I've seen you of course." She had scarcely noticed him before partly because he was always working and also because he looked quite young and was not much taller than she was. Malcolm looked at his watch and made some feeble excuse to leave, and Clare sat there alone with David and watched him draw. He drew very well, quickly and with conviction, but Clare was getting cold.

"Shall we go for a walk?" she said. "It's far too cold to stay out doing nothing." She realised that *she* was doing nothing, David was working. She knew how selfish she must sound. But David seemed pleased with the idea and closed his sketchbook without regret. They started to walk and talk, Clare making most of the conversation, since she felt David's shyness called for some animation on her part, and David seemed pleased to listen.

David, in fact, was terribly happy. It had been he who had suggested to Malcolm sketching where they did because he knew Clare might pass them on the way to her flat. He had not expected she would reappear that afternoon. He had been watching her ever since his first day at the school but hadn't known how best to approach her because she always seemed busy, or with other people, or alone, or anyway hopelessly distant. He had followed her one day as she wandered around the museum and remembered her gazing into a case full of antique clocks, absorbed in her reflection. She had turned to him and smiled dismissively as if she were ashamed to be caught looking at herself. She had glanced at him as if she thought she ought to know him from somewhere but couldn't quite place him.

Now that he was alone with Clare he didn't know what to say and was rather glad when she suggested having tea, though he was rather put out when she said they could go to the room of a friend of hers. He would have been happy to buy her tea at a shop. He was frightened that her friend would be there and they would talk about people he didn't know.

But Simon was out. Clare walked in and plugged in the kettle.

"Won't he mind?"

"I shouldn't think so," said Clare calmly. "I often do, he's almost like a brother to me. In fact he's my sister's boyfriend."

They discussed school and art and nothing in particular. Clare sensed David's nervousness and wondered why on earth he should be nervous of *her*.

Then he said, quite out of the blue, "May I look at your hand?"

Clare gave it to him, expecting that he would look at the palm, but he held it and looked across at her.

"What would you do if I said I loved you?"

And she said, as kindly as possible under the circumstances, "I hope that you don't, say it I mean." Or love me for that matter, she added to herself. Having suddenly become aware of the seriousness of what was happening, she realised that he meant it. It was rather alarming to have someone so utterly at one's mercy.

"Would you like more tea?" asked Clare brightly, disengaging her hand.

"That would be nice. I mean, if there is any."

David watched her as she poured it, her hand shaking as she did.

Oh, hell, thought Clare, what on earth do I do now? Her dread of getting hurt was equalled only by her dread of hurting someone else. Yet there was something attractive in David's intensity; she felt both powerful and impotent at the same time. She smiled as she handed him the tea cup.

"Are you happy, Clare?"

"I don't know," she replied.

"You always strike me as being horribly sad. If I could I would like to make you happy and protect you even from yourself."

"David, you don't even know me. I don't think you would like me very much if you did." Clare felt it was necessary to say this. In her heart of hearts she thought she was probably not a very nice person and she was almost certain David was. But she was secretly rather pleased at the turn of events; it is always flattering to be admired, especially so unexpectedly.

"Are you doing anything this evening? If not, I would like to take you out to dinner."

"Actually," said Clare, "as it happens I wasn't going to do anything special. Thank you very much, I'd love to go out to dinner."

David smiled and she thought he was fleetingly attractive. She added, "I think it would be fun, don't you?"

But would it? she wondered. He was, after all, rather shy and would almost certainly be intimidated by the waiters. He had looked so happy, though, when she had said she would go that she was glad she had said yes. Anyway, anything had to be better than an evening spent feeding shillings into the gas metre, lighting joss sticks and going to bed at ten out of boredom.

Dinner that night was rather a tense proceeding. However, Clare did her best to enjoy the drab surroundings (custard-coloured walls with college crests on them). After all, it wasn't often that she was invited out for a real meal. She realised that it must be costing David rather more than he could reasonably afford in order to impress her. And so she let him hold her hand in the street as they walked home but was glad that they did not meet anyone she knew on the way. She did not invite him in, in case Julia was there.

Clare lay in bed and thought about David, and if, by encouraging him, she was being unkind. Still in the dreamland of ideal love, David did not at all resemble what she imagined she wanted. He was very young for a start. She could not be sure if he was intelligent, though he could certainly paint very well. He was not tall or rich, he had no glamourous friends. But there was something about his intensity, his untouchedness almost, that made her glad that he wanted to know her. She took two sleeping pills, turned over and went to sleep.

Meanwhile David was writing a poem to her.

David invited her to his room, a cramped attic in a vast old house. It had a brass bed, an overhanging ceiling papered with faded purple roses, an easel with a painting on it, a cup with fur growing out of it, a tiny gas ring and a dirty saucepan and everywhere total confusion and chaos. Clare sat uncomfortably on the floor while David showed her his collection of animal skulls and skeletons. They gave the room its rather odd smell. His paintings littered the room, stacked, leaning, standing. She liked the room, which was totally different from most people's she knew, rooms full of contrived statements about their owners' interests and affectations. This one was merely lived in. She had no desire at all to tidy it up, was merely gratified to find somewhere more disorganised than her own lodgings. They talked about David's childhood, which had been spent in Jamaica, and which accounted for his previously unplaceable accent.

He told her how much he had hated being shipped off to England when he was seven, exiled to the biting cold and emotional restraint of a traditional prep school after the lush warmth of the tropics. He had never seen snow before, he had never been parted from Marietta, his nanny, the person he loved most in the world.

He did not talk very much about his parents, Clare noticed, but described the trees and plants and animals of that endless summer which he was still trying to recapture in his paintings. The paintings were very strange, peopled with birds and animals, half real, half imagined. They seemed to have a life of their own trapped within the confines of the picture frame. A self-contained world with little reference to the real one, an idealised world, Clare realised, a private domain, accessible only to David. She was impressed.

Clare studied David as he talked about his work, and thought for the first time that he was very beautiful. His face was not an ethereal one at all, but blunt and square, his nose short and freckled. But his eyes were lovely, a bright blue with green flecks, fringed with long dark lashes.

His hair was dark and thick, too. But he looked even younger than he was.

It was obvious that he was very nervous still, that he was frightened that Clare would not like his work, in spite of her assurances that she did. Clare, set up as an arbiter of his fate, started feeling nervous, too.

"*Do* you like them, Clare? Really?"

"I would not have said I did if I didn't."

"I thought you might merely have wanted to be kind." He kissed the palm of her hand, then held it, feeling it gently as if to understand it, to impress upon his memory the shape and texture of it. He leaned forward and kissed her mouth. Clare closed her eyes the better to feel his lips upon hers, their warmth and softness. He could not kiss her enough, touch her enough, amazed as he was at his good fortune.

He sat back and smiled into her eyes. Clare could not help smiling, too, so infectious was his enthusiasm. He looked at her as if he was drawing her, gauging the shape of her eyes and the angle of her neck, and then kissed her again.

"I love you, Clare," he said.

"I know," she said. She wondered why he had singled her out for adoration when she had been unaware of his existence.

"You don't know how long I have imagined bringing you here."

Clare hoped it was not too long. To be the object of someone's desire was rather flattering, she decided, but not very easy.

David had bought food, in metal containers, from the Chinese take-away and they picnicked on the floor surrounded by discarded drawings and unmatched socks. There was an interesting layer of fluff under the bed, Clare noticed; Mrs. Corbett would have had a fit!

"Will you stay the night with me?" David asked when the sky had blackened outside the room and the streetlights had come on, throwing orange shadows onto the ceiling.

"If you want me to." Clare by this time was bathed in the warm aura of his adoration, flattered and beguiled by his persistence.

"I was frightened to ask you. I thought perhaps you would be disgusted by all this chaos and debris. But I changed the sheets in your honour."

They were unironed but surprisingly white. Clare could see a school name tape in one corner.

"I've never had anyone to stay the night here before; I don't think the bed is very comfortable."

"Perhaps I won't notice very much."

They lay clasped together, talking and touching, until the first cold light brightened the sky. Then they fell asleep in each other's arms, in the sagging bed, warmed by each other's bodies and the promise of happiness.

Almost against her will Clare was drawn into David's world. She could not escape him nor did she try to. Because he loved her with such intensity she grew to love him and longed for the time they could spend alone together. School was a kind of torture for them both. They counted the minutes until meals, breaks and the end of the day. They tried to avoid the other students as much as possible, those other people who considered their sudden allegiance surprising and odd. At mid-morning break and lunch they ate alone in the gloomy Cadena café where no one else ate, surrounded by typists and housewives who did not know who they were and did not care.

When she was at school Clare worked very hard because working made the time seem to pass more quickly. She became a model student, avoiding the knitting ladies as far as possible and producing some passably attractive still lifes. David admired her work, and his admiration of it gave it new importance in her eyes, though she still considered it entirely secondary to her real life, which was spent alone with David, preferably in bed, isolated from the world, not needing anyone else's company or approbation.

David painted her constantly. She dwelt in the jungle, enmeshed in tropical flowers, snared by creepers, looking out at herself with great blank eyes, naked and at peace.

Clare wondered, while driving home with her father at the end of term, whether she should tell him about David; she had not told him about Max, whose conduct could never be construed as honourable however fascinating he had been.

She turned the conversation to Jamaica, where her parents had once spent a holiday, and she did start talking about David as the green, damp fields sped past the window. The fields soon gave way to the forsythia hedges of suburbia and neat gardens with improbably pink-blossomed cherry trees.

"Dad, I think he's a very good painter, but he's younger than me."

"That's hardly important, darling."

"What?"

"That he's younger than you. I don't think a month or two will matter much in the annals of world history, anyway. What does he paint? This inamorata of yours?"

"Jungles mostly and birds. His parents were very proud of his first paintings, which were exhibited in London at some society or other when he was still at school. But he doesn't want to paint pictures of birds that look like real birds and appeal to pedantic naturalists, though there seems to be money in it."

"What does he want to paint?"

"Oh, me, and pictures of animals of no definable species."

"The trouble with me, Clare, is that I like pictures to look like what they are meant to be. I don't have very advanced ideas about art, though I'm sure you do."

Clare didn't think she had, actually. She had a secret hankering for the solidity of Courbet and the diffused world of the Impressionists. Art that was based upon reality but enhanced and made rich and ripe. She could see no merit in abstraction.

"You do look rather artistic though," said her father. "I don't quite know what your mother and the worthy matrons of suburbia will make of you."

"I don't really care what they think, Dad," Clare said as unaggressively as possible. She thought she looked rather nice, though she could see that her father might have doubts about her pony-skin jacket (ex-jumble sale) which was a little bare at the elbows. She liked her wide-brimmed felt hat which she had pinned back with an art nouveau clip. She thought she looked very romantic, pale and interesting, though she rather doubted there would be anyone at home to interest.

"How is Mummy, anyway?"

"Flourishing. And the daffodils are out. She's told me the menu for the entire weekend at least twice already, but I've forgotten half of it."

Her father's tolerance of her mother's foibles never ceased to amaze Clare. She sometimes tried to imagine what her parents would think of each other, if they met now for the first time, at a drinks party, for instance. She wondered whether they would have much to say to each other or would like each other at all. How odd it would be to be in love with the same person for twenty-five years! And yet they obviously were still in love; she remembered how her father's eyes had lit up when he showed her the present he had bought for her mother's fiftieth birthday, just like a schoolboy with a secret. He had such pleasure in giving presents to people, seemed to enjoy them even more than the recipients did, Clare sometimes thought. She loved her father unreservedly. He never irritated her as her mother often did. He never asked awkward quesions or made her feel guilty except when she was rude to her mother, which she never meant to be really but seemed unable to avoid.

Clare walked in the woods, sat beside the lake and painted the water, which reflected the green shadows of the new-leafed silver birches. It was not a very good painting at all. They had been set, as a vacation project, to paint from nature. But Surrey that April seemed singularly unpicturesque.

She decided to turn the conservatory into a studio and nailed hardboard onto struts. She attempted a vast ambitious picture with five figures, sort of Augustus John out of Piero della Francesca. It was even worse than her effort with the lake, and the damp made the struts warp. She abandoned the attempt, and it remained a dusty monument surrounded by geranium cuttings, a constant reproach to her failure to achieve anything. She thought about David, and how to him painting was supremely important, more important than anything else, certainly more important than she was. She wondered why it didn't matter as much to her.

Clare hated the suburban security and comfort of her parents' house, its familiar dullness and her inability to create anything there or even want to. So she stopped trying and instead watched television, walked the dogs, ran errands for her mother and ate a lot. The holidays now seemed to her not freedom, as they once had, but constriction. She was glad that her mother had no inkling of her real life, which she now felt was outside this house altogether, on an entirely more rarefied and spiritual plane. They both did their best to be nice to one another and masked their irritation as best they could.

Eight

Lydia Hughes-Ellis turned up unexpectedly one day in Antonia's boardinghouse room, a striking vision dressed entirely in butter yellow. Antonia was surprised Lydia wanted to know her. She had almost entirely ignored her the previous Christmas when, invited by Lydia's younger sister who was her schoolmate, she had gone skiing with Lydia's family.

Antonia was kissed on both cheeks. "How marvellous that you are here in Oxford! Clare told me all about your escape and I thought I would come and look for you. But what on earth are you doing in this North Oxford hole?"

"I'm meant to be getting my O levels."

"Oh, so am I. I failed them last year. I was much too busy to read any of the books." She held out her hands from which pearlescent talons sprouted and looked at them. She obviously liked what she saw. "I live in the most perfect place you can imagine. Right in the middle of town. You must come and see it. I'm all alone at the moment. Come now. It won't take a minute."

It was indeed one of the most magical places Antonia had ever seen; in a tiny road parallel to Broad Street, a very small old house set on an ancient street with church spires visible from either end.

"It *is* wonderful, Lydia."

"That's just the point. I want to stay here and I'm behind with the rent. Would you like to live here, too?"

"Of course I would. But how much do you owe?"

"Oh, only about twenty pounds. Then it would only be two pounds ten a week. They say Henrietta Maria stayed here during the Civil War and D. H. Lawrence later on."

"What an odd pair," Antonia said, while wondering if she had twenty pounds in her bank account and how often Lydia was in debt. In Switzerland she had only spoken to Antonia when she wanted to borrow money for ski lifts and drinks. Antonia had not had a room of her own for some time except the pink room in Eileen's house, which didn't count. "I'd love to, Lydia," she said.

"Then it's settled. Can you give me the money tomorrow?"

"Of course."

"But first you must meet Mrs. Tradescant."

Mrs. Tradescant came with the house. They never knew how long she had been widowed. She was over ninety then; wizened and bent. Her husband had been a cobbler and the cellar was full of his lasts, the ancient wooden shapes of the feet of people long dead. She spent her days in the darkened front room facing the street, a benevolent presence waiting for her son to come home from the war, the first war it turned out. She had kept his bed made up for fifty years. She slept on the top floor where Antonia had her cell-like room, Antonia to the left, Mrs. Tradescant's son in the middle, and Mrs. Tradescant at the end. Lydia had a room somewhat bigger than Antonia's, next to the sitting-room which looked out over the street and into Jesus Quad, where a huge horse chestnut tree grew alight with white candles in the May air.

Antonia telephoned Mrs. Tradescant's daughter-in-law once a week; they were meant to keep an eye on her which was why the rent was so cheap, and she occasionally bought Mrs. Tradescant flowers, which she seemed to enjoy. The telephone was in an Indian restaurant which was in the next street, but its kitchen abutted theirs at the back of the house and strange smells would waft into their kitchen. Lydia would then light joss sticks in competition. Antonia thought the joss sticks were more revolting than the food but Lydia said they weren't.

Mrs. Tradescant did not bother them at all. She would sometimes wander into their sitting-room late in the night and tell them that they should be in bed, but Lydia would say, "But it's only half past ten. We can't tell our friends to go yet." It was often one or two at the time but Mrs. Tradescant did not seem to notice and shuffled off in her down-at-heel slippers, smiling faintly to herself; she was quite satisfied.

Antonia felt in those weeks that she was truly happy for the first time in her life. She would sit looking out at the tree, listening to Mahler, and try to write poetry (an activity she hid from Lydia), and wait for people to turn up as they invariably did, parades of people drawn by Lydia's beauty. She would watch the rain falling silently into the street and smell the spring air, the dampness mingling with the house's smell, pungent and sweet. It reminded her of Cornwall.

Lydia was often out, with a succession of men whom she professed to despise but whom Antonia found charming and attentive. Because Lydia was beautiful and cold they flocked to her and remained to become Antonia's friends. She did not mind being second best nor the interminable walks around St. John's garden with some of their number discussing the state of Lydia's heart, being pumped for information. She liked being a part of things, being asked out to dinner when Lydia would not go. She was glad to be noticed by Lydia's rejects.

Antonia performed many useful functions for Lydia. She cleaned the house. She was a foil to her fairness. She took messages and was a permanent audience to her intrigues. She felt herself to be quite indispensable. She couldn't understand why Lydia was so successful, why she curled men round her little finger and dropped them so callously.

Since her adoration of Simon was obviously fated to be fruitless, and she liked him too much to embarrass either herself or him, she fell in love instead with one of Lydia's cast-offs. William Grenville was a fair-haired old Etonian with square hands whose nails were bitten as hers were at that time. His eyes were clear and blue like her father's. At first she thought he did not notice her.

"Toe, do stay. Perhaps he'll go away sooner," Lydia whispered one day when William had come to visit her. Antonia hoped he would not and sat in the shadow of the beam which divided the room and gazed at him, his profile turned against the light.

"Toe, I'm going out now to see Adrian. *Do* try to get rid of him before I get back. It's getting too silly. He must realise it by now."

To Antonia, William was the embodiment of everything a man should be: decisive and funny, very rude about the foibles of the world, careless about his work and the world's vision of him. And yet Antonia felt that beneath this casual and carefree veneer he was very good and very strong. She longed for him to touch her. She did not imagine him making love to her (nothing as real or dramatic as that), just being alone somewhere talking into the night.

"Don't offer him anything to drink, Toe," Lydia said as she swept out of the room.

Antonia offered him wine or tea as soon as she heard the front door slam, glad to keep him, if only for a moment.

"Wine would be nice, I think," he said.

They sat together quite companionably as the light faded, and Antonia drank in his every gesture and all of their rather prosaic conversation.

"And so the Circe departs and it's just us, Antonia. Do you want to come for a walk?"

"I should really read tonight. I have a lesson in the morning," she said, waiting to see if he would bother to persuade her to come or was just being polite and really longing to escape.

"Lessons. Lessons. I can't think why you bother with them."

"Because I'm very undereducated, as Jeremy would say."

"Would he? He's very overeducated if you ask me."

"Yes, but he makes me feel very ignorant."

"Does that matter?"

"Yes, it does to me," Antonia said.

"I don't really like sophisticated people," said William, "particularly sophisticated women."

"Isn't Lydia sophisticated?"

"Yes."

"But you like her."

"I don't *like* her in the least, Antonia. She isn't the sort of person you like exactly, is she?"

"No," said Antonia.

"But there it is. Why don't we go and climb into the Botanical Gardens and look at the plants?"

"It's locked up at night."

"So?"

With William, Antonia thought she could do anything. He took her by the arm as they walked down the dark street together.

"She's a bitch, Antonia."

"Yes, I suppose she is."

"Why isn't she nice like you?"

"You probably wouldn't like her if she was."

"It's very stupid, isn't it?"

"Yes, it is," said Antonia, wondering if he had the least idea what she felt about him.

They climbed over the spikes by the river. Antonia was terrified of falling and impaling herself but did not say anything for fear of appearing feeble and childish. William caught her as she jumped down, her heart in her mouth. They looked at the angelica plants which towered above them.

"It's quite different at night when there's nobody here, infinitely better don't you think?" he said.

The clouds moved swiftly over the sky and the greenhouses glinted white in the moonlight. They walked hand in hand round the gardens, smelling the damp, well-tended earth.

"And what are you doing here in Oxford, Antonia?"

"Oh, I ran away from school and couldn't think of anywhere else to go. I thought Simon Varley would take me in. It turned out very well, don't you think?"

"How did you meet Lydia?"

Lydia. Always Lydia.

"I was at school with her younger sister. I met her ages ago."

"Was she always so vain?"

"Yes," Antonia said, not feeling particularly loyal to her at that moment.

"You're so funny, Antonia. Do you just sit there knowing everything about everyone?"

"A bit about some of them; Lydia's conquests."

"Don't you want to conquer people, too? Most people seem to, women anyway."

"I don't think so. I just want to be liked. I wouldn't know what to do with a conquered person. And I probably haven't any talent for conquering, if it comes to it."

"You're much better off not, I think."

They walked in silence for some time. "Do you want to go back now? I'll walk you to your virgin tower with resident witch."

"Do you really think Mrs. Tradescant witch-like?" Antonia asked.

"Perhaps, or like a dragon whom one must slay in order to proceed with one's quest."

"Do dragons wear pink nylon dressing gowns?"

"Who knows what they wear. Give my love to Lydia," he said at the door.

"I will. Thank you for the walk."

"I enjoyed it." He kissed Antonia's cheek.

She went to bed thinking about their conversation and how absurd it had been and when she would see him again. She supposed William would want her to tell Lydia all about climbing into the garden to make her think she had missed something.

When she went to wake Lydia in the morning, she saw a man's body in the bed beside her, his wild dark hair spread on the pillow. She crept out without waking either of them and went back to writing her essay on Shelley, drinking tea from a cracked Minton cup.

"Did William stay long?" Lydia asked when she emerged later in the morning.

"For a bit," Antonia said. "We went for a walk."

Lydia was too bored to ask where. She continued filing her long nails. "Can I borrow your belt," she asked, "the wide red one?"

"If you want to." Antonia hoped she would get it back, preferably undamaged. Lydia was rather careless of other people's things, particularly hers.

"It goes with my yellow blouse, don't you think?" Lydia appropriated the belt. "Am I getting fat?" she asked, turning sideways and holding her breath.

"Not that I've noticed. But please don't put it on the last hole. You'll stretch it."

"Will I? You're disgustingly thin, Toe. You should eat more."

"I don't want to get fat, either," Antonia said.

"I suppose not." Lydia pulled the belt on to the last hole and looked at herself in the mirror which was propped up on the sideboard. "Do I look okay?"

"Yes. Are you going out?"

"Yes."

"Then what am I meant to do about him?" Antonia enquired.

"Who? Oh, Spongo. Anything you want. He probably won't wake up for a while anyway. How did you know he was here?"

"You asked me to wake you up, if you remember."

"Did I?" Lydia asked vaguely.

"Yes, you did. Mrs. Tradescant will have a fit."

"Let her. Oh, do stop worrying what Mrs. Tradescant will think. It's not worth it. She'll forget almost immediately anyway."

"Doesn't he have a real name, Lydia?"

"I never asked. I suppose so. Most people do. He had some wonderful dope. Do you want some?"

"No, it makes me feel sick."

"But this is really good stuff, much better than the last lot." Lydia was being magnanimous, stubbing her cigarette out in Antonia's saucer.

She went out and Antonia was left alone with Spongo, who vomited into the lavatory and then left, too, taking his guitar with him.

"Tell Lydia I'll see her around."

"Yes," Antonia said. She cleaned the bathroom before Lydia got back. She could not imagine what Lydia could see in Spongo when she could have had William.

Lydia decided to give a dinner party. "Do you want to come, Toe?"

"Well, I could always go and hide if that's what you want."

"Oh, I didn't mean that. It's just that you look so gauche sometimes."

"I'll do my best not to. How do I look gauche, anyway?"

"Oh, I don't know. You look at everyone so adoringly. You act like some sort of puppy."

Antonia was rather hurt. "Well, I'll try not to this time. Who are you having?" She was pleased at the thought of a party at the flat. "Will you have Spongo?" She was fascinated by their dubious relationship.

"Of course not. This is a dinner party. You don't ask people like him to dinner."

"No."

"Well, I thought we could have Simon and Elinor since they've been so kind to you."

"Yes, I'd like that."

"And Jeremy Winters because he's always very good value at dinner. He'll come if William does even if he loathes me."

"Does he loathe you, Lydia?"

"Of course he does. And Liz Jacobson because she's so clever and fat. To give intellectual tone you see. She can talk Italian to Claudio."

Antonia did see. It was a plot of Lydia's to get Claudio Monseignori, whom Antonia found courtly and terrifying. Simon had said that they only let him into Christ Church because of all his money. He would be a catch for Lydia in a way.

"And I thought we could ask poor William, pining away. You'd like that, Toe, wouldn't you?"

Antonia could see it all; it was really quite cleverly done. She had to admire Lydia, a whole dinner party and no one to threaten her at all.

Claudio sent flowers on the afternoon of the party. "There are some for you, too, Antonia." Lydia sounded disappointed. "But I suppose properly brought up Italians are terribly polite and he wouldn't want to be too obvious, would he?"

Antonia was pleased because she had never been sent flowers before.

"The place does look clean, Toe! Did you work terribly hard? Did you manage to get everything?"

"Yes, your share comes to three pounds seven and eight."

"As much as that!"

"Well, I got everything you asked for."

"Oh, well. I'll pay you back in the morning."

They had not got eight chairs so Antonia sat on the edge of a trunk which they had covered with a patchwork quilt with a cushion on top. She was almost the same height as everyone else. She had chopped chives into the chilled consommé (which had come out of a tin, but no one seemed to notice). She had also chopped chives into the bottled mayonnaise to make it seem homemade. The salmon was all right anyway; Lydia's father had had it sent to them fresh. Antonia had bought the tiniest peas and the smallest new potatoes she could find in the covered market. Their guests had brought more than enough wine.

It was a great success, Lydia taking all the credit for it as was her due as hostess. She looked wonderful, dressed in old white lace, wearing enormously long false eyelashes. She was very graceful and gracious, her eyes gleaming in the candlelight. Antonia wore a black, sprigged silk dress which had belonged to her mother's mother and which she had used for dressing up as a child. It was rather tattered and she had pinned it together with a seed pearl brooch of her mother's. The stuff had originally been very good. Antonia thought it had come from Paris.

"How divine!" said Jeremy. "Are you allegories of Night and Day? Or Lydia is a Valkyrie and Antonia a wood nymph?"

Lydia looked as if she were not quite sure she wanted to be likened to a Valkyrie; however, she continued smiling.

"How frightfully clever of you to find such an exquisite place, Lydia," Jeremy continued. "Are you taking care of Antonia or corrupting her?"

"Corrupting her horribly I should think." Lydia laughed.

"Are you very corrupt and world-weary, Antonia?" he asked.

Antonia wished they would stop talking about her. She could never think of anything remotely clever to say. She went to fetch the strawberries which she had left in the cellar to stay cool since they had run out of room in the minute refrigerator. She looked at the cobwebs and listened

to conversation which was very far above her, both literally and meta-
phorically, she felt. Liz Jacobson was talking about Dante, whom
Antonia had never read, and Elinor about Florence, where Antonia had
never been.

Simon came and sat next to Antonia as they drank their coffee. "I
wouldn't worry about them if I were you, Toe. It's all a pretense, a game
really. Lydia doesn't even know what she is talking about half the time.
She just likes to hear the sound of her own voice."

"But she does *sound* intelligent at least."

Simon made a dismissive gesture. "How goes it all really? Elinor and
I worry about you a bit, you know."

"Oh, fine. You see I enjoy it all really, except when they make fun of
me. I would prefer just to listen. I'm so frightened of seeming stupid."

"Nobody thinks you are stupid. You were even quite funny about
Shelley."

"That's the whole point. I wasn't meaning to be funny."

"I rather doubt Lydia has read him at all."

"Oh," said Antonia, slightly comforted.

"People are much more easily amused when they're drunk."

"Oh, stop being nice, Simon, it makes me feel worse."

"Anyway you look very lovely. You don't need to talk."

"How humiliating, Simon, to be a part of the decorations like a
potted palm."

He smiled and went back to Elinor. Claudio was obviously entranced
with Lydia; they were comparing notes on the grander ski resorts.
Antonia knew Lydia had only been to two but did not say anything. She
hoped no one would notice where the rather lovely old table was
propped up with an unopened tin of baked beans. Jeremy was amusing
William discussing the sexual proclivities of mutual acquaintances and
being artfully verbose; Antonia thought he was funny, too.

Lydia lit a joint and passed it around wanting to seem sophisticated.
"Such a good way to end a meal, don't you think?" She exhaled slowly
and looked into Claudio's eyes through the smoke.

The night breeze crept in through the open window, smelling of
summer. Antonia took the joint inexpertly and held her breath for a
moment hoping it would make her relax and not feel sick as it

sometimes did. Lydia looked very grown up, she thought. Perhaps in two years she would look grown up, too. Perhaps there was hope for her yet.

William sat on the floor, his back resting against a table leg (not the one with the beans tin, which Antonia hoped he would not dislodge).

"Come and sit by me, Antonia." He put his arm round her shoulders and she shivered; she had waited so long for him to touch her. "Are you cold?" he asked.

"No, not at all."

"You seem cold. Shall I shut the window?"

She was in fact rather chilly, since her dress was very thin and she was wearing nothing beneath it, but she did not want him to move. He might take his arm away and not put it back. She thought he was probably drunk, pleasantly drunk, anyway very far from sober.

"Your hair smells very nice tonight." He twined his fingers through it.

"I've just washed it with herb shampoo," she said, thinking, God what a ghastly thing to say! just like someone in a television commercial. She blushed; luckily it was quite dark and no one could see.

"Lydia's in fine form tonight, isn't she?" said William.

"In her glory, I would have said."

"What do you make of all this, Antonia?"

"I rather enjoy it."

"Well, it bores me rigid," said William.

"Then why did you come?"

"To see Lydia of course; to torture myself. And to see you, too. I wouldn't miss seeing you, you know that." Antonia wanted to ask: Why are you so lovingly my friend? Don't you know that's not what I want at all? But she didn't.

He obviously did not know. "I'm drunk again, Toe. Can I call you that?" He put his head on her shoulder.

"You can call me anything you like, though I think it's rather a ghastly name. It always makes me think of feet."

"But you have such elegant feet."

Antonia had kicked off her high-heeled red shoes, which lay beside her on the dark floor. "It's funny you've noticed. I quite like them, too."

She stretched out her naked toes. "Not a very noticeable asset, though. You can't get far on feet alone."

"I do love you, Antonia."

"I know. That's the worst of it. Loving me and wanting Lydia."

"Who said I wanted Lydia?"

"You did. Everyone does."

"Stupid Lydia. Lovely Toe. She'll get her comeuppance in the end."

Antonia thought: William is making much of me to get at Lydia, and Lydia isn't taking any notice.

William was really very drunk by now. Antonia got up and poured more coffee. She wondered if she could sit down again where she had been before, or whether it would be too obvious. She knelt back on her heels and looked around the disordered, flower-filled room.

"Why did you go away?" William took Antonia's hand, with its chewed nails, in his.

Lydia said, "Look at Antonia making cow eyes at William. His Constant Nymph."

"Shut up, Lydia. You aren't worth her little finger."

"What, with its bitten schoolgirl nails? Come William, you can do better than that."

It was lucky for Lydia, Antonia thought, that Claudio was not listening. Lydia looked slightly wary as if she knew she had gone too far and was frightened of being discovered.

"Stupid cow," William whispered in Antonia's ear. "Silly bitch."

Lydia swept out of the room with Claudio. "I'm sure Antonia will take care of you all," she said, framed in the doorway, flushed with triumph. "I'll see you later, Toe."

When Lydia smiled she was quite breathtakingly beautiful, and even Antonia could feel the power of her pleasure. Elinor and Simon stayed for a moment and started to help Antonia tidy up. William sat looking out of the window.

"It doesn't matter," said Antonia, "I'll do it in the morning."

"It really was the most lovely evening, Antonia," said Elinor, kissing her on the cheek. "I always knew you could cope."

Just then Mrs. Tradescant shuffled in and William told her that he was Antonia's brother, and that he was staying for the night.

"How nice for you, dear," she said, smiling kindly and drifting out of the room.

"But you ought to go, William," said Antonia.

"Should I?" He smiled up at her. "Lovely Toe. Stay and talk to me."

"What do you want to talk about?" Antonia sat down beside him on the floor.

"Not Lydia anyway."

"Well, that's a relief." She allowed herself to smile. "I get quite bored of talking about Lydia."

"I'm sure you must." He took Antonia's face in his hands and kissed her.

"Do you want some whiskey?" she asked after a time.

"I'd love some. How clever of you to think of it."

"It's Lydia's whiskey," she said.

"Naturally."

She poured him a glass.

"May I sleep with you, Toe? Most lovely of Antonias?"

"If you want to," she said.

He kissed her again very gently.

They crept silently upstairs, past Mrs. Tradescant's room and the room of her son. William went to sleep immediately without making love to her, or, in fact, touching her at all.

"I'm sorry about last night," said William. "Was I very drunk?"

"Yes." Antonia liked William being there in the morning beside her, being alone with him in the room.

"Is Lydia back?" he asked.

"I don't think so. I haven't liked to look."

They sat later amidst the debris of the previous night, drinking coffee. There was nothing to eat but Antonia had not wanted to go out to get anything in case he left in her absence. A clock struck eleven.

"I must go," said William, touching her lightly on the cheek. She longed to ask when she would see him again but did not dare. He clattered down the stairs and out into the street.

So that's that, she thought. I will try to digest it all later when I've tidied up.

When Lydia appeared, she said, "It was wonderful, Toe. We drove to London in his Alfa and went to a nightclub. It wasn't like being with a student at all. Claudio is so unlike all the creeps we know here. William, for example, so predictable and dreary, and Jeremy so irritatingly fey, always trying to be clever. I feel so beyond all that, that my real life isn't here at all."

"I quite like William," Antonia ventured.

"Anyway," continued Lydia ignoring her remark, "Claudio has asked me to go punting on the river tonight and he asked if you would like to come, too. I can't think why except there is going to be quite a big party. Do you want to come?"

"Not if you put it like that."

"Well, it might be good if you did come. He said he liked you."

"Did he? But he scarcely spoke to me."

"Well," said Lydia, "he seems to think we are very great friends."

"Are we great friends, Lydia? I sometimes think you consider me a convenience, some sort of theatrical prop. Gracious Lydia, to have taken in poor Antonia."

"Oh, don't be stupid. Why on earth do you think that? I adore you and anyway it will be quite wonderful on the river. What shall I wear? Do I have anything remotely clean? I must look." Lydia went to her room and started to sort through heaps of clothes which were littered over every available surface. "Do help me, Toe. I do value your advice." Lydia smiled so stunningly that Antonia thought for a moment that perhaps Lydia did like her after all.

"You are having fun, aren't you, Toe? I told you we would." Lydia picked up a red silk dress which had been lying on the floor. "I suppose I'll have to iron it. Does red look very wanton?"

"Do you want to look wanton, particularly?"

"Yes, I do."

"Then it does," said Antonia.

"God, you're irritating sometimes, Toe! Why are you always so eager to please?"

"I'm not. I just hate arguing about things which aren't really important."

"You won't get far not arguing; it's so unnatural. Can I borrow your shawl? The one with the black fringe?"

"I thought I might wear it myself if it got cold."

"Oh," said Lydia fishing out some leaf-green tights from under the bed, "I suppose I'll have to wash these, too."

Antonia hated the smell of Lydia's room, cigarette smoke and spilled scent vying with each other. Lydia rarely opened the window.

"Well, if you change your mind about the shawl do let me know. And have you seen my hair brush?"

"On the sideboard where you spilled the honey," Antonia said.

"Christ, is it really? How on earth did it get there?"

"You put it there yourself when you came in."

Antonia was constantly amazed at how Lydia managed to look immaculate in public, how she could contrive to make herself such an icon, all out of such chaos. "Aren't you meant to be at school this afternoon? You have a lesson at three-thirty," she said.

"How boring you are, Antonia. Don't you ever enjoy yourself? I couldn't work now if they dragged me to it. I'll say I was ill when I next go in."

"But you've had the flu three times this term already."

"Well, it's a very difficult recurring kind of flu. They must realise that by now, don't you think?"

"They probably do," said Antonia.

"Don't you think Claudio is quite magnificent?"

"Yes. But in rather an intimidating way."

"He's not intimidating at all," said Lydia.

Not knowing exactly what Lydia wanted her to say about Claudio, Antonia went out and bicycled around the town, feeling very vibrant and alive. She half hoped she would run into William, but of course she did not.

Nine

Clare was enchanted with the house in Ship Street, though not with Lydia, whom she had long detested. "I can't think why you put up with her, Toe," she said.

"But this was her place first, she found it."

"Even so, you shouldn't let her be quite so beastly to you."

"She's quite nice at intervals," said Antonia.

"Only when she wants something," said Clare. "But who cares about Lydia anyway. I'm sorry that I haven't seen you for so long, but I've never worked so hard in my life. I feel quite virtuous, actually. But it isn't very good, my work I mean. You should see David's! You must meet him, Toe. You'd like him enormously, I think. He's not a bit alarming and he's awfully nice."

Lydia appeared, looking bored. "Oh, Clare," she said, "how is the great world of art?"

"Much as usual, Lydia, thank you."

"You do look the part, Clare. But is it necessary to go round advertising it?" She stared at the great blotches of vermillion paint spattered all over Clare's skirt, which she had obviously been using as a paint rag. Antonia had thought them picturesque and bohemian.

"Oh, God, I do look rather a mess, don't I? I never remember to change. Never mind, no one really cares what I look like there."

"Do they pay the models much? The ones that you paint from?"

"I haven't a clue, Lydia. I shouldn't think so. Why? Do you want to be painted?"

"I've thought of it, but I'm not quite sure if I want to sit about naked and be gawped at by all your spotty fellow students."

"Oh, you'd love it, Lydia. I'm sure you would," said Clare grinning. "Just think of it: your exquisite body captured for eternity in oils!"

"I'll think about it," said Lydia, glancing at herself in the mirror.

"Well," said Clare when she and Antonia were safely out in the street, "it would be rather fun to have Lydia as a model. Most of us can't paint at all well yet. She might come out looking perfectly frightful."

They walked through the summer streets to David's room. Antonia looked forward to meeting him but she wondered if anyone could ever live up to Max, whom she had never met.

David looked up as the girls entered the room, kissed Clare and held out his hand to Antonia.

"This is where we spend all our time holed up when we're not at the museum," said Clare, pushing aside a pile of unfolded laundry and making a place for Antonia on the bed. "Well, what do you think, Toe? Aren't you stunned by all this?"

Antonia looked at David's paintings, which were propped up all over the place: Clare sleeping, Clare reading, Clare looking directly out at her, and Clare in various states of undress. Clare had been quite right, her paintings were quite insignificant in comparison. She also looked at David.

"Do you only paint Clare?" she asked him.

"I used to paint jungles," he said. "But I prefer painting Clare."

Antonia saw how he looked at Clare then, a very private exchange. Clare was right, he was very beautiful.

"I'm very flattered to be someone's inspiration," Clare said. "It's all rather fun. All except Marilyn of course. She hates me."

"She doesn't you, Clare. She just doesn't want you to be here, that's all."

"Oh, but she does hate me. She loathes my guts."

"Who's Marilyn?" Antonia asked, imagining a deposed model, an outcast from David's pictures.

"The landlady," said Clare. "She lives downstairs. I don't seem to have much luck with landladies. She's a terribly sad sort of Socialist. She adopted David when he first came to Oxford and lets him have the room for almost nothing. She hasn't got any children, only cats—which is a part of the deal. He has to feed them when she goes away."

"Which I ought to do now," said David going out with a rusty tin-opener in his hand.

"He is nice, isn't he?" said Clare, collapsing back onto the pillows. "You know I never imagined myself falling in love with anyone nice. Not that I wanted to be in love with anyone horrible. But it's rather frightening being with someone you have the power to hurt. And I used to think that I preferred tall men, but it doesn't really matter, does it?"

Clare seemed to Antonia to be terribly happy. She regaled Antonia with a catalogue of David's virtues. "You know what the only bad time was?"

"No," said Antonia, thrust again into her usual role as audience.

"When I was being sick all the time," said Clare.

"But why on earth were you being sick?"

"Oh, that was just at the beginning when I went on the pill."

"I never knew it made you sick," said Antonia.

"Neither did I, but it did. It's quite funny in retrospect. I decided to go on the pill, but I didn't dare just waltz in and demand it. I thought that would be rather too brazen, besides which I don't think doctors like *you* to tell *them* what you want them to give you, do you?"

"No," said Antonia, from her somewhat limited experience of the species.

"Anyway, I crawled off to my supplier of Librium and Mandrax and muttered something blushingly about wanting to know about contraception. I think he was more embarrassed than I was. He went on for a full ten minutes describing a whole barrage of hideous devices before he eventually said he thought I could go on the pill. I wished I could have told him that straightaway and saved him the trouble. Anyway, he gave them to me, and I took them. And every morning I was sick as a dog. It's quite disgusting really, throwing up when you haven't got anything in your stomach *to* throw up. Awful yellow bile juices, pinging into tin bowls; truly revolting. I couldn't get up until noon. David brought me endless cups of tea in bed, but they didn't help and I used to slink about on the landing, longing for Marilyn to disappear for the day. I'm sure she must have known what was going on, but she never said of course. Do you think it's as bad as that when you're pregnant?"

"I suppose it might be," said Antonia. "But I don't think I've ever known anyone who was pregnant, or at least when they *were* pregnant."

"It wasn't something I could ask my mother really, was it?" Clare grinned. "But anyway, after a week of this I'd had enough. So I rang up the wretched doctor and recited my woes. 'Quite normal,' he said, 'it'll pass.' He actually sounded quite pleased about it; divine retribution for transgressing girls! I think he's a Catholic, he's got an Irish name anyway. So that was that, and it did get better."

David reappeared and the subject was dropped. They sat together on the bed (the only place there was to sit) and drank mugs of tea. Antonia didn't dare risk the milk because it looked a bit odd. She picked up a skull and examined it. "This must be a fox," she said. "Years ago I had one just like it, and a vole and a stoat, except I was never allowed to bring them into the house." She smiled; how liberating it was no longer to be told what to do all the time!

They talked, then, about their families and their various failings: Antonia's father's general lack of interest in her, Clare's parents' too great an interest, and the utter gloom emitted by the Lennoxes.

"Do you want to stay for supper, Toe? We so rarely see anyone. I think there's some ham somewhere, or there was," said Clare.

"I ate it when you were out," David said.

"Oh, well, there isn't anything to eat, but I could go out and get something. Do stay!"

"No, I really ought to go. I think William Grenville might be coming to see Lydia this evening."

"But if he's coming to see Lydia, what do they need you for?"

This was unanswerable. Antonia did not want to say that she wanted to see him herself and Lydia didn't. Clare had decided to get a Chinese take-away since she said she didn't feel like cleaning the frying pan; she walked with Antonia out into the street. "Wouldn't it be lovely," said Clare, "if we didn't have to bother about eating and things, and we could just lie in bed and never have to do anything ever again?"

"I suppose so," said Antonia, "but I'd get awfully bored by myself. No one has ever wanted to make love to me."

"They will, Toe. I'm sure they will. Don't worry about it," shouted Clare from across the road.

When Clare returned with the tin foil dishes containing the Chinese food she found David lying on the bed staring at the ceiling. His face was rather flushed and he said he felt rotten.

He looked at the contents of the greasy lidded containers and said he really was not hungry at all.

"But what have you got?" asked Clare, solicitously feeling his forehead.

"I haven't the least idea. Except it isn't very pleasant and I hope it isn't catching. I really just want to go to sleep."

Clare chewed on a bit of pink-painted duck and felt sorry for him. It seemed there was nothing she could do to make him comfortable. "Would you rather I wasn't here?" she said.

"Yes . . . though I hate to say so. I'll probably feel better in the morning."

"Well, I'll go and report on my activities to Julia and come back at the crack of dawn to wake you up." Clare liked making love in the mornings when they were only half awake and their bodies fitted together as if by magnetism with no effort and no striving.

At the flat in the Woodstock Road Julia was nowhere to be seen. It felt as if no one had been there for some time. Clare leafed through her accumulated post. There was the usual weekly epistle from her father with a synopsis of the previous Sunday's sermon and an up-to-date account of the state of the fruit cage and its contents: strawberries almost over, raspberries promising well, four blackbirds needing rescuing. Her mother was well, ditto the dogs, when were she and Elinor coming for the weekend? Her lovely father had written to her every Sunday for the past nine years except when she was at home. He fitted it in between Matins and lunch.

There was a bill from Blackwell's which she read with horror and then hid. She would deal with it next month, or the one after. There was also a thick white envelope with tea mug rings on it which had obviously been lying around for a long time; she wondered why she had not noticed it before. Perhaps it had fallen into the rubbish bin and then been fished out again. There were a few stray tea leaves sticking to it.

It was an invitation to a deb dance in Gloucestershire for the following weekend. Once she had longed for such things, now she thought she ought to disapprove of them on principle, as wasteful and elitist. Grania Mallett had an enormous bosom she remembered; it wobbled when she ran. Perhaps it would be nice, she thought, to go to one of these things just once, just to see what she was missing. But, of course, she did not want to go without David. She ran her finger over the writing. It was engraved, not printed. She put it aside and went and washed her hair.

David felt worse in the morning, very hot and sweaty with a sore throat and pains all over.

"Shall I ring for a doctor?" asked Clare, sitting by the bed and holding David's hand, very romantic in theory, in practice very boring.

"Don't bother, Clare, I'm sure it's just flu or something. I think I'll try and sleep it off."

Clare felt unwanted and useless. She picked a few socks up off the floor and put them into a plastic carrier bag ready for the laundrette, whenever she got round to it. Which ought to be soon. David had very few clean clothes left. The thought of spending a June morning amidst swirling gray underwear was not appealing. "I could go to Gloucestershire for the weekend," she said, feeling disloyal.

"Then why don't you?"

"You might need me, don't you think?"

"I'd much rather you went away and had a good time."

"I don't have a good time without you, David."

"Well, you certainly won't have a good time *with* me when I feel like this."

Clare left David surrounded by great heaping baskets of cherries which she had rushed out and bought, which she later discovered he did not like and didn't eat.

The mechanics of these dances must be so difficult to organise, thought Clare, as she and the plastic bag containing her dress got out at Gloucester Station. Grania's older sister, Flavia, picked her up in an open Land Rover. Such wonderful names, so wasted! Flavia had been very good at games like hockey, Clare remembered, and now driving through the narrow streets, with her head scarf knotted under her chin, Flavia wore the same look of absolute concentration she had worn when thundering down the right wing.

"Journey all right?" asked Flavia, not looking at Clare, stopping at a traffic light.

"Yes, very good, thanks."

"The Cooper-Smiths are having you for dinner and you're sleeping at the Shaws'. I think I've got that right anyway," said Flavia, looking round. "It's all written down at home. Is that all you've brought with you?" She eyed Clare's plastic bag dubiously.

"Yes. I hate packing, don't you?"

"I've never thought about it, really," said Flavia. "It's just something one does, isn't it?"

They had tea on the lawn of Shamley Court. Smiling plump girls in Laura Ashley dresses greeted Clare with shrieks of delight. Quite a number of them were doing secretarial courses in Oxford and Cambridge, others were learning to cook in Woking. Oh, God, thought Clare, I should have realised what it would be like. How could I have forgotten all this so quickly?

Clare was driven to the dinner party by a young man with an open Morgan and a very long name. The wind whipped her hair and made her neck feel stiff.

"Not too breezy for you, is it?" he enquired cheerfully, not expecting a reply. He was studying anthropology at Aberystwyth and was interested in gorillas, which Clare was not. But since he could not be drawn on any other subject she tried to seem attentive. He looked like Woody

Allen, she thought, plainer than Woody Allen. Was he her punishment for answering the invitation by telephone? She hoped she would not have to sit next to him at dinner.

The dinner party was not a success. In the drawing room before dinner, their host had looked at Clare's bare toes on his white shag pile carpet and had made her wish, if only for a moment, that she had worn shoes. They were a very vulgar family, Clare thought, everything was new and shiny and slightly too big. There were too many invitations on the mantelpiece, too many pink carnations in the vases, the melon was scooped into too many little balls and the napkins were tortured into water lilies (this last the achievement of the daughter of the house, Cynthia, who Clare was pleased to notice was slightly too big and too shiny, too). Cynthia was at the domestic science college in Eastbourne, where Mrs. Fane had once hoped to send Clare; Clare thanked God she had been prevailed upon not to.

Oh, David, thought Clare, why did I ever come? This isn't even funny (though she would try and make it seem so to him later). Then she noticed Nicholas, who looked almost as ill at ease as she did. He had shoulder-length hair, rather wavy, and a nice moustache. He was being grilled by Mr. Cooper-Smith.

"And where are you going this summer?"

"Nowhere," said Nicholas, "I'm working in a record shop in Oxford Street."

"Before you go up to university?" Mr. Cooper-Smith tactlessly enquired.

"No, because I want to. I meet some fascinating people."

"I'm sure you must. I'm sure your hair would not be remarked upon there."

It was clear that Mr. Cooper-Smith was not enjoying himself either. Clare thought he would rather have been watching cricket on television, with his feet up, instead of entertaining these disagreeable young people whom, he must suspect, despised him. Probably the whole evening was his wife's fault (and his, perhaps, for letting her get ideas above her station).

Nicholas Carstairs admitted that he hated the dance. He, like Clare, was only accidentally there (to please his mother, it turned out; she played bridge with Mrs. Mallett). Clare was only prevented from finding him attractive by the thought of David lying in bed, hot, miserable and missing her. She hoped he was missing her, anyway. She wondered what he would have made of the dinner party and realised he would have hated it even more than she did. He was not very good at small talk. She danced only with Nicholas and warded off his tentative advances half-heartedly. She would have liked to kiss him in fact, but did not, feeling herself to be settled and spoken for, the property of D. Lennox, Esq., late of Jamaica, W.I.

The house where she slept almost made up for the dance. It was overwhelmingly beautiful in the dawn as she crept downstairs before anyone else was awake. She sat in the drawing room looking out into the dew-filled garden through tendrils of wisteria which crept about the window frames. Flowers were carelessly arranged on the table and old Persian rugs dotted the floor. I would like a house like this one day, she thought, a mysterious old house with blackened floorboards, a house which has remained the same for centuries. She touched the keys of the open grand piano and wished she could play, could fill the air with Chopin and Debussy. She tried a few simple pieces ("Jesu, Joy of Man's Desiring," and a very poorly executed opening to the Moonlight Sonata). It was lucky no one else was up yet, she would not have known their names if they were.

She returned to Oxford that afternoon to find David much improved and missing her as much as she had hoped he might be.

At the beginning of July, Mrs. Tradescant fell down the stairs and broke her hip. Lydia found her, a crumpled heap of old clothes smelling of mothballs, gently groaning, lying in the dark hall. She was surrounded by vases of plastic flowers whose water she had replenished daily.

She was taken to hospital by ambulance and Antonia expected any moment to hear that she was dead. But she did not die. Antonia went to visit her in the crowded ward where she lay immobile and gaunt, but she did not recognise Antonia at all. The fall had damaged her mind as well as her body and Antonia did not think she would be capable of eating the grapes she had brought for her, or getting any pleasure from the magazines. It seemed very unfair that she could not die. She asked Antonia if he had come back (Antonia presumed she meant her son). She replied, as she thought she must, that he had not done so yet and Mrs. Tradescant said, "But I think he will come soon, don't you?"

"Yes," Antonia answered, "I'm sure of it."

Mrs. Tradescant took Antonia's hand in her gnarled and large-knuckled one and said, "You were always such a good girl, Gwen. You will take care of him for me, won't you?"

Antonia nodded, wondering who Gwen was and if she was like her.

They were asked to leave the house at the end of the month, which didn't matter to Lydia since she was going to St. Tropez then anyway. Antonia did not have anywhere to go. She did not want to spend the summer in London. Her father was away, she knew. He was now very rarely in England at all. Eileen was growing fat at last. Fat and rather expensively blowsy and sad. She had asked Antonia once, embarrassingly, what she could do to keep him.

Antonia had said, "How am I supposed to know? He didn't stay with Mummy and me, either. Perhaps you could *do* something?"

"What for instance?"

"Oh, I don't know. Get a job or something like that?" She thought Eileen was too bowed down to try. She had probably forgotten what skills she once had and had her confidence eroded by years of waiting for Antonia's father: doing her nails, doing nothing, flicking through magazines, having her hair done, redecorating the already overdecorated house.

"You're lucky, Toni, with all your life before you." Eileen so often talked in clichés. "You can do anything you want. Don't be like me, for heaven's sake."

"I won't be," said Antonia unkindly, though she occasionally wondered if she would be; if she would spend her entire life waiting for someone who never arrived.

No, she certainly could not face a summer of Eileen. She would stay on in Oxford, and do . . . something. Surely something would turn up.

Ten

An undifferentiated mass of people moved in time to the music and the lights. Antonia sat behind a projector dripping colours from an eye dropper onto a glass slide. She then placed another glass slide on top of the first one and inserted them both into the machine. There, the heat from the light mixed the inks into swirling patterns, marbled and bubbling, which flashed in time to the music. The design which she had so randomly created was caught on a blank wall at the other end of the room. She watched, transfixed, to see where the shapes would move, when the colours would blend together and what new hues would evolve. She was quite sure no one else was so intent upon the designs as she; perhaps no one even noticed them. It was hard to tell. Antonia felt very safe and detached, hidden away from them all. She lit a joint whilst deciding what colours to use next.

She smiled to herself and thought what an odd job it was; what fun to smoke dope and play with ink all night. She was employed (if so formal a term could be used to describe her activities) by three friends of

William's who owned a mobile discotheque. She was responsible for the light show, which was not a very onerous task.

William had introduced her, saying, "This is the magical Antonia who can do anything and needs somewhere to live. Take care of her for me." And they had. She had liked Micah immediately because he had accepted her without question and had taught her all she knew about the lights. He was small, scarcely as tall as she was herself, with a delicate, thin face framed with black curls, somewhat reminiscent of the face of the young Disraeli, which Antonia had seen in history books. His voice was unexpectedly deep and resonant.

"So you want to live with us?" he said, having explained the technicalities to her.

"If that would be all right?"

"Of course, we would love to have you."

They had spent the rest of that first day listening to the Velvet Underground and Jimi Hendrix amplified so loud as to preclude much conversation. They lay entwined on a mattress on the floor with the curtains drawn, smoking dope. And Antonia let Micah make love to her because she could think of no reason not to. She knew, from William, that he had a girlfriend who was away, but she did not mind. She had no illusions about being in love; she had come to the conclusion that her virginity was merely an absurdity to be disposed of at the first opportunity. Micah was horrified when he realised what he had done.

"Oh, God, Antonia, you should have told me."

She smiled at him, not knowing what to say. "It doesn't matter," she said eventually. "No one has ever wanted to make love to me before, that's all."

"But you know about Helen?"

"Yes. William told me. I knew. I won't say anything."

"You really are quite extraordinary, Antonia. I don't understand you at all."

"You weren't meant to. You couldn't anyhow since we've only just met." She sat with her knees drawn up to her chin, smiling down at him, her shadow obscuring the small bright patch of blood on the white sheet. The late afternoon sun filtered sideways from behind the black velvet curtains. "I feel rather special today, what with meeting you and

William going away. I feel quite outside myself." She stood up and wrapped her Japanese robe around her and went out into the kitchen to make tea.

When she came back Micah propped himself up on one elbow and said, "What will your parents think of your living here with us? Won't they think it rather too decadent and strange?"

"Oh, nothing much. I don't really think my father will care unless I cause an awful lot of trouble, which I very rarely do. And my mother died years ago."

"It must be nice in some ways, not having a mother."

"You are the very first person who has ever said that; it's rather refreshing. Most people are dreadfully sorry for me. But it does turn out to have unexpected advantages, like being able to do what I want without people fussing all the time."

Micah, it turned out, had a large-bosomed, all-consuming mother from whom he had trouble escaping, though he loved her. She had never been to his house and he hoped she never would. He often wondered, he said, if the benefits of the use of her abundant funds were worth the torture of her cloying affection.

He had bought the house one day, on a whim, without his seeing it either. It had been remarkably cheap and was in fact due for demolition. It lurked in a tiny terrace of run-down buildings, near the canal. Everything about it was small, stunted and cramped. The largest thing in the street was the van in which they travelled every night, transporting the turntables and records and amplifiers. They often did not return to the house until early morning, when they drew the curtains and went to sleep, shutting out the clean dawn air, while the other inhabitants of the street were just getting up and going to work.

There was a small overgrown yard beyond the kitchen, full of nettles and broken bottles and rusty tin cans, which Antonia imagined turning into a garden. She thought she could create a tiny green jewel, an oasis of peace amidst the squalor. She wanted to grow lilies as her mother had and longed for their smell on a summer evening, something which she could only dimly remember. Instead she had to content herself with straggly geraniums in terra-cotta pots which tomcats peed on.

The kitchen was filled with dirty mugs and half-eaten take-away food gone mouldy in its containers, and bottles of milk turned sour because no one remembered to put them back into the fridge. Antonia slept on a mattress on the sitting-room floor, a mattress which had apparently been new at the beginning of the summer but was now battered and stained with spilled wine and coffee and Antonia did not like to think what else. She did not try to impose order upon this chaos because it was not her house after all, she had no private place in it, her room was anyone's room. It depended how many people were living there at any given moment.

She looked at her face in the mirror one morning. The glass was propped on the edge of the bath and the angle was odd. She thought how strange it was that she inhabited this face, this house. She could be anywhere at all. Luckily she enjoyed this proximity with others, and could lose herself travelling and listening to music all the time and having people to sleep with who did not demand anything of her except that she be there.

Guy, the second of the three partners in this dubious enterprise, was quite different from Micah. He was tall and conventionally handsome, with a bland, untroubled, boyish look and manner with which he charmed county matrons into parting with large sums of money for the privilege of having his music at their dances.

"It's an amazingly easy way to make money isn't it, Toe?" he said one day as they sat eating breakfast at two in the afternoon.

"I suppose so," she replied, "but I've never tried any other ways, or even thought about it really."

"Well, I'm glad you're here anyway," he said, squeezing her hand. "You add a sort of waifish glamour to it all. You are so unlike all of them."

"Unlike who?"

"Oh, all those strappingly healthy, plain girls the dances are for."

"Am I unlike them? I always tend to think of them as normal; what I should be like. You see what a failure I am."

"I think it is a greater triumph not to be like them, and altogether more fun." He smiled and put on another record.

Antonia found both Micah and Guy very easy. Giles, the third partner, was not. She happened upon him one day as he sat at the kitchen table making out the phone bill.

"Who on earth do you ring up all the time?" he asked sounding very angry. "This bill is quite monumental."

"I don't ring up anyone at all. I don't have anyone *to* ring up," Antonia said.

"Are you sure?"

It was odd, Antonia thought, that things like gas bills and electricity bills were paid by people all the time. She had never thought about them before and had certainly never paid a utility bill in her life. Perhaps it would be rather nice in a way to have to. It would prove that you were real and grown up. She never felt either real or adult in Giles' presence. He tended to look at her as if she were both stupid and childish, as if she was twelve, instead of sixteen.

The summer wore on in a cloud of hash and incense. Antonia slept with Guy when Micah was not there. She wondered if they discussed her, and if they really cared about her as they both seemed to. She was very comfortable with them both.

She felt very isolated from the real world, travelling to different places every night, and not being on nodding terms, even, with their neighbours. She was permanently tired with great black circles under her eyes, and she ate almost nothing at all.

Everything was taken care of by Micah and all Antonia had to do was be there, to roll the occasional joint and sometimes to creep out and buy food if she was awake when the shops were open (which was not often). She painted what little there was of her nails black and rarely went out in the sun. Occasionally she fell asleep in the back of the van amidst all the fuses and the flexes and they would carry her, still sleeping, into the house. She would wake up with one of their arms round her and would have to discover by feel who it was.

Whilst Antonia, in those weeks of high summer, spent very little time in the fresh air, Clare grew to think she was spending altogether too much. She and David had decided to hire a punt for a fortnight and to try to live on the river, thus putting off the inevitable day when Clare would have to succumb to her mother's entreaties and return home. It was an idyllic plan, if not very thoroughly thought through. Their companions on this venture were two school friends of David's, both quite unknown quantities to Clare. She hoped they would prove to be amusing and know something about boating.

They set off full of high hopes on a tranquil June evening with a calm pink sky and the air full of mosquitoes. Clare had brought her paints with her and a selection of books. That first evening they got no farther than the ruins of Whytham Abbey. In the two miles they had travelled they discovered several things. First, that Clare was not strong enough to paddle the boat; second, that the tilly lamp was in constant danger of exploding; and finally, that Nature, though pretty, was conspiring to make them as uncomfortable as possible. Swans seemed likely to attack; gnats did. Wasps were more partial to their food than they were. And then it began to rain.

"It's only a few drops," said Clare. "I'm sure it will stop in a moment." But it didn't.

When the rain became torrential they tied up the boat and made for the nearest pub, where they were able to indulge in the luxury of reheated pies and congealed baked beans and Clare inhaled the smoke-laden atmosphere with delight.

It was growing dark when they tossed up for the tent, for only two could sleep with any comfort in the boat, and they had decided to take it in turns. David and Clare got the privilege of spending their first night on dry land, or land which would have been dry had it not rained so much. Rupert and Stephen pulled the canvas hood over the boat and played cards by candlelight. When it stopped raining at last the calm meadow seemed eerie to Clare; she had never slept in such an exposed spot before. She also felt dirty and longed to have a bath. In the middle of the night Rupert said he saw a ghost and woke everyone up. Clare, too, felt some overbearing presence and longed for dawn; she felt she was being watched. But David assured her it could only be the lockkeeper gazing out at her from the dry comfort of his house. Clare lay awake in her damp sleeping bag regretting that they had not made love; David had not wanted to for fear the others might hear.

The first week they continued up the river, waking early in the dew-filled meadows to the lush freshness of the morning. They ate endless meals of tinned mince and baked beans; everything either cold or fried. Clare managed to spill boiling fat on her foot, and it formed a gigantic watery blister which was not soothed by soaking it in the muddy, unrefreshing river.

Rupert saw ghosts everywhere: lurking behind trees, inhabiting deserted mansions, floating miasmally from the water. At first Clare tried to find his affectation amusing, but it was not. So convinced was he of their presence that Clare came to believe in them, too. One morning she woke up to find a man, standing, his feet swathed in mist, pointing a gun at their tent.

"David, wake up! There's a man with a gun." She shook him.

"There can't possibly be," he said, not looking up.

"Then it must be a ghost," said Clare, terrified.

"If it's a ghost it can't hurt you. Go back to sleep."

The figure stood watching intently, and disappeared when Clare looked away. She knew she had seen him and now she would never know whether he was real or not. She was glad when they broke camp and moved on. She did not tell Rupert what she had seen, not wanting to give him the satisfaction.

Rupert was useless on the boat, and his vagueness, which had at first seemed to Clare to be mildly endearing, now endlessly rankled. When sent out by Clare to buy more tins of mince and tomatoes at the nearest town he returned with a packet of Edwardian needles (very rusted) and a small leather-bound volume of Ruskin's *Stones of Venice*. In addition to not buying food he had squandered the entire day's supplies kitty. Clare was very hungry by now and not amused at all. She had looked forward to the doughnuts she had ordered; she did not care in the least what Ruskin thought of Venice.

"You *must* talk to him, David. I can't really. He's your friend after all." Clare was frightened of sounding bossy and carping.

"We could eat yesterday's bread," he said unhelpfully, sketching a water rat whose significance and charm Clare failed to detect.

"All right, I'll talk to him." No one else seemed to care what they ate. If she did not cook they would starve. It was her job, all the cooking. David did all the work on the boat. Rupert and Stephen did not do anything except admire the view and try to keep out of Clare's way, especially when she wanted them to collect firewood or wash up.

Clare was bored though she would not admit this, even to herself. She wanted endless physical affirmation of David's affection for her, which he was loath to display in public. Every moment he spent drawing or writing seemed a moment willfully snatched from her. She hated the very pencil with which he drew. He made records of everything they passed, more water rats, cows, grass, reeds and the sky. He did, occasionally, still paint Clare but less frequently now she was more familiar to him, and so often cross. He drew every day, and every day Clare grew more fretful.

The river, of course, was beautiful. The dawns, the sunsets, everything was felt more strongly in the open air. But for Clare, all was spoiled by the conviction that David no longer wanted to communicate with her spiritually (or physically for that matter).

They were unwashed, filthy; their hair tacky and foul, and wasps followed them wherever they went. The river and the summer had lost their magic. Clare's instinct was to hang on, never admitting that this was a mistake. She blamed everyone but herself and loathed Rupert and Stephen with an appalling venom. She felt David slipping away and herself to be fat and unappealing and miserable when they returned to Oxford after the first week, which had seemed an eternity.

Clare lay in the bathtub surveying her brown legs and white stomach, and David sat on the edge of the tub and admired them, too. In private he was charming, as he always was, attentive and attractive. If they could always be alone together perhaps everything would be all right.

"Do you love me, David?"

"Of course. How could you doubt it?

"I could, a bit, on the boat."

"You should have painted," he said.

"Perhaps I should. I thought it would be possible just to *be*."

"But it isn't enough, is it?"

Clare wiggled her toes in the luxurious clean water. "No," she said.

Whilst in the basement of Marks & Spencer buying food for the next week's ordeal, Clare ran into Max.

"How odd to meet you here," she said. "I never knew you went anywhere as prosaic as this."

"I have to eat like everyone else."

"I suppose so, but I've never actually seen you buy food before." She smiled.

"You look very well. It suits you to be brown. Where have you been hiding all these months?"

"In a garret. I did not realise you would miss me."

"I miss you very much. Come, let's go to my room and you can tell me all about it." He took her arm and she realised that she would follow him anywhere, even now.

His room was as dark as it had always been and was made to seem more so by contrast to the brightness of the streets. He lit a Black Russian cigarette and handed it to her, and poured China tea into one of the handleless cups; it was as if she had never gone away.

"You smell of sex," he said. "You look much loved."

"I am," said Clare, sitting cross-legged on the floor.

"And do you love him?"

"I don't know, Max. I really don't know." She looked into Max's eyes. "He loves me very much, I think. He even wants to marry me, or that's what he said. And I want to have everything fixed, settled, organised, so I don't have to think about anything ever again."

"Does he make you laugh?" Max asked, leaning forward and touching her cheek.

"No, he doesn't make me laugh."

Max put his head to one side and drew on his cigarette, and smiled. "Silly Clare, you have so much to learn."

"And you know everything, of course?"

"No, but I know what will not make you happy in the end. You had so much joy, Clare, and now it is all gone."

"How do you know what will make me happy?"

"I don't. Only what won't."

"You made me happy, Max, and then you vanished utterly. I didn't want to go through that again."

"But you knew that our relationship was quite other, a temporary fusing. We are too much alike, Clare. We would not do very well together all the time."

"And there was Sasha of course."

"Yes."

"So tell me what I'm supposed to do, Max, the fount of all wisdom."

"Stay and talk to me."

"I can't. David will wonder where I am. I have never told him about you."

"Such admirable loyalty, Clare. I wish Sasha had some of your qualities."

"If she is such a bitch and David such a bore, what on earth are we doing?"

"But they aren't, are they? Not entirely, even if we would like to pretend they are."

"No," said Clare. "They are the real world, and this, as you insist, is quite other."

They lay together on the bed, watching motes of dust dancing in the light, Clare enfolded in Max's arms, his heart beating beneath her cheek.

"If anything goes wrong you will tell me, won't you?" Max gazed at her, studying her face very seriously. "I will always be there."

"I know," said Clare. "You are always with me, too. I sometimes think it unfortunate—this random connection, which neither of us can do a thing about. Do many people have it do you suppose?"

"I think so, but it is not something most people admit to. There are too many people who might be hurt and not understand. David for instance."

"If David was lying now in some other woman's arms, I would feel sick. I would not understand. I would feel demeaned and diminished, which is why we can never be really honest with those we profess to love most, because they could never, ever understand." Clare put her hand on Max's breastbone and felt the hardness of his ribs, she slipped her arms around him and squeezed him very tightly. "I must go," she said. She kissed him lightly on the lips and walked out into the bright day.

As she walked out into the courtyard she stealthily wiped a stray tear from her cheek with the back of her hand. David, she was sure, would never understand.

Below Oxford the river was quite different, crowded and altogether less peaceful. Great pleasure launches full of loud and vulgar day-trippers swept past nearly swamping the punt in their wake. The wasp problem was magnified ten thousand fold, or so it seemed to Clare. Sitting down was a constant torture—nearer and nearer they buzzed, menacingly, insistently. In the evenings gnats gathered round the boat and danced in their millions, stopping only for an occasional snack from Clare's arms. David found them rather fascinating, and he would hum at a strange frequency, which the gnats found in some way unnerving, and the swarms would move off for an instant, all together, before drawing nearer again to continue their meal.

One day Clare decided to paint, to give herself something to do. She wanted to capture the elusive evening light. David was pleased that for once she was taking an interest in creation, albeit a temporary one. Painting the bright yellow grain, the blue evening trees, and the darker sky, Clare was pleased with the contrasts. They reminded her of a Vlaminck painting which had hung in the dining room at her boarding school, of a country road with a threatening sky, in those last moments of calm before the rain falls.

Clare and David walked that evening in a meadow beside the water. Clare felt rather pleased with herself for having made the effort to paint, a very mild effort to assert herself. Now, at the height of summer, she felt the seeds of decay already apparent in the dry grass and the overgrown hedges. She felt that things between her and David had become stagnant and stale, too. It was time to discuss the future.

"You know I'm going away to university in the autumn," she said.

"I have not forgotten," said David, stepping over a dry cow pat.

"Will you still love me if I go away?"

"You know I will," he replied, not looking at her.

"I must have a brain as well as a facility with paint. They would never have accepted me if I hadn't," said Clare, wondering if this was an unkind jab. Had David wanted to go to university? She had never asked. She wondered, too, if he was bright enough. She had always assumed that, being a man, he was more intelligent than she was.

"Studying things is not the same as doing them," said David after a pause. "I sometimes think it's an excuse for putting off doing anything in particular."

"But do you know what you want to do with your life? I don't really. So don't you think going to university could be valuable?" asked Clare. She had been educated to think that acceptance in itself was a mark of success in the world's eyes. Why couldn't David see with the world's eyes? Just for once.

"Of course, you must do whatever you want. But have you thought why you want to go?"

She had. First, to be considered as intelligent as Elinor; second, to impress Max; and third, because she had always been a voracious reader, and there was so much she wanted to discover. She said, "I think it will make me a better and stronger person, to understand things better. Are you afraid it will take me away from you?" She did not want to suggest that it might teach her things David did not know. She did not want to seem intellectual and threatening. Her mother always said men did not like brainy women, a comment Clare had always dismissed as absurd. But what if it were true?

David said nothing, just sat staring out over the fields.

"Are you frightened I'll have other boyfriends? What on earth are you so upset about? Talk to me, David, please."

"I sometimes wonder if you know what you are doing. If you leave it will change everything."

"Why should it? I never said I was going to leave *you*."

"But you are. That's just the point." David trudged off over the now dew-soaked grass, and Clare noticed, as he vanished into the gloom, that the night had fallen at last.

Clare burst into tears and plucked at the grass. A drop of blood oozed from one of her fingers where a sharp blade had pierced it. She put her finger into her mouth and tasted the fresh red blood, so rich and heavy and flavourless. She knew David hated it when she wept; her face became puffy and swollen. Partly he hated having the power to make her cry, but also Clare knew that it embarrassed him to have other people realise there had been a scene.

David walked back to where Clare lay in the grass, still sobbing. He knelt down on the damp earth beside her. "Whatever you think, Clare, I will always love you. I only wish you didn't have to go away."

Later, after they had made love in the tent in silence, Clare propped herself up on her elbow in the dark and lit a cigarette.

"I won't go to university if you don't want me to," Clare offered.

"You must decide, not me." He kissed her flushed cheek. David rolled over and put his arms round her soft warmth, his face tucked into the nape of her neck. They lay like spoons in a drawer, neatly fitted together. David had been crying, too.

Eleven

William sent Antonia a postcard from Turkey with a picture of the minarets of Istanbul glistening under a moonlit sky. It reminded her of the time they had walked in the Botanical Gardens. It must have been one of the last things he wrote. Soon afterwards, on one of those deceptive straight roads in Northern France where cars hide in dips until the last moment, he was killed.

Micah and Guy left for Morocco in the middle of August to spend a few weeks in the sun, and Antonia drifted to London where she worked for a short time at a club in Wardour Street, which, that summer, was a mecca for all the little girls from the suburbs who aspired to be groupies. Their parents would appear, tearful and shattered, on gray mornings when Antonia was scarcely awake, and show her photographs of smiling children in school uniforms. They all looked alike to Antonia; those little girls so innocent and staring, with names like Linda and Heather and Elaine, who had fled Streatham and Catford to try to capture the glamour and glitter of the West End. It was all very squalid and sad, she thought, as she listened to the music and took money at the door. Occasionally, one of the members of some group would mistake her for one of those children with their thigh-high skirts and painted-on eyes who were so eager to be laid. It was easy for Antonia to repulse their clumsy advances and they showed no signs of minding. There were plenty of others to take her place.

She rarely saw her father, who had recently been knighted for his services to industry. Eileen could now have Lady Acton embossed on her credit cards and the obsequious attention of shop servants, which, Antonia thought, must be a certain compensation for her father's neglect.

Antonia's father continued to give her an allowance, most of which she spent on hash and occasionally, when she felt particularly tired, speed. At the end of August, she found herself in hospital. After several days, her father came to visit her.

She lay there, gazing at the wall. The doctors were trying to get her to eat, threatening all sorts of irreversible damage if she did not. Eventually they managed to frighten her so much that she gave in and ate just a little to please them and to escape their constant prying.

Her father said, "I can't think what you are trying to do to us, Toe."

"I'm not trying to do anything to you."

Rex Acton sat by the bed, both confused and angry. "Are you terribly unhappy?"

"No, I'm not unhappy at all," said Antonia, who felt so distanced from everything around her that she truly did not feel anything much.

"But what are you going to do with your life? Don't you want to grow up and have children?"

"One day perhaps, but not now." She turned her face to the wall.

"I want you to come back and live with us. I'm sure Eileen wants you to as much as I do. She's alone so much."

"But that isn't *my* fault, is it?"

It was not a satisfactory meeting. Antonia thought of the house he had just bought in Chelsea, just off the King's Road, a beautiful tall house which Eileen had succeeded in making quite dead. There was no trace of her mother left. Even the few pieces of furniture from Field End which they had had at the mews had disappeared. She never asked where they had gone.

Antonia's next visitor was Clare, and she was very pleased to see her. Unlike Rex Acton, Clare was fascinated, not horrified, to find her lying in such surroundings, amidst fruit and flowers.

"I could paint those, Toe," said Clare, pointing to a large basket of peaches which Eileen had had shipped in from Harrods at vast expense.

"You can if you want to, Clare. I really don't fancy eating them."

"Oh, I would if I were you. They look quite delicious. May I have one?" The sweet juice dripped down her chin. "Well," Clare said, "how on earth did you end up here?"

Antonia related the events of the summer, ending with her father's visit. "And what about you, Clare?"

"Oh, I've been on the river with David. It was a bit curate's eggish— good in parts. Elinor went to Greece, which rather outdoes anything I have done." Clare smiled. "And I've decided to go to the University of Sussex."

"How exciting," said Antonia.

"Is it? I keep wondering if it is the right thing to do. David wasn't exactly thrilled, but we have reached some sort of compromise. I'll spend the week at Sussex and be with him at weekends. So I'll be able to see you a lot, too."

"I will look forward to it. I slightly dread going back to Oxford, but it seems a long way off. I've got to go to Torquay with Eileen and Justin after I get out of here."

"Have you really? Why on earth Torquay?"

"I told my father I wanted to go to Amsterdam, but he said he thought Torquay was healthier. Eileen likes it, and I do want to see Justin."

"Isn't it desperate what one does for one's family to keep them happy and at bay? You could always come and stay with us. Mummy would be sure to want to have you."

"I'd better not. I feel guilty enough as it is. Daddy thought I ended up here in order to punish him for something, because I hate him. I don't think you can actually hate anyone you very rarely see, can you?"

"So when will they let you out?" Clare looked at Antonia's transparent hands with great dips at the base of her thumbs, and bruises where the intravenous lines had been on the backs of them.

"Oh, quite soon I think. I'm getting enormously fat as it is. They weighed me this morning and I've put on six pounds. I get grosser by the minute."

Antonia built huge sand castles on the beach with Justin which the waves swept over and obliterated entirely. She played interminable games of Monopoly with him, which he invariably won, having seemingly inherited their father's business acumen. She ate cream teas to placate Eileen, and then made herself vomit them up later when Eileen was having drinks in the lounge. She let her stepmother buy her lots of clothes which she did not want to wear, and which lay in their tissue-filled boxes on the floor of her cupboard reproaching her with the waste of it all. She tried very hard to be good.

In September she returned to Oxford to study and to attempt to pass exams. Lydia was in London modelling. Antonia sometimes saw her photograph in magazines. She looked radiant and happy, and for all Antonia knew, she was. Simon and Elinor were working for their finals and she did not see much of them; she assumed they would probably get married one day and envied their settled relationship. Surprisingly, Mrs. Tradescant was still not dead, but living in a convalescent home, being taught how to walk. She still did not know who Antonia was though she seemed pleased enough to see her, and accepted with a wraithlike smile the flowers and biscuits Antonia brought her. The house in Ship Street was locked up, and Antonia avoided passing it whenever she could.

The only person whom Antonia continued to see was Jeremy, so languid and effete and amusing. She often went to his rooms to gossip or have dinner, and realised more than ever the kindness beneath his affectations.

He said one day, "You were in love with William, weren't you?"

"Yes," said Antonia. "But I didn't realise anyone knew."

"Oh, I did, because I was in love with him, too."

"I never knew that," she said.

"I didn't tell him. He would have been shocked I think."

"But he always pretended to be so unshockable."

"He was the straightest person I knew, and one of the nicest."
Neither of them ever mentioned him again.

Clare was in Sussex, or rather she was there on the two days a week when it was absolutely necessary. Most of the time she lived with David in a cottage eight miles from Oxford which he shared with three other students. Antonia went out to visit them one mellow autumn afternoon. Clare was picking apples in the orchard surrounded by a tribe of village children who had come to help her.

"I think I would like to be a farmer's wife, Toe," she said, handing Antonia a basket. "This is my rustic idyll period. I cook and clean and sweep. I have become the very model of domesticity. I get very pleased when everyone eats what I cook, just like my mother, except I'm not so good at the tidying up bit."

The cottage itself was half fifteenth century and half Victorian with an overgrown garden and a barn with doves. It was set at the end of a cart track, aloof from the village.

"Isn't it bliss, Toe? I'm beginning to think going to Sussex was a terrible mistake, but I don't dare admit it yet. I never realised I had an accent before. Do I have an accent?"

"I suppose so, in a way. Everyone does of some sort or another."

"But is it an *elitist* accent?"

"It doesn't sound odd to me," said Antonia.

"Ah, but it does to *them*. I wish my father was a Billingsgate fish porter, or something like that."

"Really?"

"Of course not," said Clare, "but it would make my life easier at the moment." She put down her heavy basket and shooed away her minions. "Let's go in and have a cup of tea. We've got enough apples to last forever and no one really wants them. This place is awash with apples."

Antonia followed Clare into the kitchen and watched her as she made the tea, swatting the occasional replete and sleepy wasp as she did so. "There aren't any wasps in Hove," said Clare, "which I suppose is something in its favour. Probably the only thing. I'm amazed anything can live there at all. Yet they seem to go on forever, those old people, and they are all either obese or emaciated and at least ninety. There aren't any real people at all. Only students and geriatrics. It's hell, Toe, the boardinghouse. My room is a dismal cell about seven feet by ten, and the only window faces a blank wall about six feet in front of it, so I have to leave the light on all the time and hazard wild guesses about the state of the weather. And I'm also utterly bored most of the time."

"But isn't the work interesting? Aren't you learning anything?"

"A bit, but everyone ridicules me in discussions because I'm not a Marxist. I almost wish I was some of the time, it would make life more peaceful. But they're so horribly nasty that I couldn't exist in a world run by them. Actually, I think they think people like me are about ripe for the guillotine and they wouldn't let me live in their utopia anyway. Oh, Lord, I don't even want to think about it. You can stay the night, can't you? I long to have someone to talk to about it all; I don't dare reveal its full awfulness to David."

"I'd love to stay," said Antonia. "My room is fairly grim, too, rather like yours in the Woodstock Road, which I thought was so wonderful at first."

"Good. You can sleep on the sofa in the sitting room; I've got some clean sheets somewhere. Mummy pressed them upon me. She's still under the illusion that I sleep on the sofa when I'm here. Her continuing belief in my purity is truly amazing."

Clare hunted for the elusive sheets in the room which she shared with David. It had once been the dining room of the cottage and had two low windows which looked out on the garden. There was a sagging double bed and a dressing table with a picture of Clare propped up against the mirror whose silvering was coming off in patches. In the painting Clare was naked, lying eating an apple in a field. She saw Antonia looking at it.

"David painted that one day in the summer, just before we went on the boat trip. It may look very peaceful but it was hell just lying there with the grass scratching my bottom." In the painting all was green and tranquil, suffused with variegated light. "Actually," continued Clare, "all the time he was doing it I kept wishing he would stop and make love to me." She picked up one of David's shirts from the floor and rubbed it gently against her face. "I wish now I could be here all the time."

• • •

Clare had made Irish stew for dinner. "One of the only things you can use really cheap meat in," she said, ladling it out lavishly and watching David as he ate.

There was apple crumble to follow. The two other men who lived there seemed to enjoy it and ate a lot.

"Clare in her element," said Christopher, "feeding the hungry throngs!"

"Well, none of you has the least idea how to cook," said Clare. "You exist on beer and Marmite sandwiches when I'm not here."

"I wish I lived somewhere as lovely as this," said Antonia, watching their faces in the flickering candlelight. "I don't really like towns at all."

"You can come out whenever you like," said David. "Clare is almost always here. It's as if she never went away."

After supper Antonia helped Christopher build a log fire in the sitting room while Clare washed up in the kitchen. Antonia glanced up and saw David with his arms about Clare's waist.

"D'you want tea-bag tea or Nescafé?" Clare shouted to Antonia. Clare didn't drink Lapsang Souchong anymore, Antonia noticed, but bought everything at the village shop where they gave out Green Shield stamps. She was saving up for a toaster she told Antonia as she carried in the tea tray. "Aren't I getting bourgeois?" Clare settled herself on the floor and looked into the fire. "I wish life was always like this," she said, putting her head on David's shoulder and smiling.

For some time Clare was happy at the cottage, since her life there was infinitely preferable to her life at university. David was increasingly wrapped up in his work and they made love less frequently than they had in the past now that their relationship seemed so fixed and settled. For Clare, who had few other diversions when she was at the cottage, this was a deprivation. She started counting the times they made love on each visit and they seemed to grow fewer and fewer.

One night as they lay in bed when she had wanted to make love and he had not and she felt rejected and miserable, Clare said, "David, do you think you could ever make love to another woman?"

He paused for a long time, considering the question. Then he said, "Yes, but I don't want to just now."

Clare burst into tears. Her stomach felt as if it had been riven by huge knives, so strong was the physical sensation of pain. She turned from him, sobbing.

David put his hand on her shoulder and said very gently, "But Clare, you asked me a question. Didn't you want me to answer honestly? I didn't say that I loved anyone else, merely that one day perhaps I would. I thought it was a general question. It isn't anything to cry about, please."

Clare lay twisting the horrible grayish sheet between her fingers and feeling sick. Then she smoked a cigarette in bed, which she knew David hated, and it tasted foul to her. "Well, I can't imagine making love to anyone else," she said after a pause.

"I don't want you to, Clare. Don't you realise that?"

"I don't know it at all. Sometimes when you are gone all day and I don't have anyone to talk to I feel really abandoned and useless."

"Perhaps you should start painting again, at least when you're here. Or perhaps you should spend more time in Sussex and try to find things to do there."

"But I hate it there. Don't you realise that?"

"But you wanted to go. Surely there must be some interesting bits to it?"

"Well, I haven't discovered any yet."

Clare still sobbed and David rubbed her back soothingly and started to make love to her. But she imagined him thinking of making love to some other woman and couldn't stop crying. She eventually went to sleep on the far side of the bed, away from him. Her nose was somewhere over the edge of the bed and she could smell the remains of her cigarette smouldering in the ashtray. She was too miserable to make the effort to move it.

Antonia looked forward to being invited out to the cottage more and more. It seemed to her an oasis of friendship, a place where she was wanted. She wondered if Clare felt that her presence was intrusive, yet she always seemed genuinely glad to see her. "You don't intrude at all, Toe. It's lovely to have another woman to talk to so I don't have to be housewiferly all the time."

Clare mostly wanted to talk about David.

Antonia went out to the fireworks party they gave where a huge bonfire threw bright sparks up into the black night sky. She watched the village children's eyes light up as they followed the rockets. Clare was rather subdued.

"What's the matter, Clare?"

"Oh, nothing. Or rather, I don't think David loves me anymore, do you?"

Antonia saw David's compact figure outlined against the flames as he bent down to throw more wood onto the fire. "Of course he does. He still draws you constantly and he has told me how miserable he is when you go away, and how he longs for you to get back."

"Has he really?" Clare wiped her eyes on the sleeve of her jacket. "I wish I didn't need constant reassurance. I sometimes think I'm such a ghastly person no one will ever really love me."

In December Clare gave a dinner party. She asked Antonia to bring Jeremy, because she said she longed to talk to someone who was not prosaic all the time, someone amusing. She was getting bored of refuelling people with shepherd's pie and baked apples. It would be an excuse to get dressed up.

Jeremy could be relied upon to raise Clare's spirits. He said, "My dear Clare, what a talent for the picturesque you have. And how divinely rustic." And so forth. Clare lapped it up. There was no one at Sussex who dared be so ridiculous. He kissed her on both cheeks. "And you do look stunning."

Clare had draped her Indian silk shawl about her and had painted huge circles of blue around her eyes, making them appear startlingly large. "I'm not surprised you manage to get yourself painted all the time," he said. Clare glowed, but was a little abashed when Jeremy continued, "And you, Antonia, look more ethereal than ever. I'm surprised no one has thought of immortalising you."

It was necessary, Clare knew, for Jeremy to consider all his friends in some way remarkable. Still, she had half hoped he might find her ethereal, too, an adjective she had never had applied to her so far, and probably never would.

Antonia did, in fact, wish David would paint her, but had never dared suggest it. She thought it was Clare's prerogative alone.

David looked uncomfortable at dinner. He either would not, or could not, join in the conversational games. He considered Jeremy affected, and could not understand why Clare liked him and had invited him to dinner in the first place. Clare was torn between loyalty to David and wanting to enjoy Jeremy's company. She was further disturbed by the presence of two of Christopher's friends, who were in the first flush of romantic passion and who could not keep either their hands or their eyes off one another.

Clare said to Antonia, as they stacked the dishes in the kitchen, "David and I were like that once but we aren't anymore." She turned and dove into the larder in search of the mousse.

David slipped past Antonia, heading for the back door, to escape to the studio for a moment. "Clare won't mind will she? There's something I really must finish tonight," he asked.

"I think she will mind terribly," said Antonia.

"No, it doesn't matter a bit," said Clare, reappearing with the pudding. "Shall I come with you? I really don't care about them."

"Don't you, Clare? I always thought you enjoyed this sort of thing. You are so much better at it than I am."

"But I can't enjoy it without you."

David went out anyway and Clare played with her pudding and drank too much wine. Jeremy was giving his usual virtuoso dinner party performance, and whilst not appearing to notice David's absence paid particular attention to Clare. But she did not find him so amusing as usual. She eventually fled into the kitchen and wept into the washing-up water. Antonia followed her to find out what the matter was.

"I wish David didn't have to work all the time. He makes it seem more important than me. He doesn't even *try* to make conversation does he?"

Antonia said, "Perhaps he doesn't want to, Clare. Perhaps he can't think of anything to say. You can't make people do things they don't know how to."

Antonia thought Clare had wanted to show David off.

Christmas came and Antonia went to London to be with her family. But aside from the pleasure of seeing her brother she was glad when the festivities were over. She was invited to spend the New Year with the Fanes in Surrey and became the sort of honorary almost-sister that she had always wanted to be. She liked Mrs. Fane enormously; she couldn't think why Clare was always so dismissive of her mother, whose unpretentious warmth made Antonia feel included and wanted.

Clare took Antonia for long walks with their dogs in the snowy woods where the animals bounded about with uncontrolled delight. Labradors were better in snow than her spaniel had been, Antonia thought, they did not collect great lumps of ice between their toes.

Quite out of the blue, Clare asked, "Where would you like to be now, if you could be anywhere in the world?"

"Actually, I'm quite happy doing this," she said. She couldn't think of anything very exotic to impress Clare with just then.

"I would like to be with Max," Clare said, smiling. "For a week at least. With just wine to drink and nothing to eat, and we would rifle his Indian sculpture book for bizarre positions to make love in. At the very end of it all I would emerge quite emaciated and very spacey indeed. That's the purest pleasure I can think of at the moment."

"But I thought you wanted to marry David?"

"Oh, I do in my real life, but in my imaginary life Max fits in so much better. He is the only person who ever made me feel I could travel outside myself. With Max I did come very near to living poetry."

"But where is he now?"

Clare suddenly looked rather grim. "Actually, he's locked up again. I write to him sometimes, but he doesn't write back." Clare kicked a snowy tussock.

"Have you told David about Max?" Antonia asked.

"Of course not."

"Well, at least David's not mad," said Antonia, wanting to defend

David, whose good qualities were becoming more apparent to her, though they did not seem so to Clare. "I would be very happy if someone as good as David loved me."

"But don't you think he's terribly dull sometimes?"

"No, I don't. I think he's very nice."

"Of course he's nice, and of course I love him. But shouldn't there be something more to it than that?"

The snow gave an air of mystery and enchantment to the usually unremarkable house. It sat on the crest of a gentle hill and the surrounding trees were bare and black against the darkening sky. The light from the drawing room windows threw out a pattern of welcoming light onto the frozen lawn.

Coming in from the cold and pulling off their Wellington boots and gloves and scarves they could hear Mrs. Fane and Elinor putting tea things on the trolley. Clare could smell crumpets hot from the grill.

"I love snow," said Antonia, rubbing her hands together, trying to get blood to circulate in their icy tips.

"So do I," said Clare, "even suburban Surrey seems less banal under a veneer of white. Rather lovely and magical."

"Do stop dripping all over the floor, Clare," said her mother. "Rose did it this morning."

Clare turned and hung her coat on a hook by the back door where it continued to drip, but now onto newspaper which had been put there for the purpose. "The nice thing about home," said Clare, "is that it is so utterly predictable. I expect my mother will be telling me not to drip onto things when I'm forty. But it's so comfortable that it makes me stop thinking, and I revert to acting as if I was about twelve, and then I really do know I ought to escape. Perhaps I will escape, but after the crumpets."

Elinor wheeled the tea trolley into the drawing room, managing to avoid scraping any more paint off the skirting board, a feat which Clare had not mastered.

"Elinor, do remind me to ask Daddy to ring up Wilson's and ask them to come and paint after the holidays," said Mrs. Fane, bending down to pick up two Christmas cards which had blown off the mantelpiece when Clare pulled the door shut.

"Why don't *you* ring them up, Mummy," asked Clare, lighting a cigarette.

"Oh, Daddy always does that sort of thing, Clare, you know he does," Mrs. Fane replied mildly.

"Or you could always paint it yourself. Or I could."

"Could you, Clare?" said her mother who had an endless supply of little men in to do things which Clare always insisted she would have been capable of doing herself.

Antonia looked round the comfortable room, at the Victorian watercolours of lakeland scenery, the corner cupboard full of lustreware, the faded rose-patterned chair covers and the Regency striped wallpaper.

"Ghastly isn't it?" said Clare grinning first at Antonia and then at her mother. "Hopelessly middle class."

"But we *are* middle class, darling," said her mother. "You can live however you want when you have a house of your own. But I really don't see what's so awful about this. Daddy and I like it."

"It's a very good example of real life," said Elinor, "and we all know what Clare thinks of that."

They heard a car pulling in to the garage and Mrs. Fane jumped up to greet her husband, smiling already. "I do like it when he gets home early, especially in weather like this. I do love it when we're all here together."

The two Christmas cards fell off the mantelpiece again when she opened the door.

Twelve

Clare had missed David but did not realise how much until she met him at Marylebone Station. He gave her an embroidered Indian shirt dress as a belated Christmas present. It was too long to be a proper shirt and too abbreviated to be a dress. Although she rather disliked it she put it on immediately because he had given it to her.

They had a very strained journey to Aylesbury. Having been apart for three weeks they wanted to make love more than anything in the world just then. At each station they hastily readjusted their clothes for fear of being discovered entangled in each other's arms. The train was terribly stuffy and they could discover no way of turning down the heat.

At Aylesbury they waited in the biting cold for a bus which would take them to within two miles of the cottage. Eventually the rural bus appeared and meandered with agonising slowness through the gathering gloom. They sat, holding hands, amidst middle-aged country women with laden shopping baskets, and felt that they were being watched.

Clare looked at David, his body hidden beneath his usual almost colourless clothes, his dark hair falling across eyes whose colour she couldn't see in the failing light. He turned and smiled at her. She looked different to him, as she always did after an absence. Now she looked white and tired and he wanted to protect her again as he had when they had first met. He was glad there would be no one at the cottage.

They got out of the bus at the top of the hill. The valley and the village stretched below them in the twilight. Mist lay in the hollows and smoke rose vertically from the cottages beneath them. It was bitter cold with a threat of snow in the air. When they reached the dank and chilly cottage it was quite dark.

They threw down their bags and flung themselves upon each other, on top of the bed they had left unmade three weeks before. They warmed each other with their bodies, but this warmth failed to permeate the sheets, which remained damp and clammy. Having slaked their pent-up passion, the damp and cold became oppressive and David went out to the barn to chop logs. They made an enormous fire which they encouraged to burn with quantities of newspaper and turpentine. Clare draped the sheets and blankets to air over the chairs and sofa. They drank hot chocolate and ate some rather stale ginger biscuits, having forgotten to buy any food. Outside it had started to snow.

Clare was very happy lying with her head in David's lap, she was warm at last and they had made love, but most of all she was happy that they were alone together. She had not realised until then what a strain it had been at home, being a dutiful daughter. She was glad her mother did not know there was a telephone at the cottage.

Going back to Sussex the following week seemed to Clare like doing penance for some obscure sin she had forgotten committing. She rode to the station on the back of David's motorcycle, the icy wind piercing her multitudinous layers of clothes. She thought how beautiful the countryside looked with the snow still lying by the hedges, and the trees, ice-coated sentinels, beside the road. If she had travelled by car, all enveloped in warmth, she would have missed all the pain but at least half the beauty.

She had made a New Year's resolution to work, and did make some effort to, though she preferred lying in bed reading Tolstoy and pretending her immediate surroundings did not exist. She had come to know and like her fellow inmates at the boardinghouse somewhat better. There was one who would haggle over the price of oranges, half-starving herself to save money to escape to America; another, the daughter of a Hampstead intellectual, professed to be an ardent Marxist and wore Biba boots (Clare idly wondered if that would be allowed come the revolution); and all sorts of other dull ones who immersed themselves in their work. Though she now quite liked them, Clare could not feel that she was a part of their world. They thought Sussex mattered and she did not.

When her period didn't come Clare was terrified and consumed with horror at the thought that she might be pregnant. If she was it was her fault, because she had stopped taking her pills at Christmas time for fear she would leave the packet lying around for her mother to find. The last thing she wanted was to be pregnant. She did not think of it in terms of having babies; pregnancy and procreation seemed to her quite separate states. She could not imagine having a baby, nor, on the other hand, could she have an abortion. Other people had abortions—squalid and frightening and illicit, as well as immoral.

After a week of turmoil she rang David who sounded as terrified as she was when she had wanted him to be strong. He did not offer to rush down and hold her hand and marry her as she had half hoped he might. Instead he said a week was much too soon to start getting all upset and he was on his way to the pub and couldn't say much; there were others in the room, possibly listening. Clare was standing at a call box in the street with others standing outside waiting to use it. She felt very far away from him and too miserable to be angry.

Late that night when she lay unable to sleep with the thought of her parents' horror ricocheting round her head, she decided to telephone Antonia. She could, perhaps, have confided in her sister but could not face the thought of Elinor's disapproval.

"Toe? Are you awake?"

"I am now," said Antonia sleepily.

"I'm sorry. I didn't mean to wake you up."

"It doesn't matter. I wasn't having any interesting dreams or anything." Antonia wrapped her nightdress closer about her and relit the roach of the joint she had used to make herself fall asleep.

"How are you, Toe?"

"Fine. But surely you're not ringing up at two in the morning to ask how I am?"

"No, I'm not, as it happens. Will you promise not to tell anyone something?"

"Of course. What is it?" Antonia drew on the joint.

"Well, it's not very cheerful news. I think I might be pregnant."

"Oh, Clare!"

"Please, Toe, don't say, 'oh, Clare' like that, you sound like Mummy. I'm sorry, really I am. I didn't mean to sound cross and vile. I'm being vile to everyone just now. I sit round playing Monopoly with anyone I can force into it, and then rush to the loo and pray for blood. Oh, Christ, Toe, what can I do?"

Antonia let Clare's words spill out of the telephone in a torrent. She did not know what to suggest at all.

"But what if I am pregnant? What then?" Clare continued. "You know all sorts of seedy people from your disco days, don't you?"

Antonia had run into a few minor dope dealers, but she was not acquainted with any abortionists as far as she knew. "Oh, God, Clare. I'm so sorry, but at the risk of sounding like David, isn't it worth waiting a little while more before you get totally panic-stricken?" There were muffled sobs from the receiver. "Don't cry, Clare, please don't. Go to bed. Smoke some dope. Try not to think about it."

"How can I not think about it? I think of nothing else. And I haven't got any dope. I've never smoked any."

"I'll send you some," said Antonia, thinking it would be something she could do for Clare, though not much.

"Don't bother. David would be furious if he knew. I never knew you smoked."

"I don't much anymore." Antonia stubbed out the last minute

remnant of joint into the ashtray and felt sorry for Clare. What the hell would she herself have done if she had become pregnant? She was too stoned to imagine it just then.

Clare took two Mandrax and eventually fell asleep.

Antonia wondered what David was feeling as she often did. She felt as sorry for him as she did for Clare. She would have liked to be able to help him if she could. She realised that she had spent a lot of time lately thinking about David and had allowed herself to wander into the museum quite often when she knew he was there, for the pleasure of being in the same building. She knew the exact times of the art school and took care to avoid actually meeting him and having to explain her presence. But the morning after Clare's call she misjudged the time, or at least told herself afterwards that she had misjudged the time, and he caught up with her as she went down the steps into Beaumont Street. He looked very tired and miserable.

"Antonia, just the person I was wanting to see. How odd to meet you here this morning. Let's go and get some coffee." He took her arm and they walked together to George's in the covered market where they could get coffee in enormous mugs, a pint or a half pint at a time. "How are you? You haven't been to the cottage for so long. I miss you."

"I'm very glad to be missed," said Antonia. "I'm very well. I'm trying to avoid reading Walter Scott, that's why I'm out. I usually quite like working, but I really can't face it just now."

"Neither can I," said David, looking at Antonia over the rim of his coffee mug, his eyes very blue in contrast to his dark hair. He hesitated, as if deciding whether to confide in her or not. "Have you heard from Clare?" he asked at last.

"She rang me up last night very late. Actually, I think it was this morning already."

"Did she tell you?" He looked down at his hands.

"Yes."

"I feel like such a heel. I didn't know what to say to her. Does she hate me?"

"I don't think she hates you at all."

"But I was very feeble and useless on the phone. I don't know what she wants me to do."

"I think she wants you to marry her, in an odd sort of way. And make all her problems go away. Puff. Just like that."

"But I couldn't marry her, Toe. Even if I wanted to. You know that."

"She does seem to think that being married is the universal panacea for all ills. I suppose she might, coming from such a family."

"But in spite of everything I do love her," said David. "I think I always will. But I can't make her happy. I can't be everything to her. She seems so miserable all the time. I wish she would find something to do with her life and not leave everything up to me."

"You should go down and see her, David. I know she'd like that."

"I know." David sighed. "I should, but in my innermost heart I don't want to. I'm afraid. I think I'm almost as frightened as she is. I will go of course."

Antonia wished she could put her arms about David and comfort him and say that everything would be all right. But then it might not be all right at all.

"You're very lucky, Toe, not to get yourself involved in such messes. You always seem so detached and untouched somehow."

"I'm not at all underneath," she said.

"Perhaps not," he said wearily, "but you make a very good show of it. Does everyone confide in you?"

"They seem to, perhaps because they know I will never say anything. I don't really have anyone to say anything to, as it happens."

"You can always talk to me if you want," said David, "if that would be any good. It probably wouldn't be, but you could try." He smiled and squeezed her hand lightly as it lay on the coffee-puddled table. Antonia looked at his blunt-fingered hand, that hand which could create such delicacy and precision.

"When you see Clare, you will send her my love won't you? And I'm sure it's all a great storm in a teacup, at least I pray it is. You know I would do anything to help Clare. I could lend her some money, too, if she needed it."

"You are a very good friend to us both, Toe."

"I know," said Antonia, half wishing she wasn't, that she had never met Clare and didn't care in the least what happened to her. She smiled briefly at David, picked up her gloves and wandered out into the street.

Clare's discovery that she was not pregnant failed to make her any more cheerful; if anything, she was more depressed. Antonia went to visit her in her bleak boardinghouse by the sea. Clare lay in bed in a faded antique nightdress which looked rather pretty at first glance but was in desperate need of mending. Her hair fell in dismal strands over the patchwork quilt which was in much the same state as the nightdress.

"How kind of you to visit me, Toe. I thought no one would ever manage to find me here." She was surrounded by screwed up paper handkerchiefs and stubbed out cigarettes.

"So you are all right, really?" Antonia said, thinking Clare was probably not.

"Oh, yes. I'm better from all that," she said gloomily. "You can't imagine the embarrassment of trailing round the campus carrying an old mayonnaise bottle full of urine, and those horrible, snooping doctors. But I'm lying in state because I've just had my tooth out." She opened her mouth to show Antonia the gap where the tooth had been.

"But surely they didn't have to pull it out? Couldn't they just have filled it?"

"Oh, it only costs ten shillings to pull it out and it's so much quicker—all over in a moment. Does my face still look odd?"

Other than being rather white Clare did not look particularly strange.

"You see people kept staring at me in the street, and I went into Boots to get some aspirin, and when I looked at myself in the mirror I had this disgusting trickle of blood meandering down my chin! Oh, God, I'm glad you're here," she said rousing herself a little. "What do you think of Brighton?"

Antonia shrugged. "It makes a change from Oxford. I'm so bored of writing lots of essays without once being asked what I really think about anything. I suppose one must in order to pass exams and so on, but it would be heaven if once, just once, I could say what I wanted to. Does it get better at university?"

"Not really," said Clare.

"But it was nice on the train. I do like travelling. I'm always pleased to see the sea. It seems to give things definition, a proper ending."

"And France is on the other side," said Clare brightening. "I was thinking earlier how nice it would be if we could all pack up and run off to Paris or Italy or anywhere warm. David could paint, you could be sensible and I could lie around looking consumptive and trying to think of something exciting to do."

"It would be nice, in a way," said Antonia thinking of Shelley's travels through Europe with Mary and Claire Claremont, and how she seemed to be the perennial third party, the one who was left out, the commentator, the expendable baggage. "But David did come to see you, didn't he?"

"Yes, he did, but it wasn't a great success. Actually I thought it might be a disaster, and it was. I hired a room on the campus where you can put up guests, but it was small and cheap-looking and falling apart even though it was quite new. I don't usually mind things being decrepit, but the room was sort of like a crippled child, everything blighted and wrong. And the room was the least of it. David seemed so out of place separated from his work, in unfamiliar surroundings. I took him to the museum near the Pavillion, the one full of stuffed birds. I had thought he would like it, but he said they were faded and moth-eaten. I couldn't think of anyone to introduce him to and we didn't seem to have much to say to each other. I knew I was stopping him from working. I was only happy when we were in bed. But you can't spend all your time in bed, can you?" At that, Clare decided to get up. She walked with Antonia along the gray seafront, where they failed to discern the least shadow of the coast of France.

"Do you really think it would be better if we were abroad?" asked Antonia. "Wouldn't we still be just us but in a different place?"

"Well, it would certainly be different," said Clare, "which would be a relief in itself. I don't know how much longer things can go on as they are."

When the spring came at last it brought the liberation of cotton dresses, the pleasure of the long light evenings and diminishing demands from the gas metre. Antonia loved the bright new leaves on the trees and the gaudy colours of the tulips. There were vivid yellow daffodils in the cottage garden, and vast numbers of narcissi, which Clare painted with a new energy.

"Does spring cheer everyone up?" Clare asked one day, wiping her brush on her paint-spattered smock.

"Well, it certainly cheers me a bit," said Antonia, putting aside her book and leaning back against the barn wall from where she could get a better view of David who was taking his motorcycle to pieces.

"Are you good at sitting still?" Clare asked.

"I don't know, I've never tried."

"Well, if you could bear to try I could put you in my painting. Your blouse is a wonderful colour against the wall and the flowers. Do try. It would be fun."

Antonia sat immobile while Clare worked. She was feeling very peaceful and drowsy, warmed by the sun. David seemed unaware of her watching him. Later he came up and looked critically at Clare's work. "You see," he said smiling, "you can paint if you want to."

"Toe is a lovely model, David. I'm surprised you haven't got round to painting her yet."

David picked up Clare's sketchbook and started drawing very quickly. He made three sketches which Antonia longed to look at, and then went back to the intricacies of his bike.

"Do let me see them," said Antonia.

Clare handed Antonia the book and then threw down her brush and ran inside the cottage. When she followed Clare into the kitchen Antonia could see that she had been crying. As she handed Antonia a mug of tea she sniffed and said, "It's hopeless, Toe. He can do in five minutes what I fail to do in two hours. It isn't fair. I may as well give up."

"I thought you were doing rather well, Clare. I thought your picture was quite like me."

"Yes, if you were deformed and had a goitre and a squint." Clare managed to smile. "It doesn't matter anyway. I've got to go down to Sussex tomorrow and I'll never have time to finish it. And when I do get back all the blossom will be over and everything will look different."

"Do you think David would let me keep those sketches he made of me? No one has ever drawn me before."

"I expect he would love you to have them if you want them. He sketches all the time. It's rather like a diary; there are thousands of them littered about the place."

Antonia already knew this. She had one of his drawings already, which she had retrieved from the dustbin. She had flattened it out and preserved it between the pages of her diary.

When Clare took the time to think about what she was doing with her life she felt ashamed. She was not, in fact, doing anything at all; neither studying, nor painting and certainly not living poetry. She was sure there was something she ought to have been doing if she could only discover what. David did still seem to need her, and he was happy when she was happy, but it was not enough. She did not know whether she had the strength to leave him. Perhaps no one else would ever want her. She did not like herself very much and doubted if anyone else would.

She went up to Oxford less frequently, frightened of imposing herself upon David. She thought that perhaps, if left to himself, he would come to need her more. She wanted the reassurance of his need of her. She tried to gauge how he felt about her from the length and intensity of his letters.

One day she received a letter, rather longer than usual, in which he wrote, "You know you always said I should paint Antonia? Well, I have been working on those first drawings I made. It is very different from painting you. You'll see when you next come up. I'm very excited about what I'm doing. I think you'll like them."

Clare wondered if she would.

Antonia posed often for David during the next few weeks, sometimes when Clare was there but frequently when she was not. Clare never mentioned the hours Antonia spent alone at the cottage with David. She spent more and more time reading, her habitual retreat when things were not going well.

·   ·   ·

When Antonia was in Oxford she found herself counting the days and minutes until she would be alone with David. At first they talked a great deal about Clare and then hardly at all, as if they had a tacit agreement not to mention her. David felt the paintings were going very well. He said he had discovered a new energy and was discovering new ways of seeing.

The first time Antonia posed naked for David she felt very awkward. She felt her body to be ugly and ungainly, but David's drawings gave her an elegance she did not associate with herself.

"I don't like my body very much," said Antonia. "I think I'm much too fat."

"You're much thinner than Clare."

"Am I really?"

"Of course you are. You must realise that." He looked at her as if she were mad. "You never eat anything. How could you be fat? But I think you are very beautiful anyway. And I am very grateful to you for letting me paint you."

Antonia sat draped in David's dressing gown, which she threw over herself between poses. He turned the easel towards her and came and stood beside her, and looked at the painting over her shoulder. "What do you think?"

Antonia turned to him and looked up into his face. Her eyes met his and she turned away.

David put his hand on her shoulder. "You never say what you think of the painting, Toe. Surely you think something?"

Antonia said, "What are you going to tell Clare?"

"I don't know what I'm going to tell Clare. But it isn't wrong, is it? It was her idea, after all, that I should paint you." He threw aside his brush. "Perhaps it is wrong; perhaps I shouldn't do it. But I want to. God, do you realise how much I enjoy having you here, so calm and uncritical? You'd better put your clothes on."

They sat in the sun, leaning against the barn wall, watching the butterflies dance across the long grass.

"I dread Clare coming up this weekend," David said eventually. "Wouldn't it be nice if it was just us alone?"

"Yes," said Antonia, not looking at him.

"I think I'm falling a little in love with you, Toe. And I don't know what to do." He picked up her hand and held it between his two paint-stained ones.

"Well, don't tell Clare."

"But I will have to tell Clare. Of course I'll have to tell her."

"But why? We haven't *done* anything after all. Perhaps I'd better go away and not come here anymore. Wouldn't that be better for us all?"

"In what way better? Better than what? There is something between us, isn't there? Don't you feel it, too?"

"Don't, David. Don't say anything or I will have to go away."

"But you don't want to really, do you?"

"I don't know what the hell I want to do," said Antonia, disengaging her hand and pushing away a tear with the back of it. "I think I'll go to Oxford and finish the essay I should have handed in yesterday."

"If you really want to go I'll take you on the bike."

"No, don't. I'll hitch. It's perfectly all right."

"I hate you hitching. It's dangerous."

"Not if you're sensible. Clare always seems to think I can be relied upon to be sensible."

Antonia stood beside the main road and cried. Great wet tears dripped down her nose and crept into her mouth. A lorry stopped for her. She got in and they drove off.

"You all right, Miss?" said the bulky lorry driver beside her. "You feel all right?" He handed her a filthy handkerchief which she felt it would have been impolite to refuse. She wiped her nose and gave it back.

"Had a row with your Mum, have you?"

"No, nothing like that," said Antonia.

Thirteen

Antonia took a train to London because she did not want to see either David or Clare, neither together nor separately. The streets were hot and dusty and the area round Paddington Station was full of litter and dubious-looking hotels. She decided to walk for a while because she was in no great hurry to see Eileen. She walked slowly, savouring the unfamiliarity of actually studying those buildings which she had seen so often, if fleetingly, before. Her daydreams about their occupants were interrupted by one of those awkward pavement confrontations where she stepped first to the left and then to the right, attempting to allow the other person to pass by. Her partner in this absurd ritual dance was a swarthy Middle Eastern-looking man whose stare could only be described as lascivious. One of her shoes was rubbing her heel quite raw. She gave up her walk in desperation and took a taxi.

She looked at the door of the house which was officially her home. Eileen had recently had it painted a surprisingly attractive shade of hot pink. The colour echoed that of the geraniums which leaned cheerfully from the window boxes. *I wonder what magazine she got that out of,*

Antonia wondered, hating herself for her petty-mindedness. Wherever she got the idea from, the general effect was pleasing. She knocked.

"You look tired, Toni," said her stepmother leaning forward to kiss her cheek. "But what a lovely surprise to see you." Eileen smelled of expensive cosmetics and nail polish remover. "I wish you had let me know you were coming. Your father will be so pleased to see you."

Thus saving himself the effort of coming to Oxford, thought Antonia.

"The door looks nice," she said, trying to think of something remotely civil to say.

Eileen smiled. "I'm glad you like it. I hoped you would."

"Is he here?" Antonia asked.

"Not now. He should be arriving from Milan this evening. I've got to go to Heathrow in a minute to pick him up."

"What was he doing in Milan?"

"Oh, something to do with import licenses, the usual sort of business thing. I never ask anymore. You don't mind if I finish my nails, do you, Toni?"

"Of course not." Antonia wished she would stop calling her Toni, a name she detested but had never dared tell her not to use.

"I've bought a new dress, would you like to see it?" Eileen said. The dress was lime green and very short. "D'you think he'll like it?" She held it up against herself, the colour harsh against her unmade-up face. "Tell me what you think."

Antonia could not imagine her father liking it.

"I could always take it back," Eileen said when Antonia failed to think up any appropriate comment.

"No, don't. I think it's very nice. It's very you. You always look nice in bright colours."

"It's not too gaudy, is it?"

Antonia was torn between wanting her to look awful out of spite, and the realisation that her stepmother was desperately trying to please both her and her father. "I always liked the pink one you got at Liberty's," she said.

"Then you hate this one?"

"I don't hate it, Eileen. I just like the other one better."

"I am grateful for your advice, Toni. You always seem to know what Rex will like better than I do." Eileen hung the offending dress back in her overfull wardrobe. "But isn't it still term time?"

"Yes, but I wanted to get away for a bit."

"You are all right, aren't you?" Eileen scanned Antonia's face and body very rapidly. "You don't look very well to me."

"I'm fine, really I am. How's Justin? I haven't heard from him for ages."

Eileen's face lightened immediately at the sound of her son's name. "He's so tall suddenly, and terribly grown up and polite. The very picture of a proper English gentleman."

"Is he?" said Antonia, not quite convinced that this was what she wanted her brother to become.

"He wants to be a big-game hunter. I took him to the zoo at half term to see the lions. We were to meet your father, but he couldn't get away. He told Justin he would take him to Kenya when he's twelve to see real lions. I mean the lions at the zoo are real, but they're probably better in their natural habitat, don't you think?"

"I'm sure they are." Antonia wondered what Justin's chances of actually getting to Kenya were; she did not rate them very high.

"But it was nice to be alone with him for a bit. I miss him awfully. I hated seeing him off on the train at the end of his weekend. He seems very young to go away."

"Does he have to go that ridiculous school, Eileen? Wouldn't you love to have him at home with you?"

"But he likes it there. He isn't unhappy," said Eileen, not sounding very convinced. "All his friends are there."

"He could have other friends if he went to day school."

"But they wouldn't be the same sort of friends."

"What do you mean the same sort of friends? There are eight-year-old boys all over the place."

"But you know what I mean."

"Of course I know what you mean, and I hate it."

"Your father thinks it's a very good school. He would have liked to have gone there himself."

"He probably would, but that was years ago. Everything is different now, or at least it should be. Are you going out to dinner?" Antonia was desperate to change the subject.

"No, I thought we would eat at home. You never know when planes will be late and the traffic is always awful on Friday nights. And he'll probably be tired when he gets in."

Antonia lay on the bed and watched Eileen putting on fresh makeup as efficiently as she had once been able to type. "Is it all worth it?" she asked, twisting the fringe of the pristine white bedspread between her fingers.

"All what?"

"All this waiting around for my father."

"Of course it is," Eileen said quite briskly, shielding her eyes as she sprayed her hair. "Would you be a love and put the oven on at half past seven? We should be back by eight. I hope so at least."

She was still excited at the prospect of seeing him, Antonia thought; bully for her. She flicked through a copy of *Vogue* and then lay in a bath full of sickly bath essence watching the London grime float up off her body. She put on one of the dresses Eileen had bought for her the previous summer which she had never worn before. She wanted to look nice for her father, too.

David wrote a letter to Clare. She picked up the envelope with his familiar writing on it and went back into her room to read it.

He wrote: "Dearest Clare, I want to talk to you very much, but lately it seems that we have not had the opportunity. Nor, I think, have you wanted to really. It is very difficult for me to explain exactly what it is I want to say. Nothing is changed between us, believe me. I still love you very much, as you should know. However, what you felt about Antonia is partially true. I think I am falling a little in love with her. If you love me, as you say you do, I think you will be able to understand. . . ." There were several more pages in much the same vein, which Clare could scarcely decipher because her hands trembled so much. There was a pain at the back of her throat. Her hatred sprang up for Antonia rather than David. She loathed the beautiful, talented, scheming, odious, predatory Antonia, who was, of course, more desirable and more lovely than she was in every way. What Clare could not understand was the physical pain she felt. She thought of the old saw from her childhood, "Sticks and stones may break my bones, but words can never hurt me." What a lie; it was the most stupid thing she had heard in her life.

Clare lay in her coffinlike room and wept, trying to stifle her cries in the sodden pillow. David belonged to her alone and he had been stolen; she felt physically violated as if a part of her had been torn away. She felt belittled and betrayed. Since she had been with David she had purposely cut herself off from the possibility of finding anyone else she remotely liked. Without David she was nothing, had nothing and could never be anything. She wanted to kill Antonia and wound David. She dared not leave her room for fear of breaking down in front of anyone she might meet. She locked her bedroom door and lay looking into the future, which stretched bleakly before her into infinity, treeless, grassless, unbeautiful and hopeless. She continued to weep although she was almost too tired to squeeze out any more tears. The hours passed exquisitely slowly. She wanted to scream but dared not for fear of being discovered. No one could help her and she did not wish anyone to try.

All she wanted was to get through the rest of her life as quickly as possible. She no longer wanted to know or feel anything, ever. She wondered if she wanted to die. She did want to die. All that held her back was a consciousness of the pain it would cause her parents. She would have wanted to see David's reaction to her death. She wanted to hurt him as he had hurt her.

Her usual antidotes to suicide filtered through her mind. Nevermore to see the sun rise. Never again to see the sun set. They didn't work. She still retained vestiges of the fear of death, but, in fact, she didn't much care. She had no wish either to continue living or to undertake the courageous step of actually dying.

She sat at her table and tried to write to David. She found that she did not know what to say. What could she say? She did not hate him but felt so distanced even from her own thoughts that it seemed an impossible task.

She looked in her drawer and took out what pills she had. There were nine sleeping pills and seventeen five-milligram Libriums; she wondered if that were enough to kill her. She hadn't the least idea, but it didn't seem likely. Still, she took a plastic beaker of water and swallowed them. She was frightened by what she had done and yet not frightened enough to regret it. In fact, she was interested to see what would happen. After what seemed like a long time lying in the dark, she fell asleep.

A faint light crept through the open curtains as she lay sprawled on top of the bed. Clare could dimly see the light and wondered what it was. Her head felt so heavy that it was impossible to lift it from the pillow; her body, equally heavy. Everything was muddled. She was obviously not dead, unless her hideous, small room and her orange-and-red-striped face cloth had followed her wherever she had gone. She had a cramp in her stomach, a gnawing pain. She swung her feet over the side of the bed and clung to the side of the washbasin. She wanted to be sick but wasn't. Her clock, dimly visible, said it was a quarter to five. She washed her face in cold water and then fell back onto the bed and wanted to scream. More than anything else in the world she wanted to scream and scream and scream. She thought it might remove the pain in her head.

Clare unlocked the door and went out onto the dark landing, and then walked out of the silent boardinghouse and down to the beach. It was cold and the sun was beginning to gild the hideous buildings and glint on the calm sea. The shingle cut her feet. She walked along the edge of the freezing water and screamed. There was no one to hear her except a drunk collapsed beneath the seawall. She continued screaming as loudly as she could until she was exhausted and flung herself face down on a little patch of damp sand. The brightening light hurt her eyes, so she closed them and lay very still.

She lifted her head at the sound of footsteps approaching across the shingle. . . . Two pairs of polished black boots swam into her vision, but she did not look up. One of her feet was bleeding where it had been pierced by a piece of glass. Her thin cotton dress was wet from lying on the sand.

One of the policemen put his hand on her shoulder. She shook it off. "Are you all right, Miss?" he asked.

"Perfectly all right," said Clare, "thank you," and started to cry again. She stood up and looked at them both. For a brief moment the face of the shorter one metamorphosed into David's face, which terrified her.

"Please go away, I'm fine, can't you see, wonderful, marvellous, tremendous . . . please go away."

The taller one tried again. "Does your mother know where you are?"

This question struck Clare as a very strange one indeed. "Please leave me alone." Clare sat down again on the sand and surprisingly, they did go away.

She lay on her bed for the rest of the day and looked at the ceiling, which was very dull, painted pea green with a sort of rippled texture. When she could stand that no longer, she tried to sleep again but failed. One of the worst things, Clare thought, was that she did not want anyone to know how miserable she was. She was humiliated by her situation. Out of pride, she had never told anyone at the boardinghouse that David was anything but the most attentive and perfect of lovers; she had wanted to appear aloof, special and above criticism. Now she was a reject, without friends and with nothing to do.

Eventually she went upstairs and knocked on the door of the girl to whom she had sold her Indian silk shawl. The shawl now lay abandoned on the floor of the cupboard amidst piles of boots and shoes, hopelessly crushed. Cathy was reading when she walked in, sat on the sofa and looked out at the sea.

"You look terrible, Clare," Cathy said.

"Do I?"

"What on earth is the matter? Are you ill?"

"I suppose so. Oh, I don't know. What day is it?" Clare sat hugging her knees, which drew her up into a ball.

"Friday." Clare realised that she had missed a whole day, but she didn't feel in the least surprised. She didn't know whether to tell Cathy everything that had happened or not. It didn't seem to matter either way. She really didn't care what Cathy thought or anyone else for that matter.

"David just wrote to me and said that he was in love with someone else and I took a lot of pills and have just been asleep for a long time."

Cathy did not seem impressed. Clare secretly wished that she had been more startled. "I'm sorry, Clare. I really am. Is there anything I can do?"

"No, nothing; I just feel terribly tired. I don't think I even care just now."

"Why don't you come to the pub with us? It couldn't be worse than staying here." It was very kind of Cathy to offer to take her. Clare hated pubs generally but was quite willing to have decisions made for her and to be taken in hand.

Clare screwed up all her courage and said that she would go. She went to her room and looked at her face in the glass; it was a red blodge which makeup did not improve.

The pub was filled with smoke and the smell of stale beer and an aura of bonhomie. Cathy introduced her to her friends whose names Clare was too incurious to take in. They all seemed very cheerful and welcoming, which Clare found very odd. Perhaps they thought she was a good friend of Cathy's. Clare drank two gin and tonics paid for by someone whose name she still didn't know. Everyone else drank beer. The drink failed to revive her. Everything seemed distant, as through a veil, and she did not take in the conversation. "You'd like to come to the cottage with us, wouldn't you?" Cathy asked her after a while.

"Yes, of course," she murmured, thinking she should at least appear to be agreeable to these people who were tolerating her company even though they held no interest whatever for her.

They piled into two cars and set off through the darkness out of the town. It was unlike Clare not to know where she was going. After a time they turned off the coast road and turned inland across a grassy hillside. She whispered to Cathy, "They won't expect me to sleep with them, will they?"

"Not if you don't want to." Clare didn't think that she did. She had enough trouble differentiating one man from another, though they seemed pleasant enough.

Clare slept on the floor of a large dim room at the cottage, behind a sofa. She could hear Cathy and her boyfriend making love in the early hours of the morning. She closed her eyes and tried not to listen. Had David and she made noises like that? She wondered, and thought not.

Clare got up very early, which seemed to her normal; everything was either very early or very late. She explored the village, wandering in the steep churchyard reading the epitaphs. It was early June, still and fine. The downs, where the hedges were white with hawthorn, encircled the village. Clare felt very remote and calm. She did not know the name of the village, and viewed it with a certain detachment. It seemed cosy and protected. Nobody knew she was there, or rather nobody who cared where she was knew.

When she went back to the cottage, she made herself a cup of tea, swilling out a tannin-encrusted mug under the cold tap. She took it out into the garden and sat under an apple tree and thought, this is very nice, perhaps they will let me stay here.

Clare did not see Cathy leave, though she heard a car going down the lane. The three people who lived in the cottage did not seem surprised to see her sitting there in the garden enjoying the morning. She was a solitary figure somewhat bedraggled and pathetic in the crushed cotton dress in which she had slept.

"Brian is away and you can have his room if you want," said Greg, a tall, thin, bespectacled figure with a Northern accent (who laughed, not unkindly, at Clare's). A couple, Chris and Ruth, didn't say anything but smiled nicely enough before they, too, left to go to the university.

Brian's room turned out to be unexpectedly clean, with a mattress in one corner and books neatly stacked. She tried to imagine him from his books. She thought he was probably a biologist, a Marxist biologist who was interested in sex and very tidy. She would have to keep the room neat. She hoped that he would be gone a long time.

Clare decided to paint, all day and every day, to stop herself from thinking about David. She walked over the downs and hitched into Brighton and bought canvases and paints and began.

Greg was kind to her. He did not question why she was there and he admired her paintings. He was gone for days at a time and shared his food with her when he was there. He ate a lot of brown rice, which Clare found dull, and a lot of raw vegetables, which became more interesting when you were not eating much else. There was no white sugar in the house, so Clare went out and bought some, which she hid amongst her paints in a cardboard box in the larder thinking the others would disapprove.

One night when Clare and Greg were alone, he asked her if she would like to smoke and she replied, "Oh, I've got some cigarettes, would you like one of mine?"

"No, I meant smoke dope, hash, whatever."

"Of course I'd love to." Clare did not want to admit that she never had before.

"Do you want to roll up while I make tea?" Greg asked.

She decided to admit her ignorance; she sensed that Greg would enjoy being a teacher, an initiator.

"I don't know how to, I'm afraid."

"Really? How odd, I imagined you were a dope fiend."

"I only do pills and prescription ones at that." What a fraud I am, thought Clare, not sophisticated at all. "What will it feel like?"

"Nothing much at first, but inhale deeply and hold the smoke in your lungs as long as you can and breathe out slowly."

"What happens if the police come?"

"They won't."

"But what if they do?"

"Are you scared?" Greg asked.

"Not at all." But she was.

Greg rolled a joint quickly and expertly. Clare always admired little tricks like that, little sleight-of-hand things which she was too clumsy to copy. He lit the joint, inhaled and handed it silently to Clare, his wrist turned at an angle so as not to burn her.

Clare inhaled and felt the smoke going down into her lungs and held her breath for what seemed a long time and then started coughing. Nothing happened. She inhaled again, trying not to make the paper too wet, which seemed rather difficult. She handed the joint back to Greg.

When it was almost finished, she began to feel its effect. Or was she imagining this? It was hard to tell, she had felt so odd most of the time lately.

"Are you getting anything?"

"A bit, I think."

"I'll roll another." He did.

Everything seemed hilarious, muzzy and strange. She thought of David seventy miles away and didn't care in the least what he was doing. Clare leaned back against the wall, the cushion beneath her, comforting and soft. She felt very safe. This is what I should be doing, she thought, looking out into the starless night, just sitting in a room, being. She looked at Greg, who was so different from David physically, so long, angular and ugly. She corrected herself, not really ugly, just ungainly. She wondered what he thought of her. As if sensing her thoughts, Greg handed her the joint and said, "Did you know that I think you're very attractive?"

"No," she said, shocked. "I didn't imagine it at all."

"But you are, very." Clare thought she should have washed her hair or shaved her legs or something.

"Oh!"

"I'd like to sleep with you."

"I . . . I'm terribly sorry, I mean I'd love to but . . . it's rather difficult. I'm in love with someone else, I mean." (He had not said anything about loving her.) Clare was profusely apologetic. She supposed it was a compliment when someone said they wanted to sleep with you. How did one refuse politely?

Greg said, "Shush, don't talk about it," and smiled.

She started to explain about David and he said, "Look, love, I don't want to know. You're here, I'm here, and it's a beautiful night; we can't concern ourselves with what's going on out there. All sorts of things are going on and whatever either of us does or thinks isn't going to make one atom of difference. So relax and forget about it."

She thought that this was very sound advice. Greg certainly knew more about things than she did. In a little while she said, "I'm going to make some tea. Do you want some?"

"Thanks. That would be very nice."

She stood up and swayed slightly and laughed. "I'm stoned," she said, tentatively, wondering if she had got the jargon right.

"You're stoned," he said, "and so am I. That's nice."

Fumblingly, she made tea, needing three spoons of her illicit stash of sugar to make it sweet enough. "Here's yours," she said slopping it slightly over the edge of the mug, which was very funny indeed. She hoped she hadn't given him the tea with the sugar in it.

"This is the first time I've seen you relaxed," he said. "You should smoke more often."

Greg looked rather nice in the light of the flickering candle, his eyes reflecting its glow. Smiling, not judging her. Perhaps it would be nice to sleep with him, to sleep with someone's arms around her comforting in the night, but she knew she could never do it. She could only sleep with David, or Max.

She felt sleepy, kind and benevolent towards the world. She looked forward to her dreams, and wondered who would come to her in them. She finished her tea, and went to rinse her mug in the kitchen. While there, she caught sight of herself in the small, cracked glass over the sink, her face, with flowers reflected behind it, very white and insignificant in the universal scheme of things. She smiled and thought to herself that it was peaceful being alone. She went to sleep and did not dream.

The weather continued fine and clear. Clare set out each morning with her cardboard box of oil paints and sat in her bikini until the sun at midday burned her shoulders. She liked what she was painting and enjoyed things in particular rather than in general. She admired the colours of shadows falling on leaves, and the patterns of grasses against the sun. She had brought her own small, black piece of hash, which she rolled, most inexpertly, into joints that were constantly coming apart at the seams. She got hungry and brought in secret supplies of non-macrobiotic food; she did not want to admit she liked white bread.

Surprisingly, she painted rather well, beautifully coloured almost impressionistic landscapes of the downs and of the village. She thought a great deal about David but didn't want to talk to him except fleetingly. Then she rolled another joint and stopped needing him.

One Sunday afternoon she went to a party at another cottage in the village where a couple with two children lived with another girl with a baby whose father no one mentioned. They ate chocolate cake in the sunshine as naked children ran amongst the apple trees. The cake had dope in it. She wondered if hashish was bad for children; they looked very happy and healthy. The baby lay at its mother's breast content and replete. The mother's long hair reached the ground as she sat nursing him in an Indian robe. Clare wondered if she would ever have a child. It looked so idyllic to lie in the sun with a child in one's arms. No one spoke much. Clare had nothing to say to them; she was frightened to break their tranquillity.

On passing the telephone kiosk on her way back to the cottage where she was staying Clare was suddenly seized with the desire to talk to David.

She fumbled with her change. She was still stoned.

"It's me, Clare."

"I know. Oh, God, I've been so worried about you."

"You needn't have been."

"I went to see Elinor. She didn't know where you were either. She was worried, too."

"I'm fine. I'm happy. I'm in the country painting—a butterfly dancing in the sunshine."

"You're what?"

"It doesn't matter. How's Antonia?"

"How am I supposed to know? I haven't seen her."

"But why haven't you seen her? I thought you were madly in love with her."

"Oh, Clare, it's much too complicated to explain on the telephone. I've missed you so much. I wish I had never written you that ridiculous letter. Won't you come and see me? I will try to explain everything, if I can."

"But why, David? Why? I really don't know if I want to see you." But she did want to see him, against her better judgement.

"Please come back, Clare. Please," he pleaded. "I never said I didn't love you, Clare. You know that I do."

But I don't know it, she thought, and wondered if she even wanted him to.

Clare went back to David to try to recapture what they once had together, but she had travelled too far from him in the weeks that she had been away. She was too hurt to respond easily to his protestations of affection.

She posed for him mechanically as he turned all the paintings he had started of Antonia back into ones of her, wiping out all visible traces of his defection.

"I never stopped loving you, Clare. Never for one moment. What I felt for Antonia was quite different, quite separate. And it wasn't what I thought it to be at all."

"But you destroyed what there was between us."

"Yes," he said wearily. "I know that now."

One afternoon Clare went into Oxford and walked over to Antonia's room. Antonia was sitting by the window pleasantly lost in a Jane Austen novel, in a circumscribed world where almost everyone knew how to behave.

"You look well, Clare," Antonia said tentatively.

"You don't. Don't you ever go out in the sun?"

"Yes, but I never seem to get brown or only a little bit." Antonia put aside her book.

Clare lit a cigarette and looked at Antonia through the smoke. "You can sleep with David if you want to," she said magnanimously.

"I don't want to, as it happens. And I never did really."

"The stupid thing is, Toe, that now I don't care."

Clare stubbed out her cigarette and smiled at Antonia. "Have you got any dope?"

"A little in the second drawer of the desk."

"Shall I roll up?" Clare was anxious to show off her newfound dexterity.

"So what now?" Antonia drew on the joint and watched little motes of dust dancing in the afternoon sunshine.

"I don't know. I just don't know. All that I'm sure of is that everything must change. I think I want to paint. I want to be free and on my own. I keep thinking about Max, and how I felt when I was with him. He made me feel that everything was possible, which David never did. I knew that I would never stay with him and that he would never want me to, but he always said that he would be there if I needed him."

"Then you should go and find him, Clare, and see what he has to say."

"Do you hate me? Do you think I have behaved as badly as I think I have?" Clare was quite stoned by now.

Antonia smiled. "I think it was inevitable, all of it. We have all behaved badly but there was nothing else we could do."

"Will you always be my friend? Whatever happens?"

"If you want me to, though I can't imagine why you do."

"Because you never judge me. However horribly I behave you seem to think I'm all right. There is some comfort in that. Do you mind if I go to sleep now? I'm terribly tired all of a sudden."

"So am I. Do you think, as your mother says, that it will all turn out all right in the end?"

"It may or it may not," said Clare wrapping the blanket around them both.

Very early the next morning while Elinor sat with Conrad, Simon picked up the telephone and dialled the number of the cottage. "Oh, David, this is Simon Varley. Is Clare there? I need to speak to her."

"No, she isn't. But I think she'll be here later in the morning. Can I give her a message?"

Simon hesitated a moment. Putting his hand over the receiver, he glanced at Elinor who said, "I think you'd better tell him."

"Yes, David, if you would. Tell her that Max Cousins is dead, that he killed himself late last night."

David asked, "But who was Max Cousins?"

"Clare will know."

After David told her Clare walked out of the cottage and down the lane. She felt assaulted by the lush magnificence of the midsummer fields. The cow parsley grew thigh high and the hawthorn hedges sprouted recklessly, even the nettles looked rank and luxuriant. She thought of rosebay willow herb, growing in bombed-out buildings, where buddleia attracted butterflies; and of yew trees growing in graveyards nourished by rotting flesh. Nature didn't care in the least what it feasted upon, just went on multiplying randomly. How thoughtless of it all!

Privet, Clare always thought, smelled like death, with its horrid little white flowers which bees seemed to like. This endless cycle of growth and decay going on and on without pause. Poppies in cornfields in Flanders and over it all clouds billowing and lowering or doing whatever clouds formlessly did. How she hated it all!

She sat on an abandoned plough in the middle of a thistle-filled field and tried not to think. But her mind was awash with images: Max dead and white; Antonia's slight limbs encircling David's; flowers growing obscenely through paving stones. How relentlessly it all went on, this turbulence, this uncontrolled fluctuation of matter! She drew on her joint and the end became soggy and a little piece of paper attached itself to her chapped lip. If she smoked any more she would be sick or go to sleep, either one preferable to this all-enveloping consciousness of pain.

After a long while she dragged herself back to the cottage where she found David sitting in the kitchen with Antonia. They drew apart when she came in, and she saw that Antonia had been crying, too.

"It's all right," Clare said. "I don't care what you do."

She flung herself on the bed and hugged her pillow to her and was swamped by alternating waves of nausea and sleep. The bed was a rocky ship being blown hither and thither by the tide but firmly anchored somewhere a long way below. Nothing remained constant but change. She knew that she must leave England.

Part Two

Fourteen

Soon after she arrived in Florence Clare happened upon the Locanda dei Cesere during one of her interminable walks round the city. Tucked away in a side street off via dei Neri, she saw the shabby notice which said "Camere, Rooms, Zimmer." In spite of its name the Locanda could never have been grand or imperial. It was made up of lots of houses all crammed together, its passages meandering and dim.

There was a desk in the upstairs lobby with a bell which Clare had rung, but no one had answered. Eventually, bored, she had followed the smell of cooking and discovered the signora chopping onions and mopping her brow. Having established by signs that she was looking for a room, Clare followed the woman's broad back through the warrenlike house and was shown at last into a small square chamber. It was furnished with a bed, a table, a chair and the most enormous wardrobe Clare had ever encountered, elaborately carved with the leaves of no tree Clare had ever known. The floor was bare red tile and the walls were white, or had once been, before the plaster had started to crumble and flake and make intricate maps of isthmuses and islands and benevolent faces.

"You like?" The signora enquired rather doubtfully, wiping her hands on her apron, as if she thought Clare might be more familiar with grander pensions with washbasins or even adjoining bathrooms. Since Clare had no desire for ornate wallpaper and framed, bad reproductions of Eurasian ladies with green bosoms, she nodded enthusiastically, liking it very much. The room was so cheap it had escaped even the most humble category of lodgings in *Europe on $5 a Day*. She took it.

It was clean and spare and nothing in it had any personality except the wardrobe. This monolith Clare decided to humour, for what if it decided not to like her? It might fall on her in the night and crush her entirely, and they would have to identify her body by the teeth alone. She stuffed newspaper into the door to keep it shut and under one leg to stop it wobbling when vehicles passed in the street.

The room's only obvious disadvantage was that it was scarcely better lit than her unlamented room in Hove. Only in the late afternoon did the sun stream in for an hour, flooding the furniture with its roseate glow and transforming what was cold and barren the rest of the day into a place of comfort and charm. When the light failed Clare would close the heavy shutters with a satisfactory thud and feel encircled and protected by the thick walls and the sturdy, uneven floor.

Now that she had a room of her own Clare bought paints and canvases and five new brushes, a mug, a jug and a huge bowl handpainted with Renaissance designs, convoluted swirls of blue, yellow and black. She bought fruit and placed it in the bowl where it sat, waiting for her to begin. Window, bowl, red apples and a lemon, acidic and sharp. She felt a small frisson of delight as she squeezed the colours onto her palette in their accustomed order and listened to the clamour in the street beneath her. She drew in the outlines first, transferring onto the white rectangle the curved shapes of the fruit—such satisfactory contrast between roundness and angularity. She could smell the paint before she dipped her brush into it, that intoxicating universal smell. She thought of Elinor saying, "You can paint, Clare, and you ought to." And David saying, "It's no use copying what other people do. It isn't a competition. It doesn't matter what other people think."

Clare painted until her back ached from sitting so awkwardly. She looked at what she had begun and was pleased. She wished there was someone to share her delight and was washed suddenly by an unbidden swell of loneliness which threatened to cancel out her joy. The light had begun to fade. She put aside her brushes and walked out into the street to be among people. She did not want to be alone.

She sat in the Church of S. Croce thinking she would sketch some *putti*, but their round bellies and plump cheeks eluded her pencil. These beautiful children who had been dead now for hundreds of years saddened her with their grace and their perfection.

Candles sputtered and glowed before paintings of saints. Each flickering light bought by someone, each one of some small significance, lit in someone's name so that they might be remembered as long as the candle burned. Clare found them beautiful and was tempted to buy one herself. An awful, Papish practice, her mother would think, superstitious and suspect. But her mother was in another country and would never know.

She dropped her coins into the box provided and lit the squat candle. She could not light it for herself she knew, that would be arrogant. Nor did she wish to light candles for the dead. She prayed instead to be included in some general benediction to be conferred by a deity in whom she could not believe. She wished there would be no pain, no loss, no hunger, no injury, no greed, no war. She prayed not for herself alone but for everyone alive.

The church's cavernous beauty, the huge spaciousness of it, dwarfed her loneliness and made her aware of her insignificance. She envied the antiquity of the shuffling old women with their heads bowed in prayer, she envied their greater knowledge of the world and its pain. She felt herself to be a fraud, a pitiful actress playing at being sad when she had nothing to be unhappy about.

She wrote to Elinor that night, telling her about the Locanda dei Cesere and its inhabitants, and that she had begun to paint. She did not mention the great calm which had come upon her in the church, nor did she mention the fact that she was lonely, not wanting her sister to think she was bored. She wanted to appear strong and independent; perhaps by pretending to be so she might become what she was not. She turned her painting to the wall and slept.

Gradually her days acquired a rhythm and a routine. She rose early to the accompaniment of metal shutters being drawn up at the adjacent shops and dressed quickly in order to sneak into the bathroom before anyone else got there. The lavatory, which Clare visited as infrequently as possible, had the most appalling scratchy gray paper and an all-pervasive stench of mis-aimed urine. She took great care never to touch anything at all with her naked hands for fear of the innumerable germs eager, no doubt, to invade and conquer her.

Then she would breakfast at Vivoli's, having taught them to make tolerable hot chocolate by diluting half of their bitter black potion with half a cup of warm milk, and then putting vast quantities of whipped cream on top. Thus fortified, she would paint until lunch. The *rosticceria* on via dei Neri served vast platters of lasagna which Clare washed down with mineral water. Unable to converse with the other diners, Clare spent the meals reading the labels on the water bottles; they promised cures for every known ailment (possibly even those Clare avoided contracting in the bathroom). She was on nodding and smiling terms with the proprietors of both of her refuelling stations but still could not hold a proper conversation with them. She felt quite worn out communicating by gesture alone.

Clare was accosted one day by a slight Italian girl named Giuliana Russo, who wanted to practise her English. Giuliana was pleased to latch on to someone as free and bohemian as she seemed to imagine Clare to be. At first Clare was grateful for her company, for the fact that her painting was going well did not entirely compensate her for being alone so much. Giuliana lived with her family still, though she was twenty, and when she was invited to Sunday lunch with the Russos, Clare could think of no reason to refuse.

Clare walked to Giuliana's house, which was almost out of the town and turned out to be an apartment in a tall, modern block of flats which Giuliana insisted was called a palazzo, though it did not look much like a palace to Clare. The Russos were most welcoming, all of them: Giuliana's brother, Giuliano, who eyed Clare speculatively (she was Northern European after all); her father, whose chief delight was in shooting small game and songbirds almost too small to eat; and her mother, who managed to overlook the fact that Clare had given her white chrysanthemums quite unaware that these were funeral flowers, reserved for the decking of graves.

They invited Clare to lunch three Sundays in a row, each meal more elaborate and indigestible than the last, until she could bear it no more, and spent most of the meal wondering how she could avoid them in future without giving offence. They really were awful people, Clare decided, in spite of being so kind. The apartment was full of cushion covers that Mrs. Russo crocheted in vivid acrylic yarns, and calling Giuliana's brother Giuliano seemed to hint of an almost willful lack of imagination. Mr. Russo wanted to talk about the war a lot, a subject, Clare felt, which would have been better avoided. Giuliana herself seemed to think that by being Clare's first friend in Florence she must remain her most important one, privy to all her secrets and holding a most privileged position in her life.

After the third of these unending lunches Clare was walking along the Lungarno wishing she had not allowed so much food to be forced upon her, and thinking how difficult it was to feel spiritual with a waistband dividing her in half so uncomfortably. She was struck by the sight of a girl even more miserable than she was.

This strange girl stood hitting her hand against the stone parapet with such fury that Clare thought she must surely have made it raw. She was muttering under her breath, and her face, when she turned to look at Clare, was bloated with tears. Clare wondered whether she should offer to help her since the mutterings sounded as if they might be English, and had she, herself, been weeping in such an exposed place she would perhaps have wanted comfort of some kind. Clare hesitated for a moment.

The girl turned on her and hissed, "Are you English?"

"Yes, I am, actually. But how could you guess?"

"You looked at me in such a fucking superior way, that's why." The girl's voice softened a little. "And anyway, if you were American you wouldn't have been wearing a dress."

Clare was rather sorry she had not been taken for an Italian and that her Englishness stood out so obviously. "But you are American," she said.

"How clever of you to guess," said the girl who was fat and dressed in ill-fitting jeans and a sweatshirt which accentuated her bulk. She held out her hand to Clare. "I'm sorry, I didn't mean to accuse you of anything. I'm Laura Pierson by the way, and I'm fed up with this whole fucking town. All this art and beauty and nothing but shits in it. And the worst of them all is English."

"That's hardly my fault," said Clare.

"No, and I apologise. You don't know Alisdair Turnbull, do you?"

Clare said that she did not. Laura fell in step beside her. "Shall we go and get some coffee? I want to talk to someone, anyone, just now."

Laura sounded so desperate that Clare agreed, hoping nonetheless that she would not be harangued endlessly about the shortcomings of her compatriots. She had had enough of that at lunch from Mr. Russo. Perhaps Laura was a lesbian or a lunatic or, worse yet, both.

Once Laura composed herself behind a small table at Gilli's she revealed herself to be much more prepossessing than she had at first appeared. She had a dignity befitting her stature and ordered pastries in rapid and perfect Italian. Her face, now that it was no longer red, was a luminous white with even features and almost alarmingly even teeth. Clare wondered if her teeth had always been like that, or spoke of years of the most expensive orthodontia. Had she not been so grossly over-weight Laura would have been beautiful; perhaps she was, even now, if you looked at her face alone.

"I'm sorry, I never introduced myself. I'm Clare Fane."

The pastries were having a remarkably calming effect upon Laura. She smiled at Clare over her teacup. "And why are you here?"

"Which here?" asked Clare. "Having tea with you, or in Florence in general?"

"Both."

"Well, first because if I was miserable I would like to think I would have the courage to pick up total strangers in the street. And second, because I wanted to get away from England."

"But what do you do?"

"I try to paint," said Clare.

"And I try to write. Just think, someday all this will be the stuff of a rather bad novel, my bildungsroman, or something like that." Laura's smile was enchanting. "I really shouldn't let myself get deflected by people like Alisdair."

It was a long story to which Clare listened with some interest. Alisdair Turnbull, it emerged, was exquisitely beautiful, or so Laura said; an art historian who had been extraordinarily attentive upon discovering Laura was one of the Boston Piersons but who had, after capturing Laura's affections, casually revealed himself to be homosexual. He had come to the elaborate dinner designed by Laura to ensnare him into her bed, had eaten well and talked far into the night, and then departed on the arm of Enzo, Laura's Sicilian lover, who had unfortunately appeared when he was supposed to be in Rome. Enzo, Laura said, she could forgive; he had merely been a subplot to enlarge her experience for the book and was known to hump anything that moved. With Alisdair it was different. Laura had decided he was the real thing; she had been bowled over by the wit and the charm and the elegance of him.

"He was supposed to meet me this afternoon to explain everything," she said. "But he never turned up. Probably there isn't anything *to* explain is there? He is probably in bed with Enzo right now, discussing me and saying how clever it was of me to introduce him to someone so sumptuously divine, so lissome, blah, blah, blah. I feel like *The Heiress*."

Because Laura threatened to get tearful again, Clare said, "And are you amazingly rich?"

"My family is. Which is why it is so easy for them to dispatch me to foreign countries when they get bored with me at home."

"It must be very nice to be rich," said Clare. "I never have been, but of course I've never been exactly poor either. My family seems to fall into the dull middle bit, erring on the side of bourgeois respectability."

"And burning with a desire to do good?"

"That, too."

Laura laughed, revealing all her perfect teeth. "I have very little self-control," she said, ordering more cakes. "I either feel ecstatically happy or else totally miserable. God, I hate fags don't you?" Laura chased an errant crumb round the plate with her finger.

"No, I rather like them, actually," said Clare, "though it's a pity they are so hopeless in bed." Clare thought of the time she had flung herself upon Jeremy Winters with no result at all. "Do you know lots of people here?"

"Every creep, sponger and deadbeat in town."

"How lovely," said Clare. "I don't know anyone at all except of course the perfectly appalling family I had lunch with."

"Well, you know me now," said Laura. "I'm sure we shall be very good friends."

Clare's room became another stop on Laura's circular itinerary of the town, and she visited often. She said it was impossible to write for more than three hours at a time, and so in order to fill up her day Laura went visiting her material.

Clare said, "I don't much want to be material, and very raw material at that. Thanks anyway."

"Oh, you would never recognise yourself, I promise you."

"That is some sort of relief."

"But tell me everything about yourself anyway. Some of it might come in handy some time." Laura lay on Clare's bed eating from a large bag of pastries, getting crumbs on the blankets, which she doubted Clare would notice. "Are you a tragic figure do you think?" she enquired, munching.

"Good heavens, no! Why ever should I be?" Clare tended to feel tragic on her own but never in company. She rather regretted telling Laura so much of what had happened in England, and she dreaded to think in what form it might reappear.

"Max was a tragic figure. Incomparably tragic," Laura suggested.

Clare put down her paintbrush. "Yes, he was, but not to me. He couldn't have gone on shining like that. Not for very long. I don't think middle age would have suited him very much."

"And David, what about him?"

"Not in the least tragic, Laura. I do wish you would stop trying to make out that everyone is wildly romantic. He was very nice in lots of ways. But I think I would be very bored if I was with him now. He did stop me from painting."

"Do you think it's possible to be really creative when attached to a man?"

"Of course not," said Clare. "Well, I suppose some women might be able to. Whenever I'm with a man I just want to give up and luxuriate in sex and reflected glory."

"How feeble of you," said Laura, scattering crumbs all over the floor. "You're not a feminist at all."

"Should I be?"

"Don't you realise how horribly oppressed most women are?"

"Yes, they probably are, Laura. But the thing is, I am not and neither are you. Neither one of us has the least idea of the conditions under which most people live and it is bogus and hypocritical of us to pretend we do. All I want to do is to paint and be loved. That seems quite enough for now."

"You should sell your paintings, at least. You can't just do heaps of them, like a hobbyist. You should be a part of the economic system. It makes everything more real."

"But everything *is* real. You can be most exasperating at times. Will you sell your novel?"

"Of course, when it's finished. It will change the way people look at the world and at youth." Laura had the grace to smile.

"God you're pretentious, Laura."

"If I didn't believe in what I was doing I would do something else."

"Well, you should stop moping about after Alisdair. You can't believe in that, surely?"

Clare's time was up and Laura sauntered off to visit her next victim or piece of material, and Clare wondered why she put up with her. But Laura had the habit of saying, amidst a lot of ridiculous claptrap, things which were true. She had confirmed what Clare had been thinking for some time. If she was to be a real artist, not just a schoolgirl pretending to be one, she must attempt to sell her work. She could not put off what she dreaded much longer.

Laura's friends and acquaintances became Clare's. She met the wonderful Alisdair Turnbull, whom she liked. She discovered they had friends in common in England, and in spite of his rather irritating insistence that Clare's family were some sort of fallen members of the gentry, they got on very well. She met the promiscuous Enzo, too, was charmed by his attentiveness and managed to deflect his amorous advances with a minimum of fuss.

The person she enjoyed most was Sergio Manzini. He was a musician of undoubted talent which he squandered nightly at an awful nightclub called the Red Garter whose chief clientele were Americans studying at the many dubious educational establishments which dotted the city. Clare would go and watch him play feeling smugly superior: She was a friend of one of the band; she actually *lived* in Florence. She now spoke halting Italian and Sergio adored her. He called her "walking spirit," which she thought was rather flattering, but she did not fancy him at all. Physically, he was a great shambling bear of a man with large soulful eyes and wild curly hair, constantly dishevelled. He wanted to be a painter as well as a musician; his enthusiasm was unbounded. He was in love with a married woman, whose husband, he insisted, had sent men to pursue him. He would not tell Clare where he lived; it was too dangerous, he said. Laura said he was paranoid, that his pursuers were entirely fictitious, but since he spoke of them with such conviction, Clare was prepared to believe in them, too.

One evening Clare stood playing pinball in Bar Colonine. She saw Sergio standing at the bar drinking liquor in large quantities. Clare was cheerful, but Sergio obviously was not. The nasty "Tilt" light came on, and Clare abandoned the game. Her thighs were bruised enough from fighting with it.

She went over to Sergio and slipped her arm around his considerable girth. "So? How goes it?"

"It's a long story." He sighed.

"It always is. But why are you miserable? Tell me."

They wandered out into the street arm in arm and Clare listened to the continuing saga of Sergio's life—the threats of the unnamed woman's husband, the impossibility of playing proper music to Philistines, his brother's erratic behavior, the weather, his liver. His plump hand searched for hers in the capacious pocket of his coat.

They ate dinner at a restaurant run by one of Sergio's many cousins and both drank too much. He became increasingly melancholy. "So you don't care about them anymore? Those men?"

"What men?"

"All your departed admirers."

"Good God, Sergio, you know as well as I do that I came here to get away from all that."

The night had turned cold and they took a last drink at a deserted bar. Not wanting to break the evening's affectionate companionship, they walked together back to the Locanda dei Cesere, to Clare's room.

Sergio stood behind Clare looking into the flawed mirror on her wardrobe door, his hands on her shoulders. "I've dreamed this before," Sergio said. "A particular dream of you and me together."

The glass distorted their faces and Clare thought how odd it was to be part of someone else's unconscious. She was not surprised when he kissed her. But she would not make love to him, thinking it would ruin their friendship forever. She did not love him except as a brother. She would not raise hopes she would be unable to fulfill. Clare thought briefly that it would be nice to fall in love with Sergio, convenient. But Clare knew she had had enough of demented people, however charming.

Sergio sat at the end of her bed and admired Clare's paintings. Clare placed her pictures in a row against the opposite wall and came and sat beside him.

"We will choose four first," he said, "and Mauro will frame them. How professional they will look."

"Do you think so, really?"

"Of course. How can you doubt it, little spirit? And then we will sell them. Perhaps Mauro will buy one himself, he often does. That's why he's so poor, with a whole clutter of things in the back of his shop."

"Go on. You choose first," Clare said.

He picked one of the biggest paintings. In it a round table was set in front of a window, with the light shining from behind the fruit and flowers, and to the right sat a somewhat slimmed down version of Laura holding a letter. The next one he chose was a pen-and-ink drawing, meticulously detailed, of apples in the Renaissance bowl, washed with delicate colours. The third was of the open window, looking out into the street with the occupants of the house opposite dimly suggested as they went about their everyday business. Clare chose the fourth, a very bold painting of flowers gleaming against a dark ground.

They were interrupted by the appearance of Giuliana, who stared round the disordered room with veiled disgust. "Oh, Clare, I'm so sorry to disturb you at such a time."

"You aren't disturbing us at all. Sergio and I were just discussing which pictures his cousin will frame up for me."

"Oh," said Giuliana, her tone expressing incredulity. "Well, I only stopped by to invite you to lunch on Sunday. My mother is worried about you since we haven't seen you for so long."

Clare's excuses were getting thinner and more preposterous as the weeks went by. "Well, this Sunday might not be so good. I'm going to Arezzo with Laura and Alisdair."

"She'll be very disappointed, you know. She worries what your mother must think of you living like this." Her eyes scanned the clothes littering the floor and the bottle of Sambucca open by the bed. "She thinks you come from a good family."

"I'm sorry, Giuliana. I really can't come."

"She thought you were so nice, Clare. She took such an interest in you."

Clare wished Signora Russo would find someone else to take an interest in. She did not deserve to have her feelings hurt of course, and Clare did not want to appear aloof and ungrateful. But she did not feel capable of sitting through another lengthy discussion on the general superiority of Italian family life, which, if the example of the Russo family was anything to go by, was even more suffocating than suburban family life in England. Clare had travelled all this way to avoid getting bogged down in that. Clare knew that Giuliana found her friends unsuitable, if not dangerous, but Clare felt quite capable of taking care of herself without anyone else's mother worrying about her. The letters she received from her own were bad enough.

"Do tell her I'm most frightfully sorry. I'll try to come next Sunday." By next Sunday she might have dreamed up another excuse.

When Clare returned to England for Christmas she took Laura with her. Mrs. Fane was happy to ply them both with food, which Laura enjoyed almost enough to compensate her for the absence of snow.

"In Dickens it always snowed at Christmas," Laura said.

"Did it?" replied Clare vaguely. She had not read any Dickens for years. "I can't think why people imagine an English Christmas to be so much better than any other sort. All I know is that it has become disgustingly commercial."

"But nothing to America," said Laura, helping herself to another mince pie—a delicacy she had not previously encountered. "*There* it starts almost before Thanksgiving and ends in a flash the day after."

"I wish it did here," said Clare. The Boxing Day variety programmes on television were beginning to pall and the shops were shut for an additional two days. "It does seem to go on a bit."

The following week, having exhausted the possibilities of Guildford, Clare took Laura up to London where they walked miles in the damp, took in the King's Road from the top of a bus and then sauntered through the Victoria & Albert Museum where Clare lingered before the Pre-Raphaelite paintings.

"You know I always wished I had hair like that," Clare said, "opulent billowing masses of it. It seems awfully unfair that Elinor got the hair genes as well as the brain ones. Do you remember that girl Antonia I told you about? These pictures always remind me of her—that amazing pallor and a sort of spiritual look that I could never achieve in a thousand years. And, as well as the hair, she's awfully nice."

Clare had been feeling guilty about her neglect of Antonia for some time. "Would you mind awfully if I rang her up? She doesn't live so very far from here."

"To tell you the truth," Laura said, "I think I've had just about as much art as I can manage for one day."

Antonia's number was busy, which Clare took as a good sign. If someone was on the phone they were certain to be in. Clare and Laura boarded the bus for Sloane Square.

Clare, never having met the dreaded Eileen, wondered whether she could really be as unappealing as Antonia had painted her. When Eileen opened the door Clare was struck first by her youth and second by her prettiness, by the immaculate façade she presented to the world. (She probably looked quite different without makeup.)

"Toni, how lovely! Some of your friends," Eileen called out. "I'm ever so pleased to meet you, Clare. Do come in. I've heard so much about you."

"Clare, is it really you?" Antonia held out her arms and embraced her friend. "I thought you had vanished entirely." She drew back and smiled at Clare, her face lit up with pleasure. "I thought perhaps . . . oh, never mind. . . ." She held out her hand to Laura as Clare introduced them.

Antonia led the way into the sitting room where the metallic Christmas tree glistened. She grinned at Clare half apologetically. "Harrods' best," she whispered as Eileen disappeared into the kitchen. "Oh, Clare, I am so happy to see you."

"And me you. I feel that I owe you an apology, vanishing like that. It was just that after Max died I couldn't face any of the people who had known about him or any of the places he had been. I had to get away from everything."

"I thought perhaps you hated *me*," Antonia said.

"Never that. It seems so long ago now, all of it."

If anything Antonia looked more lovely than she had in the summer. If physical beauty were sufficient to make one happy in this world Antonia's life should have been without flaw. "Did you stay on in Oxford, Toe?"

"Yes, I took the Oxford and Cambridge entrance exams this autumn. I worked incredibly hard but God knows how I've done. I won't hear for a while and even then I'll have to get wonderful results in my 'A' levels, which are coming up. So much work, Clare! But it's too boring to go into. I missed you and everyone so much. I long to hear about you."

Clare turned to Laura, hoping she wasn't feeling excluded. "Oh, you should ask Laura about Florence, she is the storyteller. She has wonderful tales about all the weird people we know."

Laura, thus launched, and fortified by the sherry Eileen had produced, kept the conversation afloat until lunch was served. Clare studied Antonia as Laura rambled on and realised anew what a wonderful audience Antonia was, had always been, how her attention once given allowed others to shine. She realised, too, how much she had missed her.

"What about Elinor and your mother, are they well?" Antonia asked Clare.

"Both exactly the same. Mummy domestic and Elinor beavering away, being successful and doing everything right. Daddy is being awfully good about Italy though Mum still thinks abroad is rife with terrors. She was quite relieved when I quit Sussex, hoping I'd suddenly become sensible and would sit at home waiting for Prince Charming to arrive on his steed to sweep me off to a life of unmitigated bliss in Surbiton."

Antonia smiled. "Is Italy really that much different from England?"

"Isn't it more romantic to part with your lover on the Bridge of Sighs than in some car park outside Ilford? Really, things are quite different there. And for the first time in my life I feel independent. It's good, Toe. Couldn't you come and visit? I'd show you all the sights."

"I'd love that, but I really must work tremendously hard. I've got thousands of books to read before the exam." She shot a look at a pile of them lying in front of the fire.

"Is it very important to you, all this work?"

"Yes," said Antonia.

In the middle of the afternoon nine-year-old Justin appeared clamoring to be taken skating at Queens' and the four of them spent the rest of the afternoon gliding over the ice, or rather the three English ones stumbled and giggled whilst Laura sailed over the ice like a galleon in full fig with amazing aplomb—Boston's cold winters and years of lessons having paid off in the end.

Mrs. Fane was ironing her husband's shirts for the week ahead. In a fit of guilt Clare had offered to help her mother and had done all the easy things, like the handkerchiefs and the tea towels, before her mother appeared.

"Oh, darling, that was kind of you. There always seems to be so much more to do when you're home, though of course I don't mind."

Clare sat on the bed in the spare room and watched her mother. "What an awful fate, Mummy, having to iron shirts all the time—all those awful fiddly bits like the collars and cuffs. Couldn't you send them to the laundry or something?"

"You get quite used to it in the end, and anyway the laundry is dreadfully rough with them; they wear out in no time. No, it's thinking about food which really drives me mad."

"But I always thought you enjoyed that. You spend enough time doing it."

"I ought to get more organised, I suppose." Mrs. Fane folded the last shirt and carried the pile to the airing cupboard. She returned to dismantle the ironing board, which always stuck and threatened to squash her fingers. "Are you really happy in Italy, darling? I sometimes think you ought to have finished your degree. It does worry me terribly you being so far away and not knowing what your life is like. I mean, I do like Laura, but isn't she rather odd?"

"She's quite mild compared to some of my friends."

"And whatever happened to Antonia? I sometimes see her father's picture in the *Telegraph* and think of her. How ghastly for a child not to have a proper mother."

"She wants to go to university if her exams are good enough. Her mother was there years ago. I think it means a great deal to her."

Mrs. Fane looked at Clare sprawled on the bed, wearing jeans for a change, which she thought looked so much better and healthier than the droopy garments her daughter managed to discover amongst the piles of jumble sale clothes. Perhaps it was partly her own fault; perhaps Mrs. Wilson could keep the boxes at her house so Clare wouldn't be able to get at them. "Do you really have to go back to Italy, darling?"

"Yes, Mummy, I do."

"You'll promise me you won't do anything really ghastly, won't you?"

Clare grinned at her mother. "What do you classify as really ghastly? Or daren't I ask?"

Mrs. Fane sighed. "I do wish one of you would get married. Then I could stop worrying about you both so much."

"Does being married solve everything, Mummy?"

"It did for me."

"But things are so different now. Quite different from when you were young."

"You're being arrogant, Clare. Things are not different in the least. I suppose you think I have forgotten entirely what it was like to be young. Fashions change, and manners, but not what people really need. I wish you would find someone who makes you as happy as Daddy has made me."

"But didn't you ever want to be anything in your own right? Something important and interesting? Did you always want to just be a wife and a mother? Didn't you want to have a job?"

"I do have a job. I look after my family and my house. I'm endlessly busy."

"But is it all worth it?" Clare asked. "Is that enough?"

"It is for me, Clare, whatever you think. One day perhaps you'll understand. Don't you think I criticised my mother, too, when I was your age? I used to arrive home and want her to change everything about the house. I thought her drawing-room curtains were awful for one thing."

"Well, at least the drawing room here's all right," Clare said. "Though I'm bit dubious about this room."

Elinor called them both down to tea.

Fifteen

F lorence was much colder than England. Bitter winds from the Alps swept between the tall buildings, and it was painful to be outside. The one radiator in Clare's room gave out little heat, and she looked forward to the evening when she would eat out with her friends in a variety of cheap restaurants where delicious smells wafted from the kitchen and her hands would thaw out at last. The wine and the noise were benisons after her isolation during the day.

It was on one such evening, when surrounded by her friends, that Clare first saw Richard Adler. He was sitting alone at the far side of the room reading a book which so absorbed him that he was not conscious, at first, of Clare watching him. At intervals he took out a pen and marked passages. Clare was fascinated that he hardly looked at his food yet managed to eat without dropping any of it on his book. When he did at last look up he stared across the room, through the raucous crowd of diners, and smiled at Clare. She smiled back and then went on with her meal. She knew neither his name nor his nationality; she did not bother to guess his occupation. It would not matter in the least what he did; he might breed pigs for all she cared.

She saw him often after that, striding down the street, his hands thrust deep into the pockets of his long coat, his head bent against the wind. They always smiled, recognising each other, but they did not speak.

Clare did not mention him to her friends, did not ask if they knew the tall fair man whose high cheekbones gave an ascetic cast to his thin face. He was always alone, and Clare felt there was something formidable about him. It seemed inevitable that they would meet eventually.

Selling her paintings proved not to be as difficult as Clare had thought it might be. Mauro, the owner of the *cornichia*—that glorious dim hole of a frame shop smelling of varnish and polish and gilt and antiquity—did buy a painting. It was a small one which Clare quite liked, and he took it in part exchange for the other frames. Mauro was a leathery, wrinkled, dwarf of a man, with eyes of the most startling green, bright and astute. He took Clare by the arm and showed her the paintings he collected, heaps of them in the most amazing array of styles and techniques. He pointed out the merits and defects of each one, attaching to them painters' names and the dates on which they were acquired. He talked of them as if they were his children and had characters, each one individual and remarkable. Clare felt very honoured to be admitted to such a company.

Encouraged by Mauro's enthusiasm Clare approached two small galleries and Pineider, a rather grand stationery shop in Piazza Signoria which sold paintings upstairs. All three places took a couple of paintings on consignment, and no one was horrid to her. Clare had thought that if her reception had been casual or unfriendly she would say that the paintings were the work of a friend, some mythical other, invented for the purpose of protecting herself. How different from England! There, shops and galleries acted as if they were doing the artist the most enormous favour even to glance at one's work. Clare knew this from the times she had trailed round with David feeling that they were grovelling intruders, despicable and beggarly. Clare was amazed at her good fortune and began to think her work rather good after all. When framed it looked quite different, as if it had been produced by some other person who bore little relationship to the real Clare, who felt uncertain and incompetent. Two small paintings sold the first week.

Clare decided to take Laura and Sergio out to dinner with her newly acquired wealth. She bounced down the street with a friend on either arm. "I'm real at last!" she said, "like that blasted rabbit, only he was made real by being loved and I did it myself!"

"Which rabbit, Clare?" Sergio was being swept along by Clare, who by now was almost drunk on two glasses of wine and a great deal of goodwill towards the world in general.

"Oh, the velveteen one in a book I read as a child. I don't think you'd know it."

"I always thought it was a horrible book," said Laura. "What if you were a toy no one ever loved and you fell apart before anyone cared about you at all?"

"You'd just have to keep on waiting I suppose, and anyway you wouldn't fall apart if no one touched you, would you? I mean it's only by feeling things you can get damaged. Oh, God, this is getting depressing isn't it? Where do you want to eat?"

Luckily Laura was easily deflected by the prospect of food and they turned off the street into an alley and approached the brightly lit doorway of Anita's.

"Ho! Sergio." He stood at the corner in the lamplight, the collar of his coat turned up against the cold.

"Riccardo, *come stai?*" The two men embraced with much slapping of backs and many exclamations of delight. Sergio said, "I didn't know you were back."

"I have been, for some weeks, but I've been very busy."

"Clare, Laura, this is Richard Adler."

Richard smiled at Clare and held out his hand, which she took, meeting his smile. "I know you," he said, "though I didn't know your name."

He turned to Laura and shook her hand, too, and they went inside to eat.

Anita's was very crowded that night and the four of them were obliged to sit very close together at a small table near the kitchen door. Clare looked at Richard's hands, large peasant ones, oddly at variance with his face, which was so finely made. Richard drew on his cigarette and stared at Clare through the smoke. She met his eyes without smiling and crumbled the bread she held in her hand. Christ, she thought, this is it. What on earth do I do now?

Fortunately Laura had cheered up and Sergio was at his most gregarious. There was food to be eaten and wine to be drunk. No one seemed to notice that Clare had very little to say.

Sergio asked Richard about Africa: how he had got there and how he had got back, and Richard replied with stories of Tunisia and Morocco, of nights spent in stalled trains and in the back of trucks full of chickens, of hours spent sitting beside the road with nothing but the desert stretching to infinity around him.

"You must be glad to be back," Laura said, "to be somewhere semi-civilised at least."

"I always come back here in the end," Richard said, "because I can be quiet and nobody bothers me."

"Clare is a painter," Sergio said, wanting to include her in the conversation.

"I guessed from her hands." Clare thought what a mess she looked and how the smell of paint hung about her all the time as the smell of scent hung about other women. "But I must go now. I have someone to meet," he said, pressing a scrap of paper into Clare's hand. Richard put on his coat and walked out into the cold night.

"Who is this Richard you greet with such enthusiasm, Sergio?" Clare asked very casually, as if she didn't much care.

"I don't know, Clare, just an American who comes and goes. I suppose I've known him for about three years off and on. I think he's a writer of some sort."

"You acted as if you had met him before," Laura said. "Have you a secret understanding? Why does he give notes to you and not to me?" She smiled at Clare and shovelled the last of her zuppa Inglese into her mouth. "You're lucky. He looked rather interesting."

Clare did not know if she was lucky. The scrap of paper bore his name and address.

. . .

She sat on her bed and looked at her scattered possessions, the things with which she differentiated herself from other women. She examined her meagre supply of clothes and eventually chose a black silk dress whose background was sprinkled with minute flowers and whose shape became her. She scrubbed her hands as clean of paint as they had been in some weeks; her face was bare of makeup, her hair newly washed. She looked at herself in the mirror as she put on the hat whose floppy brim she clipped back with an antique pin. She thought she looked entirely blank.

The afternoon air was bitter cold and the shops were shut for the long midday break. The streets were almost deserted. She imagined families wrapped snug in their homes. She glided unseen between the beautiful tall buildings whose severity was both impenetrable and mysterious. She crossed the icy square where her breath billowed round her in clouds and the cold hit her throat like an impediment.

She followed the directions Richard had written on the now dog-eared scrap of paper, turning off the barren street into an enclosed courtyard. The building, she saw, was at least in part a church. There was a long cold flight of steps marked by the indentations of eight centuries of feet. She climbed upwards in the blackness as the stairs twisted and turned, and came at last to a metal door set flush in the wall, a door which, had one not known it was there, might have been mistaken for a mere plate put in to reinforce the crumbling structure of the building.

As she knocked Clare thought, what if this is not real at all? It echoed the day, so long ago, when she had knocked on Max's door. The day had about it the quality of a dream.

Richard opened the door almost at once and let her into the room. On a small deal table were set two mugs of tea, steaming, waiting. "How did you know I would come today?" Clare asked.

Richard shrugged and smiled, and they sat, the two of them, at either end of the table and looked at one another, ignoring the mugs whose contents chilled, untouched.

"Has anything this strange ever happened to you before?" Clare asked.

"No," Richard said, still staring at her. "I wish it would stop."

Clare's hand shook as she lit a cigarette. "I feel," she said, "that I'm not acting of my own volition. Do you feel that, too?"

They rose together and Richard put his arms around her and they stood a long time rocking slightly. Clare could feel his breath on her hair and the nape of her neck. He was very thin, the bones of his chest were flat and hard against her face.

He drew back and looked into her eyes and she did not know where she ended and he began. She saw herself from outside and watched herself quite separate from her body.

The huge room dwarfed them, shadowy and dim. They lay on the bed still fully clothed, holding each other's hands, waiting for the strangeness to subside. But it did not.

From the street far below Clare could hear a car careening over the icy cobblestones, a welcome sound anchoring her in time and space, in a world where there was traffic and other people. She felt the roughness of the blanket which covered them and the uneven thumping of her heart. She could smell Richard's body encompassed in wool, the smell of warm flesh.

She wanted to touch and feel and hear and smell before her soul was snatched from her and she ceased to exist.

"Do you want to sleep?" he asked when hours had passed and the trumpet had sounded through the thin air over the rooftops from Forte Belvedere, and the midnight streets were empty of cars and people and the city was silenced.

"If I sleep I might never wake up. I feel drunk, stoned; everything is spinning wildly out of control and it won't stop. You are totally familiar to me, Richard. That is what frightens me most." She burrowed her head against his shoulder, butting the muscled flesh. "Make it stop."

"I can't," he said. "I can't do anything."

She touched his face with her hand.

"It's all right," she said, that being the only comforting thing she could think of to say as a shudder passed through her.

The moon, now risen, shone through one of the seventeen windows, cutting his face into four equal parts. His flesh looked ghostly and bloodless.

Later she watched the dawn make visible the outlines of the room, etching the objects on the table into a frozen tableau. Real things, ordinary things: cups, ashtrays, the sugar bowl, an open packet of cigarettes. She felt Richard's warm breath on her cheek and the solidity of his body and, at last, she slept.

The next afternoon Clare removed all her possessions from the Locanda, gave up her room there and moved in with Richard. It was all accomplished in one trip, in a daze. Clare felt moonstruck and ridiculous. She threw her books, clothes and paintings into a great heap on the floor and climbed back into bed with Richard.

When they emerged much later and night was drawing in again, they sat side by side with their backs against the kerosene stove, which warmed only a small portion of the cavernous room. Richard said there were bones buried in the walls, the remains of nuns who had perished in the plague seven centuries before. There were black metal hooks hanging from the ceiling from which hides had been suspended in the sixteenth century when the room was used as a leather tannery. In spite of its many previous incarnations the room felt benevolent, its atmosphere benign. Richard had very few things, no ornaments, no pictures, only the few objects that were necessary to his life: a battered typewriter, piles of paper and enough dishes and mugs to suffice for his solitary existence. It would have been arrogant of him, he said, to feel that he was anything more than a transient inhabitant of the room.

When at last they became hungry they went out to the supermarket, which neither of them had ever entered before, and bought fish fingers and bananas, throwing things randomly into the cart. They did not want to meet anyone they knew.

Clare drew the room on countless sheets of paper; tight, detailed drawings in pen and ink: ten packets of cigarettes and a quart container of honey, lemons in the Renaissance bowl, the moonlight falling through one of the seventeen windows onto the table; everything seen with an almost surreal clarity. She captured every nuance of the table's clutter.

She looked up from her sketchbook and saw Richard watching her. "I know so little about you," she said.

"Come here. Sit beside me." He took her two hands in his.

"You will discover everything in the end," he said.

Slowly the outlines of Richard's life began to emerge: the secure suburban childhood outside Chicago (the greatest gift, he insisted, that anyone could be given); college; the discovery of other worlds, other lives; and his departure five years before from an America he found stifling and in many ways terrifying in its greed and materialism. He had wandered through Europe and the Middle East, eventually getting as far as Vietnam, after his brother's death, to see it firsthand. Clare wondered if they could make him go there again, draft him this time, force him into the army. He replied that they could try but he would not go. One son sacrificed to politicians' ineptitude and self-aggrandisement was surely enough for any family. But he could no longer go home, though he missed Hershey bars and baseball and a vast array of little things.

His income, such as it was, he derived from three sources: from the articles he wrote for *Rolling Stone*, the *Village Voice* and various radical publications, in which he reported on his view of the world, and the folly of most of it; from the checks his grandmother sent him from the rest home in Florida in which she was incarcerated (but these he feared would shortly stop since his father was in the process of having the eminently sane old woman declared incompetent to stop these contributions); and from casual jobs he picked up (building walls, painting houses, clearing land), anything, in fact, which provided money to enable him to eat and pay the nominal rent for his room. He did not worry about money, he said. What did he need, after all? He had no use for electronic devices to open garage doors, or tie racks which spun round purposefully. (These last two items, Clare discovered, were the Christmas presents his father had received just before Richard left home.)

"I would like to be warm though, once in a while," he admitted, gathering Clare into his arms as they lay in bed, watching their breath-mist, visible in the frigid January air. "I think being warm is an impossibility in Europe in winter. I guess America has something going for it after all."

In those first weeks together they had no visitors, nor sought any, and they rarely left one another's sight. They went everywhere together, on the most trivial of errands, to buy paint, or replace the *bombola* which gave gas for the two-ringed burner that comprised the whole kitchen. They walked arm in arm down the street, both tall and fair and so alike that they might have been taken for brother and sister.

One day Richard turned to Clare and said, "We must go out into the real world quite soon and confront it."

"But not yet, surely?" Clare asked. She unwound his arms from her waist and continued with the washing up.

But slowly the strangeness wore off as their lives assumed a pattern. Clare painted and sold her work. Richard wrote and sold some of his work, too. How comfortable it was, Clare thought, to be with someone whose work was so entirely different from her own. Richard liked her paintings, though occasionally he chose to disparage them, saying she should deal with some larger theme and not be so literal and so happy all the time.

"But I was miserable quite a lot before I met you, and my paintings were the same. I want to enhance the world not make it more dismal than it so often is."

Clare filled the room with the hordes of people she had been unable to invite to the Locanda dei Cesere, the motley expatriate collection of misfits whose conversation delighted her. Richard did not seem to mind.

"You were very morose before you met me," she said. "You should enjoy people more."

"But I don't need throngs of others to make me happy, Clare. You and my work are enough to satisfy me."

"Oh, I'm sure I could be happy without them. It's just that I'm happier with."

They continued to arrive, Laura and Sergio and Enzo and countless others, and Clare fed them all, and listened to their stories and was very happy indeed. She was happier still when they departed, leaving her and Richard alone.

"Do you realise, Richard, that this is what I've always wanted? To work and love and have friends?"

"I'm glad that you're happy," he said, "and the ridiculous thing is that I am, too."

• • •

"How important is this thing with Richard?" Laura asked.

"I haven't the least idea," Clare said. "It's too weird to discuss just now. All I know is that it is the most liberating thing, not having to search anymore. Not to be always looking for something and not knowing what it is."

"Are you going to marry him?"

"What an odd question. You sound like my mother. I can't imagine someone like Richard married, can you? Signing bits of paper and making what should be private, public. All I know is that I was quite hopeless on my own."

"I envy you," Laura said. "I haven't got anyone to have even a rotten intrigue with just now."

Clare placated her with some *biscotti*.

Sixteen

One morning in late September Antonia sat at a small table in a room in a rather dismal pensione on via Cavour. Before her lay a large notebook with marbled covers which she had bought the previous day very soon after her arrival in the city.

The book was entirely empty. She wrote her name in it. See, I exist, she told herself. I am a name in a book. What else? A failure—too stupid to be accepted to Oxford, too indifferent to accept the place offered at East Anglia. She thought back to her abortive visit to the windswept campus outside Norwich on a blustery February day when the cold swept down on her straight out of Russia. How utterly charmless the new buildings had been! She had told her father that she might go there if nothing else turned up. Nothing had. After spending the summer in the dispiriting company of Eileen she had allowed her father to think she was taking up her place there. It was no one's fault but her own, she knew, this inability to feel enthusiasm for anything. She admitted now that Eileen had done her best to comfort her. Eileen had said, "Going to university isn't everything, Toni, there are lots of other things to do."

"Like what?" Antonia had replied, feeling her own unkindness as she said it. Eileen had never been offered the possibility of college. Neither of them had been able to come up with anything Antonia really wanted. Eileen had suggested modelling. But Antonia hated being stared at. She felt her looks to be a curse rather than a blessing.

So now she sat with the blank book before her, regretting her flight from England and feeling sorry for Eileen who would bear the brunt of Rex Acton's disappointment.

Outside the room incessant rain fell from a bleak gray sky, puddling the pavements.

I must do something to justify my existence, Antonia told herself. First I will learn Italian. I will try to understand all I can about this foreign place. I will try to make sense of Florentine painting, of the past, of myself.

The next day she sat in a library, her book still empty except for her name. Outside, the Italian street bustled, roared, scurried and thumped. Antonia looked at the faded, gilded decorations of the room—still dignified in their decrepitude—and thought that she was very privileged to live her life surrounded by beauty. She opened a grammar book and wondered if these alien words would ever mean the same things to her as English ones did.

She wandered round the city, walking through cloisters which were quiet and empty, far removed from the turmoil in the streets. She sat in the sun in the amphitheatre of the Boboli Gardens warming herself like a lizard on the stone. She was always alone but kept hoping that Clare would appear from nowhere to discover her. She wanted Clare to be surprised at her turning up so unexpectedly. The last address she had for Clare dated from April. When at last she climbed the many stairs to that room, she missed the unmarked door entirely and retreated, not knowing whom to ask in the labyrinthine building, certain none of them knew English.

After a week of waiting for Clare to materialise she knocked on the door of the only other address she had, that of the billowing and insatiable Laura. She stood rehearsing her Italian sentence, realising that she might well not understand the reply if one were to be given. She knocked.

"*Buon giorno. Voglio trovare* Laura Pierson."

"Oh, Laura, well she's not here," said the boy who had opened the door. Antonia was sorry her Italian was so bad that he knew immediately that she was a foreigner. He, himself, was American from his accent.

He turned and called into the room behind him. "Enzo! There's someone here for Laura."

Antonia was ushered into the bare white room where a half naked youth lay upon a mattress in the middle of the floor. There was no other furniture in the room.

"So you're looking for Laura?" He gazed up at her enquiringly.

"Well, either her or Clare Fane. I want to see Clare more really."

"I haven't seen Clare for some time, and Laura is in America."

Enzo looked up at Antonia as if deciding if she was worth the effort of helping. Having come to the conclusion that she was, he got up. "Excuse me while I go and dress," he said, adding as an afterthought, "Sit down if you like."

There was nowhere to sit except the bed. Antonia remained standing. Enzo returned, clad only in his jeans. His feet were bare on the tile floor. "And who are you?" he enquired.

"Antonia Acton, a friend of Clare's."

"Would you like some wine?" He smiled and filled a glass from the bottle he had brought with him into the room and handed it to her. He observed her through half-closed eyes. "You're all so alike, you English girls, always so tall."

Antonia thought this was untrue. What if she replied that Italian men were always so small? Neither fact was universally true. She hated being stared at like this, summed up and stripped.

"Have you been long in Florence?" he asked.

"No, not long. But I would like to see Clare if you know where she is. I have got some sort of address for her but I couldn't discover the exact place."

"I'll take you there if you like."

He did not seem to have anything better to do. There were no signs of any activity in the room except a flute lying discarded by the window.

When they had finished their wine they went out into the street. Enzo took Antonia's arm and she felt glad to be walking with someone beside her instead of alone.

"Shall we go to a bar?" Enzo suggested hopefully.

"If you like." Antonia did not want to really but thought it might be rude to refuse. Enzo ordered two coffees, which were brought to them in tiny cups that could be downed in two gulps. Antonia was getting used to eating and drinking standing up. It had seemed very strange at first.

"Where are you staying?" he asked.

Antonia told him about the pensione, which he said was ridiculously expensive, though it had not seemed so to her.

"I'll help you look for an apartment if you like. They are very hard to find, but I know everyone."

"Thank you," said Antonia, hating being taken over like this. Being abroad did seem to put you at the mercy of unlikely people.

Enzo continued to stare at Antonia as she towered above him, feeling English and aloof. She wondered what Clare made of Enzo, and if he intended sleeping with her.

They walked across Piazza S. Croce and to the left of the church whose side steps were covered in dog dung and horribly malodorous.

Enzo knocked on the door of Richard's room but there was no reply. Antonia's heart sank. "Thank you for trying to help me anyway," she said as they stood in the courtyard, having navigated the treacherous stairs in the dark. Enzo had either not known where the light switch was or had preferred to descend in the gloom, the better to touch her under the guise of guiding her.

"I'm sorry we couldn't find her. I remember now, I think she must still be in Venice. Perhaps she will come back soon."

"But when?"

"Boh!" He shrugged. "Would you like to come back to my apartment?"

Antonia had nothing to do and the thought of her empty notebook in the pensione was not enticing. "I'll come, just for a minute," she said.

In Laura's absence Enzo had filled her apartment with a selection of his friends, three Italians and two Greeks who were all between lodgings and found the place as convenient as any other and a great deal cheaper than most. They were all, apparently, studying at the university, though there were very few books, or notes, or anything to indicate work was being done.

Enzo was most attentive and took Antonia out to supper at a small restaurant on the other side of the Arno where they ate coarse white bread with salt sprinkled on it and spaghetti with clam sauce. Antonia had not eaten in a Florentine restaurant before but had existed on snacks bought in bars or little squares of pizza bought and eaten in the street.

As they ate Enzo enjoyed showing off his English, which was surprisingly fluent but highly idiomatic. She could hear echoes of Laura, and also some of Clare's very English expressions.

"You must stay with us while you look for a place," he said.

"But where would I sleep?" she asked. There seemed to be a vast number of people living in the apartment as it was.

Enzo's hand found hers as it lay on the table. He looked into her eyes as she sought a suitable moment to remove her hand. "You could always share my room. I would sleep on the floor."

Antonia felt quite sure, he would not.

"It's terribly kind of you. But I'm quite all right where I am."

They walked through the dark streets and then sat eating ice cream on the Loggia de Lanzi watching the people who wandered the streets, chatting, happy and mostly in pairs. Antonia thought she was getting very clever at guessing people's nationalities before they spoke. There were American girls with sensible hiking boots and ill-fitting T-shirts; Italian girls with silk scarves knotted just so. Antonia felt ashamed of her compatriots, with their nylon shirts and gray synthetic trousers and gray faces.

They went to another bar and Enzo ordered two Sambuccas, anise and sweet. They walked beside the river, arm in arm, looking at the lights reflected in the water. He is being so charming to break down my resistance, she thought. The evening seemed to have gone on for a long time, but Antonia was half amused by his attentiveness and was putting off her inevitable loneliness in the room she shared with three other women, where she felt excluded because she could not talk to them. She liked Enzo and could feel now that he might be fleetingly attractive to someone, but it wasn't her.

She let him persuade her to go back with him to Laura's apartment where they drank yet more wine. Enzo was becoming quite insistently physical, constantly touching her when she did not want to be touched. She hoped she was not being too rude rebuffing him. She was trying to be subtle about it and kept leaping up to look out of the window, which did not have a view but merely gave on to the apartments on the other side of the courtyard.

The two Greek boys were there. Alexis rolled up a small joint and they talked into the night. Enzo leaned against Antonia, stroking her cheek and her hair. She decided she should have left long before and got up. She thanked Enzo for the supper.

"But surely now you will want to stay here?" He looked quite crestfallen.

"No, really, all my things are there."

"You could fetch them in the morning."

"But I'd rather go."

"As you please, English Miss," said Enzo, still smiling. "I'll walk back with you if you like."

Antonia was getting quite frantic to leave by now. "It's all right. I know my way." She did, by daylight; she trusted she would find it in the dark.

Enzo got up and kissed her on the cheek. He had aimed for her mouth but she had managed to turn away in time.

"Come and see me again very soon," he said.

"I will," she said, relieved to be escaping from his clutches, glad to be out in the cool night air alone. She had wondered if she would ever get away. She heard footsteps behind her and turned to see Alexis, one of the Greek boys, following her.

"I like to walk in the night, don't you?" he said, falling into step with her.

"Yes, usually. But I'm not quite sure that I know my way."

"It's easy. I'll show you."

They walked in silence for some time. Antonia looked into shop windows admiring the elegance of the clothes.

"What do you think of Enzo?" Alexis asked.

"I like him. He was very kind to give me dinner."

"But you don't want to sleep with him?"

"Why on earth should I? I hardly know him anyway."

"He thought you would. We were laying bets on it. I think you have hurt his feelings," he said.

Antonia thought it was rather distasteful to be discussed in this way. "I'm sorry his feelings are hurt, but I'm not usually bought by a meal alone." She had to smile, Alexis looked so serious about it.

"Do you want to go to look at an apartment with us tomorrow? It's quite large. Very nice, very reasonable. It would be me and my cousin, whom you met, and you. You could have your own room, Antonia. No one would bother you."

Antonia thought about it and was tempted. She wondered whether she had been foolish letting them know how much money she had. It seemed it was necessary to have three months rent in advance to sign for an apartment. But she did want to get away from the pensione very badly, and to have a room of her own. She could not wait indefinitely for Clare to appear.

Alexis said good night to her very politely at the door of the pensione. She had liked him very much and she fell asleep thinking about him and looking forward to seeing him again. Alexis was very beautiful she decided, and he had not pawed her, like Enzo. She would go and look at the flat with him in the morning.

The morning light was very bright as Antonia walked out into the street. It had rained in the night and everything looked newly washed and pure. She felt elated, that something was going to happen today. It was almost like the way the beginning of autumn term had seemed to her as a child after the endless summers. Things beginning again which she could not stop whether they were good or bad.

The apartment on via Torta was far lovelier than Antonia had been led to expect. There were two large rooms between which was a pink bathroom, and each room had a window. One opened onto a courtyard and the other onto the street. The rooms were painted white and the floors were bare red tile. In the room which she wanted there was a huge cupboard almost like a smaller room, and there were bookshelves let into the wall. The shuttered window let onto rooftops, ancient and red, with pigeons fluttering down onto them.

"It won't be at all expensive," Alexis said, "not when we divide it three ways. But," he added, "you will have to take it in your name, since you've got all the deposit money. We will pay you back each month. The landlord's agent need never know."

There seemed no reason why he should. And they signed the papers that afternoon in the minute cavelike room the agent called his office. There were quantities of papers all with official-looking stamps on them.

Stratos, the other Greek boy, who was Alexis' cousin, translated everything for Antonia. After the signing they went to a bar with the boy who had given up the apartment. The conversation was held in Greek, and Antonia felt excluded. Then Alexis turned to her and said, very cheerfully, "You see how easy it is when you know people!"

Indeed, he had made finding somewhere to live very easy. All she had contributed was money.

Antonia studied Alexis' face as he talked with his companions. He had brilliant dark eyes with immensely long eyelashes, a thin nose and a wide curved mouth that tilted upwards at the corners when he smiled but was rather sulky and petulant in repose. He wore tight jeans and an old brown sweater which accentuated his thinness. He was much the same height as Antonia. She noticed that he never sat still, was always twisting his hands as he talked. His long brown fingers were elegant and fluid.

They went back to the absent Laura's apartment where Antonia felt suddenly tired and longed to go to sleep. Drinking so much wine in the afternoon made her feel very stupid. The men continued to talk and Antonia watched the discussion raging between them; she could not understand a word of it, but Alexis' animation was fascinating. She found she liked to watch him.

After some time the three young men went out and Antonia went to sleep on Alexis' narrow bed. She had not the least idea where they had gone; she assumed that they had classes at the university but could not be sure.

She awoke to find Alexis standing above her beside the bed, staring at her. She sat up and stretched, still full of her dream, which she could not recapture.

"Would you like me to give you a back rub?" asked Alexis.

"Yes, that would be wonderful," said Antonia, feeling very lazy and sleepy and sensual.

"I'm very good at back rubs," he said.

"I'm sure you are," she replied.

He was, indeed, very good at it, very gentle and soothing. His fingers massaged her neck and every vertebra in her long spine. It was a delicious and mellifluous feeling. She wished that he would go on forever. He maneuvered himself onto the bed and looked into her eyes. "Did you like that, Antonia?"

"It was lovely," she said, smiling back at him languidly.

"You see how clever I am." He twined his fingers in hers and she longed to touch his face and feel the softness of his hair. "You are the most beautiful English girl I have ever met," he said. "No wonder Enzo was so angry you wouldn't sleep with him."

"But I didn't want to sleep with Enzo. You know that."

But she did sleep with Alexis before the sensuality of his massage had evaporated and because she wanted his body so badly. She had never seen anyone as attractive as he was to her then.

"Did you always have long hair?" he asked.

"Always," she said as he twisted its heaviness in his hands.

"You are like a witch," he said, "so seductive."

"I just wanted you, that's all." She smiled.

"I suppose that's reason enough. Do you have lots of boyfriends, English Miss?"

"Don't call me that. That's what Enzo called me. I don't like it. And no, I don't have many boyfriends; that is, I don't have any just now."

"You've got me." He looked triumphant.

"Yes," she said, "I've got you." She laughed up at him.

They lay together until it had become dark in the room and she realised that she was rather hungry and her mouth was dry. She put on her dress and went into the kitchen to get a glass of water.

Enzo was there pouring himself a glass of wine. Antonia wished he had not been, and hoped he could not smell the semen which was sliding down the inside of her leg.

"So, Antonia," he smiled, lifting the glass to his lips. "Welcome to Florence."

Seventeen

On October afternoons it was still warm when the sun was out, turning chilly only after dusk. Antonia walked every afternoon to her Italian lessons, which were held in a dank palazzo on the other side of the Arno. She sat there for three hours of conversation and study and was amazed as her confusion slowly lifted and things were revealed to her, like the sun burning the mist off a shrouded beach. She liked the enormous enclosed courtyard behind the schoolrooms with urns darkened by verdigris and the decay of the summer's flowers.

She would walk home at half past six, pausing on the bridge to look down the length of the city as all the lights were beginning to come on. She held her books under her arm and watched the magic of the dusk transforming everything from day to night, but so slowly, so gently, as to be almost imperceptible. She liked looking into the shops in the early evening and reading their names: *farmacia, cornichia, lavanderia*. Even the most mundane seemed transformed, each shop a bright cavern carved out of the gloom, full of jewelled objects like flower gardens seen in the distance.

She used to walk home wondering if Alexis would be in. She never knew if he would be and never liked to ask. She bought an *etto* of prosciutto and some large red apples for her supper. Alexis usually ate at the university cafeteria where she had occasionally gone with him at first. It was cheaper, he said.

She climbed the stairs to the apartment and threw down her books.

"So how goes it, Antonia? Learning Italian?" Alexis smiled.

"Oh, all right, I suppose. I really do think I'm beginning to understand it, some of it anyway. It's so much easier than Latin or French."

He kissed her. "And what are they like—your fellow students?"

"All very different, all nationalities: Swedish, Japanese, Swiss, Iranian. Some of them are quite old. But it's very frustrating not being allowed to utter one word of English, because I'm quite sure Bruno, our teacher, can speak it very well, though he never will."

"So you like him, this Bruno?"

"Of course."

The next day Alexis came to collect her from the school which she thought very kind of him, though she missed going to a bar with some of the other would-be linguists as she had planned. She was very pleased that Alexis wanted to be with her.

Days passed, as Antonia happily drank in and tried to absorb the city. She spent the mornings looking at things in the museums and discovering courtyards and secret gardens and buying fruit and meat in the market. (She hated to see the songbirds strung up, so dead and so delicate, in rows high up at the butcher's.) It seemed impossible that a whole city could be so inexhaustible. She walked past doorways with brass plaques. The one which fascinated her most was the one that said piano teacher. The doorway was heavy and forbidding and was never open though wafts of music would spill out of the open windows and fill the street. She could imagine schoolchildren standing in front of that door waiting for their lessons, terrified, as she had always been when she had not practiced. She imagined the huge room with the vast black piano and the teacher who could force stubby fingers to become nimble and bold.

Antonia wrote to her father eventually and sent him her address. She thought he must have gathered by now that she would never go to the University of East Anglia. She told him she wanted to spend the year in Italy and would reconsider going to university after that. In fact, she had no idea at all what she intended to do. She did not mention Alexis.

Her father wrote back enclosing a cheque and saying how much he had enjoyed Florence years ago with her mother. Her allowance continued to arrive, but it no longer seemed as generous as it once had, now that she was paying rent and for her lessons. But she did not want to ask for more. It was odd for Antonia to have to think about money; she had never had to before. At first she rather liked it.

Clare appeared at Antonia's apartment one morning at the beginning of November when Antonia had almost given up hope of meeting her.

"So, your introduction to Florence was meeting Enzo?" Clare grinned.

"Yes," said Antonia, smiling, too.

"Oh, well. I expect he was very nice to you?"

"Yes, he took me out to dinner and showed me the sights."

"I'm sure he did. And did he try to seduce you?"

"Yes, he did that, too."

"What? Try to or actually do it?"

"He only tried."

"He is rather humourous, isn't he? Do you think he lies in wait for foreigners who are at least six inches taller to pounce on? As a sort of hobby perhaps?"

"I didn't know he did that to everyone," said Antonia.

"Of course he does," said Clare, hugging her. "But anyway I'm so glad I've found you. I only got back from Venice yesterday."

Later Clare showed Antonia the room which she shared with Richard, the room which was so vast that it was scarcely a room at all but one huge space most of which Clare had turned into a studio.

They sat drinking coffee and Antonia admired Clare's new paintings. Some of them were enormous, great explosions of colour, rather wild and expressionist with heaping bowls of fruit and flowers more magnificent and vivid than in life. Even Clare looked bigger to Antonia, plumper and a great deal happier than she had ever been before.

Richard said very little, as Clare filled in for Antonia the time since they had last met. He cringed slightly as Clare described their meeting but laughed as she waxed lyrical. "So you see, everything does turn out all right in the end!" Clare said, holding Richard's hand and smiling at him. "Richard makes everything possible, and I stop him being so pessimistic all the time. We are good for each other, I think."

Clare's latest scheme was selling her smaller drawings on the Ponte Vecchio, which was illegal but not particularly risky. It usually brought in enough money for lunch at least. She took Antonia with her one morning when the sun made it feel as if the day were midsummer and not the middle of November. Antonia was nervous but Clare said she ought not to be. She explained how quickly it was possible to roll up the velvet cloth on which the drawings were displayed and stand, nonchalantly, gazing down the river when the police passed, and how quickly it was possible to set the display up again. There were others there, too, some Italian, some American and a sprinkling of those whose origins were difficult to ascertain, selling belts and beads and pottery. They all seemed to know Clare. Antonia envied their easy camaraderie. A tall wistful boy played plaintive tunes on a flute while an elderly Oriental man set up his easel and started to paint.

Clare was a very good saleswoman, very cheerful and encouraging. She made everything look easy.

The first thing Antonia sold was a watercolour of a garden with urns. The would-be purchaser, an American woman, bedecked with cameras, smiling in a polyester pantsuit, asked if it was a garden in Florence.

"Yes," said Antonia, trying to be helpful, "you can tell by the urns. It's rather lovely, isn't it?"

"Did you do it?" the woman enquired hopefully.

"No, but I wish I had," said Antonia. "I wish I could capture all this beauty. Don't you?"

The woman took the painting and seemed pleased with it. Her husband produced the money without quibbling about the price and agreed it would look very nice in the den.

Antonia said, "You can look at your picture and think about Italy."

"Oh, I will," said the woman. "Have a nice day," she called as she vanished into the crowd.

When she had gone Clare turned to Antonia and said, "You know that drawing you just sold?"

"Yes."

"Well, it wasn't Italy at all. It was a garden in England. Rather Italianate I'll agree but in Sussex nonetheless."

"Oh, dear," said Antonia, sorry for what she had done.

Clare laughed. "Actually, it doesn't matter at all. They can hardly get us under the Trades Descriptions Act, can they? All that matters is that she likes it and thinks that it is Italy. It's just an illusion after all. That's all art ever is. A depiction of what one thinks things are or ought to be. I often wonder where my stuff ends up. A den in Cleveland might be quite a nice resting place." They sold two more drawings and by the end of the morning they had made over ten thousand lire. The stone they were sitting on was becoming cold and hard under their bottoms.

"That's enough for today," said Clare, stretching. "I'm starving."

They bought sandwiches and ate them sitting in the sun in the Boboli Gardens. "So Antonia, tell me about the wonderful Alexis."

"There isn't much to tell."

"You know he never liked me," Clare said.

"Why on earth not?"

"Actually, I think it was because I was not impressed with some of his ideas and used to argue with him." Antonia knew Clare did not like Alexis any more than he liked her. It had not yet occurred to Antonia to question his theories about the state of the world. She decided to change the subject. "Do you think I should get a job?"

"Why, do you want one?"

"In a way. You see, I don't really do much. I just wander around looking at things and tidying up and reading, ordinary things like that. Alexis says I'm being a parasite and it is necessary to do things."

"Oh, so the job is his idea? Why can't *he* get one then?"

"He can't. He's studying."

"Is he?" Clare sounded incredulous. "I never saw much sign of it. And he thinks *you* are being a leech and living on the spoils of capitalism and being idle off the sweat of the oppressed, et cetera, et cetera."

"Something like that. But I do have more free time than he does."

"He's full of shit, as Richard would say."

"But I think I would like a job, Clare—I don't want to rely on my father forever. I just can't think what I could do."

"Well, if you are really determined to subsidise the creep you could work in a shop. They always want people who speak both English and Italian."

"But my Italian isn't that good yet."

"It's okay," said Clare. "No one will complain."

"I sometimes wish that they would. If they never complain I never know what I have said wrong."

"Well, at least it's better than the French, who complain endlessly so one never dares say anything at all."

Antonia had to agree.

Clare found Antonia a job in a sweater shop opposite the Palazzo Pitti, where she worked from eleven to five. It catered to the tourist trade and so did not have the usual long lunch break. It was run by an American woman who had lived in Italy for years and who certainly did not need to work but in whom the taste for business was so strong that she could not happily remain idle. She seemed to like Antonia, and Antonia liked the sweaters, some of which had fanciful designs of deer or fir trees on them and other equally elaborate patterns. They were very soft to the touch and very expensive. The women who hand-knitted these sweaters lived out in the country. Antonia knew they were paid very little and felt sorry for them, but there was nothing she could do about it, though Alexis insisted she ought (but failed to explain exactly what).

Antonia sometimes wondered what her father would think of her working in a shop but anyway Alexis was pleased, particularly with the money. She thought that perhaps now, with some extra cash available, they would go out more often together in the evenings, but they did not. Alexis, though, often stopped in at the shop during the day to see how Antonia was, or, as Clare said, to check up on her. Antonia was pleased to see him anyway and thought Clare uncharitable.

Antonia would walk home in the evenings through the darkening streets and shop for her solitary meal, enchanted with her newfound ease in speaking Italian, buying food she had not tried before or wine for them both to drink.

When Alexis appeared after supper and she had tidied up the apartment they would spend the evening making love. It was the time of day she most enjoyed and Antonia would count the minutes until she heard his step on the stairs. Being alone in bed with him, with the door shut and Stratos far off in the other room (or, better still, out) made the rest of the day without Alexis seem trivial and insignificant. Her room and her body seemed secret and miraculous. She had never loved anyone with such violence and such passion, nor had a lover so insatiable and so pleasing. She felt very happy in bed with Alexis.

He often went out at night to bars where Antonia soon realised she was not welcome, and she would lie amidst the disordered sheets waiting for him to return and for it all to begin again.

Very few people came to the apartment, and Antonia did not want them there. She wanted the place to remain secret and private. Occasionally Antonia went out with Clare, whom Alexis did not make welcome in the apartment. When they went out they would pretend to be innocent tourists and fend off the tiny Sicilians who found Clare irresistible. Clare taught Antonia the delights of pinball and her thighs became as bruised as Clare's in ineffectual attempts not to make the machine tilt while still jiggling it about satisfactorily.

Sometimes they would spend the evening at Clare and Richard's place. The contrast with Antonia's apartment was quite striking. The studio was constantly strewn with clothes and plates and paintings and people. Clare would occasionally make vague attempts to tidy up, but she did not care really. The loft was so vast it could swallow up quantities of debris. Brushes and knives were lost for weeks and not missed, and then hours were spent looking for them. There was a constant stream of people passing through. Clare now spoke fluent if somewhat ungrammatical Italian. Antonia was amazed at her energy.

Richard, on the other hand, remained taciturn, in a world of his own which few people ever managed to penetrate. Antonia never knew how he managed to work surrounded by Clare's circus but he did. He accepted Antonia, as he did all of Clare's hangers-on, without comment, but she was aware of his acute powers of observation and tried not to appear too foolish and ignorant before him. One of the few people Richard publicly argued with was Laura, whose schemes for the betterment of mankind he found almost as absurd as Alexis'. Antonia had learned not to say too much about Alexis when she was there. She was happy with her lot and saw no reason to change it.

One evening, when Richard was out and she was alone with Antonia, Clare said, "Are you really as happy as you pretend to be?"

"Yes, I am."

"But he's such a shit to you, Toe."

"Is he? I've never noticed." Antonia could feel in her mind the flatness of his belly and the insistence of his tongue. She could not discuss those things even with Clare.

"Of course he is," Clare continued. "You must realise that. What happens when the first fine flourish wears off? What then?"

Antonia could not imagine their relationship changing. "Do you love Richard?" she countered. "Is my relationship with Alexis so very different?"

"I think it is," said Clare. "We help one another, and also leave one another alone. I don't hover about and wait on him hand and foot. Being with David taught me about that."

Antonia quite liked waiting on Alexis, handing him his coffee and seeing him smile. He very rarely said thank you. He would have considered it demeaning, Antonia thought.

The evenings were dark now, even before Antonia left the shop. "Christmas again," said Clare. "It does seem to recur with appalling frequency of late. Just think how we used to look forward to it. Actually I still do in a way. What are you going to do?"

"I'm not sure," said Antonia. "My father has sent me a cheque and wants me to come and stay with him and Eileen because he's going to

New York for six months just afterwards. He says he would like all the family to be together. It is a fantasy of both of ours that we all love each other very much, so I suppose I will go. And I do want to see Justin at least." Antonia's brother had started sending her long letters from his prep school full of useful information about Jones Minor who had had chicken pox as well as failing Common Entrance, and the team that had won the interhouse rugby matches. "You can't imagine how gothic it will be, or perhaps you can, Clare. Eileen's parents will turn up from Forest Hill and disgust my father, mostly I think because they remind him of his own parents, whom he is doing his best to forget. And they will all give Justin horribly expensive presents like electric train sets with all the bits you can imagine so he'll have none of the pleasure of lusting after bits he hasn't got. And Eileen will produce that wretched silver tree again."

"You could always come to us. Mummy would have great pleasure in trying to fatten you up, and Daddy could tell you all his antique jokes. Actually we're all going to Norfolk to stay with my grandparents but no one would mind someone extra—that is, if you could bear to play hockey on Boxing Day and all that."

"You don't know how tempting it sounds, but I can't. I ought to try to be nice to them both especially since I won't have to see either of them again for six months."

Antonia did spend Christmas in Chelsea and it was quite as depressing as she had thought it would be. She was relieved when Clare rang her up on the twenty-eighth. "Are you having a wonderful time, Toe?"

"No," Antonia said shortly, not wanting to enlarge at that moment. Eileen was hovering nearby, arranging anaemic and unseasonable pink roses in a cut-glass vase.

"Good," said Clare cheerfully. "Then I'm sure you would like to come to Venice with me on our way back to Florence. No one else seems interested at all. It should be quite mythical and gray, swathed in mist in the dead of winter."

"But I told Alexis I would be back on the sixth," said Antonia.

"Oh, I never tell Richard exactly when I'll get back and so he's good and longing to see me when I do turn up."

"How clever of you, Clare. I would never dare risk doing a thing like that."

"But you do want to come, don't you." It was a statement not a question, and Antonia was tempted. She had not been to Venice since she was six. She wondered if her memories would mesh at all with the reality of the city. She let Clare persuade her. She would only be two days late returning to Florence.

On the way to the boat-train Clare and Antonia went to dinner with Elinor and Simon in the house they were restoring in South London. It was a beautifully proportioned Regency house in a most squalid street, and they were in the process of discovering wonderfully solid doors, wood floors, and even a real marble fireplace, all of which had been hidden beneath layer upon layer of orange and green paint, flocked wallpaper, Formica and autumn leaf carpet. They ate in the kitchen by candlelight while Simon described what it was necessary to go through in order to become a barrister. Antonia was sure he would be a very good one; he could be quite intimidating when not being funny. Elinor was employed as a sort of general dogsbody for a publishing firm and said she thought it would lead to better things if she stuck it out, as no doubt she would, and it would, too. Antonia could not imagine Elinor not getting what she wanted.

Antonia tried to describe Alexis to Elinor as they drank their coffee. Elinor's reaction was rather dubious, but Antonia had hardly expected her to be enthusiastic.

"He's very charming when he wants to be, Elinor."

"I'm sure he is, Toe, they all are. But do take care. Anyway I'll probably meet him if we come out at Easter. Simon, we are going to Florence for Easter, aren't we?"

"I hope so, if I can get away."

Simon and Elinor seemed to Antonia to lead such busy and purposefully occupied lives. They made her feel idle and useless. She couldn't think why they liked her at all.

Venice was lovely and mysterious, as Clare had promised it would be, but bitter cold with thick wet fog sweeing in from the lagoon.

Antonia's gloves were always damp and soggy and the cold permeated her bones. Clare kept getting lost and arriving at places they thought they had left behind and lost forever; she refused to use a map since she had just spent two months in Venice and had no intention of being taken for a tourist. Antonia was rather pleased when she knew where they were more often than Clare did. As it happened, there were very few people about who could have taken them for tourists or anything else for that matter. The Accademia was almost deserted and Clare showed Antonia around as if they were in her own private domain and the paintings were hers alone.

To ward off the cold they drank cioccolata con panna in Florian's and Quadrii's.

"How Laura would love this," said Clare ordering another pastry. "We should have rung her up and asked her to join us."

Antonia was beginning to miss Alexis very much.

Clare and Antonia arrived back in Florence on the eighth of January. They parted at the station. Antonia was so eager to see Alexis again, she took a taxi to her apartment. She bounded up the stairs and flung open the door praying that he would be in and as thrilled to see her as she was to see him.

The bathroom door opened and a girl clad only in one of Antonia's bath towels stepped out.

"Who are you?" the girl asked, pleasantly enough.

"Antonia. I live here." She could see Alexis' naked shoulder emerging from the blankets on her bed. "Hello, Alexis," she said, putting down her bag, which now seemed very heavy. She took in the confusion of the room and the crumpled sheets. It was three in the afternoon and an open wine bottle was set on the floor by the bed.

"I didn't know when you were coming back," said A exis, as if that explained everything.

The girl, who had long straight hair parted in the middle, went and sat on the bed by Alexis and looked first at him and then at Antonia. "I'm Cindy," she said extending her hand, which Antonia ignored. She obviously had not the least idea how things stood between Antonia and Alexis. Antonia knew he was hardly likely to have told her; Antonia felt fleetingly sorry for her whilst wishing her dead.

"I'll come back in an hour," said Antonia, as neutrally as possible under the circumstances, and went out.

She stood on the stairs feeling sick and wondered what to do next. It was obvious that they had just made love. She should have expected it, but she hadn't. Antonia walked and walked, then sat on the steps of S. Croce away from the dog muck and wrapped her coat tightly around her. She had never felt so cold in her life. At exactly four o'clock she went back to via Torta and knocked on the door. Alexis opened it looking contrite. Everything was immaculately tidy and there was no trace of Cindy. There was even a bunch of flowers stuck awkwardly in a jar on the bookshelves.

"Didn't you get my letter?" Antonia asked.

"No, I didn't. I expected you back two days ago. I thought you were never coming."

"I see I am very quickly replaced," said Antonia icily.

"Don't be silly, Antonia. I was longing for you. You don't know how lonely I've been. And you look more lovely than ever," he added placatingly.

Antonia thought this unlikely since her eyes were red from crying and her nose raw from the wind. Alexis came and stood by her, put his arms about her and kissed her very slowly on the lips. She melted at his proximity. He undressed her hurriedly and they made love quite ravenously. Antonia hated him then but she had missed his body so much. She loved him, too, and was consumed by jealousy.

"Who is she, Alexis?"

"Oh, nobody, Antonia. I was so lonely without you. I missed you so much." He made it sound as if it were Antonia who had wronged him by deserting him when he most needed comfort. "It won't happen again," he said. And she believed him.

They took photographs of themselves in bed that night, holding the camera at arm's length and grinning idiotically. Antonia wondered if the camera shop would process such pictures. But she wanted pictures of herself and Alexis together.

Alexis did not ask her about England and she did not ask him how he had got on in her absence. He surely had not been as lonely as he had suggested.

When Antonia went to take her pill that night she discovered that she had left the packet in Venice, in the paper bag in which she had stashed the six months' supply which she had got from her doctor in London. She did not tell Alexis because she thought he would be furious at her stupidity. He never used condoms.

And so she became pregnant, though she would not believe it at first. She had often missed her period, especially when she was not eating. She put her tiredness down to standing in the shop and lying awake into the night waiting for Alexis to come home. She could not think why her breasts were tender, though they were bigger, which Alexis liked. She had always been very flat-chested before.

Clare said to her at the beginning of March, "You look ghastly, Toe, are you all right?"

"I'm perfectly all right."

"Are you sure? You look different somehow."

A week later she told Clare that she thought she might be pregnant.

"Why on earth do you think that? Have you been sick?"

"I left my pills in Venice."

"Oh, my God," said Clare, "then you probably are. You should find out, you know, before it's too late."

"Too late for what?"

"To have it dealt with of course."

"But I don't want it 'dealt with' as you so euphemistically put it, Clare. If I *am* pregnant, which might not even be the case, I don't want an abortion." Antonia had heard about abortions in Italy done in milk vans travelling at night on deserted roads and women bleeding to death as a result. She wanted to have Alexis' baby, to have a family and never to be alone. She fantasised about Alexis asking her to marry him, their having a cosy life together somewhere. She thought it might make them feel more connected, that he would not dare to leave her and sleep with other women then. She thought of Elinor with Simon and of Clare with Richard and the strength of their relationships, the exclusiveness of them. She thought how sometimes when she was with them as couples she felt left out and deprived.

A week later she went to a doctor who confirmed what by then she was sure of. The baby was due in September, a reality not a fantasy anymore.

"Congratulations, Mrs. Acton," he said, and Antonia left his surgery feeling very powerful and happy.

"You've got to tell Alexis soon," said Clare, who was waiting for her in the street. "God knows what he will have to say about it."

Antonia could put off telling him no longer. The waistbands of her skirts were getting tight and her jeans were unwearable. She waited until late one night when they were lying together in bed having made love exhaustingly for hours. She liked him the most at such times, lying together, spent and companionable.

She sat up and looked at him. "Alexis, I've got something very important to tell you, very wonderful news. I'm going to have a baby."

"It's not true," he said. "It can't be. Is it mine?" He sounded shocked and not so delighted as she had somehow imagined he would be.

"Of course it's yours. And it is quite true." Antonia looked into his eyes.

"But surely something can be done about it, Antonia? You can't have a baby. I can't marry you. You must be quite mad to have let it happen."

"Then you don't want our baby? You want me to kill it?"

"I want it never to have happened. You know you can't have a child." His mouth turned down at the corners.

"But it's too late for an abortion, Alexis." She wished she could say it was not true, that she had not trapped him, that it was entirely her fault and had nothing to do with him at all.

He sat with his head in his hands thinking. When he looked up Antonia saw a glimmer of a smile in his eyes. "It's very clever of me to have made you pregnant, isn't it?"

Antonia did not think it took brains particularly. He smiled. "I like children," he said. "Will your father pay for it?"

"No," said Antonia, "because I'm not going to tell him."

"But babies are expensive. They don't cost nothing."

"I'll find the money somewhere," said Antonia, not knowing where. "I'll have it in England on the National Health. That doesn't cost anything."

Alexis looked glum again.

"Are you very angry?" she asked, hugging her knees to her, concealing her stomach.

"No, I'm not angry anymore."

Antonia could see he was warming to the idea and very pleased with himself.

"Would you get me a cup of coffee?" he said.

And Antonia went into the kitchen to make him one, although she did not like the taste of coffee herself any more.

Eighteen

Antonia liked being pregnant, though she did not see any more of Alexis; if anything he became more elusive, and more evasive when he was there. Stratos was kind and would occasionally go out and buy Antonia supper from the *rosticceria* when she was too tired to buy anything for herself. She felt newly in tune with her body and spent as little time as she could thinking about the future. Perhaps when the baby was born Alexis would want to be seen in public with her again; perhaps being seen walking in the street with a pregnant woman would diminish him in some way, though she could not imagine how. When they were alone he still liked her body very much.

Elinor and Simon arrived to spend Easter with Clare, and they drove Antonia up to Fiesole to have lunch with them and to admire the city glistening beneath them in the spring sunshine. But Antonia could not go out in the evenings with them in case Alexis came back to the apartment when she was not there and wondered where she was.

Simon met Alexis when he came to via Torta to collect Antonia for an outing and did not like him at all. Simon did not need to put his sentiments into words. Antonia managed to ignore his expression.

Another day Antonia went with Clare and Elinor to the Uffizi and spent hours wandering amongst the paintings, each girl wanting to share with the others those paintings which she particularly enjoyed. Clare stopped before the portraits of Battista Sforza and Frederico da Montefeltro.

"You see," she said, "how it all comes together, the people and the landscape both utterly of their time. I think having them in profile was meant to make you think of Roman coins, or even Greek ones, although I suppose they *had* to do poor Frederico that way because half his face had been taken off by a cannon ball."

"They do look rather fierce," Antonia said. "And yet sometimes I see people in the streets who seem to have jumped straight out of a Renaissance painting."

"Who would you have wanted to paint you, El?" Clare asked.

"Bronzino, so I would look aristocratic and frosty."

Antonia, who had spent countless hours in the museum, led the sisters to Botticelli's "Primavera." "I always come back to this picture. I do wish I'd worked harder all those years ago when we did the Greek myths at school. I've never quite fathomed exactly what this is about."

"I think Botticelli meant to be enigmatic," Elinor said. "But you must know Flora. And those are the Three Graces."

"And what, exactly, were they meant to symbolise?" Clare asked.

"It all depends. They were alternately the daughters of Zeus or of Dionysus, the handmaidens of the gods, or the personifications of the desirable feminine attributes. Sort of universal rent-a-nymphs. One, I think, was meant to symbolise beauty, another wisdom, and the third, fruitfulness." Elinor glanced at her watch. "Didn't you promise Laura we'd meet her for lunch? It's almost one-thirty. She'll be ravenous and eat without us if we don't hurry up."

The evening before Simon and Elinor were to return to England Elinor asked Clare what she was going to do about Antonia.

"What can I do, Ellie? What right have I to do anything?"

"You could persuade her to tell her father."

"But she really doesn't want to. And he's in New York until June," said Clare.

"How could she be so stupid?" said Simon. "I always thought she would land on her feet in the end."

"I think there are all sorts of reasons, Simon. She wants to be fixed, settled somehow, and she wants someone to love, someone who won't desert her—ever."

"Which counts Alexis out."

"Actually I think Alexis hardly comes into it. I think she wants the baby far more than she wants him, though she wouldn't admit it."

"At least she said she would come to England to have the baby," said Simon. "I've been looking into it, and if she had it here it would be the most awful legal mess. The baby would have no nationality if it was born in Italy to a Greek father and an English mother."

"So you see," said Richard, who had been observing the sisters together, "how governments do nothing but fuck up and complicate our lives."

"Never mind governments, Richard. Think of Antonia," said Clare.

"And how will her feckless father react to all this?" asked Elinor.

"God knows. I expect he will be horribly embarrassed. He's beginning to dabble in politics and has adopted the most appalling right-wing views."

"You know, Ellie," said Clare, "I am only just beginning to realise what a relief and a salvation it is to have dull but reliable parents who always do the right thing."

"Well, make sure you ship her off to England by the end of August," said Elinor. "I made her promise to come to us—that is, unless you convince her to tell her father before that."

"How kind you are, Ellie."

"Well, don't *you* do anything ghastly in the meantime," said Elinor. "Mummy is worried about you enough as it is. She wonders if either of us will ever get married and make her a grandmother. But don't for heaven's sake go and do the breeding bit first."

"Mum can always practice on Antonia's baby," said Clare. "I don't want children for years and years."

Spring became summer and Antonia borrowed Clare's loose cotton shifts and stared at other pregnant women in the streets. She saw dozens of them every day; it seemed as if half the world was pregnant. It was odd she had never noticed before. She watched mothers with their babies in prams and pushchairs, and thought how lovely most of them were, those red-faced infants with besotted mothers. She swore she would be more restrained in her admiration for her offspring, in public at least. She looked at baby clothes in shops but never bought anything; she was far too superstitious for that.

August was intolerably hot and Antonia would plan her trips to the market so as to keep under the cover of overhanging buildings. She dreaded the glare of the sun, its unyielding beating on the stones which gave off heat even after the sun had set. Everyone seemed to be getting as excited about the baby as Antonia was. Clare knitted a multicoloured bonnet for the baby which she was rather proud of though it was not particularly well made; it had all Antonia's favourite colours in it, ones she had admired in Clare's paintings. Laura went out and bought a complete layette at a fabulously expensive shop and then sent the bill to her parents, which caused the most awful transatlantic consternation since her parents mistakenly assumed that the clothes were for some child that Laura herself was about to produce.

Antonia felt increasingly bovine and stupid and more unwieldy by the day. She read and reread all the books about childbirth that she could lay her hands on. She waited for the baby to move inside her and would poke and prod at her stomach if some hours passed without movement. She didn't like the doctor she went to very much because he treated her so matter-of-factly. She resented his attitude, thinking to herself that now she was very special indeed.

Alexis was fascinated by Antonia's body, by the dark line down the centre of her stomach, and her big breasts. He took photographs of her sitting naked in a chair by the open window on August afternoons as she tried to catch the least glimmer of breeze in the oppressive heat. Antonia knew he was dreading her departure. She asked him if he would come to England with her because she wanted him to be there when the baby was born. But he had never been anywhere outside Greece, except Italy, and said he did not have enough money to travel. When Antonia offered to try and scrape up enough so he could accompany her he said he did not want her filthy capitalist money. She could not buy him, he said. Antonia wondered if he was frightened of being in a strange country and out of his depth. He was only nineteen after all, only one year older than she was herself. He had given her a ring for her birthday in June. It was a charming ring, thin gold in a delicate design, and he had been thrilled at his own generosity, but it was not meant for the finger on which wedding rings were worn in Greece. Antonia wore it on her ring finger to deflect the beady eyes of stout Italian matrons in shops and was pleased with it nonetheless. She often gazed at it when Alexis was not there, remembering the look on his face when he had given it to her.

"Are you excited about going to England, Antonia?" He kissed one of her brown nipples, which sometimes leaked a clear fluid.

"I'm looking forward to the baby but not to leaving you," Antonia said, twisting the ring on her finger.

"But I'll wait for you, you know that. I won't sleep with anyone else while you are gone." He sounded as if he were bestowing a great honour on her with this offer of fidelity so lightly made. "I hope it's a boy," he said stroking her stomach very gently.

"I don't care what the baby is," she said, "as long as it is healthy." She secretly thought she would have a girl. She could not imagine a male body springing out of her own.

"I'm sure it's a boy. Listen to how strong his heart beats!" He put his head to the bulge and listened intently.

It was very awkward and sticky making love on those August nights, but his desire for her had not diminished as hers for him had. She did not want him to realise this. Knowing that her thoughts were so often very far from him, she could not deny him her body, too.

Alexis grew increasingly attentive as the time for her departure grew nearer. They went to the seaside on the train one day. A real day trip to Viareggio, and Antonia swam in the dirty sea like a great whale. Then in the evening they ate pizza in a park where lights strung from the pine trees illuminated the dusty ground.

It was dark when they got back to Florence and walked together by the Arno as they had so often in their first weeks together.

"You will come back to me, Antonia. Do you promise me that?" He held her face in his hands and looked into her eyes.

"Of course I will," she said. "Why ever wouldn't I?"

"I love you so much," he said. "Please don't leave me."

"I love you, too, Alexis. Don't you realise that? I could have had an abortion, everyone told me to. But I wanted to give you something very precious."

He bought her an ice cream with his own money and they sat in the Piazza S. Croce and looked up at the stars in the clear night sky. They did not make love that night. Instead Alexis rubbed her back, which ached from the train and the weight of the baby, and he stroked her hair, which was still full of sand from the beach. She had been too exhausted to wash it.

Antonia left for England two days later and Alexis saw her off at the station. He had put her bag up on the rack and seemed genuinely solicitous for her welfare. He looked very small, standing waving on the platform as the train drew out. Antonia saw that he was crying, pushing the tears from his eyes roughly with the back of his hand. She wished that he were coming with her. She felt very desolate and alone amongst the crowd on the train and very frightened of what lay ahead of her.

Simon met Antonia at Victoria Station and drove her to the house he shared with Elinor in Herne Hill. It was a calm oasis amidst South London's decay. The room Elinor showed Antonia to was tall and square, painted the palest shell pink and furnished with odd bits of furniture which Antonia recognised from Simon's family home in Cornwall.

"What bliss it is to be still after that filthy train," Antonia said, slipping off her shoes. "Elinor, you don't know how grateful I am to you and Simon. I can't think why you put up with me."

Elinor laughed. "Neither can we actually. I suppose it's got to be a habit."

"But it still is good of you."

"I know. Being good is our specialty." Elinor produced a card upon which was written the time of Antonia's appointment at the hospital clinic. "As well as being good I'm efficient. Do you want some supper?"

"I couldn't face it," said Antonia. "I do thank you." She slept for a long time in her room which felt like home.

Two days later Antonia presented herself at the ante-natal clinic of the hospital where her baby would eventually be born.

The waiting room was full of women of every colour and shape, all looking beaten and worn, with coats and shopping bags and children filling the spaces between them. A crisp white nurse sat at a desk shuffling through papers trying to avoid catching the eye of any of her unwilling flock. Their numbers slowly increased until every seat was taken. Occasionally, numbers would be called and women would get up with varying degrees of awkwardness and disappear into another room.

When Antonia thought she had sat there for a very long time she went up to the desk and waited for the nurse to notice her, which it took her some moments to do.

"Yes?" she said, rather frostily, glancing back at her papers.

"I'm Antonia Acton. I have an appointment for nine-fifteen."

"Well, do take a seat, dear. We'll be with you in a moment."

"But I've been here since nine and it's ten already." Antonia tried not to sound whiney or impatient. She knew it would not do her any good.

"We do see a lot of people here. I'm sure they'll get to you soon. What number are you?"

"I haven't got a number."

The nurse looked at Antonia properly for the first time. "Oh, dear, surely you have?" She was obviously put out.

Antonia took out her clinic card and the letter telling her when to present herself. "I haven't been here before," she said.

"I thought you must have." The nurse's eyes travelled from Antonia's stomach to her face. "Let me see your letter."

Antonia smiled placatingly, but the woman's eyes were already on the letter. The nurse stood up with some majesty and departed without a backward glance. The three women who had formed a pathetic small queue behind Antonia looked cross. She wanted to explain that it wasn't her fault; she hadn't meant the nurse to go away, but there didn't seem much point in apologising. After what seemed like hours the starched creature reappeared.

"You can go back to your seat. We'll be with you in a moment."

However, Antonia's place had been taken by a huge black woman whom Antonia thought must be expecting triplets at least; she could not ask her to move. Antonia tried to read, but her attention was caught by a small Indian child standing holding his mother's skirt in one hand, the other stuck in his mouth. He was looking about him quite impassively, watching the other children, who, having nothing to do, were whining and chewing on bottles and dummies. One was tearing pages out of a tattered magazine, her mother quite oblivious to this destruction. Antonia hardly thought it important either. It was probably a copy of *Lifeboat Monthly* from 1956. The Indian child suddenly removed his hand from his mouth and gazed at Antonia and offered her a magnificent unblinking smile. She was immediately cheered and grinned back. He was the only person who had looked at her with anything but irritation all day.

"Mrs. Acton?" A young man with the build of a rugger player dressed in a white coat stood there looking around the room. Antonia turned to him. He, too, smiled at her and she thought her luck was improving. "I'm Edmund Reilley. If you would come with me, I need to ask you some questions for your chart."

"Of course." Antonia retrieved her sweater from beneath the huge woman who had crushed it hopelessly without seeming to notice.

Antonia followed the young man's broad back into a small room which was painted in shades of institutional green. He opened a folder with her name on it.

"It's horrible out there, isn't it?" he said. "I don't know how they can all put up with it so stoically." He seemed rather nervous and she wondered if he was a real doctor. Most probably a medical student she decided.

"It was rather dull," Antonia admitted. "Not at all what they lead you to believe in the brochures: those happy mothers chatting, with toys for the children."

"So many things are not what one expects," he said, while Antonia sat studying his face. He looked up at her and smiled again. "But we had better get on with this form. Is all this correct? Mrs. Antonia Acton, 19 Wordsworth Road, SE 24. Date of birth: July 12, 1952. And your baby is due at the end of September?"

"Yes, but I'm Miss Acton, actually."

"It doesn't matter for the form," he said. She liked his smile. It was nice, not professional but real, she thought.

They proceeded with the usual litany of childhood illnesses, all of which Antonia had had, through VD and TB which she had not, to her family history. They touched briefly on Alexis' medical history, but Antonia did not know it beyond the fact that his parents were still alive. Antonia almost wished that her pregnancy had been exotic or interesting so as to have something to talk about. But it had not been, except to her, a fact for which she was grateful. They spoke briefly about Italy where Edmund had once been and which now seemed so very distant and alien. The baby moved inside her and she could see his elbow or knee sticking up at an angle beneath her thin dress.

"And so you're not worried about anything? And you feel quite well?" He looked at her quite intently.

Antonia could never think of questions to ask at moments like this though she could generally think of dozens later. "I'm fine, really I am."

"Then I suppose you will have to go back out there and sit with the crowd." He closed the folder and put it under his arm. He directed Antonia towards the now-overflowing room. "Perhaps I'll see you again," he said. "Good luck."

Antonia stood thinking how much she had liked him. It had been a relief having someone's attention directed to her face rather than her belly, but she thought it unlikely that they would meet again in such a large institution. There were so many people whom one met briefly, she thought, who had the right to know all about one but did not know anything at all, really.

She waited for another hour feeling cheerful and did not mind when she was examined in a cubby hole by two other students who scarcely glanced at her face, and who talked amongst themselves and referred to her as "mother." They treated her as if she were an idiot and not connected to her womb.

Antonia caught a bus back to Elinor's and played a very elaborate series of games of Patience, which she managed to win by skill rather than by cheating. She never sank to that, tempting though it occasionally was. She tried to recall Edmund Reilley's face but it was already fading. Antonia felt very lazy and lay on her bed in the afternoon watching the horse chestnuts high up in the trees forming their glossy globes, now hidden from sight. She fell asleep and did not dream.

The baby decided to begin its journey into the world one late September morning when the air was crisp and cool and the leaves were beginning to turn colour. Antonia had felt strange light contractions all night but had not wanted to bother Elinor, who left for work early. She could not decide at first whether what she was feeling was the real thing or a mere rehearsal for it. Simon had been in Edinburgh for a week. He was due back that night. Antonia left a note for them on the kitchen table beside a jug of asters, so they would know where to find her.

She went to hospital on a bus. She felt it would have been overdramatic to call an ambulance and too extravagant to call a taxi. She felt very competent and in control; the contractions had not really begun to hurt.

For the first time they seemed very kind at the hospital and Antonia was quite willing to abdicate all responsibility to them. They should know what to do; it was their job. She liked the midwives who smiled and were encouraging and attentive. She was very cheerful. She thought she would cope very well.

"Would you mind if a student delivered your baby?" one of the midwives asked.

"Not at all," said Antonia, very willing to be helpful and behave as they would wish her to. The baby did not seem very real to her then, though it obviously did to the hospital. She could see little plastic wristbands like the one on her own wrist, but so much smaller, in the envelope on the door with her chart in it.

Antonia put aside her Patience cards, which she had brought in with her to while away the time. They did not interest her. She walked to the window and looked out at the park where the leaves were brilliant in the sunshine. There were very few people in it. She saw an old man with a dog and a woman with a baby in a pushchair pointing to the ducks on the pond. Antonia would have liked to have been out there with them, not imprisoned in this sterile and stuffy room. She held on to the windowsill as she felt another contraction and wondered why they were so euphemistic about it and avoided saying pain. It hurt, not unbearably, but a lot. Crouching, she felt her way back to the welcoming bed and pulled the sheet over her face and waited for the pain to subside.

She heard the door open and looked up. The midwife came in with a young man whom Antonia was sure she recognised from somewhere but whom she could not immediately place.

"Mrs. Acton, this is Edmund Reilley; he will be delivering your baby."

Delivering, what an odd word. Like a package, she thought. She wondered what it would be like. Not like a parcel, she knew. She sat up and shook hands with him. "I'm sorry if I'm rather stupid, they gave me some pethidine. It all seems to be taking rather a long time."

"That's all right. Don't worry about it. I have nothing else to do today either." Edmund sat down on a chair by the door and the midwife went out.

"What time is it?" Antonia asked.

"Almost one o'clock," he said, looking at his watch. She had not noticed it had got so late, though the shadows on the wall had altered.

"I've met you before," he said. "The first time you came here. Do you remember?"

"Yes, I do," said Antonia, feeling another pain starting. A tear formed in the corner of her eye but did not fall. She clutched the sheet. "I'm so sorry," she said.

"There's nothing to be sorry about. I'll examine you in a moment if I may." He called the midwife.

"Of course."

His hands were cool and soft. "I'll be as gentle as I can," he said. "I'll try not to hurt you."

Antonia wondered why he was so concerned about not hurting her. She was sure it was going to hurt a great deal more than this before it was all over.

"And so you live in Italy?"

"Yes," she replied. "It's very beautiful in the autumn. I remember you said you had been there once."

"But that was in the spring. My mother always wanted to spend Easter in Italy. My father would have preferred Wales, I think."

"Wales is very pretty, too," Antonia said, wondering why they were having such a polite cocktail party conversation. Perhaps the pethidine was making her very stupid. She went to sleep for a moment. When she woke up, she said, "Do people ever scream when they are having babies?"

"Yes, quite a lot of them, actually."

"I won't scream," said Antonia.

"I wouldn't say that now if I were you. You may regret it later." He smiled.

"I suppose so. Have you seen many babies born?"

"Yes, hundreds."

"Really?"

"Not hundreds, perhaps, but quite a few."

"And were they all alive?"

"Yes."

She knew he was lying, but it did not matter. "I think my baby will be dead. Do many people think that?"

"Yes, quite a lot. But very few are, you know."

"Yes," she said. "Do you mind if I close my eyes for a minute?"

"Do anything you want. It's your day after all."

Antonia felt that all this was a dream. The only reality was the pain which was increasingly hard to bear.

"Do you want me to telephone anyone for you? I could, you know. Your husband or your mother?"

"I don't have a husband or a mother."

"No, I remember you don't. I'm sorry."

"Don't be sorry. It isn't your fault."

"Is there anyone you want to be with you?"

"No, nobody. I want to do this on my own."

"Are you sure?"

"I just didn't realise it would hurt so much." No one had warned her. She had never had a friend who had had a baby.

"I'll stay with you until the baby is born. She will be born today, you know."

Antonia wondered why he said *she*. But it made a change. And so the afternoon wore on. She was glad Edmund was there. She did not want to be alone after all, she discovered. She was very frightened now.

"Are many people frightened?" she asked.

"I think so. It would be surprising if they weren't. But babies are very tough really. I wouldn't worry about it if I were you."

But she did. She drew her legs up towards her chest and counted. She felt quite exhausted by the pain. She wished it would end.

"Did they ask you if you wanted an epidural?"

"Constantly. I said that I didn't."

"I don't think it's too late if you do want one."

"I don't want a needle stuck in my spine," she said. "I didn't want any drugs. I feel stupid to have had the pethidine. I feel a failure."

"I don't think it's stupid not to want pain when you can avoid it."

"No, I suppose not." Antonia waited for another contraction to pass. "Then you don't think I would be a fool if I had one, an epidural, I mean?"

"Not at all."

Clare's friends in Florence were constantly extolling the virtues of natural childbirth, particularly Laura, who liked to keep abreast of feminist literature. But of course neither of them had had a baby. Edmund went out to find the anaesthetist. Antonia felt bereft without him. She tried to go to sleep but the pethidine had worn off and she could not. The anaesthetist came and examined her spine and went away again. He said he would come back.

"Would it be all right if I held your hand?" she asked Edmund, wanting some human contact. His hand was as cool as it had been before.

"Am I squeezing very hard?" she asked.

"Yes," he said, "but it doesn't matter."

The midwife came in and strapped Antonia to a fetal monitor, very cumbersome and full of wires.

"Why don't they tell you about this?" Antonia asked rather crossly.

"I thought they had," Edmund said.

"Of course they did, but I didn't realise it would be as bad as this. I'm sorry I'm being so cross."

"I don't blame you. I think you are being very brave."

"Thank you. But where's the anaesthetist anyway?" She wanted the epidural now or any kind of drug. She didn't care what.

"He had to see another patient. He'll be back soon."

But he wasn't.

"Couldn't I have some more pethidine?"

"No, not now."

They wheeled her into the delivery room still attached to the monitor. Edmund told her to push.

"I am pushing," she said.

"Well, push harder."

Antonia tried but nothing happened. "I think I'm going to be sick," she said. A black nurse held out a kidney basin and she threw up into it. Much more than the basin would hold. It was awful but she did not have enough energy to feel humiliated.

"For God's sake push, Antonia." Edmund had put on a mask. She could only see his eyes. Antonia held the hand of an Indian nurse, so delicate in comparison with Edmund's large one. Antonia lay watching the fetal monitor, willing her child's heart to continue beating, watching the rhythmic movement of the fluctuating line which meant he was still alive. Then the heartbeats got weaker and weaker and less frequent however hard Antonia willed them to appear. They suddenly turned the monitor away from her and one of them said, "Turn it down so she can't hear."

"For Christ's sake, push now."

"I am pushing, can't you see?" Antonia shouted. But nothing happened.

More people came into the room and a voice said, "I'm just going to make a little cut. I'll give you an injection first." The injection burned like fire. Antonia could feel the knife cutting into her flesh and the warm blood gushing. She wished she was dead. The baby must be, surely. She saw the sweat stand out on the doctor's broad black brow as he stood before her and pulled so hard on the forceps that she thought her entire body was being torn apart. She held the gas and air mask to her face but kept dropping it. Her son was born and taken to the other side of the room.

"Is he dead?" she asked, but nobody answered. They brought him to her covered in blood, but breathing. A dark round head nursing at her breast.

"He's very beautiful," someone said. And indeed he was.

"We've got to take him from you for a little while so we can stitch you up."

Antonia did not care. He was alive.

Nineteen

Antonia lay on a trolley in the corridor with Benjamin beside her in his perspex bassinet waiting to be wheeled down to the ward. She wished she had done it all better and had not cried; she had not imagined such pain was possible. She watched her baby breathe. There could not be anything wrong with him if they would leave him alone with her, she thought. But she did not dare sleep in case he died when she was not watching him. In the ward, she left her light on all night so she could see him. She fell asleep as the dawn lightened the room, she could stay awake no longer.

When she woke up two hours later she moved the cradle nearer; she could not bear to have him at the end of her bed as the others did. She fed him whenever he woke up. He very rarely cried.

In the afternoon the curtains surrounding her bed parted and Edmund came and sat beside her. "Benjamin is a very lovely baby," he said.

"I think so anyway," said Antonia, but this was false modesty. She was sure everyone must be struck by his amazing beauty; it was very obvious. "I'm sorry I was so bad yesterday," she said. "I feel very humiliated by it all."

"But you were wonderful. We have far worse than you every day. You did very well."

"But I was very rude to everyone and threw up."

"So do lots of other women," he said.

"No one ever told me that."

"Well, it's true anyway. And lots of women are far ruder than you, too."

"I'm glad of that, at least." Antonia smiled.

"Do you feel all right?" Edmund asked.

"Yes, I feel wonderful, though rather battered, as if I have been in a car crash or something like that. Rather shocked."

"Did you sleep last night?"

"Not much. I was too excited. But tell me what happened at the end when Ben was being born. It was all such a muddle and I do want to know."

"His head got stuck and you had to have forceps. The senior registrar delivered him and did your fancy stitches for you because he had such a crowd to admire his handiwork."

"So you didn't deliver him?"

"No." It was Edmund's turn to smile.

"Have you delivered many babies?"

"No," he said. "Yours would have been the second. I only started work on this ward yesterday."

"But you didn't tell me that then."

"I didn't think it would have inspired much confidence if I had."

"But anyway I'm very glad you were there. I don't think I would have coped very well on my own."

"I think you have, Antonia. You seem quite self-reliant to me." Then he asked, "You don't want me to call you Mrs. Acton, do you?"

"No, please call me Antonia."

"Is anyone coming to visit you?" Edmund asked, looking at the top of her locker, which was bare of flowers unlike the others in the room, which groaned beneath the weight of wilting bouquets tied with the appropriate pink or blue ribbons.

"Oh, Elinor, the girl whose house I'm living in, will come later I think and probably Simon who lives there as well."

"Will Alexis come?"

"No," said Antonia. She had hated Alexis the night before for not being there. She felt very far away from him though she had sent him a telegram that morning. She wondered how much she had told Edmund about Alexis; not much she thought. She could not remember their conversation very clearly, nor anything else for that matter. She remembered that she had told Edmund that she was frightened of dying before she could see the baby.

Edmund stood up. "Well, I must go now," he said. "I'll try to get in to see you again before you go home. Because even though I failed to deliver him, Ben is sort of mine."

"That would be nice," said Antonia. "Please do come."

He smiled down at Benjamin who continued sleeping, his hands in tight fists. "He is the most marvellous baby," Edmund said.

Antonia was glad that Edmund shared her opinion of her son.

"Do try to get some sleep," he said.

"I will," said Antonia, feeling very close to him since they had been through so much together.

Margaret Dawson, the girl to whom Edmund was engaged, sat at the kitchen table marking piles of grubby exercise books. She smiled at Edmund briefly as he kissed the top of her head. "I'm sorry I forgot to get the things from the laundrette," he said. "I'll go out and get them later." He sat down wearily at the table opposite her.

"It's all right, I will," she said. "You must be exhausted."

Though in theory the house was run by both of them equally, Margaret tended to end up doing more of the tedious chores, which made Edmund feel guilty.

Margaret pushed aside the heap of books with a sigh. "Do you think it really matters if they ever know the difference between *their* and *there*, and *hair* and *hare*, and *where* and *wear*? I sometimes think I'm merely keeping them off the streets so they don't get pregnant at fourteen and give you lots of extra work. And how was your Italian waif today?"

"She isn't Italian, she's English. And she seemed very cheerful after all she went through last night. It's quite a relief to know I will never have go to through all that. The baby is lovely though."

"But what will happen to them? It makes me shudder to think sometimes of the fecklessness of some of these people breeding so randomly and bringing children into the world without a thought."

Edmund poured himself some more coffee. "I don't think Antonia is feckless exactly. I think she wanted the baby very much." He thought of Antonia's fragile face, those vast blue eyes and the love pouring from them as she looked at her son.

"But surely these things should be planned?" Margaret said.

"Of course they should be, but they aren't always." He closed his eyes for a moment. With Margaret everything was ordered, organised. She felt she was battling against an encroaching tide of lawlessness and ignorance. She liked being a teacher and no doubt she was a good one, but she felt it was her duty to impose some order upon other people's muddled lives. She was sturdy and comfortable and he had allowed her to organise his life. They would be married the following summer. Mrs. Dawson, her formidable mother, had already ordered the tent. She had put a deposit down on one with pink candy stripes in the interior and flaps which could be raised if the day was fine.

"I think I'll go to bed," said Edmund. "I hope you didn't make anything special for supper."

"No, go ahead. I'll just finish these books if you don't mind." She took the shepherd's pie she had made out of the oven and let it cool on the table. They could always eat it the next day.

Antonia had not realised how overwhelming the love she felt for Ben would be. She had read all the cautionary tales about how one had sometimes to learn to love a child. But she had fallen in love with her son instantly and totally. He was so perfect in every way that she could not believe that he would live. And yet he did.

Life in hospital was far removed from an ordinary existence, a hothouse life where only orchids thrived. And in that strange world Antonia recaptured an intensity of feeling she thought she had lost forever. She wished, fleetingly, that Alexis could see her son (she thought of him now as her production entirely). She knew he would be very proud of him and be charmed by his novelty. But she did not want Alexis as the father of her child, not every day. She wondered if she had been very wrong, had sinned against him, by bringing him into the world without a father. She began to think so, seeing other fathers with their children.

When the nurses found her weeping on the third day, Antonia was most apologetic. She did not want them to think they had upset her because they had not. She knew it was normal. Perhaps I'll go mad, she thought—she had read all the books, after all. She did not go mad but just lay in bed and cried uncontrollably and indulgently, blood and tears and milk flowing out of her. She felt like some primeval mammal linked with all the other mothers in the history of the world and was not entirely displeased with the notion.

Elinor and Simon came to visit her every day, bringing wine and fruit and toys for Ben. He was particularly taken with a knitted teddy bear Elinor's mother had bought at a church bazaar, or so it seemed to Antonia. Antonia was glad to have visitors. Elinor suggested that Antonia call her father and tell him the news, but she did not have the courage. She wondered how he would react to being a grandfather.

As each day passed Antonia felt her connection to Alexis fading. She started thinking for the first time of the rest of her life. She had been waiting for Ben to be born for so long. It had seemed too substantial an event to think beyond. But now she was entirely responsible for another person's welfare and it frightened her. She lay awake at night watching Ben as he slept, so still and so white. She would touch his long eyelashes with her finger very gently to see if he would react, to make sure he had not slipped away when she was not looking. Sleep seemed to be the last unattainable luxury, better than food or drugs, and more satisfying. She felt tortured by the lack of definition between night and day. Antonia saw Edmund just once more, very briefly as he was on the way to see some of his other babies, ones he had actually delivered himself.

When he turned and walked off down the bleak institutional corridor Antonia was sorry that she would never see him again.

The outside world came as a shock to her when she was discharged, such a mass of humanity walking in the streets, and so many cars and noises and buses and sirens which she had not noticed before. Now she heard it all with Ben's ears and wanted to protect him.

Elinor had filled her room with flowers, which looked very welcoming as Antonia lay in bed and admired the autumnal colours. But she felt utterly exhausted and panicked at not being surrounded by potential sources of help as she had been in hospital. When Elinor and Simon left for work Antonia longed for the midwife's visit. When she eventually did arrive and had checked both Ben and Antonia's stitches, Antonia offered her a cup of tea, hoping she would stay, but she could not; she was very busy and had other mothers to see. Antonia was entranced by Ben's growing loveliness, but she longed for Elinor to get home so she would not be alone with her onerous responsibilities.

One day she fainted in the bathroom when she was alone, which terrified her. What would have happened if she had been holding Ben? She imagined his head cracked open like an eggshell and his brains spilled on the carpet. Antonia rang the midwife who told her to stay in bed. She continued to bleed, which the midwife said was normal but she imagined her life blood dripping away. And what would happen to Ben if she died?

After two more days Antonia thought she should get up. She could not lie in bed indefinitely like someone in a Victorian novel. She decided to go to Brixton to buy a sterilising unit. She had convinced herself this was necessary though it obviously was not since she had a horror of bottles and the germs they bred and had never used any of the six she had been given. But the midwife had said she should have one, and so she must. Elinor would watch the baby, but still Antonia was reluctant to leave him.

It was a Saturday and the streets which had once seemed friendly and interesting now seemed very crowded and overwhelmingly alarming. It took Antonia a very long time to chose which steriliser to buy, which she knew was absurd since there were only two kinds. But she had not been into a shop for ten days and they seemed very alien and the queues very long. Perhaps Ben is crying for me, she thought, perhaps something terrible has happened. The house might be on fire for all she knew. A fat Jamaican woman stood in front of Antonia in the queue, blocking her view of the cash register. Antonia thought the woman at the till was dawdling to provoke her. She looked into the woman's basket; so many things she could not possibly need! Surely she would let her go first if she knew how important it was, but Antonia did not ask. She paid for the steriliser and rushed out the door, up past the shoe shop to the bus stop. There was the usual crowd of housewives with laden shopping baskets, old men in shabby suits and boys lounging in Woolworth's doorway.

She could see a bus coming under the railway bridge and strained her eyes to see what number it was. It was not the one she wanted. She braced herself against the bus shelter as the crowd surged past her, knocking into her with their elbows and their baskets. She clutched her awkward parcel to her, fearing it would be knocked out of her hands by the mob.

She saw Edmund walking towards her, smiling, and thought at first that she must have imagined seeing him, so fortuitous was his appearance. She was surprised he recognised her out of bed, standing up, wearing clothes. He looked taller than she remembered.

"Antonia! How lovely to see you." He took the parcel from her. She started feeling very dislocated and distant. She did not think she could deal with the crowd anymore; she could not stand up anymore. She started to see blackness clouding his face. She clutched his arm.

"I'm terribly sorry," she said, "I think I'm going to faint." And did.

The crowd at the bus stop was fascinated to see someone lying on the ground not drunk or stabbed.

When Antonia felt a little better and could walk they took a taxi from the rank outside the library back to Elinor's.

Elinor let them in, laid Antonia unceremoniously on the sofa with a rug over her and turned to Edmund. "Oh, Lord," she said, "do you think she's all right?"

"I expect so," he replied. "But perhaps you could ask the midwife to come over this afternoon to check."

"Are you Edmund?" Elinor asked, since Antonia had not felt up to making formal introductions.

"Yes. How could you guess?"

"Oh, Antonia told me all about you. Rather bad luck to waste all that time and miss actually delivering Ben. Do stay for lunch. I was just making it."

Antonia loved Elinor, and wondered, as she so often had, what it would take to throw her utterly. Nothing so trivial as collapsed bodies being hauled into the house by total strangers, she knew. Ben had slept through the whole thing with characteristic unconcern.

It was warm enough to eat in the garden, and they had bread and cheese and fruit amidst the pink and blue drifts of Michaelmas daisies and the falling leaves. After lunch Elinor disappeared into the house to catch up on her reading and left Edmund and Antonia alone with Ben, whom Antonia fed. He went peacefully back to sleep. Antonia was amazed at his goodness and docility.

Edmund then told Antonia all about his family, who lived in a genteel suburb of Birmingham. Antonia could picture his parents as he described them: his mother, her beauty now faded, who had once been a nurse and who now kept their house as sterile as a hospital ward, and his serious, distant father, who was the headmaster of a Grammar School. He was their only son, their gift to posterity. He described them very well and with great humour. Antonia could almost feel that enclosed world of real but dutiful affection. It sounded quite soothing to her. He described his room, which his mother kept as a shrine to his boyhood, full of photos of cricket teams and soccer teams and rugger teams full of boys with short hair, grinning, trying to look tough. She had seen such photos in Simon's room in Cornwall long ago. She envisioned the bookshelves full of adventure stories and old copies of *Beano*. Edmund said it was all there quite intact.

He described the garden, which he said had once seemed full of jungle creatures and romance but was now clipped into lines of polite rigidity. There was a fish pond which had once had fish in it but no longer did, and a stone birdbath full of moss. His parents' neighbours (to whom they rarely spoke) envied his father his weedless lawn. They had created their own private kingdom, inviolate. Nothing ever changed, he said, not the food nor the curtains, nothing. Antonia wished that she had a home which never changed.

"Do you go there often?" she asked, wondering what it would feel like to have lived in the same house all one's life.

"Not very often," he said, "though they look forward to seeing me, I think."

Antonia, in turn, told Edmund about her family, how she had hated leaving Field End and most of what had happened since. He seemed very interested, which Alexis never had been. She studied his face, with its straight nose and dark brows, much darker than his hair. His eyes were gray, the colour of an overcast sky, but amused. His face, which at first had seemed ordinary, was no longer so to Antonia.

"Do you live near here?" she asked.

"Very near, in fact."

"Do you live alone?"

"No, I live with someone who teaches in Peckham. It's her house. She bought it two years ago just after we left university." He told her quite a lot about Margaret, and the unusual children she taught. Antonia thought she sounded very nice and very sane. She envied Margaret living with someone so kind. She thought she would have liked to meet Margaret. She supposed if she were going to stay in London she might but then realised she would not. She longed to know what Margaret looked like, but Edmund did not tell her and she did not ask.

"So, you're going back to Italy soon?"

"Next week, I think."

"Are you looking forward to it very much?"

"I don't know. But I must show Alexis his son. And the city is so much more beautiful than London."

That afternoon in the garden, hidden from the street and the filth that littered it—the crushed cigarette packets, the fish and chips wrappers stained with vinegar and ketchup—even Brixton had a certain charm. Reluctantly, Edmund looked at his watch. "She'll be expecting me," he said. "I seem to have been gone a very long time for someone who was only going to buy pickled onions at Tesco's."

He said good-bye to Elinor and thanked her for lunch. Elinor said she hoped she would see him again since he lived so near. He and Margaret must come to dinner very soon.

When he had gone Elinor said, "What nice people you seem to pick up in hospital. I must have a baby some day and see who turns up."

Antonia went to her room and started planning her departure.

It was nearly four o'clock when Edmund returned to the house in Herne Hill.

"Thank heavens you're here at last," said Margaret, rather flustered. "I thought I reminded you Mummy and Daddy are coming for supper."

The house was immaculately clean, and Edmund realised that Margaret had probably spend the morning sweeping and dusting and had even attacked the inside of the oven, which was her least favourite task; the acrid smell of oven cleaner still lingered in the air.

"I'm sorry. I went to the pub with Bill and quite forgot the time." It was the first time he had lied to her. It was lucky that she had her back turned to him when he answered and was too busy looking for the fish knives her mother had given them the previous Christmas to notice his expression.

Edmund went into the sitting room and plumped up the cushions on the sofa, which was unnecessary since the room was perfectly tidy already. He felt he had to do something. I am suburban already, he thought, tamed, subdued. I will never do anything exciting, ever.

An hour later Margaret's parents arrived and were quite pleasant to him, as they had become ever since the engagement had become official in the spring. Prior to that they had been rather frosty (understandably, Edmund thought) to someone who had so defiled their daughter. Mr. Dawson drove a Jaguar, the kind of car which Edmund's father could never have afforded (even if he had wanted one). Mrs. Dawson talked about bridesmaids and how many layers they would have on the cake.

Margaret looked her apologies to Edmund over the dinner table. "I know they are boring," she seemed to say, "thank you for being so patient." Kind Margaret, in her sensible dress from Marks & Spencer's, the perfect daughter who would do her best to be a perfect wife.

Later, when they were getting ready for bed, Margaret said, "I promise never to become like her." But Edmund knew that she would.

"You seem very depressed, Eddie." She nuzzled his shoulder. "Is it something I've done?"

"No, nothing. Really." He rubbed her freckled back and thought that he should make love to her, but he could not. "I'm sorry, Margaret, I hope you won't mind. I'm still terribly tired."

"Eddie, you don't have to make love to me to show that you love me. We know each other better than that."

Edmund slept and dreamed of rows of little Margaret clones with sturdy legs, doing homework round a vast kitchen table. One of them turned her broad cheerful face up to him and said, "I know that you love me, Daddy."

And the worst of it was that he did.

Twenty

Antonia, like Clare, had always liked trains and the adventure of travel when everything was suspended. Rather like waiting for the baby to be born, Antonia thought, when everything was concentrated on a final point.

She watched Ben sleeping in his carrycot. She had taken off his knitted cap and could see the pulse beating beneath his thin unprotecting skin and the sparse hair which was flattened against his fragile skull. He breathed easily, lightly, and occasionally his mouth moved, searching for food in his dreams. Antonia stroked his hair very gently, not wishing to disturb him. Pink and white flesh and a pale blue babygro, and tiny unused fingers made into fists in sleep. He was so perfect and so small. So you're going to see your daddy, Ben, she thought. I think he will like you very much. How could he not?

Antonia did not regret leaving England, as the flat Kentish hop fields sped past the window. She thought of the last time she had made this journey alone and how different everything would be from now on.

Miraculously she found a porter to help her with her luggage at

Folkestone, but all the clatter woke Ben up with a start and he began to wail. Antonia hated hearing him cry and looked for a suitable place to feed him, away from prying eyes. The boat was full of boisterous public school children whose voices grated on Antonia's ears. How confident they sounded, how they pushed themselves forward, how arrogant they were! She would never allow Ben to become like that. Everything would be quite different when he grew up she was sure, but she did not know exactly how.

The train drew into the Florence station at four the next afternoon. Antonia felt filthy and wondered if Alexis would be there to meet her as he had said he would. She knew she did not look her best for him but did not care. She just wanted to stop moving and lie down. She looked out of the train window and Alexis was there, waving wildly. He helped her down out of the train and with the carrycot and her bags.

"I've waited so long to see him, Antonia." He kissed her cheek hurriedly, and when he looked for the first time at his son his face was quite changed and rapt, amazed at what he saw, at such perfection.

"He's beautiful," he said. "Marvellous. But I had not imagined he would be so small. Is he all right?"

"Oh, yes, he's quite all right. They are small at first, you know. He'll grow."

Alexis studied the small sleeping form. "My son," he said, as if trying out the words for size. "My son," he said again, smiling ridiculously broadly.

Antonia winced because Ben was hers, too, but she did not say anything. Antonia was surprised at the foreignness of the familiar station; everything seemed different than when she had last seen it: the newspapers, the advertisements, even the smell. It was warmer than London and the wind blew dust into their eyes from the pavements. Antonia was exhausted and wondered if it would be extravagant to take a taxi. Alexis carried her bags and Antonia pushed the pram.

"I've got enough money for a taxi," Antonia suggested.

"We don't need one, we can walk."

Antonia did not know if Alexis ever took taxis, it was the sort of thing she had never known about him. He was so bouncy and full of energy. They eventually compromised and took a bus.

Alexis had arranged a large welcoming committee for his son, mostly men and mostly Greek. Antonia could not understand much of what they were saying and was too tired to care. She drank a large glass of wine (though she would have preferred tea) and left them admiring Ben while she fled to the bathroom and attempted to wash some of the smell of the train off her face and hands. She heard Ben crying. They probably frightened him, she thought. She wished all of them would go away and leave her alone. She went into the room and rescued her baby. She could not bear alien hands to touch him. His nappy was soggy; he was tired, too, and only wanted to suck and sleep.

Alexis was ecstatically happy; it was beaming all over his face. He looked very attractive and very young. He was so proud.

"Please make them go soon," Antonia whispered to him when she could bear the noise no longer.

"Why? Don't you want to show off our son?"

"Of course I do, but not just now. All I really want is to go to bed."

He smiled, quite misunderstanding her, and his friends were persuaded to leave. Antonia collapsed onto the bed. It was heaven to lie still, not to move. Alexis came and sat by her on the bed.

"We are very clever, you and I, aren't we?" he said.

"Very."

Alexis looked into his son's face and Antonia's heart melted with happiness. Alexis rolled onto the bed and lay beside her, stroking her breast; he was hard already.

She had dreaded this moment. She should have been prepared for it but was not. She had suppressed the thought of making love, and at that moment did not care if she never did, ever again.

"I'm not meant to, not until Ben is six weeks old." She smiled at Alexis placatingly, wondering how he would take this deprivation.

"But I won't hurt you. I will be very gentle."

She could deny him nothing then, he was so happy. She was not prepared for the pain and smothered her screams in the sheets. She hoped he would finish quickly, she did not know how much more she could bear. Every moment was worse than the last, her fingernails scraped into her palms, drawing blood. At last it was over. He rolled onto his side.

"I've waited so long, Antonia. I haven't been with anyone else. Was it good for you, too?"

Horrible! Horrible! "I'm so glad to be back," she said. She liked the thought that he had been constant to her even as she doubted it. It was enough that he thought he had been.

Morning: the sound of metal shutters being drawn up, of cars in the street and a pattern of light on the red-tiled floor. Antonia threw open the shutters and looked at the houses opposite. She washed her hair before either Ben or Alexis were awake. She made coffee in the percolator, strong and black. She felt more cheerful and alive than she had in days. She discovered that there was nothing to eat in the apartment, only a stale heel of bread with mould on it which Alexis had been too idle to throw out. She felt very hungry but did not like to risk going out in case Ben woke up and cried for her. She would ask Alexis to go out. He usually did not like running errands, but she thought perhaps he would today. She looked at him sleeping, the long dark lashes which Ben had inherited spread out on his cheek. He did not look at all like her image of what a father should be. He awoke as she stood staring at him.

"Come back to bed. It's much too early to get up." He made a place for her beside him and nuzzled her flesh. "You were gone so long. You don't know how I've missed you. Let's make love before the baby wakes up."

"Please, Alexis, really I can't. It hurts too much."

"It didn't hurt too much last night, did it?"

What could she say not to hurt him? Not to disappoint him?

Luckily, just at that moment, Ben woke up and wailed.

"I'll pick him up." Alexis leapt naked from the bed and lifted the soggy baby very gently. Ben continued howling, protesting Alexis' unfamiliar smell.

"I think he wants you." Alexis looked quite crestfallen.

Antonia changed and fed the baby, his heavy head wobbling against her breast, smelling of warm toast.

"There's coffee in the pot, Alexis." She usually brought it to him but she could not then, feeding the baby. "I'm starving, too. Could you go out and get us something to eat?"

"Of course. What would you like?"

"Oh, I don't know, anything will do. You could try at the bar on the corner."

He was eager to help her as he had been when they were first together. Alexis went out and brought back buns wrapped in pink wax paper.

"I remember which kind you liked," he said in case she had not noticed the effort he had made for her.

"Thank you, Alexis."

He was very pleased with himself that morning, with life in general, with Ben and with having Antonia back. He said that he had been worried that she would never return, that he would never see his son. He was glad that he had a son, not a daughter. It made him more of a man, he thought.

"What shall we do today? I won't go to the university. We'll make a holiday just for us."

Alexis' idea of a holiday consisted of making a long tour of his friends and acquaintances. Antonia carried the baby in his sling and un-wrapped him at each stop where Ben's beauty, and Alexis' remarkable cleverness in producing such a fine specimen, were duly noted. They ate lunch sitting in the sun in the Piazza S. Croce on the warm steps of the fountain.

"How was England?" Alexis asked. He had not seemed interested before.

"Oh, fine," said Antonia, "quite sunny in patches." She did not like to go into her bourgeois life there.

"And what does your father think of our son?"

"Nothing. He doesn't even know he exists."

"So he didn't give you any money?"

"No." Antonia knew Alexis hoped she would have extracted some money from her father. He knew her father was rich, and the rich have their uses, even to those who do not subscribe to their system. Antonia knew Alexis was disappointed, though of course it was against his principles to say so. They went back to the apartment, which they had

245

to themselves. Stratos had gone back to Greece to visit his dying grandfather. It was sad for Stratos of course, but convenient for them, a positive luxury to have two whole rooms and a bathroom to themselves.

Antonia settled Ben for his rest and started to do some washing. "Don't do that now," said Alexis. "Surely it can wait? Come here." He lay on the bed looking up at her. "What does it feel like having a baby?"

"It hurts." It was the only thing she could think of saying just then, she was so cross with him.

"You look beautiful when you are angry, Antonia."

"Oh, God, Alexis. Where did you get that line from?" She had to smile. She thought he probably meant it.

His tone to her that day was so soothing and persuasive that she could not refuse to make love to him though she knew she ought to. It still hurt, burning and tearing. She could still feel where the stitches had been, or still were, for all she knew. She saw blood on the towel when she washed herself afterwards, fresh red blood in bright spots on the white towel. She put it to soak in the bidet with the nappies. It hurt when she sat down.

"Well, Antonia," said Clare as she stood in the doorway beaming. "How wonderful to see you. But you look ghastly, if I may say so. How are you?" She hugged Antonia and then handed her the huge bunch of white daisies she had brought her.

"Actually, I'm fine," said Antonia putting the flowers in water.

"And where is Ben, the infant marvel?"

"Asleep. You can look at him if you like."

"What a wonderful-looking baby, but we all expected that." Clare looked about her. "Where's Alexis?"

"He's asleep, too. So we can talk in peace."

"So how did it all go? Elinor told me a bit on the phone, but I want to hear all of it, every gruesome detail."

Antonia thought how nice it was to have a friend who was so genuinely riveted by her life.

"And what are you going to do now?" Clare asked at last.

"Oh, it's much too soon to think about all that. I only got back yesterday after all."

"I gather you didn't get any money," said Clare. "You won't be able to work. You'll have to think of something to do at home."

"The only thing I can think of is stringing beads, but I don't think I'd find that very fascinating after a few days."

"I can't imagine you with Ben selling them on the Ponte Vecchio like one of the gypsies," said Clare, smiling.

"No, I can't either." Antonia did not want to think about money just then and changed the subject. "How's Richard?"

"Very well, and longing to see you and Ben. He suggested that perhaps you could model for me, and I could pay you a little bit if you need the money."

"Thank you. I might need it, but I would hate to take it from you." Antonia knew the precarious state of Clare's finances and thought she would have to be very desperate to take Clare up on her offer. Like Mr. Micawber, Antonia always thought something would turn up. "But tell me what you have been doing, Clare."

"Much the same as usual. Painting like a fiend and wandering about. I'm doing all still lifes at the moment, working on the effects of light, and the paintings are getting vaster than ever. Some of them are rather good. I hope you like them."

Alexis went out, slamming the door behind him. He had not bothered to say hello to Clare. He probably thought they were discussing him, which they did once he was safely out in the street.

"And how goes it with Alexis?"

"Fine, Clare. He thinks Ben is the most marvellous thing he ever beheld. He's very pleased with himself."

"Does he realise yet how much work a baby is?"

"Luckily he hasn't the least idea," Antonia said.

"And you really feel okay?"

"Okay-ish. The stitches still hurt."

"Has he tried to make love to you yet?"

"Yes—and that hurt, too."

"Oh, my God, Toe. You're so stupid. Why on earth did you let him? You shouldn't have."

"Of course I shouldn't have. But I didn't know what to say that wouldn't make him miserable and make his face crumple up like a child whose sweets are taken away."

"Let it crumple, for Christ's sake. He's got no right to hurt you. Didn't he realise?"

"I didn't tell him that it hurt if that's what you mean. I chewed on the sheet," Antonia added lamely.

Clare was quite furious by now. "I think you are demented. I really do. Why don't you leave him?"

"But he's so pleased to have us back. Besides which he's so proud of himself for being faithful to me in my absence."

"Well, he wasn't." Actually Antonia knew this already. She had found some Tampax in the bathroom cupboard. Other than that he had covered his tracks very well. She did not want to know any more.

"Oh, Clare, I do want to believe him when he is trying to be so nice."

They sat in silence for a moment. Then Antonia said, "I'm afraid of being alone, Clare. And he's so charmed by the idea of being a father."

"He would be. I wonder how long that will last."

"Why are you always so nasty about Alexis?"

"Because he's fairly nasty himself. He's got you exactly where he wants you, barefoot and pregnant and in the kitchen . . . well not pregnant anymore, but anyway, for all his fine talk about equality between the sexes et cetera, et cetera, he's an absolute Fascist when it comes down to it."

"Don't you think I know all this?" Antonia burst into tears and Clare held her. "But what can I do?"

"You could come and live with us for a bit while you decide." Clare patted Antonia's shoulder.

"That's terribly kind of you, but I'm all right, really I am. Perhaps Alexis will become a reformed character and a doting daddy. You never know." She wiped her eyes with a spare nappy. "Let's go for a walk. I'm sure Alexis won't get back until at least nine."

Antonia put Ben in his pram and they walked out into the street. Night was slowly falling over the magical city and they leaned over a bridge and saw the lights reflected in the dark water beneath them.

"Do you think the rats are still there in this weather?" Clare asked.

One of her summer evening pastimes was watching the ugly creatures scampering in the mud beneath Ponte Santa Trinita.

"I think they are always there," said Antonia, who wanted to be in Florence even with its rats. "I missed the city physically, you know, Clare. I longed to see it again. I feel quite at home now amongst all the chaos and the beauty of it."

They ran into Laura dawdling down a side street. "Let's go to a bar," she said, glancing at her watch. "I haven't eaten for at least an hour. I'll buy you both doughnuts."

"I'm so glad Antonia is back, aren't you, Laura?"

"Certainly," said Laura, and Antonia looked at the sugar on her chin and laughed.

Antonia kept hoping that things would get better, that her stitches would not hurt, that Alexis would have more patience and come to terms with the changes the baby had brought. She wished that Alexis would come to love him as a baby, not simply as an object to be shown off. In a way, Alexis did love him. Antonia would catch him gazing at Ben's naked body as she bathed him in the sink or when he lay kicking on his rug by the open window. She was furious with Ben when he cried when Alexis held him. But how could he realise how important it was for him to be good for his father? He could not do that anymore than he could refrain from waking up in the night, or remain dry, or smile at Alexis, or need her less than he did. She tried to shield them from each other, took Ben into the other room to nurse him in the night. Heaven knew what would happen when Stratos reappeared and needed his room. She washed the nappies before Alexis woke up in the morning and never asked him to buy things for the baby or carry the pram up the stairs (all thirty-two of them). She never asked him where he had been, though he felt quite justified in asking her where she had been if she was not there when he returned. She had been back ten days when he said, "Don't you love me any more, Antonia?"

She looked up from folding some of Ben's clothes. "Of course I do."

"You don't seem to, not like you used to," Alexis said, petulantly.

Antonia wanted to say everything was different now that she had Ben to look after but didn't. She was so tired. She had not had more than four hours' sleep at a stretch since before Ben was born. And she worried constantly about him. What if she fell down the stairs when she was carrying him? What if he just died one day when she was not looking? She was still incapable of leaving him for an instant and was constantly checking his breathing and touching him to make sure he was still warm.

Alexis began to stay out all night. In a way Antonia did not care. It saved her from having to make excuses not to make love or else to go through with it unwillingly. But she wondered where he was and with whom. The apartment was still in her name and the rent was paid until the middle of December. Then she would have to decide what to do.

Eventually, since her money had dwindled quite alarmingly, Antonia agreed to model for Clare. The small sum that Clare was able to give her was enough to buy coffee with. Antonia realised all at once how expensive everything had become. Alexis continued to tell her she was stupid not to talk to her father. She was getting thinner than ever though she thought she was eating a great deal. She knew she had to, for Ben's sake. She was so tired that she stopped thinking very much and felt that getting through each day was an achievement in itself. She was glad she did not have a clock. She did not want to know how often she was awakened in the night, and preferred to time her day by the noises in the street. So distinct were they that she could gauge almost exactly what time it was by bells, carts, shutters and the clatter of children being dismissed from school. She started reading a great deal. She would lose herself in books which she chose by size alone; she felt quite bereft when she had not got one to hand. When not reading or posing she wandered around the city letting Ben breathe in the crisp autumn air.

Antonia was too proud to let Clare know how bad things had become. But one day she fainted while posing in the studio.

"I'm sorry, Clare. It's only the position I was in. I should have moved sooner." She lay on Clare's unmade bed, amongst the heaps of clothes and stared out of the window.

Clare made tea, stirring the mugs with fury. "I know what I'll do, Toe. I'll send Richard back with you to talk to Alexis."

"Don't," said Antonia. "It won't do any good."

"Well, he certainly won't listen to me. He hates any woman who doesn't think he's God."

"I don't think he's God, Clare."

"No, but you allow him to think he is. His mother has quite a lot to answer for."

"I think all Greek mothers do."

"But you're not Greek."

"No, I'm not. But I still don't think Richard talking to him would do any good. Rather the reverse in fact."

"Do you feel better?" asked Clare.

"Yes, I feel fine. I really ought to go now. Alexis said he would be home early this evening."

"What if he is?" said Clare, spoiling for a fight.

"He'll wonder where I am."

"Well, let him wonder for a change. Why are you so spineless? You don't endlessly ask him where he has been."

"But that's different."

"Why different?" persisted Clare.

"You wouldn't understand."

"No, I really don't, as it happens."

"Oh, Clare, stop it," Antonia screamed. "I can't bear it." She burst into tears. "I want him to love Ben so much," she said between sobs.

"He does according to his lights," Clare conceded. "He's just too young; he doesn't want responsibility. He wants the freedom to fuck anyone he fancies and have you to go home to."

It was all true. Antonia knew it but was too tired to do anything about it. Yet it was obvious she could not go on soothing first Ben and then Alexis and then fighting about it all with Clare. She stood up, picked up Ben and hugged him. "I must go home now, Clare."

"And that's another thing. You will persist in calling it home. It's not home, just two rooms with someone who treats you like shit. You must see that."

"Don't you realise, Clare, that I haven't *got* a home? That that's what all this mess is about?" She could not see for the tears which were streaming down her face. "Good night, Clare. Thanks for the tea."

"Don't mention it. Oh, you infuriate me sometimes."

"And you do me," said Antonia. But beneath it all she knew that Clare was the best friend she had in Florence, or anywhere else for that matter. It was almost—but not quite—like having a sister.

Of course Alexis was not there when she got back to via Torta. She decided to wait up for him and ask where he had been, like a jealous wife.

She fell asleep in the armchair and was awakened by his return in the dead of night. The town was quite silent and there was no way at all to tell what time it was.

"Where were you, Alexis? I thought you said you would be back early tonight?"

"Out, visiting friends," he said shortly.

"Then why couldn't I come?"

"You wouldn't have enjoyed it."

"How do you know? You never ask me if I want to come."

"We were talking about politics all the time, and in Greek. You wouldn't have been able to understand."

She was fed up with the endless arguments between Alexis and his friends. It was true. At first she had taken them very seriously, she'd thought they were important. And she was fed up, too, with Alexis' moral condemnation of her while he continued to enjoy her body—and her money when she had any. It was all talk she had come to realise. If they were so keen to overthrow the colonels, what on earth were they doing in Italy, supposedly studying, while spending their parents' money? Richard had pointed this last fact out to her. It would have taken her much longer to discover it for herself, she was so willing to give Alexis the benefit of the doubt.

Alexis was angry. He had not expected to be met by anything but welcoming flesh. He went into the other room and read, sitting sulkily on the floor under the lamp. Antonia knew he was doing it in order to provoke her so she ignored him and went to bed.

Eventually he came to bed, where Antonia lay, pretending to be asleep.

"Are you really asleep?" he said, coaxingly.

"No, actually I'm wide awake," she snapped.

"Are you very angry?" he asked in his best little-boy-wheedling tone. He managed to look charming and wistful.

"Yes, I'm furious. You exclude me entirely from your life. I never know where you are or who you are with. You are never here, and you expect me to be all smiles and leap into bed with you at whatever hour you deign to turn up."

"And all you ever think about is yourself and Ben. You should hear yourself." He mimicked her voice. "I must feed Ben. I must change Ben. Ben needs some fresh air. Ben this, Ben that."

It was true the baby was very time-consuming, but he needed her, as Alexis did not.

Alexis turned to her. "Why are you so cross all the time? Didn't having the baby make you happy?"

"Of course it did," she said and sighed. She was so tired. She wanted to sleep, to sleep for twelve hours at least, to wake when she felt like it.

"Then cheer up and we will make love."

"I don't want to," she said.

This threw him. She had never confronted him so directly before. "Then I'll go and sleep in the other room." He stamped off into Stratos' room taking the one warm blanket with him.

Ben woke up and started crying and would not be soothed.

"Can't you ever get that baby to shut up?" Alexis yelled.

"He's your baby, too, if you recall," Antonia shouted back. Since Ben was already crying she did not have to worry about disturbing him.

"How can you be so sure, *putana*," he said very nastily.

Of course she was sure. She would not have put up with his tantrums for so long had she not been.

Alexis went out very early the next morning without speaking to her, leaving his coffee cup on the floor for her to pick up. She did not see it and kicked it and it broke on the red tiles and cut her toe. There were no adhesive plasters left and she had to staunch the blood with toilet paper. She felt lucky she had not dropped Ben, who smiled his amiable confused smile. He looked slightly puzzled as his blue eyes scanned her face.

"Well, my angel, at least I didn't kill you this time," she said, sinking her face into the warmth of his neck.

She sat in the armchair by the window trying to coax another smile from him, holding out flowers for him to look at, which he tried to grasp with his hand but failed.

Clare arrived carrying a bottle of wine. She poured out two glasses and handed one to Antonia. The December sunlight caught her face and fell weakly onto the floor. "I have been offered an exhibition in London, Toe. You must congratulate me!"

"But that's wonderful, Clare. Aren't you thrilled?"

"I would be if it was at a more prestigious gallery, and of course it's only a joint exhibition. But it is something after all." Clare smiled. "Fame at last," she said. "Actually it's with three other women, one of whom I knew in Oxford. I think they are going to call it 'Women and Light,' which sounds perfectly ghastly to me but never mind."

Antonia could tell Clare was pleased however dismissive she thought it necessary to sound. She wanted everything she did to appear effortless and easy when Antonia knew it was not. She had been working very hard lately and was beginning to take her work very seriously.

"And in the same post," said Clare, "I got a wonderfully funny letter from Elinor telling me how furious Mummy is getting about neither of us getting married. Apparently, one of the things Mummy finds most difficult is trying to think what to call Simon when he goes there to stay and how to introduce him. And she also wonders when she will ever meet Richard. All this living together is getting to be too much. El says she thinks Mummy wants to call it living in sin but daren't. El also said, and this might interest you, that she and Simon had your wonderful Edmund to dinner the other night with his girlfriend, and that they both thought he was charming, and she was, too, if a bit on the dull side."

"How nice for them," said Antonia. "I thought they would get on. Edmund was incredibly nice to me, you know."

"Was he? El said he was very interested to hear how you were. She got the impression he was rather taken with you."

Antonia smiled. "As I was with him actually." She got up and went into the next room to retrieve Ben, who had started whimpering miserably.

"You liked him very much, didn't you?" Clare said, following

Antonia into the other room. "What amazes me, Antonia, is that you never actually do anything to try to save yourself."

"But what could I do, Clare? Even if he does like me, what of it? He is in England living with someone with all sorts of estimable qualities whom he never once said anything the least derogatory about. And I am here in an awful trap of my own making with Alexis and Ben, which I feel quite incapable of springing."

"So you admit you think about him?"

"Of course I do, Clare. But I don't want to; it makes me too miserable."

"Have you mentioned Edmund to Alexis?" Clare asked after a bit, while idly demolishing the bunch of grapes Antonia was saving for supper.

"Of course not. Do you think I'm quite mad? What should I have said? Oh, by the way, Alexis, while I was in England I fell madly in love with someone who is as good as married. Of course I'm not going to do anything about it, but I thought I'd just let you know." Clare giggled and finished the bottle of wine. Antonia did not know whether to laugh or cry.

Just then Alexis came in looking disgusted at all the mess Clare had managed to create in the short time she had been there. And she did not leave as Antonia half wished she would, but just sat there chatting about her family and England while Alexis got crosser and crosser. He eventually went out again.

"I wish you wouldn't make Alexis so angry, Clare. He's only viler to me later."

"But it's your apartment. If you let him get away with being so bloody all the time he'll only get worse."

"I suppose so. You are good for me, Clare. It's about time the worm turned, isn't it?"

"Wildly overdue if you ask me." Clare tossed the empty wine bottle into the wastepaper basket, which rolled over and spread its contents on the floor. She went out and bought paint and spent the afternoon fantasising about becoming rich and famous, wishing everyone could be as happy as she was.

Twenty-One

"**D**o you want to go to India, Clare?" Richard lay on his back looking up at the hooks which had once held the skins of dead animals.

This is what she had been waiting for and had dreaded; Richard had never remained in Florence for so long. She propped herself up on one elbow and looked down at him. "What do you mean, Richard? Are you asking in a general sort of a way or in particular?"

"I was asking if you wanted to go with me."

"Do you want me to?"

"I don't know."

"Then that makes two don't knows." Clare added, "But I'm glad to have been asked."

"I've never asked anyone to travel with me before," Richard said.

"I did realize that." Clare rolled over and buried her face against Richard's chest and hugged him; he was here now, at least. "I suppose you have to go. I always knew you would sooner or later. But I had hoped it would be later."

He rubbed her back with his hand. "I asked if you wanted to come with me."

"But you don't want me to, really. You want to be by yourself, unencumbered; you always said you experienced things better on your own."

"If you don't come I will miss you, but if you do we might well end up hating each other. I don't want that, Clare."

When Antonia went to the studio the next week Clare was not there. "Where is Clare, Richard?" she asked.

He looked up from his typing, as if angry to be disturbed. "She left for England last night. She lost a filling and her grandmother is ill."

"Is it serious?"

"No. Nor was the tooth. I can't imagine why she thought she had to go to England. There are dentists here but she's convinced they're all butchers."

"I suppose you'll miss her," said Antonia. Clearly, Richard was on edge and this flustered her so she could only come out with banalities.

"Yes. I will." Richard looked at Clare's things scattered about the studio—her canvases and her clothes, all disordered from her hasty departure. "Did Clare tell you that I'm going to India in January?"

"No! Is Clare going with you?"

"I doubt it."

"But you will come back, won't you?"

"I always have." Here Richard smiled for the first time and Antonia realised that his irritation masked his real feelings.

"What on earth will Clare do without you?" Antonia asked.

"I'm sure she will find something."

Clare's reasons for going to England were many, though not necessarily those she had announced. First, she wanted to make arrangements for her exhibition and did not want to tell Richard about it until everything was fixed and certain. Then, she wanted time to digest the implications of his need to travel—and his invitation to her. One part of her wanted to follow him wherever he went. But another part of her whispered insistently that if she were ever to become an artist, a real one, not someone playing games, this was the time to work. (Her mother would not understand her dilemma, but Elinor would.) And, of course, she did prefer to get her tooth capped by the family dentist in Wimpole Street, for whatever Richard said to the contrary, she could not trust an Italian one. She also wanted to reassure herself that she had not made her grandmother ill by telling Richard she was. Finally, she wanted, if at all possible, to meet Edmund.

When Clare arrived in South London she telephoned her grandmother who proved, at eighty-one, to be exceptionally fit and walking her dogs at least three miles a day. So that was all right. Elinor was as thrilled about the prospect of Clare's exhibition as her sister had hoped, and arrangements were soon settled between Clare and the gallery. Clare's dental work was completed with a minimum of pain and fuss.

Clare knew she should not meddle in other people's affairs but just this time the temptation was too great. If Antonia would do nothing for herself, then she—and Elinor—would have to.

"Why don't you have Edmund and Margaret to dinner, El?" she suggested as they sat alone after supper one night.

"We've only just had them."

"Well, you could have them again. I promise not to do anything ghastly."

"I won't, even for you, Clare." Elinor smiled. "I dread to think what you will say."

Luckily for Clare, all three of them were asked to supper while Clare was staying. Elinor made her sister promise to be discreet. Margaret was their hostess, after all.

The meal which Margaret had prepared for them was delicious, and Clare had to admit she was a very good cook as well as being very nice. Edmund, Clare decided, was one of the most amazingly English people she had ever met, very inscrutable and controlled. She found him hard to read and had no opportunity to talk privately with him until after dinner when Margaret was in the kitchen with Elinor scraping plates (a thing Clare never did until hours after a party).

"You have not told me how Antonia is," he said, turning to Clare.

"Oh, beautiful and wan and waiflike as usual."

He smiled, and when his full attention was directed towards her, Clare realised how attractive he was. "And is she well?"

"No."

Elinor and Margaret appeared with coffee, and in the general conversation which followed Clare realised how nervous Margaret was and how she kept saying things like "Didn't we" and "won't we" to Edmund, talking always of them as a couple, a pair, incapable of individual action.

Edmund seemed slightly nervous, too, and Clare was not altogether surprised when he arrived the next morning to talk to her just as she was about to leave for Victoria Station.

"I had to see you before you left, Clare."

"Yes." Clare made coffee and they sat in Elinor's scrubbed kitchen and talked for a long time. Surprisingly, they did not discuss Antonia very much. Instead, Edmund told her how he had spent his whole life being good and pleasing other people and doing the right thing and how he felt incapable of being dishonest any longer. "You seem to do whatever you want and you don't hurt other people."

"But I have," said Clare. "My mother thinks I'm leading the most dissolute life."

"But you don't change it to please her."

"No, I'm fed up with all that. I tried to do what I thought I ought to do. Go to university and all that, and be like El. But it wasn't any good."

"Do you think it's possible to do whatever you want without hurting anyone else?" His gray eyes searched her face.

"If you mean, do I think it is worthwhile being dutiful, Edmund, if that is not what you want most, the answer is no."

"I don't know what I want," he said.

Clare felt very proud of her self-restraint in not saying more.

"And is Alexis a shit?" he asked as they departed. "Is she very miserable?"

"Yes," said Clare. The taxi stood impatiently at the curb.

. . .

Antonia did not know what to make of Clare's visit to England. On one hand she was glad to have news of Edmund, but on the other she wished she had not because she was constantly thinking about him. And she knew it was no use. Clare had said that he seemed well, if tired, and had asked after her.

Clare did not say anything else since Richard had warned her that her idle speculations on the romantic possibilities of having lined up a knight in shining armour for Antonia might do more harm than good.

"But you can't imagine how miserable *he* is, Richard," Clare said.

"That's his problem, Clare, not yours. Why don't you get on with your painting and mind your own business?" He smiled as he spoke, which took some of the sting out of his words. Clare realised he was not angry with her so much as generally out-of-sorts.

"But it would be nice if he came to save her," she said.

"All sorts of things would be nice. It would be nice, for example, if my father decided not to visit us next week, but I can't think of any way of putting him off. Can you?"

Antonia saw that Ben was growing daily to be more of a person. He held his head up quite strongly now and smiled a lot. Antonia found herself having long conversations with him when they were alone and even making herself believe he could understand her. Alexis was very rarely at the apartment at all now. He would leave his clothes to be washed, or want to make love and then disappear for days at a time. Rex Acton, having returned from New York at last, wrote to Antonia suggesting that he should bring Eileen and Justin to spend Christmas in Rome where she could join them. Antonia knew she would have to confront her father very soon and was dreading it. She had almost no money left and did not know how much longer she could continue living as she was, but kept putting off from day to day making any real or sensible decisions.

On a beautifully sunny day in the first week of December, the sort of day which comes as a gift in winter and makes one think that spring is near, though one knows of course, that it is not, Antonia got dressed to go out, noting the shabbiness of her clothes as she did. She remembered when it had been fun to wear old clothes, an elaborate charade. Now she put on a beautiful Liberty wool skirt (or rather it had once been beautiful, but the fabric was getting thin in patches and would not last much longer), and a T-shirt which had once been red but had faded through constant washing to a delicate salmon. It was in that soft state of utter comfort just prior to total disintegration. She put a nappy pin in the waistband of her skirt. No one would look at her anyway; a mother with a baby was not fair game. She could not remember when she had last worn makeup. She flung on her coat and bundled up Ben and carried his pram down the stairs, feeling dizzy at the bottom.

She met Clare and Laura at Bar Colinine as she often did when Alexis was not there in the mornings.

"You look rather lovely today," said Clare stirring her hot chocolate. Someone else might have looked ill, but as Antonia became thinner she merely appeared more waiflike and appealing.

Antonia was secretly pleased. She thought she had probably turned into an old hag by not caring. Laura was on her second doughnut.

"You should have one while they're still hot, Antonia. You're much too thin," said Laura.

"I don't like doughnuts, Laura."

"But it's one of the things which makes living in Italy so worthwhile."

Antonia sometimes thought Laura could spend all day on food, buying it, preparing it, eating it and recovering from the effects of it. Clare had become infected with Laura's delight in it, and often had to rush out and replenish her still lifes when she discovered she had eaten significant parts of her props.

Clare said, "I often think I like food as much as sex. I wonder which I would hate to do without most."

Enviable round Clare, enjoying herself, quite different from the Clare who had left England two years before. Antonia wanted to talk to her very much.

"What are you going to do today, Clare? Do you have time to go for a walk with Ben and me in the Boboli Gardens? It's such a delicious day, much too good to waste."

"I would love to, but I can't. I've got a thousand things to do and at least a dozen people coming to dinner. Richard's father and his aunt are in town on their way to Rome and want to see *la vie bohème* at close quarters. You couldn't possibly come this evening, could you? You'd enjoy it I think. Mrs. Wilder is rather nice and I think she would find you quite fascinating."

"I'll try Clare. I'd like to very much."

"There's no reason why you shouldn't."

Actually there were a lot of reasons, the most obvious of which was Alexis and his ridiculous jealousy. Antonia could not face a scene in front of Richard's family, or anyone else's for that matter.

She walked over the Ponte Vecchio where she had once sold paintings with Clare, past the sweater shop and up into the gardens to think. The gravel crunched under her feet as she walked. She was the only person there. She sat in the amphitheatre and gazed at Ben and wondered what she and Alexis would argue about next. Probably something as trivial as running out of sugar. She hated him when he was so bad tempered about such insignificant things, things which were so inconvenient and that she had to go out and fetch, carrying Ben down the stairs and up again. If she asked Alexis to buy groceries, he would forget, to punish her, and then sulk.

She felt tears pricking her eyelids. She must get away from Alexis before she became a complete jelly, incapable of doing anything. She thought of all the possibilities. She could go and stay with Clare, but she did not want to impose on her. She could ask Alexis to leave, but knew she would never have the strength to do it. She could get Richard to throw him out bodily, as he had often offered to do. But what about Stratos when he came back? She couldn't live alone with *him*. She could try to find another apartment, but she did not have enough money for the deposit, even if one could be found, which she doubted. Antonia had realised very soon how lucky she had been to find the one she had now. She could throw herself on her father's mercy but that would be to admit she had failed, to succumb utterly to his power over her. She could kill herself, she thought, becoming melodramatic between sobs, but she knew she could never kill Ben. And what would happen to him then? She could think of no one to whom she could entrust him. No one could ever have loved a baby, she thought, as much as she loved hers.

She sat cross-legged on the stone which was cold and damp beneath her and drew her skirt round her knees. Ben woke up and looked at the clouds floating high above them. He waved his hands as if to reach them. She stood and began once again to walk down the stately avenue of evergreens, which were so magnificent and calm, not having come to any rational conclusion at all.

When she got back to via Torta at two, Alexis was waiting for her with a letter in his hand.

"Who is Edmund?" he asked.

"Let me see the letter. It is for me I suppose?" Her heart had leaped up at the mention of his name.

"Yes," said Alexis.

"Then why did you open it?" He had never opened her letters before, had not sunk to that.

"I didn't know you knew anyone called Edmund in Florence."

"You don't know all my friends," she said. He did actually, but she was not ready to admit it just then. "Give me my letter."

"Not until you tell me who he is."

"Oh, a friend. A friend from England, someone I know."

"You never mentioned him." Alexis looked furious.

"Why should I, Alexis? Just give it to me."

He handed it to her.

She took the letter upstairs, locked the bathroom door with trembling fingers and read what Edmund had written.

"I will wait for you at four, on the steps of S. Croce. I hope you will be able to meet me. If not, leave a message for me at Hotel Sforza in Piazza S. Maria Novella. Edmund." No love or anything, just "Edmund." She folded the note very carefully and put it her pocket.

Antonia had often dreamed of meeting him, but these were muddled dreams which she had been unable to recapture on waking, which had left her with a residue of emotion which she could not confront directly. Her need of him was too obvious.

Alexis stood outside the bathroom door, and grasped her arm as she emerged. "Are you going to meet him, Antonia?"

"Of course. Why ever shouldn't I?"

Alexis slammed the door of the apartment and stamped out. He went downstairs and slammed the *portone*, too. Antonia had not asked him where he was going. She did not want him to have the satisfaction of not telling her.

She lay on her bed with Ben, listening for sounds which would indicate that it was nearly four o'clock. She thought of each of her meetings with Edmund and how opportune they had been. She thought of his face, which appeared and disappeared before her. She tried to recapture the touch of his hands, but however hard she tried she failed.

Twenty-Two

Antonia walked out into the clear cold afternoon and turned into the square. She saw Edmund almost immediately. He was leaning against the façade of the church, his black coat distinctly outlined against the pale marble. His face was turned towards her and she saw him step forward as he recognised her. He ran down the steps and into the middle of the square. Antonia could not run with the pram. She waved instead. "Hello, Edmund," she said. They stopped and stood about two feet from each other.

"Hello, Antonia," he replied, looking into her eyes and smiling the most devastating smile she had ever seen.

She could feel her heart thumping in her chest as if it were trying to escape. "It's very nice here in the sun," she said, though it was in fact rather cold. She held on to his hand, which felt warm in her cold one. "I'm so happy to see you," she said, and burst into tears. She could hold them back no longer.

He put his arms round her, and she could feel his heart beating beneath his thick coat, which smelled of England and airports. "I thought you would be pleased to see me, Antonia. Please don't cry."

"I am pleased," she said between sobs, "that's why I'm crying." He produced a handkerchief from his pocket and handed it to her. She took it and leaned against him in the pale unwarming sun. They stood for a long time saying nothing.

And then Antonia saw, out of the corner of her eye, Alexis' slight figure, dark and malevolent, against the buildings at the side of the square. She panicked and sprang away from Edmund's arms, grabbed the pram and turned into Borgo S. Croce and ran down the darkening street still half blinded by her tears. Edmund caught up with her, put his hand on her shoulder and turned her towards him. "Why are you running away from me? Talk to me. Tell me what it is."

"I can't now. He was watching us." She shook off Edmund's hand and looked back. The pram hit a bump and Ben woke up and cried out miserably. They fled through the winding streets narrowly avoiding lingering tourists and speeding cars.

"Are you very frightened of him?" Edmund asked, and Antonia realised that she was. They made their way to Edmund's hotel where they locked the door of his room, shutting out Alexis and the stout, black-dressed signora at the desk who had looked at Antonia with disgust as they had come in. They shut out all of the insignificant world.

"Whenever we meet, something dramatic happens. I wish we could meet normally like other people," said Antonia. She tried to catch her breath, and looked up at Edmund.

"I don't think you are like other people, Antonia," Edmund said, reaching out to touch her face. "Not ordinary at all."

They lay on the bed together in the gathering gloom, until it was quite dark and they could no longer see each other's faces clearly, could no longer look into each other's eyes. Antonia hugged his body to her and buried her face in his chest. He was so substantial compared to Alexis or Ben. She wanted to dissolve into his body and never move again.

Edmund switched on the light and sat up. Antonia noticed how tired he looked, as if he had not slept well for a long time. There were black rings under his eyes.

"Does Margaret know where you are?" Antonia asked.

"Yes," he replied, looking bleak. "She knows I've come to find you. It was no good, me living with her and thinking constantly of you. It was unkind to let her continue to suppose that I would marry her. God knows she is good and comfortable, but it wasn't enough." Edmund looked at his hands, which were holding both of Antonia's.

"It must have been hard to leave her." Antonia felt very sad.

"Probably the most difficult thing I have ever done. But I can't talk about it. It wouldn't be fair. She is terribly hurt and angry. I tried to let her see it coming. I wanted to make it easy for us both, but it wasn't. There was no way it could be."

Antonia rubbed the back of his hand against her cheek. "Poor Edmund," she said, "I'm sorry."

"You still look very tired, Antonia," he said taking a stray strand of her hair and pushing it very gently off her face.

"So do you."

They rolled together into the middle of the bed, too excited to sleep and too exhausted to think or talk. They lay still for a long time.

They were suddenly disturbed by a loud knocking on the door. The signora stood there looking in horror and disgust at the rumpled bed upon which Ben lay gurgling cheerfully. She asked for Antonia's passport, and then launched into a long tirade of abuse. Antonia was glad Edmund could not understand what the woman said though she supposed he could guess the general drift of it from her demeanour. Of course Antonia did not have her passport on her.

"All right, I'll go," Antonia said, when the woman had finished at last. She did not in the least care what the woman thought of her morals. She did not care if she was turning the hotel into a den of ill-repute; she rather hoped she was. Edmund told the woman to get out in English, which the woman did not speak but seemed to understand. She said she would be back in half an hour with her husband to throw Antonia out bodily if she were not gone by then.

"It's no use Edmund, I'll have to go. Some of them are quite obsessed with rules and regulations. Most of them are all right, but she obviously isn't." She put on her coat and picked up Ben.

"I'll come with you," said Edmund, throwing his few things into his suitcase. He paid the signora as Antonia stood by the door, longing to get out, while the woman counted the money with greedy fingers.

"Don't worry about her. We'll find somewhere else." Antonia sat down on the steps and put her head in her hands and cried. Edmund sat down beside her and put his arms round her. "Don't let her upset you. There are hundreds of other hotels."

"That's not the point. I don't have my passport. They all want it or they won't let you in. It's quite hopeless. I can't go back to via Torta to fetch it. I can't face Alexis now." She wondered if she would ever be able to, whether she would have the strength. What a mess, she thought, what a terrible mess. She imagined spending the cold December night walking the streets alone with Ben, and Ben freezing to death, and being found white, cold and still in the morning.

Edmund's arms enveloped her. "I'll find somewhere, Antonia. There must be somewhere we can go. It isn't as bad as all that."

Antonia suddenly thought of Clare. She had been asked to dinner with Richard and Clare that night. It seemed aeons ago, in another life almost. "We could go to Clare's." How Clare would relish the drama of it all, Antonia thought. "She always said she would take me in if I left Alexis."

Perhaps she had blundered by saying she had left Alexis. Would Edmund think she had thrown herself on his mercy forever? She still did not feel her decision to leave Alexis was irrevocable; perhaps it was not, even then.

"Would Clare mind my turning up unexpectedly?" Edmund asked.

"No, of course not," Antonia said, "she'd love it."

They walked through the dimly lit streets, through the whole city, with the pram and the nappies Antonia had run into a *farmacia* to buy, and Edmund's bag. They walked past bars full of people drinking and fruit shops just being closed up for the night. Antonia stopped under a streetlight on the corner of via dei Pepi.

"It's not far now," she said, looking up into his face. "You don't have to come with me, you know."

"But of course I will come with you."

They walked on in silence, their footsteps echoing in the deserted street. They climbed the twisting stairs which seemed to go on forever.

Antonia knocked at the metal door. Clare opened it, wiping her hands on a towel.

"I thought you would never come, Toe." She kissed her cheek. "You look funny. Are you all right?" Then she saw Edmund. She wiped her hands again, grinning, pleased with herself, and held out her less garlicky one. "Hello, Edmund," she said.

"Well, Clare," he said, smiling at her.

"God, you took a long time about it!" she said. Then, looking at his suitcase, she said, "You're staying of course?"

"If Antonia does."

"Let's have some wine to celebrate. There's some open on the table and Richard said he would be back in a moment. At least I hope he comes back soon. I'm fed up with doing all the work for his wretched family without him." But it was obvious her heart was not in this complaint.

Edmund looked round the cavernous room with the table set near the door with plates and fruit and flowers and wine. Salads were massed in huge bowls. It was difficult to tell where the room ended; there were only shadows in the far reaches, which were lit by dozens of candles flickering in the dark.

Clare poured them some wine and then went back to crushing pignoli for pesto in a mortar.

"Can I help you, Clare? You seem very busy."

"That would be nice, Toe. You can make some more salad if you like." There seemed to Antonia to be a great deal of salad already.

"So how do you like Florence, Edmund?" asked Clare, mashing rather wildly.

"I haven't seen much of it. I came to see Antonia, not the sights."

Antonia started slicing tomatoes into a bowl, adding olive oil and basil. Edmund watched her as she worked, while Clare rattled on about nothing in particular, as if this was an ordinary day and everything had not changed.

Richard returned very soon accompanied by Sergio, a short fat little man whose complicated name Clare could never remember although he was purportedly some sort of a count, and a third man who looked oddly familiar to Clare. "I didn't think you'd mind me bringing guests for dinner, Clare. The most extraordinary thing, I've met a man who's just got back from Goa, one of the places I rather want to see."

"Oh, no, not at all; the more the merrier." Clare wiped her hand again, held it out to the stranger and smiled.

The young man, whose hair was tied back in a ponytail, smiled, too. They looked at one another quizzically.

"I'm sure we've met," Clare said. "Aren't you Nicholas Carstairs? From Gloucestershire? Do you remember that perfectly ghastly dance which we both hated so much, thousands of years ago on another planet?"

"Clare, isn't it? Clare Fane."

"So we both escaped England—and deb dances—in the end," Clare said.

"Actually I'm on my way back there," Nicholas said.

"But not straightaway, I hope. You must stay and enjoy Italy for a bit. It's much too good to miss. What fun you've turned up tonight. I'm so sorry I won't be able to hear all about your travels right now. But you will come back again to see me, won't you?"

Nicholas smiled.

The dinner party lasted until three in the morning. Richard spent a long time grilling Nicholas about India while his father and aunt became very drunk, or anyway as drunk as visiting middle-aged Americans could allow themselves to be. Antonia missed a great deal of what was going on by gazing at Edmund while at the same time trying to converse with Mrs. Wilder. Edmund watched Antonia all the time as the conversation hurtled round him in a confusing mixture of English, French and Italian. He did not attempt to join in.

A great deal of food was eaten and wine drunk and at the end of the meal the table was littered with fruit skins and the ashtrays were full to overflowing. Joints were passed round with the coffee, and Clare whispered to Antonia that she hoped Mrs. Wilder would not be able to recognise the smell.

"Richard is about to become very famous," Clare shouted to Mrs.

Wilder. "One of his long articles about European student politics is about to come out in the *Voice*."

"What is the *voice?*" asked Mrs. Wilder of Antonia, to whom she seemed to have taken a liking.

"A paper, I think," said Antonia, who was not sure.

"I am fond of Richard," said Mrs. Wilder, "but sometimes I'm very glad he's my nephew not my son. I can enjoy him without feeling he's my responsibility. I do think his life-style, if that's what you call it, is odd. Just when you think he's settled for a minute, off he goes again."

"But he does work very hard," said Antonia, not wanting to get into a discussion of life-styles just then.

Clare was glad Mrs. Wilder did not seem to want to go to the bathroom because there wasn't one. People vanished behind a distant screen at intervals. Luckily Richard's aunt had not seemed to notice. She appeared to be a far easier-going person than Richard's father. Or Richard, for that matter.

Antonia sat holding Edmund's hand. "Are you enjoying this, Edmund?" she asked.

"Yes, oddly enough I am," he said. "Though of course I would prefer to be alone with you."

Ben woke up and Antonia brought him to the table to sit with them all. He looked astounded at the number of people. He was used to being alone with Antonia in the evenings.

"What a lovely baby," Mrs. Wilder said, looking at his rosy round cheeks and endless dark lashes. "Does he take after his father?" She looked at Edmund in some perplexity. "Yes, he does rather," said Antonia, not enlightening her. She wanted to change the subject before more was asked of her. "Are you staying in Florence long?"

"No, unfortunately we leave for Rome tomorrow."

Clare had told Antonia this already, but she was quite happy for Mrs. Wilder to chatter on. Her brother, she confided, was cross with Richard for not spending more time with them, but Clare had done her best to make up for him.

"Richard always says Clare could be a tour guide if she gave up painting," said Antonia.

"But I won't give up painting," said Clare. "Why ever should I?"

Antonia could see that Mrs. Wilder was still trying to place Edmund, but she did not explain him to her. He was discussing Afghani Black with Richard and Nicholas. Antonia did not explain that either. Mrs. Wilder did not need to know.

Richard was at his most mellow and almost animated. Clare leaned back against his shoulder and felt his arm about her waist.

The party eventually broke up and the guests departed. Clare showed Edmund and Antonia a battered mattress on the slightly raised platform where the dome from the basilica beneath arched into the room.

Antonia sat in the moonlight at four o'clock, feeding Ben, as the Florentine "deficients" cleaned the streets. She could hear the swish of the brushes as the cart swept the road. She could see the faint outline of Edmund's profile against the white sheet as he slept. She watched his regular breathing. She could not stop looking at him.

Early the next morning they sat at the table amidst the debris from the night before. Clare had cleared a small space for herself and was buttering new bread. She was dressed in a Chinese robe and still seemed half asleep. Antonia sat holding Ben wearing Edmund's sweater, which swamped her, and rubbed her chin against its soft warmth. Richard was still asleep.

"Well, what the hell are you going to do about Alexis?" Clare asked, reaching out for the jam. Edmund did not look at Antonia.

What indeed? thought Antonia. Ben was his child, too. "I just don't know, Clare. I must think."

"Richard could always go round and smash his face in," Clare suggested unhelpfully. "He's been longing to do it."

"Oh, be serious, Clare. What good would that do?"

"Not much I admit," said Clare, munching.

"I've got to go and see him. Alexis is entitled to some sort of explanation."

"Is he?" said Clare.

"If you must go, Antonia, I will come with you. You can't go alone." Edmund stirred his coffee, which was as black as night.

"You haven't the least idea what he can be like. It would be better if I went alone."

"You cannot go without me," Edmund said. Antonia agreed finally that he could come if he promised to wait outside.

She decided to go straightaway before her courage failed her. She fed Ben and left him with Clare. She, too, was frightened of what Alexis might do. She would have liked Edmund to stay with her all the time, but that would not have been fair.

Edmund and Antonia took another coffee at the bar on the corner. He wanted her to eat something, but she could not. Edmund ordered a cognac. As she stepped out into the street, Antonia could feel his eyes on her back. It was eleven o'clock.

She climbed the many stairs to the apartment and let herself in. At first she thought Alexis was not there, then she saw him lying on the bed, with the blanket half covering his face, curled up like a child. She had read once that it is impossible to watch someone sleeping without feeling some impulse of tenderness towards them, an irrational urge to protect. She sat down on the edge of the bed and shook his shoulder gently. He turned slowly towards her, she saw that he had been crying.

"I've come to collect my things, Alexis. I'm going away."

He looked tired and broken. Antonia felt sorry for him, he seemed so small and desolate.

"Why, Antonia?"

"How can you ask that? I'm going because it is no good between us. You know that as well as I do."

"But I love you, Antonia. I always have." He had in his own way— that was the worst of it.

"You can see Ben tomorrow. You can see him whenever you want."

Alexis roused himself a little. "And who is he, this Edmund, this Englishman?" He said "Englishman" with such disgust, he almost spat it out.

"I don't want to explain. I can't."

"Is he good in bed? Better than me, heh?"

Antonia did not stoop to answer.

"Can't you see what you are doing to me?" he asked.

"No worse than you have done to me, Alexis."

"I never left you," he said.

273

Antonia started collecting her things and putting them into her canvas bag. She did not take much, anything which could be said to be both of theirs she left. Alexis came and stood in front of her.

"Look at me, Antonia." Their eyes were on a level. He took her chin in his hand. "Look at me and say you don't love me."

She had to say it. "I don't love you, Alexis." It was a very cruel thing to say, and not entirely true even then.

"Make love to me, Antonia, just one more time." She felt his body against hers; his penis erect already under his jeans. She flinched.

"Don't touch me. Please don't touch me."

"You were happy enough to fuck me before you met him. Did you fuck him in England?"

"Of course not. Don't be stupid. What do you think? Let go of my arm." He was holding it very tightly, his fingers biting into her flesh under Edmund's sweater. She saw his eyes searching her face, pleading with her. And then she saw them harden when she would not weaken. He slapped her face very hard with his free hand.

"You bitch," he said, and spat in her face.

"Let go of my arm, Alexis. Let go of me now."

He hit her again, much harder, and she could feel the blood spurting out of her lip and dripping down her chin. He let go of her then and she continued putting things into the bag, stopping only to wipe her chin on her shoulder. She could scarcely see anything. Her eyes were full of tears of pain and humiliation. Her throat ached. But she was not angry. She felt she deserved all this and possibly more.

"I hope you have got everything," Alexis said. "You needn't bother to come back." He dropped an ashtray she had bought for him onto the floor where it shattered into a thousand fragments. "Get out, Antonia. Get out. I never want to see you again." He flung himse. back onto the bed and covered his face with his arms and sobbed.

Antonia zipped up the bag and closed the door behind her. She slipped the key back under the door. She could still hear Alexis' muffled sobs. She sat down on the stairs and wept, too. Great tears of pain and relief wracked her. She wiped her nose on the now filthy sweater. She took it off and dabbed at her face with it. Her cheekbone ached dully and she hoped it was not broken; she would probably have a black eye. She was glad Ben was too young to realise.

She continued sitting dazedly until she heard footsteps on the stairs beneath her. Edmund appeared. "What has he done to you, Antonia?"

"Nothing," she said, standing up, leaning against the wall, hiding her face. "I want to go back to Clare's. I just want to get away."

"All right, let's go." Edmund picked up her bag and put his other arm around her. He sounded very angry. When they were out in the light, he said, "I want to see your face." But she kept it turned from him. When finally he managed a glimpse he dropped the bag and turned back towards the apartment.

"Don't Edmund. Don't do anything. What good would it do? For Christ's sake leave him alone. We've done enough already, don't you realise?"

They walked in silence back to the studio. Edmund bathed her face with cold water. She winced at his touch; the skin was broken and puffy on her lip and cheek. All things considered, she thought she had got away very lightly.

"I could gladly kill him," Edmund said.

Antonia sighed.

Ben lay in his bouncing cradle by the window smiling beatifically around him, grasping a piece of newspaper and dropping it whenever Clare handed it back to him. He was enjoying the game very much.

"I must go back to London next week," said Edmund to Antonia. "Will you come with me?" He said this lightly, as if he were asking her if she wanted an ice cream or a glass of wine.

Antonia was very quiet. Though posed so simply, the question was utterly serious.

"I want you to be with me always. I love you, Antonia."

"Do you realise what you would be taking on? Me, and another man's child."

"I realise all of it, Antonia. None of it matters." He had obviously thought it all out. "I loved you from the first moment I saw you in that dismal waiting room full of fat women. I thought I was going mad, that it couldn't be true, but it is."

"I need you too much, Edmund. I thought you were just being kind, professional. I never expected you to fall in love with me."

"But I have," he said. "I'm not just being kind. I can be very unkind." He thought of Margaret. He looked at Antonia.

"Probably," said Antonia, stirring her coffee. "And could I become a suburban housewife?"

"You could become anything you want," he said.

Her face hurt when she smiled.